OUT FOR BLOOD

TEMPLE STONE SERIES: BOOK ONE

JOLENE GRACE

Contents

Praises For Out For Blood

"The fast-paced, efficient police procedural's likable hero lends emotional weight to a gruesome case," – – KIRKUS REVIEWS.

"In the midst of darkness, light persists." *Mahatma Gand-hi*

–

Chapter 1

The new person on the desk was vague. No surprises there.

"The caller is waiting for you at Franklin Park," Dispatch said. "Head there, 1443."

Not even an hour into their morning shift, officers Brenda Westcott and her partner, Danny Stevens, set off to canvas the area on foot. Westcott blew on her hands to keep them warm. Stevens sipped on a hot coffee. Both strolled, their pace leisurely.

"Dispatch, 1443. Do you copy?" Stevens said into the portable radio.

"Go ahead, 1443."

"Did the caller say where in Franklin?"

After a few seconds of crackling static, Dispatch returned, "By the stage. According to the notes in the system, the city is hosting a running convention today in Franklin Park."

"Can't be that serious. Probably a false alarm." Stevens glanced at her partner.

Westcott transmitted, "We're rounding the corner. Copy. Over."

"Don't put too much into it," Stevens said. "We get a lot of prank calls. Kind of absurd. It's like a new trend. You'll get used to it eventually."

Westcott rounded 8th Street, the park entrance coming into view. Stevens, unbothered, slurped his coffee.

"See?" Stevens said. "Nothing to stress about. After we take her statement, I vote we beat it back to the squad. Can't feel my toes from the cold."

"Dispatch sent us to check it out, Stevens. Can't always take the easy way out," Westcott said.

"I sure can try."

Freezing rain began to drizzle down. She reached into her side pocket and opened a bright yellow rain poncho. She donned it.

"You like being a cop, Westcott?" Stevens asked.

"Why do you want to know?" she replied and pressed the crosswalk button.

"You can jaywalk, rookie. No one's going to give you a citation. There isn't a soul but us in sight."

Westcott waited for the walk signal to flash green. "It's out of principle."

As Brenda Westcott stepped onto the street, she felt a surge of worry in her shoulder blades.

We're not alone.

The raw April wind blew into the banners, and they rustled noisily. She thought back to the academy and her training — *situational awareness* and how easy it would be for a sniper to take her and Stevens out from one of those empty buildings. The silence of the park didn't help calm her jittery nerves.

She stopped abruptly and studied the drab rooftops.

"Would you relax? Enjoy Boston being so quiet. No racing cars, no rushing buses. How many times can you say Boston was a vacant parking lot?" Stevens smiled wide. "Hurry, my balls will freeze off if we stay out here."

They entered Franklin Park. Up ahead the two spotted the mega stage, banners, and band equipment sprawled out. White tents, signs, and folding chairs took up most of the greening lawn of the park.

Westcott squinted. She picked up her remote radio. "Dispatch, unit 1443, no visual of the caller. Do you have a number for her?"

"Stand by."

Westcott pointed. "There. The woman at the top of the hill. Could be her? Go check it out. I'll take the stage."

They split up.

Westcott was starting to think her partner might have a point. Prank calling was a trend. She should get used to it.

She jumped over a metal railing and circled around to the back of the stage. Assessing the danger level to be low, Westcott proceeded. She eased her way to the main stairway. At the top, a gust of wind almost snagged her hat off. Westcott managed to cross over the myriad cables, sound equipment, and musical instruments until she grew closer to the center, marked X in white chalk paint.

What is this?

She squinted — on a single folding chair, a woman in white sat motionless.

Nearing it, chills danced up Westcott's neck and reached the top of her unruly black hair. She peered into the woman's face, or where her face should have been.

Oh, God...

A flock of winter-gray birds flapped their wings and flew away. Terrified, Wescott turned around, attention trained on the city rooftops. It took several seconds before her nerves calmed slightly. She glanced at the chair.

"Westcott — that was the caller. She's hysterical. I spoke to her husband. He's coming down to get her," Danny Stevens said, approaching. "The witness said she thinks she saw a dead — Jesus, so it's true!"

Westcott pressed her lips together.

"Poor thing..." Stevens mumbled. "I think I'm going to be sick."

Westcott frowned. "Suck it up, officer. I need your head in the game. I haven't called it in yet."

"What are you waiting for? Go on. The sooner Homicide takes over, the sooner I can begin to forget her."

Westcott nodded. She tended to agree.

"Doesn't she look cold to you?" Stevens asked.

"My father used to say the cold only bothers the living." With that, Westcott unhooked her portable radio and transmitted, "1443 to Central. Do you read?"

"Affirmative, 1443."

"I've got a 10-33. Dead body. White female. Late thirties to forties. The cause of death is undetermined at this time. She's wearing a white lacy dress. Her face is blocked by a..." she paused, "mask."

"What type of mask?" Dispatch asked.

Westcott and Stevens exchanged concerned looks. Westcott replied, "A Halloween mask. Like the Grim Reaper or the Slasher. One of those. Not sure which one." Westcott scanned the area around the chair. "No personal belongings. And no visible trauma to the body." She paused again, longer this time. "Correction — I see bruises on her wrists, ankles, and around her neck. Requesting field supervisor, Homicide, and a bus."

"Copy, Westcott. Hang on. I'm paging Detective Temple Stone, Homicide. He's the lead. New and no answer. Go figure."

Stevens noticed the pockets of people first. Small groups at the edge of Franklin Park. He tapped his partner on the shoulder. Westcott understood.

"Dispatch be advised — runners and spectators are starting to show up," Westcott said.

"Secure the scene as best as you can. I'm still paging Detective Stone. Nothing yet. I'll keep trying. Sending you additional units. En route. One minute tops. Do you copy, officer?"

"Affirmative." Westcott exhaled with relief.

"Who do you think she is? Was." Stevens stared at the female body, which appeared nearly frozen.

"No idea. I feel bad for her though. Left half naked in the cold for the world to see. Judging by the mask, her death was no accident."

Stevens took his police hat off out of respect. "It's moments like this I'm glad I'm not a Homicide detective. Too much death is not good for the heart."

Westcott nodded. "I'll stay with her. Can't leave her alone. You secure the crime scene perimeter until our backup shows up."

Alone with the dead woman, Westcott peered into the hollow eyes of the mask and tried to imagine the face behind it. The person before someone had played God and ended her life.

She didn't want to think about what the vic had been through. And while monsters still existed in the world, Wescott felt safer with her gun locked and loaded.

An unexpected sound caught her attention.

Hard soles of boots climbing up. A faint male voice dictating schedule lines. Wescott rushed over and found herself facing a man in a black turtleneck.

"Boston PD. Stop right there!" she yelled.

Turtleneck jumped back, holding onto the railing, a cell to his ear.

"Good grief, officer!" He laughed it off. "The gun is overkill, dontcha think? I'm the assistant event director. Showtime in an hour."

"This is a crime scene. Go back, sir."

"Excuse me, lady? I don't think I heard you right. I swear you said 'crime scene,' but can't be?"

Wescott looked back to the park set up for a celebration. There would be none of that today.

"You'll have to cancel the convention," Westcott said.

"If this is some kind of joke," Turtleneck began, "I don't find it amusing. Now, if you'd excuse me, I must prepare for one of the *largest* running events in the nation."

"Can't let you go through," Westcott said.

"Listen, I'm growing tired of your grandstanding. I don't see a crime. Move or I'll call your supervisor."

"My supervisor should be arriving shortly. You can speak to him in person then," Westcott snapped.

"Get ready for the fallout. Boston won't get over such a travesty. You will not get away with this. Wait till the mayor hears about this. A major upset. Read my lips, officer W-e-s-t-c-o-t-t — a humiliating loss for you." Turtleneck skedaddled to one of the parked trailers.

In the distance, Wescott spotted the first wave of flashing blues and reds. Soon, the scene would be hot with cops and detectives. Maybe the field supervisor would cut her loose, and she'd be able to return to her post and try to forget about the freaky mask. But she doubted it. There was no forgetting a murder like that.

Chapter 2

It was sometime before nine on a Tuesday morning, bright and sunny, a rare Boston spring day. I was fidgety, swiping between apps on my phone, waiting for the heart doctor to see me.

Dr. J.P. Giovanni had been my primary ever since he saved my life after I was shot. So, when his office called me out of the blue requesting that I sit down with him, I consented without putting much thought into it.

There was nothing terribly interesting on the news. I spent several minutes checking the sports section, reading over last night's basketball scores. Disappointing season all across the board, I quickly concluded. Mildly bored, I shut the phone and picked up a car magazine. My wife had been on my case to get rid of the old truck and buy us something more reliable. What she actually meant was something suitable for a family.

"Mr. Stone," a nurse called me, "Dr. Giovanni's ready for you. Right this way."

She walked me to the doctor's office.

Dr. Giovanni stayed behind his desk looking unusually stiff. He muttered, "Detective," and pointed to one of the two chairs in front of his desk.

"If you don't mind, I asked my colleague, Dr. Hoffman, to join us," Giovanni said. "She's coming down now."

The concern painted on him made my own back stiffen up. If Giovanni hadn't saved my life, I would have blown off the appointment, especially today of all days. First day on as Boston's newest lead homicide detective. A chance I would have missed out on if that bullet had hit an inch closer to the center of my chest.

The door opened and closed behind me. Giovanni stood up and came around his desk. Beside him, a stern woman in a white coat gave me a forced smile.

"This is Dr. Hoffman," Giovanni said. "She's a world-renowned cardiologist."

"A cardiologist?"

"A heart doctor." Hoffman lowered herself into the chair next to mine.

Giovanni slid a couple of black and white X-rays over to her. "I think we discovered the reason for your blackouts. It's your heart. The part over here is concerning," Hoffman explained. "A small bullet fragment, undetectable before, has worked its way to one of your valves."

I studied her eyes, expecting her to tell me it's nothing to worry about; suggest new meds, changes to my exercise regimen.

"As concerning as they are, I'm afraid the blackouts are the beginning of something far more serious," Hoffman explained. "I'd like to operate today and remove the fragment."

My neck tensed. "The look on your face tells me there's more you haven't told me."

A hesitation. Then, "As much as I would like to take you to the OR for an emergency extraction and repair, the truth is your heart sustained a tremendous amount of damage from the bullet. It's practically a miracle you're here with us today. Your previous team of surgeons put you back together, but they weren't able to make you whole. It's the reason why we've observed you so closely."

"You expected this?"

"Yes — to a degree."

"To a degree?" I asked Hoffman.

"Correct, detective. The bullet fragment is a new discovery. Due to its size and previous position, we weren't able to detect it with our usual standard protocols. But after your last blackout, you must have hit the ground hard and somehow dislodged the fragment. It shifted. I'm not sure how, and we might never figure it out. But it's now visible on your scans."

I glared at the X-rays and studied the tunnels snuggled around my heart, still of firm opinion that Giovanni and his grumpy sidekick had read the scans wrong.

"We prepare for the worst and hope for the best," Giovanni said kindly.

"Wait, a minute. Prepare for the worst?! How serious is it?" I asked.

"It's a situation that shouldn't be taken lightly. The human heart has four valves that help the blood flow..."

"Doc, give it to me straight," I cut off Giovanni. "I'm a murder cop, not a science guy. This feels like a medical lecture, and I was never the best student."

"Fair enough. What answer would you like me to give you?"

"How about the truth? Let's start there. Am I going to die?"

Hoffman trained a worried expression on me. "The operation I'm proposing is experimental. I've performed it twice in my career on far healthier and less complicated cases than yours. Full disclosure — your heart is extremely weak to go under the knife. It hasn't had time to fully heal. The shifting fragment is the wild card for you medically." Hoffman added, "First, I'd like to begin with some blood work..."

"Temple," Giovanni cut in, "is it okay to address you by your first name?"

"Yes, sure," I replied pointedly.

"Your blood is another matter we have to talk about. It could complicate things for us, medically, down the line."

"How can my blood complicate things for you?" I asked.

"According to your chart, you're O negative."

I remembered. "The most common blood type. Anyone could receive it. What's the issue?"

"Right. It's also the most popular blood type a hospital uses. And currently, there is a shortage of O negative in the country."

"Can't I get one of the other types?"

Hoffman exhaled slowly. "Any other blood type, yes, but O negative can only get O negative."

"So, what you're trying to tell me is I'm screwed."

The gravity of my medical situation zapped me in the spine. I waited for Hoffman and Giovanni to offer words of encouragement. Half considered that they might tell me someone was playing a sick prank on me. I looked at the heart scans again — could it be a lab mix-up?

My phone lit up. I glanced at it, distracted. Work. I wondered if I should get it. Left it unanswered.

"The blood order is in the system. After we're done, the nurse will come in and draw several vials, and then we wait to see what the panel shows us," Hoffman said.

"Best and worst outcome?" I asked.

"If the bullet fragment continues to shift, it could cause irreversible damage to your heart. A sudden heart attack is not something we can count out. If we delay and don't take action now, you could be walking down the street tomorrow and drop dead," she said. "I'd like to start you on IV meds. It might require you to spend a week in hospital where I can keep an eye on you."

I shot up. "Out of the question. Shelly — my wife — is due any moment." I felt lightheaded. "And what about my work?"

Hoffman bit her lower lip. "You're Boston's latest murder cop. I thought I recognized the name. Your promotion was in the paper last week."

Giovanni tuned in. "There might not be a workaround for the hospital stay."

"And if I refuse?"

My phone went off again. I didn't even bother checking it.

"Look — you can try and put off the surgery, it's your right..." Hoffman continued, "But you're putting yourself in great danger. Your health comes first. If you ignore the problem, it won't solve itself on its own. Quite the opposite. It will make it worse — "

Her spiel was interrupted by the incoming avalanche of text notifications on my phone.

"Do you mind turning that off?" Giovanni asked.

I scanned a few of them briefly. "It looks like a 10-33 at Franklin Park. I'm ordered in."

"Detective Stone — "

I looked up at Hoffman.

She continued in a cold, measured voice meant to hold my attention. "I'm not sure I can sign off treating a patient in your condition who isn't fully committed to recovery." Hoffman got to her feet. "The waitlist to see me is long. Think it over. Speak to your wife. Clear it with work. Then call me in the morning."

I stood up quickly as she excused herself. Late for her rounds, she headed for the door. My knees felt wobbly from standing up so fast. I dropped back down in the chair. Giovanni offered me a bottle of water. I sipped it, thinking about the 10-33, the Boston Police code for homicide; a dead female found on a stage in Franklin Park.

"Do you have questions?"

Giovanni's voice brought me back to the present moment.

"One — what am I supposed to do about work? I'm maxed out on medical leave."

"At this moment," Giovanni sighed, "you should look on the bright side."

"There is a bright side, Dr. Giovanni? Excuse me, but I must've skipped right over it."

Giovanni tugged on his ear, irritated. "Blood work first. Then, we let Doctor Hoffman tell us what's our next step. Switch to light duty, desk assignment, until further notice. I strongly suggest you avoid chasing criminals, take as many breaks as you need, eat plenty of protein-packed meals, and most important of all — avoid stress." He held up his hands. "I know — you're a cop — and stress is rocket fuel for you. But do your best. Now is not the time to be the hero. Do I make myself clear? Your life depends on it."

My cell rang one final time. I saw the lieutenant's personal line. Fat chance I'd let him leave a voicemail.

"It's my boss. If you don't mind, I have to take this," I muttered.

"I'll tell the nurse we're done, and she can come in. When the blood results are in, I'll be in touch."

I hit the answer button. Lieutenant André Jones barked at me on the other end.

"Party's over, Stone. We got a fresh vic. Where the hell are you?"

"I'm on my way."

"The captain's asking what happened to her lead detective. Can't cover for you forever. Get over here fast," Jones said. "Temple — whoever committed this has a seriously twisted mind."

Chapter 3

I couldn't recall how I got from the Cardiovascular Center at Boston Medical to the crime scene. But twenty-four minutes later, my police vehicle came to a stop next to the barricaded front entrance of Franklin Park.

The entire block was flocked with police trying to control the crowd. What in the world was going on?

A cluster of uniforms stood guard in front of the center stage, while runners shouted angry questions, waving their hands in protest.

I showed my badge to an officer. He lifted the police tape, and I ducked under it. Ten paces in, I spotted two detectives from Robbery — Webber, a short, plain-spoken cop on his last tour of duty, and his latest newbie partner, Tanaka.

"What are all these people doing here?" I asked Webber.

"You didn't hear? The rookie who found the dead vic shut down some running convention. They're pissed off, if you can't tell," Webber said.

"Some sicko chose the main stage as his body dump," Tanaka joined in. "The boys were talking. I circled out back to see her." His eyes grew bigger. "She looked freaky."

Webber studied the buildup of people behind the barricades alongside me. "The mayor's shitting bricks. She wants Boston PD's head on a spike."

"We need to establish a larger crime scene perimeter. As is it won't do."

Webber glanced at me. "Heard them calling you on the radio." He focused on the gold badge hanging from a chain around my neck. "The rest of the suits are up on the stage. Take the stairs and go to your right. You can't miss it, *big guy*."

"Hold the line, Webber," I said, already walking away from him.

A few moments later, I reached the staircase. But I hesitated.

You can do it, I encouraged myself. *It's just another homicide. You've solved plenty of them*, I tried to spur my confused mind into action.

Only I couldn't actually take the first step.

Frozen, I breathed in fear, doubt. *What if I suck? What if I fail?* Giovanni's grim words about my fatal heart condition circled on a loop in my head, sabotaging any attempt at self-confidence.

A gust of wind tangled the badge across my chest. I smoothed it out, calmer now as the dread-pumping shiver in my veins began to thaw.

Giovanni hadn't yet confirmed the results of the blood test. It could all be a big whoop for nothing.

And until told otherwise, I decided not to let uncertainty dictate my actions. Because nothing that snooty Doctor Hoffman said made sense. One minute, I was a medical miracle after a bullet hit my chest. The next — I was told a fragment left undetected until now could explode my heart and kill me.

The more I thought about it, the more I convinced myself things would work themselves out.

Relax, Temple. You have a killer to catch.

I scanned Franklin Park before I headed up. *People,* I observed, *and lots of them.* I frowned. Any physical evidence left behind by the killer might be gone by now. The size of the scene was already beginning to complicate my investigation.

Up on the stage, I encountered a wall of more cops. Too many people to conduct a solid prelim. Quietly, I ordered everyone but the necessary personnel to stay. I brushed past Callum Baker, the head of the crime lab unit. If they brought him here, it was big.

My eyes locked on André Jones and Captain Gail Mercy. They were huddled off to the side of a mountain of band equipment. They looked like tsunami survivors.

Captain Mercy met my stare with an upset glare of her own that said I'm in hot water.

"How nice of you to join us, Detective Temple. On behalf of the entire homicide division, I'd like to apologize for dragging you away from whatever was more important than this murder."

"It won't happen again, captain."

"You can stake your entire career on it. If you're not ready to lead, fine, I'll send you back to your desk. And quickly promote someone who wants the job more than you."

Captain Mercy was fifty-one; fit, but stout. Four years ago, she had clawed her way to the rank of captain after successfully suing the Boston Police Department for discrimination. But despite her brilliant police mind, she walked around with a chip on her shoulder, as if she had to prove her worth at every turn. She'd bust anyone's balls if they slacked off on the job.

"Roger, ma'am. I'm good. One hundred percent here. Ready to hit the ground running."

André dragged a handkerchief over his neck. "Franklin Park is a nice, family park. Lots of young kids play here. We caught a lucky break. We found the vic before some youngster could point her out." His eyes fell on the floating river of upset runners. "They've been asking us if they could still use the other end of the park for their convention. As if!"

"Bring me up to speed. What did I miss?" I asked.

"I will. But first — how do you feel? Last week you blacked out on the podium, hit the ground hard."

"Ah you know — the physical therapist had worked me hard that morning. But the doctor says I'm fine. Tip-top shape. He's changing my meds, and he seems to think the blackouts are over," I said, not looking André in the eye.

He seemed to believe me. "She's over there. I'll take you to her."

"I want a team of boots to start canvassing the park. We'll have to empty the grounds for that."

He nodded. "White, female, late thirties, early forties. No obvious trauma to the body. Waiting for the medical examiner to determine the cause of death. A lady spotted the vic. Called us in. Two officers on their morning patrol caught the call. Danny Stevens and a rookie, Brenda Westcott from the Roxbury division."

"I'd like to speak with them," I said.

"I have them on standby. I'll get them after you've had a chance to see the body."

"Have we IDed her yet?"

André shook his head. "No ID on her. The fingerprint scanner didn't get any hits."

In the center of the stage, a group of sweepers vacuumed, dusted, and bagged physical evidence. After they finished, they departed.

And I saw her.

"Jane Doe, huh? Hopefully not for long," I said to André.

"Pity," he replied.

I knelt next to the lifeless victim and studied the body. She was seated on a black folding chair. A simple white cotton dress spilled down to her ankles.

"No one moved anything. You see her as Officer Westcott found her."

I slowly stood up and leaned forward to examine the Halloween mask blocking her face. I reached over and pulled it off. Her honey-brown hair with streaks of some gold came loose and fell right below her shoulders. Her lips painted poppy red. Barefoot. Her toenails matched the red on her lips.

"Bag." I handed André the mask to secure in an evidence bag. "Take it to the crime lab immediately. I want to know everything there is to know about the mask. Where did it come from? What store sells it? Any fibers and fingerprints, I want it run against the state criminal database. And if we get nothing, then the lab should run a nationwide search."

As André sealed the bag, I stared at the lifeless gaze of Jane Doe. Gray and cloudy, her eyes held the mystery of what had happened to her. A mystery I was determined to learn.

I scanned the rest of the body, ready to wrap up, when André led in a female officer.

"Officer Brenda Westcott," she introduced herself, trying her best not to look at Jane Doe.

"Nice to meet you. I heard you single-handedly shut down the convention."

She flinched with surprise, perhaps anxious that I'd chew her out. "Well, they were starting to gather, fast, and so many of them. Stevens, my partner, and I had to do something. Backup was taking their sweet time. I was worried about her." She nodded towards Jane Doe. "But I was mainly scared I was screwing it all up. First shift on my own without a supervisor. Man, how much trouble am I in?"

"Relax, Westcott. You played it by the book."

"Dispatch sent us to Franklin Park at 5:40 a.m. Told us a call came in for a woman possibly dead. We were here to try and locate the potential victim. We were looking for the caller. Eventually, we spotted a woman in pajamas up on the road. My partner went to check in with her. I searched the stage. Found her sitting alone, in a white dress and a Halloween mask. Didn't know what to think of it at first. A practical joke, maybe. But she seemed real to me. Too real." She angled herself to face Jane Doe and pointed at the vic's feet. "Saw the bruises. And the ones on her wrists. Figured, to hell it with. She needs help. Our help."

"So you called it in."

"Bus, supervisor, and Homicide. Yes, sir. I did. Followed protocol."

I had her kneel beside me. "Do you see anything else, officer?"

After a second, she replied, "No sir. Should I?"

I took my flashlight and pointed at Jane Doe's fingers. "You found all the big bruises. But this little one — has my attention."

"A bruise around her ring finger," Westcott said. "Sorry, I missed it. Nerves and all. What do you think it means?"

"The obvious right now — given her age, she was most likely married. A special someone was in the picture. Could be our killer. Too early to make any predictions. Did you see anyone else?"

Westcott paused to think about it.

"Maybe someone watching you? That early in the morning, the park's practically empty. He would have stood out," I said.

"No. Not really. In the academy, they teach us about situational awareness. And so I got a funny feeling, like you know, in the pit of my stomach, that maybe — he, the killer was nearby. But I didn't actually see him." She put a hand on the butt of her gun. "I did have a word with the assistant stage manager, I think he said. Threatened me with the Mayor's Office. I set him straight. Set him right."

I held back a smile and told her she could go back to her patrol duty.

Before she left, Westcott said, "I want to be a detective too one day. Years down the line. My partner thinks seeing too much death is bad for the heart, but I can't think of anything more awesome than slapping justice on an asshole who kills for sport."

Chapter 4

I put a hand on my chest and walked around the body. "It took time staging her. This killer sure loves attention, or is it a cry for something else?" I said to André.

"A cry to go straight to jail, do not pass, and do not collect," André said.

"I think he's confident he won't go to jail. Why this stage? Franklin Park? Public and family friendly. Lots of questions." I stopped in front of her. "He didn't kill her here, given the fact that we haven't discovered blood. Can't rule out strangulation. Have a detective check the overnight logs for 911 calls reporting a woman shouting. If it was a random attack, someone might have heard her struggle with her killer. The dress she's wearing — I want to learn everything about it. Who made it? Sold in stores, online, or both? It looks new, but I see some frayed edges on the sleeves, and the fit is slightly off. Wouldn't you agree? Like it's two sizes too big? Was it hers or part of her killer's fantasy? The small clues will help us solve her murder."

"I will have the medical examiner hand over the dress to the crime lab as soon as she transports the body to the morgue," André said.

"Ballsy move, the whole production he put on," I said.

André received a text, and he read it. "As of an hour ago, no one reported a woman missing in the last twenty-four hours," André said.

"Odd. She doesn't seem the type to go off willingly with a stranger. Maybe a spouse." I concentrated on her fingers, slender and delicate. A ring missing, but she wore one at some point. So, indication of marriage, relationship, commitment. Did the killer take it to keep as a memory? Or did she walk out — the relationship over? "Maybe someone got dumped," I observed.

Chatter over the radio broke my concentration. André turned his unit down.

"I want to formally interview the caller, the woman who found Jane Doe. Have a car bring her down to the station. I need to write the report. I'd like to include her official statement in it. Set up the murder board later."

"Alright people, make some room," a woman ordered. "Move, please. Stretcher coming."

Tessa Wu, the Boston medical examiner, looked winded. Dressed in jogging shorts and sneakers, I suspected Wu got the same *get-your-ass*-ASAP call as I did.

"Let's take a look," she said without any fuss.

The ME performed the initial exam efficiently, not disturbed by the hundred pairs of eyes observing her work. She jotted down several notes and took measurements of the body.

"Rigor mortis has set in," Wu finally remarked. "I'd say the vic expired in the last twenty-four to thirty-six hours window. Hold that thought. Something's off."

"What's wrong?" I asked.

Wu probed the vic's joints and neck muscles before answering. "This will sound strange, but she hasn't started to decompose. The natural response a body goes through hasn't kicked in. Weird."

"Do you think it's something the killer did to her?"

"I think so, yes. Once I get her open, I will be able to figure it out."

"In that case, how about COD?"

"I can tell you right now — he held her in restraints for several hours after her death. Same bruises on her ankles. Shackled. I'll need to perform more tests before I can give you a full report."

"She does smell fresh — warm water and soap." Wu bent one knee. "Sponge bath, most likely. I've seen it done before in sexually motivated crimes. The killer was trying to dispose of evidence."

"That's sick." André fixed his tool belt.

We both watched Wu while she managed to hike up the white dress over the vic's body.

"Makes perfect sense." Wu pointed to a dime-sized hole in Jane Doe's ribcage. "A puncture wound between the fifth and sixth rib means he targeted her lung." Wu peeled her gloves off. "Hate to say it, but she suffered a slow, horrible death. Given her height and weight, it didn't take long before the lung collapsed. She was soon incapacitated, unable to do anything to save herself." Wu draped a sheet over Marathon Jane. "After that, he had her all to herself and did God knows what with her. When

I get her on the table, I intend to extract every shred of evidence the killer tried to erase but left behind."

Once Wu and her team wheeled the body to a van, André let one hand rest on his holstered gun. His serious eyes landed on me.

"Okay — you're up, kiddo. What do you want to do now? You heard the captain — you got yourself a blockbuster case right out of the gate. This investigation could make or break your career. There's still time to turn down the promotion before we hit the ground running."

Determined, I said to him, "I'm all in all the way."

Chapter 5

It had started as a warm morning, and then it had all gone downhill, including the temperature. The doctor with news of the shifting bullet fragment threatening my heart, next a grisly murder on my first day after a hard-earned promotion, and a city sizzling mad over a canceled sporting event.

Caught in the crosshairs, I decided to throw myself into my work. Staying busy is the best medicine. I would solve the biggest murder of my homicide career and leave the medical stuff to the pros. I saw it as a win-win.

"The captain already left. City Hall ordered her in to update the mayor. I'm staying with you." André secured his hat on top of his head. He looked ready to melt, despite the cooling afternoon.

"She wants eyes on me?"

"It's a big case. Generating lots of publicity, and not the good kind. It's her neck on the line if the homicide division drops the ball."

"It's not just that," I said.

After a brief moment, André agreed. "Your blackouts might have something to do with it. Don't take this as a vote of no confidence in your skills as a detective. You proved how good you are at tracking killers a long time ago. You earned your position as a leader."

We left the stage together and walked across the lawn. The sun had started to slowly settle between a curtain of graying clouds. Yellow tape sectioned off where the crime scene started, about a mile in each direction. There were some people still hanging around on their phones, livestreaming the police.

"Start prepping a list of witnesses, André. We need to find Jane Doe's real name. Probe her life for enemies, a jilted lover, or a stalker," I said.

"Get me the name of the company in charge of the show. The concert event coordinator. Westcott mentioned exchanging words with an assistant. Get me his name too. The people in charge of the convention, we'll have to speak with them too.

"And I want a photo of Jane Doe so we can show her to them. Maybe she was a runner. Is she from Boston or here for the convention? The sooner we know these details, the sooner we can begin to build a profile of her killer."

"Who do you want to start with?"

"The 911 caller. She could have seen the killer but didn't realize it. I want to speak with her while her memories are still fresh. Make sure Westcott and her partner — Stevens, did she say? — write their report and send it to me."

André typed furiously on his phone. A message followed, then another, and one more before he told me.

"Alright, I have some initial information. The Groove Factory is the name of the company in charge of the show and the stage."

I shook my head. "Never heard of it. Based in Boston?"

"Yeah. The main office is on Trenton and 11th."

"Trenton and 11th." I stopped walking. "That's three blocks from here."

"Four."

"Four blocks. Not exactly far. I most certainly want to speak to as many of their employees as we can line up."

"I pinpointed the backstage crew foreman, the head of sound engineering, the stage director, and several of the event PR people," André told me. "And a woman who said she works for the Run America convention. She's tracking people down for us. I gave her your phone number to get in touch with you."

"That's a solid start. We interview them as we work to find out Jane Doe's identity."

"Maybe we'll get lucky and someone has already called her into missing persons," André said.

"And unicorns are real," I said.

We took my car back to the station.

"Jane Doe didn't look like the transient type. On the contrary. Well groomed, physically fit — an all-round impressively maintained woman. A woman like her — someone's missing her already. But why haven't they phoned us? What's holding them back? The killer had to have snatched her twenty-four to forty-eight hours prior to placing her on the stage. That's a long time to go without hearing from a loved one."

André rolled down the window, inviting in a gentle draft. "What are you thinking? She's not from around here?"

"I don't know yet. I'm playing out several scenarios in my head," I said, loosening my tie. "A woman like our Jane has friends, co-workers. There must be a trail of people worried sick. A mailbox somewhere in a nice, quiet, picture-perfect neighborhood, piling up with uncollected mail."

At that moment, André's phone buzzed with a text. "Mercy says she's held up in a meeting with people from the Mayor's Office. She wants a briefing the moment she's out."

At the station, we rode the elevator, discussing the natural next step in the investigation.

"Hotels. Let's check with the higher-end establishments and see if they got a visitor who hasn't checked in, missed their reservation without an explanation, or someone late to check out. I'd assume most guests will be leaving tomorrow or the day after. By Monday, Boston should be back to its normal volume of tourists and visitors. But we should try to get a leg up and speak to as many people as we can while they're still in town." I stole a glance at my thinning frame reflected on the elevator wall.

André exited on the third floor, the admin division. I rode two floors up to Homicide.

The murder division had recently gone through extensive renovations. In the end, the city had gifted its murder cops a spacious and airy area with modern equipment, flat screens bolted to the walls, and rolls of new, modern black desks. The second half of the space was reserved for rank and file — anyone a step above detective had an office, not much bigger than cubicle. But it came with a glass door, its own AC, and a flat screen.

Every office had been claimed except one. It had stayed empty for almost a year until the department officially selected its next lead homicide detective.

I entered the bullpen — bare, empty, and quiet. Unusual for the time of day. Near the end of shift, the space usually crawled with grumbling detectives like ants at a Sunday family picnic. Anecdotes of the day's calls, phones ringing off the hook, chatter, tittering. Where had it all gone today?

I told myself to drop it. Not to take it personally. But I did. I had imagined giving a speech to my detectives — rallying the troops, offering my sage wisdom and guidance — "This marks a new dawn, a new day, a new era for our department. Never let a murder case go unsolved."

Instead of the store-bought cake I expected in the break room, I found someone's wife had dropped off homemade M&M cookies. I took two and got a soda from the vending machine.

I hit the lights of my office and closed the door, then turned around to scan the empty desk in front of me. And I frowned at the sign on the door. In gold letters with a black outline, someone had spelled my name wrong — 'Temple Ston,' the E missing at the end.

A small inconvenience. Easy to fix with a short call. Upset, I bit into the cookie. The sugar rush hit me right away. But my mood remained flatlined and on life support.

At that moment, I spied Bradly Walker strolling in. He had been up against me for the promotion. We haven't spoken since the announcement, but I assumed there were no hard feelings between us.

"Walker," I called out.

His thick shoulders, sculpted by a vigorous weightlifting routine, flexed upon hearing my voice. He threw his jacket over his chair and dropped into it.

With no time to be ignored, I left my office, walked up to him and planted myself at the foot of his desk.

"Walker — I need you to take a list of names from André and start running them down. When you're done, check with the lab and the morgue for the status on the Jane Doe we caught this morning. I want us to hit this case hard from all sides."

Bradley Walker opened the top drawer of his desk, pulled out a pink OT slip, flicked his name across the signature line, and stood up.

"Can't do it. Captain wants me to stay on the museum shooting from last month. Catch you later."

He casually strutted through the front double doors, called the elevator, and as he turned, our eyes connected for a second. The smug look on his face stayed there until the elevator doors closed.

Just then, the evening news came on. Footage of the Franklin Park homicide rolled on every monitor in the homicide division. I watched it with interest. The cop cars, the trove of disappointed and confused people, expecting answers; some explanation of who'd do such a horrible thing to another person.

About to walk to my office, the video switched to a still of my face ducking under the yellow tape. The thick red banner on the screen showed my name and title — Lead Homicide Detective Temple Stone with Boston Police. As the newswoman announced my promotion and skimmed over my career with the BPD, I focused on myself, shaking my head in disapproval, trying to be less self-critical — *you don't look that bad. It's a blurry image of you.*

In fact, I looked winded, even disheveled; still reeling from Giovanni and Hoffman dumping their grim prediction on me. The longer I stared at that photo, the more I began to think I seemed out of place, somehow partially damaged —the recently discovered hidden defect in me making me the wrong choice for the job.

"Detective Stone," a male voice said behind me, interrupting the self-deprecating critic in my mind.

Lem Needham, a junior detective also on his first day on the murder floor, nodded at my clenched fist crushing the M&M cookie.

"Heard you're taking the reins on the body from the park," he said.

He wore a dusty brown suit straight out of the seventies, right down to the flared pants. His hair was wavy, kind of on the longer side and barely acceptable by Boston PD standards. His sideburns were razor-edged.

"Every once in a while, the rumors are true." I dusted my sugary hands off in a wastebasket.

"I want to offer my services." His gaze pinned me to the spot. "After a full day with my current partner, we both could use a break from each other. You'd really be doing me a solid. I can do all the grunt work, you know — working the phones, prelim interviews, checking alibis. Pretty much anything you don't want to do, I'll do."

I glanced over to the desk Lem Needham shared with his inept partner, a flabby pencil pusher who came to work solely for the free coffee.

It was an offer I couldn't pass up. The number of potential suspects and witnesses had my head spinning. At this stage of the game, it was hard to know who was who.

And judging by Bradley Walker's warm welcome, I might have to prove myself to some of the other detectives before they started to trust me and follow my orders.

"Sure. That'd be a big help." I took a seat behind my desk. "Jones is downstairs, but I'll get his approval later. I'm sure he won't mind you joining the case."

Lem had a funny look on his face I couldn't quite figure out. Then he said, "André Jones, your old partner?" Lem shook his head. "Water under the bridge for you two then? Never underestimate the power of forgiveness."

The falling-out between me and André was well documented between the walls of this department. He didn't get to a shoot-out in time when a vengeful husband killed his wife then turned the gun on me and shot me three times. The blunder had been nearly fatal for me. I had survived by the skin of my teeth. And according to my doctors, the battle for my life was far from over if the shifting bullet fragment changed trajectory and ended up in my heart.

"It was a test of our friendship..." I left it at that. "André's working on a list of suspects we need to interview to kick off the investigation. He has some of them coming in this afternoon. Take some of his. Have you worked a murder case before?"

"I've assisted on a few. Technically I'm still in training," Lem said.

"Alright. Run everything by me. We can't afford any screw-ups, or both of our careers could end up in the can. I want background checks on those with immediate access to the site. The killer had uninterrupted time with the vic on the stage. So, he must have knowledge of schedules, who's coming and going."

"You think it's an inside job?" Lem asked.

"Hard to say. We must immediately start to eliminate possibilities until wc are left with one. The killer thought of everything — hair, make-up, wardrobe. The whole kit and caboodle."

I stood up. "Come get me if you need me. I'll be in the conference room setting up the murder book."

I didn't get far before a dizzy spell stopped me in my tracks. It swooped in out of nowhere and left my knees soft. The head fog lasted only seconds but cloaked my mind in a blurry veil. Too afraid someone might notice my inability to stand on my own two feet, I crumbled in my chair.

After five minutes of cradling my head in my palms, I started to feel good to go. Just then, I noticed the blinking message line on my desk phone. I punched in the code and listened.

It was Dr. Giovanni with more bad news.

Chapter 6

I had no choice but to put off thinking about Doctor Giovanni's message until later because André entered my office. The 911 caller and her husband were growing tired of waiting and asking to leave, he informed me.

"Long shift, huh?" André said. "Longer for you after being off for months."

"I like being back. It makes me feel useful. It gets old to be stuck inside the house for months. You look like you can use some time off, though."

He handed me a file. "Alice, fifty-four and Geoff Hatchet, fifty-six. They're in interview room 1A."

"What do we know about them?" I asked.

"Clean records, both. Seem like a nice couple. She's a hairdresser and he works as a managing editor for a local magazine. And according to their driver's licenses, they live on 8th and Pearl. She has been rather upset over the whole thing. But her husband's been keeping her steady."

"Directly across Franklin Park," I said.

After a quick knock, I let myself into the interrogation room. Alice Hatchet stirred as she saw me. She lifted her head resting on her husband's shoulder and sniffled.

"More cops, Geoff?" she said, reaching for her Starbucks coffee.

"Is this really necessary? We've been at it for hours. My wife's tired, and I'd like to take her home," Geoff said to me.

"I am sorry for the inconvenience. I will try to be brief. My name is Detective Temple Stone, and this is my partner André Jones." I sat in one chair, André took the other. "I am in charge of this investigation."

Alice ran a tired hand over her gaunt face. "Well alright then. I don't know how much more I can say. I spoke with a police officer at the park. Told him what I saw." She sighed. "Wish I hadn't seen it."

"And you are on 8th and Pearl? Is that so?" I said.

"By the park, yes. We've owned our house for twenty-four years. My husband's parents owned it before that. We've never had any issues," Alice said.

"You made the call to the police at 5:15 a.m. Are you always up at that time?"

"Only when my husband's out of town," Alice said.

"I was in Maine, writing an opinion piece on a new five-star resort."

"We will need the name of the hotel," I said.

"Sure. I checked in on Saturday. Stayed only one night. I wanted to get back to Alice. She doesn't like to be alone in the house."

Alice Hatchet trembled lightly. Geoff put an arm around her and drew her closer.

"I'm up all night long. Every light in the house is on. TV's on. The noise, hearing other people talking, calms my nerves. Sometimes I travel with Geoff if we can add in a few extra days; a getaway for us. But since he was traveling to Maine and I had a client early in the morning, I stayed behind."

"I see in my report you're a hairdresser. What salon?" I asked.

"Lady's Cut. I own it. It's on Trenton Street. Not far from where we live. I usually walk to work."

"And I work for *Boston High Life* as a managing editor."

"What happened this morning, Alice?" I put down the field incident report.

She seemed frozen and distant, as if she stood in front of a locked door she didn't want to open. Geoff rubbed her hand, urging Alice to speak.

"Onyx, our poodle, was scratching at the door for fifteen minutes. I couldn't get him to stop. I thought he might need to pee. He's on some meds for his age — eighteen — and his bladder is not what it used to be. I opened the door and he bolted. I have only seen him go that fast after he sees a cat, but the years have slowed him down significantly. He made a beeline for the park. I panicked. Onyx is practically blind and deaf. I was worried he'd get lost and I'd never see my sweet boy ever again. I ran right after him, wearing my house shoes and pajamas. It was still dark outside. Cold too."

"Did you know Franklin Park was hosting a running convention?"

"I knew something was going on at the park. Saw them putting up the stage and setting up the tents. But I don't pay those events any more attention. After two decades of living across a busy park, you kind of go on autopilot with stuff like that."

"Where was Onyx?"

"He ran off towards a path he likes. It leads to the water. Since he was a puppy, our Onyx loved the water. More so now since he's been getting sicker. I could hear him barking. I thought it was a cat. It didn't occur to me that it could be something else."

"Miss Hatchet, did you see what Onyx was barking at?"

She folded her hands in front of her chest, her eyes misty.

"No...no. But...but as I was getting closer, I heard a thud. A kick. Onyx whimpered and scrambled back. He jumped into my arms, shivering. I told him it was alright and started for the house. As I passed the stage, that's when I saw her. A woman in a white dress and a Halloween mask. My God! It was awful. Horrible. I screamed for help. As soon as I got to my house, I called 911. Told them to come quick. She needed help."

"There. My wife has told you everything. Are we done now?" Geoff kissed her hair.

"Not yet, sir. I have a few more questions. Alice, I know this must be hard. But I really need you to think about this morning. About what you saw. Did you see anyone else in the park?"

"No. No. Just Onyx. Running off. His favorite path. After a cat."

"So no one was around you?"

"No. There was no one. She was there. The dead woman. Alone. I can't bring myself to think what she went through."

"Alice, try to think some more. The thud. What did it sound like?"

She pulled away from her husband and withdrew into herself. "It could have been a kick. Like someone kicked my Onyx. He looked petrified when I picked him up. But I saw no one."

She started to say something else, then stopped to think it over. "I don't know if this could help you or not. But I heard a car engine idling on the street by the park. It was there for an hour, maybe longer. It drove me crazy. I must have dozed off at some point because I woke up startled from Onyx scratching at the door begging to be let out."

"A car? Are you sure about that?"

"Yes. It never occurred to me to look out the window, so I can't give you a make or a model. But there was a car parked at Franklin for some time overnight."

"Do you think you can remember the time?"

Alice glanced at her husband. "Geoff...can tell you. I sent him a text."

Geoff took his phone out. "3:40 a.m. Alice said 'I can't wait for you to come home. It's been a night.'"

"Yes, 3:40. I remember; I fell asleep shortly after."

"Thank you for waiting around. I know you want to go home."

"Do you know who she is? The murdered lady?"

"We are still working on identifying her. Take my business card. If you think of anything else, give me a call. If you don't have any questions for me, you two are free to go."

Before we left, André asked Alice, "How's Onyx?"

"Hmm?" Alice replied. "The whole thing gave him a big fright. I don't think he will be chasing after any cats in the foreseeable future."

I regarded André intently while we walked through the hallway to my office.

"It might have started with Onyx chasing a cat, but the dog might have surprised our killer. I want a team to go to Franklin and search the path Alice Hatchet told us about. Have them check the shrubs and the garbage cans. The killer could have fled in a hurry, worried Alice saw him, and left evidence behind. I'd like a patrol car stationed at Franklin Park tonight. He might be back to pick up after himself, and if he does, I'd like us to be waiting for him."

"We also need to talk to Alice and Geoff Hatchet's neighbors. Chances are if Alice heard a car engine overnight at the park, someone else could have too."

The phone was ringing when I entered my office. André stood waiting by the open door.

I picked up. "Detective Stone."

"Mercy's coming up. She wants that brief now," André mumbled.

"Got it. Thanks." I hung up. "That was Tessa Wu from the morgue. She wants to see me. The brief will have to wait."

"Did she say why?" André checked his phone.

"Not really. But I sensed she'd rather speak with me sooner than later," I said, fixing the collar of my suit.

André's jaw flexed. "Gail Mercy is not to be tussled with, Temple. She insisted on a brief first. Anything else second. If you try playing games, she won't hesitate to throw you off the case."

I shrugged. "The ME won't take that long. If it makes you feel better, I'll ask for her forgiveness when we come back..."

"But not for her permission." André followed right on my heels.

Chapter 7

A lot of murder cops I know can't stand the smell of formaldehyde wafting about the Medical Examiner's building on Albany, but I rather liked the pungent odor. For whatever reason, it helped settle down the headache hammering my head.

André swiped his ID across the security scanner, and the building guard let us take our guns from the plastic bins at the end of the conveyor belt.

"Bradley Walker would've been my first choice," André muttered. "Needham's green in the field. And his file's light on casework."

I didn't want to get into Bradley Walker blowing me off. But inside I was still seething over Walker's punk-ass move. "How else would he learn if not by holding his feet to the fire? It's how you and I gained experience. No one held our hand. They threw us to the wolves and passed the popcorn waiting to see who survived."

A smile bloomed on André's lips. "Run it by Mercy. She might want Needham assigned somewhere else." He stopped abruptly and pointed a finger at my chest. "And if her answer's no, accept it and move on. She has a lot on her plate. I got a whiff of her conversation with the mayor's emissary," he exhaled, "it sounded ugly."

I brushed aside his guidance. A lead detective should be able to assemble his own team.

"Mercy's a tough egg to crack. She stands head and shoulders above the rest." I left it at that.

I scanned the main lobby. Some visitors were taking their shoes off to walk through the body scanner. A bank of elevator doors parted. Tessa Wu stepped out, dressed in a gray skirt suit, and looked up from a stack of papers in her hands.

"That was fast. Usually it takes you a few hours to show up. Walk with me," she said.

"I'm in desperate need of good news. Got any for me? Otherwise, I wasted a trip and possibly riled up Gail Mercy," I said.

Wu offered a quick nod and pressed her index finger on the fingerprint machine. A blue light flashed, and the compression doors glided apart. She led me into the autopsy examination room.

"Why don't I show you? Remember to put on PPE," Wu said, stuffing her arms into a white medical coat.

"I think I'd rather stay outside," André said, a hand resting over his bulging gut. "Breakfast hasn't settled yet."

"Jones still can't handle the dead, huh?" Wu donned a clear shield over her face.

"Brilliant detective mind, not so good with exposed flesh and, well...guts." I glanced down at the open cavity of Jane Doe.

"Do you know her name yet?" I studied the murder vic lying flat on the metal gurney.

"Not yet, I'm afraid. But at least I can give you more background to point you in the right direction. Jane Doe was in outstanding form. She kept up her fitness routine."

"So, one of the runners then?"

Wu pointed to Jane's exposed bare feet. "Can't tell you for sure. Her scans show no runner's knee, and her joints don't look inflamed. Marathon runners go through extensive training before they participate in a world-renowned sporting event. Jane loved to exercise, but if I had to take a guess, I'd say Pilates most days, and occasionally yoga.

"She had an office job. Her skin shows a lack of vitamin D, which indicates her body didn't get enough sunlight. And I noted early-onset arthritis in her fingers. She did something that required an extreme amount of typing," Wu said.

"She looks peaceful and calm. The missing ring on her finger suggests that she was in a committed relationship. Engaged, married. But they got into a fight. He killed her," I said, focused on Jane Doe's restful features. "Why did you come to Boston? For the running convention? Or are you from here?" I asked Jane.

"Given that she's dead and she won't give you an answer, I can tell you why she looks so peaceful and calm — I'm warning you, it's as bad as you might imagine. The toxicology report suggests the killer doped her out of her mind. She was zonked out to oblivion. A total zombie. Her last hours were spent in a catatonic state. High, low, and everywhere in between."

"What are we talking about? Illicit drugs?"

"A good mix of everything. Whatever he had on hand, he gave her. One dose more of this or that, she'd have ODed," Wu said.

"Are we dealing with an amateur or a pro?" I asked.

"Can't be a hundred percent sure, but I think the killer got a lucky break."

For several moments, Wu worked in complete silence. The only noise was coming from the air conditioning system blasting a polar breeze from the vents.

Wu placed Doe's liver on a scale, measured it. "Healthy female, around forty. No other internal injury to the surrounding organs. That and the clean cut in her ribs tells me she's probably not his first.

"A nervous slasher usually plunges the weapon with too much force, causing damage to the heart. Don't see that here," she told me.

Wu adjusted the magnifying lens and trained it on the cavity. She motioned for me to step forward. "Take a look. From the point of entry the blade has to be extremely sharp, small, the tip slightly elongated. He nicked her fast. She probably never saw it coming. By the time she could do something about it — it was too late."

"Was she sexually assaulted?" I asked.

"No signs of rape," Wu replied.

"What else have you got? Can you give me the type of weapon?"

"That's not an easy question to answer. And I'll need more than just a few hours."

I let the ME work. Fixed my gaze on the dark bruises along Jane Doe's wrists. Similar markings on her ankles. I had noted them at the crime scene. Under the fluorescent lights, they appeared more sinister and wicked.

Pointing them out, I asked her, "What can you tell me about these?"

Not shifting her attention away from her work, Wu said, "He held her in restraints for some time — though I don't see why. She wasn't going anywhere. She couldn't escape or fight him. Her injuries incapacitated her enough that she would have gone along with whatever sick trick he had up his sleeve."

Images of Jane Doe struggling against metal shackles scattered in front of me until I moved on to her fingers. "Red nail polish. Shelly paints hers red when I take her on a date."

"I don't think he painted them. They seem salon quality. But I will take samples and submit them to the crime lab. Maybe they could give you the manufacturer. As far as the broken nail — it's defensive."

"A chance then that she fought him? Tried to defend herself against her attacker? It's possible she clawed a piece out of him."

"There's always a possibility, but I found no human cells under her fingernails when I scraped her. It could be he cleaned her nails. Scrubbed them when he bathed her."

"Haven't seen the crime scene report yet, but on first observation — he left a tidy crime scene. Careful. Mindful of details. Do you still have her dress?" I asked.

"I sent it off to the crime lab as soon as I undressed her. I want to find out who she is as badly as you do. Trust me," Wu said. "Any leads on your end?"

I placed a thumb under my chin. "The woman who found Jane Doe — Alice Hatchet — reported a car engine idling at the park for several hours. I have detectives talking to her neighbors to see if anyone else can corroborate."

"So you don't suspect Alice Hatchet?" Wu asked.

"Both she and her husband have clean backgrounds. Older couple. She's a hairdresser; he's an editor. Husband was out of town. In Maine. We're checking his alibi. If it pans out — then I'm confident I can take them off the suspect list."

Wu puffed and broke my concentration. I caught her inserting her hands inside Jane Doe's body and extracting a perfectly preserved heart. My own broken heart skipped several beats at the visual. Doctor Giovanni's voice started to sound off in my brain, and I needed to shut it off. I couldn't allow it to distract me.

"How soon can you run her DNA? I'm striking out with her fingerprints. Nothing in the police database," I said.

A sharp knock on the glass panels startled me.

"Mercy called. She can't sway City Hall to hold off the press conference until we have more evidence. She wants you to be there." He pointed at me. "How much longer Doctor Wu?"

"I'll be done in ten, Lieutenant Jones. Wrapping things up. Can you wait that long?" Wu pulled off her stained gloves, walked to a metal sink, and turned the faucet on.

"Lemme ask."

"Might be a while on the DNA," she said.

I tensed up. "Doctor, this case is a priority one. We need her name. We need to know where she came from. The longer we wait, the colder the trail to her killer gets."

Wu inhaled patiently. "Slow down, Stone. Look," she pointed to the heart on the scale, "notice any anomalies?"

I shook my head while staring at the perfectly healthy non-operational heart outside Doe's body. "Isn't that odd?"

Wu threw a knowing glance at the heart. "Very. Kind of why I wanted you to see for yourself." She went back to Jane Doe. "He drained her blood. Not a single drop in her. Squeezed her out like a lemon. So if you want to ID her fast, I suggest detective, that you think of another option. You have no choice." Wu returned to measuring the heart, muttering, "Have you ever seen anything like that?"

Bloodless victim. No, I have not.

Chapter 8

I've been a murder cop for over a decade. I thought I'd seen every kind of murder imaginable. But Jane Doe's bloodless cavity sent chills down my spine.

My eyes shifted to her restful features. I could imagine her walking her dog, buying a newspaper, waving hello to the mailman. Then what did she do or didn't do to catch the attention of her killer? Something about her attracted him to Jane Doe. He had gone through a lot of trouble to stage her. In his imagination, I mused, Jane Doe had given him something another woman had taken away. I shook my head, my chin resting in my hand — turning details of the case over in my mind. Her soft white dress, her fresh floral scent, nails painted to match her lips. He had tried to bring beauty to her after she died. What about the Halloween mask? Kiddish and far from scary if you saw it in a store display, but on a dead woman, it took on an entirely different meaning. The whys in the case were beginning to drive me crazy.

André joined us.

"Mercy's banging her head against the wall with City Hall. They've locked horns, and neither party is interested in reaching a compromise. She won't allow the mayor to dump on the department. But a public, full-out war with the mayor could blow up in both their faces. So, they've reached a temporary truce until," André stared at Wu with questions in his eyes, "the doc can tell us something more concrete we can take to the press. Hate to put you in a tight spot, doc — "

"No, you're not, Jones. Drop the act." Wu offered a phony smile. "I have a department to run like the rest of them. And I won't allow it to be dragged into their dog and pony show. Feel free to quote me to your supervisor. Besides, what I have so far," she hung up her heavy-duty apron, "I'm not certain you'll want to be made public at this time."

"The investigation got hit with a major complication," I started to say when André's phone lit up with a happy melody.

He declined the first and the second call right after that. "My kids." He shut it off and slid it into a pocket. "Driving my wife up the wall."

"I've been doing this job for six years..." Wu said. "But this autopsy wiped me out emotionally."

She pointed to her office adjoining the examination room. "We all could use a seat. Coffee?"

"Black, one sugar," André said.

Wu came back with two cups of coffee, one tea.

"The murder is the cleanest of my career. The cut he made was small but deadly. He knew exactly how to use the tip of the blade," Wu began.

"And yet he felt compelled to restrain her," I mumbled.

"Correct. The bruises on her ankles and wrists match what I've seen in other cases involving shackling. As I was saying earlier, that poor woman on my table was surely bleeding out. She wasn't going anywhere. Why the perp felt the need to put her through needless torture is beyond my professional expertise. Cuffs are usually used by a physically weak attacker, and he needs to exert dominance over his victim.

"I see nothing weak done to Jane Doe. Quite the opposite. The chains were tight, and judging by the color of the bruises on her extremities, he kept them on for several hours after she died. She was only five-four."

"So, he's physically capable. Strong. Not weakness but cruelty motivated," I said, gathering a second wind under my wings.

Wu's thin black eyebrows curved. The amber light of the desk lamp illuminated the medical examiner's intense mocha eyes as she swept a stray piece of dark hair away from her face.

"Excessively cruel," she remarked. "Jane Doe developed a pneumothorax quickly after he attacked her. It's not a lot to go on. And there's no concrete evidence suggesting he was a gun for hire. But my gut tells me your guy has done some killing before."

"More dead ends. The pneumothorax is specific enough for an MO. Might be something we can work with back at the station. We will search the national database for other victims murdered in the last year matching Jane Doe's injuries." I glanced at André while my brain circled through all my options. "Doctor Wu believes the stabbing was decisive. He's skilled with the blade."

"A pneumothorax, huh? Sounds like an awful way to go," André added.

"That's right. In a nutshell." Wu set aside her tea. She picked up two sheets of paper and placed them side by side. "Imagine air pushing up against your left lung." Wu crumbled one of the sheets. "The pressure causes the lung to weaken, leading to a collapse. Nowadays, if medical assistance is rendered, a pneumothorax can be repaired. But in this case, I'm afraid the collapsed lung was intentional. His postmortem capabilities are remarkable. What he did with her is quite intricate to accomplish. Masterful. You two have your work cut out for you."

André rubbed his clean-shaven face, examining the balled-up paper. "I get the feeling that I'm still behind."

Wu nodded to the body outside her office. "Before you walked in, I was showing your partner, Detective Stone, what I think the killer was really after..."

"Her blood," I filled in the rest.

Dead silence followed. André gazed towards the open doors leading to the medical exam room. His attention landed on Jane Doe. "The SOB's out for blood." A long pause. "That's one heck of a complication."

"I'm worried she might not be his first. Based on Doctor Wu's initial findings. Clean-cut, collapsed lung. He drained her blood for Christ's sake," I said.

"Your killer definitely has a certain set of skills...unique ones. He's well-acquainted with handling a dead body. I haven't found any rookie mistakes or deliberate harm done to her. He killed her, yes, and I'll swear that was the intent, but the work he did on her after she expired is beyond comparison. Which brings me to the next issue."

"There's more? C'mon doc, you're bleeding me dry over here," I groaned.

"At the scene, I suspected the killer had done something to Jane Doe. Slowed down her decomp. He has. She was embalmed postmortem. Again, top-shelf stuff. You can't get that type of fluid off Amazon. Distributors usually sell to businesses — funeral homes, mainly. But a case or two could get bumped off a truck. Make a few extra bucks on the side selling *overstock*," Wu suggested.

I blinked several times. "Excuse me, what? Are you saying that he not only drained her blood but he also embalmed her after?"

"I'm afraid so."

"The press definitely can't know that. Never heard of anything stranger," André said, sobered.

"When we get back to the office, you and Lem get on the phone with the national distributors. I'll take the funeral homes and see if any embalming fluid walked off their shelves unaccounted for," I told André.

"Then we'd better head out. City Hall won't wait for us. And Mercy gave me her marching orders — Boston's top homicide dog must stand beside her when the cameras roll."

Wu's computer dinged, and she put on her reading glasses. "It's the chem lab. Hold on, this could be interesting." She read the report for several moments. "Let me print you a copy."

I scanned the chemical work-up on Jane Doe. Drug crimes weren't my specialty, but murder and drugs usually went hand in hand. A few names on the list like diazepam, ketamine, and propofol, I recognized without trouble. There were several others I'd never heard of.

Wu added context to the report. "Her system resembles a mixology of over-the-counter and prescription meds. Like I've been saying, she went through a very rough deal." She paused. "Interestingly enough, some of these meds are prescribed to cancer patients."

"Someone, somewhere, had to have written the script for two of these," I said.

"From what I'm told, the dark underworld of controlled substances is booming. But we can speak with Narcotics. Pull them in and ask for assistance. Their CIs might come in handy." André skimmed the pill names over my shoulder.

I hoisted myself up. My eyes met Wu's serious glare. "There are only three chemical companies nationwide that specialize in embalming fluid. I'll have my assistant fax you their names and contact info."

"Thanks, doc. If you get anything else — "

"You'll be my first call."

On my way out, I swung by Jane Doe one last time. The shocking nature of her death, mummified practically alive, chilled my spine again. The killer wanted her dead but preserved. Another troubling why.

Chapter 9

I was reaching for the coffee canister in Homicide when someone shouted, "Detective!" I hurried to Mercy's office.

"Captain!" I said, closing the door behind me.

"What the hell was that? Those reporters tore me apart in front of the mayor and the damn city. You didn't think a little heads-up would have been in order? I didn't even know the killer stabbed Jane Doe to death." Mercy's voice sizzled with fury. Her face was flushed red, her fuming stare pinning me down, demanding answers.

"Jones and I rushed over to the press conference as soon as we left the morgue. There was no time. Someone leaked it to the media — and the leak didn't come from Homicide."

"It's out there now. For Christ's sake. It's all they will talk about for weeks," Mercy said. "Okay, sit down and brief me."

"Jane Doe, early forties, white female, left dead at Franklin Park. The medical examiner found a stab wound to the ribs. He punctured her lung. The official cause of death is pneumothorax. A collapsed lung. Based on the angle of the stab wound, we have the killer's approximate height. Taller than our vic. Jane Doe is shy of five four. It's not enough to eliminate suspects, but it's a start," I said.

I powered on the iPad and handed it to Mercy. She swiped between the crime photos and the autopsy notes.

"The eyewitness report is in the system. Alice Hatchet, fifty-four, a local hairdresser, lives across the park. Her husband was out of town on a business trip. They have lived in their house for the past twenty-four years. No issues or criminal reports on either of them. At this time, I don't consider them suspects."

"What was Miss Hatchet doing in the park at 5 a.m.? Seems an off time for a woman to be walking alone."

"She wasn't, ma'am. Their dog, Onyx, ran off. Alice thought he saw a cat, but I think he might have encountered our killer. Alice never saw a person, but it sounded like someone kicked Onyx."

"And you think the killer heard the dog's barking, his work interrupted, and hid?" Mercy shook her head. "Alice Hatchet could have been killed if she decided to confront the person who kicked her dog."

"I agree. Walking back to her house, Alice spotted the Halloween mask on Jane Doe and freaked out and called us immediately. Officers Westcott and Stevens took the call."

"Yes, I see their names. From the Roxbury station. Don't know them personally." Mercy eyed the photos of the bruises on Jane Doe. "What can you tell me about these?"

"He held her in restraints for hours, even after she died. Her tox screen came back — and looking at the meds he gave her, Jane Doe wasn't going to make a run for it. I think he knew that, which leads me to believe the restraints add to the fantasy. Some twisted kink he played out. Maybe he likes to watch his victims suffer. Gives him a thrill."

"How lovely," Mercy said sarcastically, scrolling to the next page. "Anything else on the killer?"

"Doctor Wu believes he is skilled with the blade. Knew how to use it. He caused no other injuries to the organs. He targeted the lung. The rape kit came back clean. So he didn't force himself on Jane Doe. Murder seems to be the pure motivator behind the crime," I said. "She was bathed by him, scrubbed under her nails."

"To dispose of evidence. Just perfect," Mercy said.

"Looks like it. He cleaned the crime scene in the park too. The main focus was Jane Doe. She played a key role in his fantasy, I think. White dress, make-up, bath — he thought of the details, cared for her postpartum. And here is where things turn really weird."

"Halloween-mask-wearing dead woman in the center of a public park not weird enough for you Detective Stone?"

"It's weird, ma'am, but it gets worse," I answered.

"Before you go ahead — do we have an ID on her? DNA? How long does Wu need before she gets the results?"

"That's not happening, captain. The killer drained Jane Doe's body."

"Come again, drained? What does that even mean?" Mercy peered at me over the iPad.

"He removed her blood."

"Holy shit! Why?"

"The medical examiner has a pretty good idea."

"Do share it."

"He embalmed Jane Doe. That's why she looked so alive and well... fresh."

"He drained her blood and then embalmed that poor woman in the park? Am I hearing this right?" Mercy went back to the crime scene photos. "The media will dub him Bloodless. I can already see the headlines once they sniff it out. We can't keep this from the public for long. Work fast."

"Yes ma'am. The killer has a certain set of skills. Fingerprints are our only option at the moment, unless someone calls in and reports her missing. I have detectives checking past reports to see if we can find a name for her. I discovered a small bruise on her ring finger. I think she was married. And the killer took the ring after he killed her."

"So Jane Doe is still a Jane Doe?"

"I'm afraid so. At least for the next several hours. We are checking with the DMV and expanding the search nationwide. I will put in a call to the FBI and have them check their fingerprint database. It's only a matter of time before we learn her name. Meanwhile, I have a couple of patrols guarding Franklin Park in case the killer comes back. And we are going door to door, talking to Hatchet's neighbors to see if someone saw something in the park," I said. "André is working on a list of people we can interview tomorrow. And I'm checking to see if we can link a collapsed lung to any other unsolved murder cases."

"Good. Hit this investigation from all sides. We can't allow it to go cold."

Mercy threw her head back in her chair. "And don't think I forgot about you going over my head and running to the ME when I told you to wait for me. I distinctly remember saying first brief me, second the ME, then anything else."

I gulped. I guessed it was time to ask for her forgiveness rather than for her permission.

"It won't happen again, captain. I only went to see Wu because she called and said she had something to show me. And Jones said you were tied up with the mayor."

She exhaled; a long, suffocating sight. "That woman's draining. Doesn't know the first thing about policing or how crime-solving works. But she loves to tell me how to do my job."

"I imagine demanding bosses can be a pain in the ass." I set my empty mug on her desk.

"Stone, I know you know better than sassing me — "

"Meant nothing personal," I said.

"Good." She shuffled some papers and files off her desk.

Her phone rang. I stood, expecting the meeting to be over. "Hang on. This will take a second."

Five minutes later I was still waiting for Mercy to conclude the call. She was locked in a furious argument with someone named Rivers. From the back and forth I gathered that Rivers worked for the mayor in the capacity of chief assistant. Mercy despised her. After another several moments of barbed exchanges, Mercy slammed the handle in its cradle.

"Go to hell," she murmured.

"Ahem," I said.

"Sorry you had to hear that. City Hall chips away at our budget year after year. Cut, cut, cut. And when the city falls on hard times, they turn to us for answers," Mercy said, staring out the window of her office. Smoky night skies hugged the building roofs of the Boston skyline.

A knock at the door interrupted us.

André let himself in.

"Lem Needham's looking for you. He says he's completed backgrounds from his list. Wondering if he should wait for you or leave? His shift officially ended an hour ago," André said.

Mercy's brows connected. "Who allowed Needham near this case? Do I even need to ask?" She planted her hands on her desk. "Detective Stone, only I have the authority to take detectives off their cases. Another infraction, and you'll be this close to being removed from your own investigation. Don't make me repeat myself again."

"Yes, ma'am. If that's all, I should go back to my office..."

"I'll go with you. I finished interviewing a few people connected with the event. There are another eight left for tomorrow," André said.

"A lot more to go through. If the mayor wants us to move fast with the investigation, we will need the manpower," I said to Mercy.

"Budget cuts. That's all you need to know."

"I can use at least one more detective on the case. Lem Needham's young, capable, and the experience he'd gain working this homicide will only make him a stronger murder cop."

"Alright, Lem's in. No one else until I've had a chance to go over the overtime pay and see if we have anything left in our rainy-day piggy bank." She waved us away with a hand. "Dismissed."

I returned to my desk, bone tired and depressed, stared down by the sad eyes of Jane Doe gazing at me from the murder board. By anyone's standards, my first day as Boston's lead homicide detective had been a total and complete disaster. I had nearly been kicked off my own investigation twice by the captain for trying to run it with little to no oversight from her. And despite my best efforts, I haven't discovered a single clue to help me catch the Bloodless killer.

Don't worry Jane. I'll get the bastard, I said to the pinned photos of Jane Doe as I started to gather my belongings. In the paper tray, I saw a typed report signed by LN.

I unclipped the report and glanced at it. Lem Needham had attached a stack of one-sheet summaries of people on his list. Neat and organized, I noted.

A tiny tap on the glass prompted me to look up. André poked his head in, a friendly smile on his face.

He approached, keeping something behind his back.

"Leaving for the night. Before I sign out, I almost forgot to give you my gift. Meant to surprise you with it earlier, but then we caught a murder and it slipped my mind."

"You didn't have to."

He revealed a tall bottle of clear Casamigos tequila, like the one we had shared in Mexico ten years ago. Right out of the police academy on a whim, I had dragged him to the Yucatán Peninsula off the Gulf of Mexico for a weekend of deep-sea fishing. At the end of the trip, we had caught no fish, only a raging tequila-induced hangover.

I accepted the gift, grateful. Part of me wanted to tell André about my heart condition, but I couldn't quite yet bring myself to declare out loud that my life might be nearly over. So, I kept my mouth shut. "It means a lot."

"Don't drink it without me."

Holding the bottled memories of blazing sun, azure water, and painful tan burn mugged my eyes. I placed the alcohol in the bottom drawer of my desk, locked it in, and shut the lights off. I threw the photographs into my work bag so I could study them at home. As I closed the door, I sensed Jane Doe's woeful eyes on the back of my neck.

Chapter 10

In the dead of the breezy night, I drove the police Ford Explorer into my driveway and parked it next to our always-in-need- of-expensive-repairs 1999 Chevy Silverado. An owl cooed from a tree branch when I switched off the engine.

I dropped my beat-up bag on the ground after spotting a business card for 'Junk Busters' lodged between the Silverado's wipers. Choosing my battles carefully, I hid the card in my back pocket. Running on fumes and feeling sapped, I had no intentions of arguing, especially not with my wife.

A swarm of mosquitos took a chunk out of my neck. Rushing to get away from them, I stumbled through the front door of my house a little after eleven, long after the end of my shift. The front room was dark aside from the small Tiffany lamp glowing amber.

I tossed the car keys in a seashell and slipped out of my shoes. As I undid the top button of my shirt, I reached for the freezer handle. The cool air slapped me across my hot face. An image of the dead vic, white gown, Grim Reaper mask, washed over me. I pushed the crime scene memory to a corner of my brain for later.

But I couldn't do the same with Giovanni's call. A part of me wished I'd never played his recording, leaving the bad news for the morning, giving myself a night of rest before I faced the damning truth.

No matter how hard I tried to avoid thinking about what Giovanni had said — I couldn't. My life had changed forever with a single phone call.

I looked around the walls of my living room and stopped at a framed photo of Shelly and me laughing in each other's arms. It was taken at the Boston courthouse on the day of our wedding. By then, her baby bump had been visibly pronounced. What would I tell my soon-to-birth wife? Shelly was already freaked out by my job. I was no longer just chasing killers, one lived in my chest. Giovanni's words rang in my ear — *you're a walking time bomb, son!*

Why did I even listen to his message?

I scooped out some vanilla ice cream and ate it. The cold felt good melting down my throat.

In the bathroom, I shed my work clothes and got myself into something more comfortable: a pair of running shorts and a tee. As I tied the string on my shorts, I noticed how loose they fit on me — had I really not detected the sudden weight loss until now?

I walked past the garage door, the light still on. I poked my head in. Tempted, I immediately shut the lights off after I saw the treadmill asking me to jump on. The weights station looked somber at my firm rejection. I doubted I'd be doing any serious running or working out any time soon.

I went back to the fridge in search of food, finding a tray wrapped in silver aluminum foil, a yellow note stuck on it — 'chef's special.' The corner of my eyes dampened. *Hold it together, man!*

My wife, Shelly, was a beauty, with rich milk-chocolate-colored eyes, sandy light brown hair, and a face dotted with a thousand tiny specks of freckles that made me weak in the knees to this day. As drop-dead gorgeous as she was, Shelly lacked every basic human instinct in the kitchen. No other person would think to mix tuna and BBQ beans and bake it until it was charcoal. I was staring at the charred, vile mess she had proudly made for me.

Armed with a fork in hand, I probed the blob, but it smelled unbearable. I dumped it in the garbage and covered it with used paper towels and a rotten banana peel.

I filled a pot with water to boil, threw a pack of ramen noodles in it, and let it steam. While I waited for my amazing dinner to cook, I walked towards the back room and entered the only other bedroom in our fixer-upper. The floor was blocked by a half-open box, the baby crib. I might not be around to see my kid grow up. The least I could do is build the baby a sturdy bed. The idea of dying punched me between the shoulder blades and I kneeled, heavy. *Why me?* crossed my mind, but after a minute of no answer, I tore the box open and fetched the directions booklet.

There was nothing more satisfying than screwing the bolts in tightly, imagining putting a healthy little baby down for a nap. I was nearly done — last bolt — when I stood up too quickly and my head spun. I dropped the stupid bolt somewhere on the floor. Without it, the crib shook like a flimsy cardboard box.

Oh, come on. Seriously! I grumbled under my breath, scanning the beige carpet for the silver bolt. After a while, I gave up. It was lost forever, like all small important things tend to grow legs and disappear.

I wiped my sweaty brow, and a shooting pain in the nape of my neck told me that my body needed rest more than finishing the crib tonight.

I poured the noodles into a bowl and fetched a glass of milk from the fridge, then dragged them to the backyard patio. Shelly and I lived in Rivera, a seaside town close enough to be a suburb of Boston, but homes sold at a significant discount. You got a lot of square footage for your buck, and the killer ocean view wasn't bad either. And tonight, I lay back in the chair, one foot resting over the other, marveling at the thousand and one twinkling lights of the city across the water.

Suddenly, the sliding door glided open, and I heard the crackly noises of the patio planks. A hand rested on my shoulder. I bent down and kissed Shelly's soft skin.

"When did you get in?" Shelly asked as she came around and plopped into the neighboring chair. "I must have dozed off watching the NASA channel. Did you know the scientific term for the astronomical birth of a star is called nova? Latin for 'new'. It's startlingly beautiful — the cosmos beyond the sky."

"I'm looking at something startlingly beautiful right now."

"I'm as big as a ship; can't find a spot that's comfortable. Wouldn't call that beautiful." Shelly rubbed her belly. "Everyone we know has been calling me for hours — wanting to congratulate you. They must have seen you on the news."

I blushed. "The press conference? What a circus. I didn't even have a speaking role."

"With looks like yours, handsome, speaking is optional. You're the perfect cross between Chris Hemsworth and Jamie Fraser." She twirled her fingers in front of my face. "Those high cheekbones, sharp chin, eyes as gray as the moon," Shelly pressed her hands over her heart, "head full of almost blonde wavy hair. And those occasional misplaced curls that refuse to be gelled in place...I married a total heartthrob."

"Stop, Mrs. Stone — you're the one with the looks in our family. I'm an average Joe who scored big time when you married me."

Shelly leaned forward, resting her face on my chest. Her eyes gazing into my own, she said, "I heard about the woman killed at Franklin Park. I know the place. It sounded awful. Is it true? The mask alone is enough to give me night terrors. Don't want to imagine what his victim went through."

I ran a hand through my hair. Escaping the Bloodless murder would be pointless. I couldn't shut off my brain. Jane Doe refused to be filed away and allow me a peaceful moment at home. I breathed in, closed my eyes, and unloaded.

Shelly had been listening without interrupting me until I mentioned the ME's observation of the killer's skill set.

"He sounds experienced. With lots of practice." Her shoulders trembled against the night breeze blowing in from the ocean. I reached over and covered her with a blanket. "And there could be more Wu thinks...gosh, it's too terrible to think about."

"We don't know if he killed more women or if he gained practice through other means."

"What other means could there be?"

I shrugged. "Animals. He could be a hunter. They drain the blood from their kills. Or he could work for a funeral home — according to Wu, the vic's body was pumped full of top-shelf embalming fluid. Kind of like a modern-day mummification."

"Bloodless corpse, Halloween mask, and there could be others. It's much worse than what they said on the news."

"We didn't give them all the information on purpose. Not until we know who we're dealing with."

"I get it. A panicked city could slow roll the investigation. I'm learning," Shelly said.

"You've always been a quick study." I softly kissed her lips.

She concentrated on me. "How's that for a quick study — it's my husband's job to catch him and put him away. Of what you told me about the Bloodless killer..."

"Let's not call him that, please."

"He's exactly that — a blood-hungry monster, and my husband's in charge of hunting him down. I'm no fancy cop, but I know if you get close to him, there's a good chance he'll turn it around and come after you!"

I dismissed her words with a wave. Shelly was known to have an overactive imagination, which caused her to jump at the sight of her own shadow. Not once in my career did I feel threatened by a criminal. Even when that criminal held a nine-mil loaded Glock and released three rounds into me. I had been certain I'd recover, go back to my job, and move on to the next case. That's what stand-up cops do — always chasing after the next case, never stopping until the day they order us to turn in our badge.

"So, then I won't give him the chance to turn it around."

"Temple, take it seriously, okay? Promise me. Your track record of act first nearly cost you your life once before."

"Shelly, I had no choice. She called the station for help. If I had listened to her, told her to get away from him, she would be alive today."

"You did try to tell Jones. He blew you off. It was his case. She was his case. Not yours."

"It doesn't work that way, Shells," I said.

"Yeah. Yeah, it does, Temple. For other cops. You — you had to be the hero. And what did you get for trying to save her? Three shots to the chest."

I rubbed her back without saying a word because I realized I hadn't confessed to her about the doctor.

We embraced for a long time, then Shelly felt a kick. I felt it too. Strong, decisive, and determined.

"That baby's feisty, like her mother," I said and kissed the bump.

Shelly looked out to the water. She spoke over the sound of frogs croaking. "How long do you think she'll stay in? The doctor's saying the first baby is always late." She twirled some ramen noodles onto the fork. "Yum! Hey, wait a minute — how come you're eating dehydrated pasta?" Shelly asked suspiciously. "I can go reheat dinner for you."

I hated lying to her, but if I didn't want to end up in the ER with food poisoning, I thought it was necessary. "I'm stuffed. Your best meal to date. Oven-baked Bosh's beans and canned tuna. A distinct taste."

Her eyes smiled. "Phew! I thought it was odd, never seen those two mixed together, but after I burned the beef pierogi last month, I followed the cookbook recipe faithfully."

Bless her heart!

I watched her casually polish the rest of my dinner for me and wondered how I could tell her what the future had in store for us.

"Mmm, I can go for a slice of cake. Did you bring any home?"

I put my hands together, finding it hard to admit how bummed out I had been about not receiving an office party. It was silly. Silly to get worked up over it. But after putting in ten years in the police department, earning a promotion I rightfully deserved even after a life-threatening injury on the job, no one had bothered to buy a cake and a few balloons for me. The sting of Bradley Walker's self-absorbed attitude still gnawed at me.

"You okay, Temple? Where did you go just now? If you didn't remember I totally understand — after the day you had, it's understandable. I almost forgot the mechanic called about the truck — bad news — he wants four grand to fix the engine issues. I'm worried the Chevy's dead. If you're not home with the work car, I have no means of transportation."

I glared at her. "Is that why you left the neighbor's junk removal card on the truck?"

Her serious brown eyes narrowed at me. "Thatcher and Merrill stopped by as I was talking to the shop. They overheard the conversation and felt bad for us. He promised to remove the truck from our lawn for free. He left his digits without telling me. What's the big deal?"

Feeling a tinge of guilt, I dropped the conversation. It wasn't Shelly's fault I was stubbornly trying to hold on to something that was broken. But after my parents died in a boat accident seven years ago, something told me to hold on to their truck.

Their bodies were never recovered. And since they drowned in a lake in New Hampshire, I had no jurisdiction over the investigation. With no witnesses and no evidence to suggest anything off happened to them, the NH staties stopped looking.

And unless I brought forth new evidence, their case would remain closed. I had suspected the Chevy might help me understand who or why killed them. Several painful years and expensive fixes later, the heap of metal had produced zilch.

"I'll take care of it," I said.

"Yeah, right, I've heard that before. You're lucky you're so damn fine Detective Stone."

She scooted closer to me, threw the blanket over our feet, and placed her hand on my chest. "It's beating so fast. Almost as fast as our baby when the doctor listens to it on ultrasound."

I could tell Shelly was starting to doze off again. Between dream and waking, she mumbled, "Giovanni, your primary — how did it go with him? Clean bill of health?"

An electric wave of shock zapped me, this time straight into my heart. "Shelly, there's something I need to tell you. And I need you to listen, okay?"

She nodded.

But I couldn't bring myself to actually speak. Overwhelmed, I hunched over, face lying in her open palms, and for the first time that day, I allowed myself to cry.

Chapter 11

The night had dragged on after I told Shelly about the bullet fragment threatening my heart. She had insisted on hearing me repeat it over and over until eventually, she fell asleep, her cheeks still wet from the tears. Exhausted, I had tried to nap beside her, but by 4 a.m., I kicked off the bed cover and walked upstairs to fetch coffee.

Out the kitchen window, the trees were illuminated by the full moon slowly withdrawing to make way for the sun. The coffee maker beeped. I poured myself a cup and settled into the well-worn loveseat in the living room, the Tiffany lamp glowing as I unzipped my work bag.

Maybe in the wee hours of the morning, I could make sense of Bloodless's killing of Jane Doe.

I started with the initial report filed by the first officers on scene — Officers Westcott and her partner Stevens. Routine patrol until Dispatch dropped the Franklin Park call on them. A concerned citizen requesting a well-being check on a woman.

Westcott had discovered the body seated on a black folding chair. She had been dressed in a white lacy dress, her face hidden under a Grim Reaper Halloween mask.

Without an ID, we classified her as Jane Doe. After the initial shock had worn off, Westcott requested backup and Homicide. Her partner Stevens began securing the crime scene perimeter.

Officer Westcott stayed with the body, stepping away only to deal with a testy assistant event coordinator. The two had exchanged heated words. After screaming at her, the coordinator hoofed off the stage, and she never saw or spoke to him again.

I made a note to track him down. It might be nothing, but unless I spoke to him, I wouldn't know.

Other than the missing name of the assistant event co-ordinator, their report had been above board; thorough.

I turned my attention to my laptop and checked my email for the crime lab report, looking for the status on the physical evidence. I needed to know if the techs had lifted any fingerprints from the victim's white dress. I found no unread emails. I would have to call Callum Baker from the station.

I unclipped the stack of crime scene photos attached to the murder book and flipped through each one, pausing in between to draft notes to myself. According to the medical examiner, Jane Doe had been in her early forties. In good physical health. Probably had an office job. A big question mark if she was a runner. The ME leaned more to 'No', but there wasn't enough to rule it out completely. Without a name, a DNA test, or fingerprints match, I couldn't make a positive ID. It also meant I lacked a solid starting point homicide detectives need to kick off an investigation. The slow progress frustrated me.

Sipping my coffee, I stared at Jane Doe until I lost myself in my thoughts. I couldn't see her doing anything to get on the bad side of another person. She seemed like the type who kept to herself, the woman in the office everyone was drawn to because of her sincere disposition, which screamed reliable and trustworthy.

The more I observed her, the more out of place things began to seem. The dress, for instance, wasn't the right fit for her. It was a little loose around the waist and tighter in the bust. I figured a woman like her who obviously took care of herself, given her physical regimen, probably knew her size. So, I doubted she'd throw money away on a dress that wouldn't fit her right.

The make-up seemed to be another ripple. Milky powder too white for her porcelain skin, thick black mascara over-coating her wispy eyelashes, and the poppy red lipstick didn't fit her style — at least not how I imagined her.

The medical examiner had suggested the killer was skilled in killing. So maybe he had killed before. Other victims. Jane Doe could be a pattern. There was something about her the killer liked. Did she remind him of another woman? Could be? *Why not*, I decided.

The Jane Doe from Franklin Park could be a surrogate, a substitute for the real woman the killer desired. He had tried to fix her up to look like someone else. A perfect version, but not the original, or so my thoughts dictated. Again, without the bare basics — my speculations could be wrong.

My mind produced images of Jane Doe struggling to free herself against the shackles he held her in. Fighting to breathe as her lung collapsed. Certainly, she could tell death was near, I imagined, and I felt sad for her.

I chugged the rest of my by-now cold coffee while glancing over the background reports Lem Needham left in my office. All four were involved with the running convention. Two men and two women. Runners. Nothing peculiar about them jumped out at me, but I'd personally interview them before clearing them off the suspect list.

The sun had climbed in the cloudless sky when I placed the case notes back into my bag. After I washed the coffee mug, I prepped myself a light breakfast — a peanut butter and jelly sandwich with a sliced green apple on the side.

Shelly continued to snooze after I was done with my shower and slept through me searching the closet for a clean undershirt. My lips brushed against her soft skin as I kissed her goodbye. I felt how damp her cheeks were, and a lump of guilt lodged in my chest, cutting off my breathing for a second.

Outside I rolled down the window of the Ford Explorer and backed it up onto the road. In the meantime, Thatcher, our neighbor, and his raven-haired wife, Merrill, were loading the back of their new SUV. Thatcher threw his hand in the air in a friendly wave, but I ignored him completely, annoyed at him for sticking his business card on the Silverado's wipers with an offer to drive it off to the junkyard for free. "What right did he have?" I grumbled to myself as I sped off.

As I was cruising on the highway, my phone beeped.

"Detective Stone," I answered.

"Detective, we have a 13-40, disturbance at Franklin Park. I was told to notify you immediately," Dispatch said.

"What's going on?"

"All I know is a unit called for backup. About a gathering of some type at the murder site. He's asking if the murder scene has been turned over to the public?"

I threw the grill lights on and hit the horn on the wheel, yelling at the cars in my lane to move over. "Heck no. Tell the officer to keep civilians back. Be there in ten," I said to the dispatcher.

Chapter 12

"A group of about twelve of them, detective. Showed up together with flowers and candles. Several left stuffed toys. Didn't see who placed those signs," Officer Diaz said to me.

I kneeled down, eye-level with the shrine the gatherers had erected in memory of Jane Doe. Most of the signs said they prayed for her and hoped she was in a better place. I stood up and dusted off my pants.

"The lady in the pink cap is who I dealt with." Diaz pointed to a woman of average height, in a white and pink tracksuit, clutching daisies. "Olivia Masters according to her driver's license."

"Miss Masters?" I approached. "Lead Homicide Detective Temple Stone." I showed her my badge.

The group stopped their chatter and studied me. Olivia Masters made a point of lifting my wallet closer to her eyes to read my name.

"We weren't doing anything wrong, you know," she said as she let go of my ID.

"No one said that you did."

"The officer over there said we did. Told us to leave." Masters pointed at Diaz.

"Officer Diaz was following orders. This part of the park is still an active crime scene. The department hasn't opened it to the public. How do you know the victim?"

"I don't. None of us do," Masters said. "We're runners. A mix of pros and enthusiasts. But we are all runners. And a woman was killed at our event. I thought someone should do something for her. Pay our respects."

"So you don't know if she's a runner? If she's from Boston or flew in for the event?" I asked.

The group behind Masters began a lively chatter. They quieted the moment Masters spoke. "I'm the Boston chapter's leader. If she's from the city, we would have met. Unless she chose to train by herself. A possibility. Though I still think I would have seen her at other races."

"What about anyone else? Do you think you have seen her before?" I asked the group.

"Like I was telling Sonia a second ago...the dead woman is a doppelganger of my neighbor. Honestly. I saw her photo on TV last night and fell off my chair," said a tall, lean man wearing reading glasses.

I showed them a close-up of Jane Doe on the medical gurney, draped in a white sheet.

Horrified sighs and gasps. The guy with the reading glasses held the picture. "I don't know anymore. My emotions are all over the place. At first, she reminded me of Lacy. That's the woman who runs in my neighborhood. Lacy told me she was interested in checking out the convention. Thinking of making running more than a hobby now since her divorce settled."

"Have you spoken to Lacy recently?" I asked.

A head shake. "I haven't seen her in several days. But I don't keep up with her. I had a race to focus on," he mumbled. "Holy smokes. You don't really think it could be her, do you?"

"We will have to check it out," I said to him. "An officer will need your name and address, sir."

I waved to a pair of officers to give me a hand. "Get their names and contact information for a follow-up."

André Jones exited his squad car at the top of the park entrance. He spotted me.

"Well-wishers, huh?" André said.

I led him away from the group for some privacy. "One man says Jane Doe might be a woman from his neighborhood. He's not sure. The woman in the tracksuit is the Boston chapter's leader, and she's never met the vic. But all twelve felt they needed to do something nice for Jane." I studied the tiny pile of flowers near the steps of the stage.

"I came from the station — the crime techs searched the shrubs where Onyx, the dog, got kicked. Baker didn't say much, but he thinks a person had been standing there. The dirt had been disturbed, and there were some broken tree branches. No footprints to lift. He can't give us a time frame."

"This means the dirt could have been disturbed by a number of factors — people, things," I said, disappointed.

"There were paw prints. His team made molds."

"If they match Onyx, that pretty much clears Alice Hatchet," I said, my eyes trained on the homes across the street.

"We have a patrol canvasing Hatchet's neighbors right now."

"Good. Why don't you go knock on Miss Hatchet's door? See if she's home. Ask her to walk the scene with you. Maybe she will remember something she forgot during her interview."

André left me by the shrine. I spent another few minutes reading the signs strangers had written for Jane Doe. A gust of wind swept across the ground. The flames in the candle jars trembled but refused to go out.

I looked over at Olivia Masters and her group. About two feet away from them, I spotted a heavy-set man watching the stage. He seemed physically strong, and I estimated his height to be around six feet. He wore a rugged workman's jacket and baggy jeans, with a Sox cap pulled low to block his eyes.

Where did you come from?

I headed over to speak with him.

Behind me, a cop shouted for help. Assistance. For a split second, I took my eyes off the guy to check on the cop.

"Get 'im. He's getting away." The cop was struggling to hold down a male in a beige hoodie and black jeans.

A swift kick to the groin and the cop curled up in a ball on the grass.

"Suspect on the run. All units — officer in need of assistance. Franklin Park," Dispatch announced over the radio.

Beige hoodie rushed the lawn and charged towards the shrubs, tearing up the dirt. Officers bolted after him, shouting orders to stop and put his hands in the air. I sprinted too, joining the chase. Light on my feet, I edged ahead, but the guy picked up his pace. He jumped a row of flowers, but he lost his balance when he landed on the running path between the waterfront and the park.

I sped after him, faster. I nearly had him, but he reversed sideways and took off again as I repositioned my feet.

We both broke into a sprint. But his strides seemed to widen the distance between us. I told myself to hold on, keep up, don't let him out of sight. My heart rate quickened. I could feel heavy beads of sweat soaking my neck and drenching my shirt.

For a split second, he turned back and I could see his face — on the younger side, white, sharp chin, long, slim nose. The wind knocked his hoodie off. He had short-cut ginger hair and a ginger beard.

At this point, he surged ahead of me enough that I thought he would get away. I bounded with whatever energy I could summon and leaped. My hands snagged his hoodie and I used my momentum to propel myself on top of him. We rolled on the ground several times. He flung his arms to push me off and nearly threw me aside. But I jammed my right knee into his side and pressed down hard. He moaned.

"Okay, okay — I'm done. You got me," he breathed heavily. "Get off me."

I spun him around and locked one wrist behind his back. He cried out. I twisted the other wrist, bound them together, and secured them with my cuffs.

"Let me go you freaking loser!" he shouted in my face. "I've done nothing wrong."

"Running from the police is doing something wrong," I managed to say, fighting for air. "Assaulting a cop is doing something wrong."

Officers reached us. They stood him up on his feet.

"Search him for his ID," I ordered.

"Hey, you can't do that. I have rights. Stop. This is illegal. I don't give you permission to search me."

I ambled to the water, bent at the waist, taking deep breaths. Sweat oozed off my skin. I closed my eyes for a second, my attention lost to the darkness of my scattered thoughts. I heard the sound of my notebook splash in the water. I tried to fish it out, but the guardrail stopped me.

"Temple — you okay?" André put his hand on my back. "Wowza, you should have seen how fast you were going! I guess you're back to full strength."

I didn't reply because I knew I wasn't back to full strength. I could feel my heart tearing up in my chest.

The cold water at the station's bathroom helped me some. I walked back to my office, where André was waiting.

"Meet Danzel Fierra. Age thirty-nine. New Hampshire resident. Currently unemployed. An officer caught him watching people at the park. When he was asked to identify himself, Danzel resisted. Tried to run. You know the rest," André said.

I scanned the report. "Let's go talk to Mr. Fierra."

Sitting across from Danzel Fierra in interview room 1A, I engaged the recorder.

"Danzel Fierra, is that how you say your name?" I asked.

"Yeah, why? Who are you?" He was chewing his fingernails.

"I'm Detective Temple Stone, lead homicide detective with Boston PD. Spell your name for the record."

"D-A-N-Z-E-L — F-I-E-R-RA."

"Thank you for that. Can I get you coffee, water?"

Danzel kept chewing his nails. "What I want you can't give me," he said.

"So that's a no on the coffee and the water. Okay. Danzel, last night a woman was found in Franklin Park. Stabbed to death. You were standing not too far from where we suspect her killer hid."

"She wore a Halloween mask. You forgot to say that," Danzel leered.

"So you know her?"

"No! I didn't say that. Cops. Always twisting your words. Always. I didn't say that." He jabbed his finger on the table.

"You didn't have to." I showed him an evidence bag containing a Halloween mask and a second bag containing a six-inch knife. "Is it a hobby of yours to hide in bushes, carrying knives and Halloween masks?"

Danzel Fierra eyeballed the bags. He stiffened in the seat, grinding his fingernails with his teeth.

"Nothing to say, Mr. Fierra? Okay then. My job's done. I can take you in and book you on homicide charges. How very nice of you to turn yourself in."

"Hey, wait a second, sir. I killed nobody. You cops are all the same."

"Yeah, Danzel, how's that?" I asked.

"I found the mask on the ground," he said.

"And the knife?"

"I found the knife too."

"You found the knife and the mask on the ground, Mr. Fierra? We have a sales associate who IDed you. At 9:18 this morning, you purchased the mask at their store. And I'm sure your kitchen knife set is a knife short. Am I wrong Danzel?"

"You have nothing. You can't hold me."

"Why were you in the park, hiding?" I asked.

Danzel didn't reply for several seconds.

"This morning the news guy told me Jenny would be at Franklin Park. I went there to surprise her."

I sat back and rubbed my stiff neck. "Did the news anchor tell you to bring the knife and the mask too?"

"Yep. Sure thing. Said Jenny would think I was less of a man if I didn't go."

"Is the voice asking you to hurt Jenny? You can be honest with me, Danzel."

Danzel Fierra chewed off a piece of his nail.

"Sometimes," he paused and quickly added, "but I never do. You have to believe me. I didn't kill that lady last night. I swear."

"I believe you." I stood up.

"Can I go home now? My show's about to be on," he told me as he started on another nail.

"I'm afraid not," I said and shut off the recorder.

Chapter 13

I stepped into the control room. Mercy pinched the bridge of her nose where she stood in front of the one-way mirror.

"Who's Jenny?" she asked.

"Jenny Fierra." I consulted the file. "We called her. According to her, Danzel began hearing voices some time ago. He held it together for a while, but he stopped taking his meds. She packed up the kids and left. He's been on his own for months living in the family trailer at a campsite."

"Order a psych eval. And send him to the hospital. See if they can place Mr. Fierra in a ward. He can't take care of himself." She studied Danzel Fierra, then peered at the evidence bags I brought in with me. "The mask and the knife?"

"Danzel purchased the mask at a local party store this morning. Verified by an eyewitness, video, and a receipt."

"What about the knife?"

"It doesn't match the stab wound on Jane Doe. Wu checked. The knife is not a match. But we might have a potential new lead." I reached for my notebook in my inner pocket. Remembered it fell in the water. "One of the runners at the park thought he recognized Jane Doe. Lacy something, he didn't know her last name. I have officers driving by his house to see if they can locate Lacy."

"Good." Mercy smiled briefly. "Heard you took down Mr. Fierra. You were fire on your feet. Seems even after three bullets to the chest, you're unstoppable. It's good to have you back with us, Temple."

"Thank you ma'am."

André entered through the door. "There could be a new development. One of Alice's neighbors caught a car on his front-door camera. I have the video."

"Was Alice Hatchet able to give you anything else?" I asked André.

"She also thinks she might have seen a car pulling away. But she was running after Onyx, didn't pay attention. White. And that's a big maybe."

We gathered around a TV monitor in the control room. André plugged in his phone, and I turned the screen on. A low-quality video began to play. Night time. Panoramic view of the street partially lit by the street lamps. A line of parked cars. Nothing moved for twenty seconds.

"It's coming up," André said.

The next second, all three of us saw a banged-up white van pull away from the park entrance and drive off. It lasted less than six seconds.

"The time stamp overlaps with the time we think the killer left the vic on the stage," I said. "André, take the video to the video unit and see if they can work their magic. Give us at least the make and model of the clunker," I said. "And I'll get Lem Needham to run background checks on everyone who was at the park this morning."

"Keep a good eye on Lem. He's green," Mercy said.

"He wants to learn," I answered, examining the bag with the knife. "We still have no name for her."

"Yeah, that part's slowing us down. Nothing from missing reports?" She put a hand on the door handle.

"We went back a full month. No one matches her description."

"And we can't run her DNA?"

"I heard back from the FBI — she's not in their system. DMV's my last hope. If she ever drove, they'll be able to find her," I said.

"Go detective. Get me some answers," Mercy ordered as I started for the door. "One more thing. A pesky reporter has been hounding me for an interview with you. Up close and personal about the case — "

"Not a chance in hell..." I protested.

Mercy put her hand up to stop me. "I also don't think it's a good idea. I will keep dodging her requests. But it might not be for long. The chief likes the camera, and if the six o'clock news queen goes crying to him, we might be ordered to do it."

I rolled my eyes.

"Get used to it, detective. You're the lead homicide detective for the Boston PD. Part of the job is media relations. So, take your best suit to the dry cleaners and be ready at a moment's notice to charm the pants off the media," Mercy said.

I knew nothing about charm, even less about charming the media. I'd much rather sprint after a knife-wielding homicidal maniac than talk to the camera.

In my office, I prepped a cup of coffee, rolled up my sleeves, and picked a stack of names of people who worked at the running convention.

For several hours I worked without a break. I cleared about eight names on the list. They either had a verifiable alibi or didn't match the physical parameters to commit the murder.

Jane Doe had been watching me from the murder board. I took off her photo.

In his cubicle, I found Officer Chester Panzoli — the man in charge of missing person reports. He flicked a friendly nod when he saw me walking up.

"I have nothing new on your girl, Stone."

"She has to be somewhere in there," I said.

"No females matching her. Okay? I've been looking. She's not here."

"Look again. Go outside the city limits."

"You're telling me how to do my job now, huh? I have another six detectives waiting for leads on their cases. What makes yours a priority? I've told you she's not here. Go suck up to Captain Mercy. You don't give the orders around here. Not to me anyways."

I pointed to his badge; it said 'Homicide'.

"Never have I ever pulled rank before in my career until today. But I'm the lead homicide detective for the station. And you are still a homicide detective, which means, Detective Panzonli, you report directly to me.

Since you feel so emotional about it — I expect to see your transfer request papers out of Homicide by the end of your shift. I am sure they can use you down in Robbery or Sex Crimes," I said. "I am trying to catch a killer who will very likely kill again. If he hasn't killed already. That makes this case a priority. Do I make myself clear?"

Panzoli tapped a command on his keyboard.

"I haven't checked the paper-file room yet. Sometimes not all files are digitized. People still like to use pen and paper. Maybe her missing person report is there."

Back in my office, André showed up.

"What was that all about?"

"Talent management," I grumbled.

"The video unit's got something for us. I came to get you."

Two detectives greeted us sitting behind their desks. André helped himself to a slice of day-old pizza while they lined up the video for us.

"It's a home camera, and not a good one. We couldn't get you anything off the tape you dropped off," one of them said.

"Don't give me the long face yet, guys. Do you think we'll have you take the elevator to the ground floor for nothing?"

"It crossed my mind," I replied cynically.

"There's your car." The other detective pointed to a wall of flat screens. "A white Ford van. Ran every red light pretty much from Franklin to the turn-off for the highway."

"And you're sure it's the same vehicle?"

"The driver made a right turn on Pearl. It's a one-way off Franklin." He pressed a button on a remote. "And here is the street camera. The driver is making a right turn on Pearl, just from a different angle."

They walked us through the car's movements until it entered the highway and we lost the visual.

"Any chance you can give us his license plate?" I asked.

The printer spat out a page. One of the detectives handed me the printout. "What did I tell you — you don't come to the ground floor for nothing. Can't let you leave empty-handed. We have a reputation to uphold." They fist-bumped.

My cell phone vibrated in the elevator.

"Stone," I answered.

I listened briefly.

"Have her sit and wait in one of the interview rooms. I have a few things to follow up on before I can chat with her. Get her coffee." I hung up.

I glanced at André and told him a walk-in had come in. She worked for the company hired for the concert. Jane Doe had been found on their stage.

"Contessa LaPerla, Gena said," I added.

"She's one of mine. I left her a few messages. She's the concert coordinator. Mind if I tag along?"

"The more the merrier."

On the Homicide floor, I ran into Lem Needham.

"What are you working on right now?" I asked.

"Not much. Waiting on a few people to call me back from the list of names you gave me."

"Head to the DMV with a photo of Jane Doe. Have them run her fingerprints. We got nowhere using the state and national criminal database."

"Understood." He put his jacket on.

"Lem, don't let them jerk you around, you hear me?" I said, taking in the Homicide room. "It's time we make some noise."

Chapter 14

"What do we know about Contessa LaPerla?" I asked André as we headed in to interview her.

"Didn't get the chance to talk to her. Left a message briefly explaining why we need to speak with her."

"Detective Stone. Wait. Hold on," Chester Panzoli called to me from his cubicle.

I ignored him.

"Wait!" He followed me. "Stone! Will you cool your jets?"

"Panzoli, I am going in with a potential witness. Whatever you want to gripe about, see me later."

"You can be such a dick," Panzoli said.

I arched a brow.

"Sorry — no offense. I'm getting used to your new rank."

I spotted the piece of paper he was holding.

"None taken for now. What do you have there?"

"Son of a gun, Stone, I found her. Your dead girl with the Halloween mask and the white gown."

"It was more like a dress," I corrected him.

"Huh?"

"Forget about it. Let me see what you have," I said.

I quickly scanned the piece of paper. "Brad Connolly?"

"Keep reading," Chester said with a smug look on his face. "The address listed on the form. It's the reason why I didn't find her sooner. I still got it, though. I'm just that good."

"If you're done self-congratulating yourself, detective, I'd like for you to try Brad Connolly's phone and his fiancée's — Dana Miller. If you get nothing, move on to their cell-phone providers. I want all the data they can send over to us. Request as far back as a month."

Chester Panzoli uttered a few words under his breath, stalking away.

After he left, I turned to André.

"Brad Connolly's father reported him missing at the police station in Charleston. But Brad's not a Mass resident. His fiancée — Dana Miller — is."

"Do we have a picture of her?"

"No. Only of Brad. She's not even listed as missing. His father wrote down — Brad and Dana were supposed to go to Paris. But after Brad didn't call home for four days, his parents started to worry."

"So we don't know if it's her?" André asked.

"The general physical description is a close match. But yeah — we need more." I picked up a phone handle and dialed.

Lem Needham answered.

"Nothing yet, sir. But I'm giving them hell like you ordered."

"We might have a name for Jane Doe. I want the DMV to run a check on Dana Miller. Charleston resident. Text me her details if you get a hit."

I stared at the names listed in the missing person report. "Hopefully Lem can confirm Jane Doe is actually Dana Miller. Address in Charleston — after this interview, we could drive over there, check things out."

I entered interview room 1A. At the table, Gina, the department civilian assistant, had seated a tall, slender woman wearing a vintage Beatles tee over distressed white jeans. Big gold hoops dangled from her ears when she tossed her long, glossy amber hair. She studied me with curious sapphire eyes I was certain could break a few hearts.

"Miss LaPerla, I'm Detective Stone, and this is André Jones. We're working a homicide case together."

"Contessa works. Thanks. And I think — Detective Jones, you left me a very insistent message," Contessa said and reached over to shake our hands. "Here I am. What can I do for you? Though, I must inform you, I have a plane to catch, and I can't stay long. My job's sending me to the Maldives to oversee our newest account. A project I have to ace. I'll be tied up abroad for some time. Please be brief."

"I appreciate you coming down. The interview is a formality, and as long as we get what we need you should be good to go," I said.

She rubbed her lips together, smudging off some of her pink pearl lipstick. "No one that I know is recently dead.

Everybody is alive and accounted for, as morbid as that sounds."

"On Sunday night, a woman was murdered and left on the stage at Franklin Park. The folks at the running convention told us they hired your company, The Groove Factory, to put on a show. That means The Groove Factory was in charge of the stage. Are you with me?" I asked.

"I saw it on the news Monday morning. Hoped it wasn't true. It's truly despicable what some people are capable of. But I'm afraid I don't see how I could help. I didn't have anything to do with this."

"As I've said, the interview is a formality. Can you tell me where you were last night between midnight and six in the morning?"

Contessa shook her hair again. "Are you serious? Am I a suspect? Look at me — I'm not capable of murder."

I remained silent.

"I was at home. Stressing over the concert, drinking too much box wine, and drunk dialing old flames. Pretty much nothing I'm proud of. I left the office around nine thirty or ten, took an Uber to my apartment. Ordered Indian, paid with my credit card — check my receipts. I worked some more, mainly putting out fires. Routine stuff.

"The stage director had an issue with the engineers who were pissed off at one of the acts who didn't show up for their mic check. The assistant event coordinator called every two seconds. It seems the whole world was on fire that night," she said.

"And what would his name be? The assistant?"

"Georgie Stavros, a hot-blooded Greek God with looks to back it up. He's kind of everyone's assistant."

"Was he at the stage that morning, say around six? Is that unusual?" I probed.

"Look, Stavros had nothing to do with this murder."

"How can you be so sure?"

"Because he called me that morning. Scared shitless. I could hear the fear in his voice. He had no clue what your officer was talking about. All we knew was that the police wanted to shut down the convention, but we didn't know why. Stavros is not your man."

"So you knew about the murder at Franklin Park? You just said you learned about the dead woman from the news on Monday morning."

"Okay. Whatever. I lied because I didn't want to get involved. Stavros called and said there were cops everywhere. Someone left a body on our stage. I freaked out. I'm not paid enough to deal with that crap."

"So what did you do?"

"I told Stavros to get the F out of there. Go home and let the boss deal with it. Then I called my boss. He didn't answer. Typical. Left him three, maybe four messages. When I didn't hear back from him, I figured he had handled it. But after your partner," she glanced at André, "called me, I realized things were far from handled. There, you happy? Now you know everything. May I go now?"

"We'll need Stavros's contact details."

"Fine. Fine. I'll give it to you." She began rummaging through her huge purse. "If you're hunting for suspects — you really should be looking at my boss's shady partner.

If anyone could kill, it'd be that guy. Or my boss's wife. She's a nut job. Or pretty much anyone else but me and Stavros."

"I like your spirit of sharing and cooperation, Miss LaPerla. Mind if you stay a few extra minutes? It seems we have more to chat about."

Contessa glanced nervously into my eyes. "I was only joking. My big mouth. Can we forget what I said? Rewind a few seconds. I give you Stavros's number and you cut me loose."

"Why don't I get us some coffee? We will be here for a while," André said.

"Gee, you people. Alright, so I swung by the office on Sunday night, around eleven, eleven thirty. Wish I didn't. My boss, Charles Isles, was arguing with his shady partner. A mob guy. That's all I know about him. And that's how I want it. Now this guy is legit. Serious trouble. They were arguing. About a woman. One of them said he'd slit the little bitch's throat. Then, the mob guy threatened my boss, Charles. They got into it. A third guy stepped in to break them up."

"What were they arguing about?"

"Money, I think. I think I witnessed a shakedown. But Charles Isles is broke — it's an open secret at the office. The Groove Factory was about to file for bankruptcy. We're all jumping ship. Charles was looking to get out of the business, skip town maybe."

"What else?" I pushed.

"I took my stuff and ran out of the office as fast as I could." She tugged on the hoop in her ear, avoiding my stare.

"You're doing well, Miss LaPerla. We're almost done. Do you have a name for the man Charles argued with?"

"No name. He's a creep. Drugs, prostitution, illegal gambling. I'm sure you can find him on your own without my help."

"How about the third man? You said there was a third man that night."

"Big guy. Always tags along with the mafia dude. I figured it's his enforcer." She trembled. "Can I go now? I've told you absolutely everything. I have a plane to catch."

"Do you think you can recognize the two men putting the squeeze on Charles Isles if we show you some photos?" I asked.

"I think so."

My phone beeped as André returned with the coffee. A text from Lem. I read it, then showed it to André, who nodded in approval.

"Thank you, Miss LaPerla. You did well. Before I leave you with my partner — take a look at this photo. Do you recognize the woman in it?"

Contessa LaPerla gaped at the photo. Her face turned pale, fear and confusion crossing her face. André and I noticed the shift in her.

"Mmm...no," she said.

I shoved aside the murder folder. "Miss LaPerla, I've been doing this job for a while. I can tell when a witness is afraid to tell me the truth. Her name is Dana Miller.

She was killed somewhere else and then dumped on the stage you were in charge of. Now, I'd like nothing more than to find out who did this to her and why. Take another look. Miss Miller had a family, loved ones who would want the police department to catch the perp responsible for her murder. Wouldn't you if someone in your family was *unaccounted* for?"

"I think I know her. My goodness. I can't believe it's actually her." Another thought crossed her mind, I suspected. It scared her. "He didn't. He couldn't have." She mumbled to herself. "Dear Lord, I shouldn't say anything else. I'm done speaking."

"I assure you now is not the time to stop cooperating with my investigation. If you have vital information that might help us solve her murder, and you withhold it, I'll consider bringing you in on obstruction. Forget about making it to your flight."

LaPerla slipped off one of her beaded bracelets and started to rub the beads between her fingers. "She's a consultant. An accountant. You hire her if money goes missing from your company. Apparently, she can find every last red cent. That's it. She never introduced herself. Worked nights when everyone was supposed to be gone. Please, you have to promise me. If they find out I'm the leak, I don't know what will happen to me. I don't want to end up like her. I have a pet fish."

"Calm down, Miss LaPerla. No one is going to hurt you because you cooperated."

LaPerla stabbed the image of Jane Doe with her sharp acrylic nails. They were painted purple. "Tell that to her.

She was investigating The Groove Factory and my boss over money gone missing. Dana, you said her name was. She looks like a Dana. The quiet type. She stayed away from the rest of us. Didn't socialize with the crew, and we tried to be friendly. I approached her. Chatted to her several times, but she gave me a go-away-and-don't-bother-me stare, so I left her alone.

"Then, last Friday was apparently her last day, or so we thought. I happened to walk behind her when we were both leaving for the night. She seemed freaked out. Upset at something or someone. She acted spooked. I should have talked to her. At least asked what was wrong, but she had shut me down before, so I didn't bother. Gosh, I feel terrible."

"And you have no idea what might have happened to her?"

LaPerla shook her head. "None whatsoever. The office has been mostly empty. On Friday, she left around 10 p.m. I wanted to take the elevator with her. But she put her hand up, nearly crying, and asked me to wait for the second one."

I glanced down at the photo of Jane Doe. Dana Miller had cried the night she was supposed to leave for Paris with her fiancé Brad Connolly. *What happened to you that night Dana? Who hurt you?*

"I am not getting on that flight, am I?" LaPerla asked in a shaky voice.

"No one's going anywhere, Miss LaPerla, until we know who killed Dana Miller," I replied.

Chapter 15

I stepped into Mercy's office. Lem joined me. Mercy was talking on the phone but casually motioned for us to take a seat. I opted to stand, leaning against the window sill. A damp night had fallen over Boston's skyline. The weather looked uninviting and raw. Heavy rain lashed the streets.

"I only have a few minutes before I'm needed upstairs. Give it to me short and sweet. I'm afraid that's the only way I can take it right now after the day I had," she said.

"We have a name for Jane Doe. Dana Miller," I said as Lem handed her Dana Miller's DMV report.

"From Charleston. If the address is up-to-date."

"And we linked her DMV record with a missing person report."

"At least you can notify the family. Tell them that unfortunately she's not missing." Mercy let out a sigh and crossed her fingers.

"About that, captain. She wasn't reported missing by family or friends. It seems her father's fiancée reported his son missing. Dana Miller was mentioned as the last person to be with his son. Dana Miller and Brad Connolly were going to Paris for the weekend."

"The city of love, huh? And is this Brad Connolly still unaccounted for or have we spoken to him?"

"Detective Panzoli's on phone duty. I have him calling their cells and soliciting data from the phone companies. After I'm done writing my status report, I was going to call Mr. Connolly, the father. He lives in Connecticut."

André joined us. "The witness made a positive ID. Both men."

"Potential suspects?" Mercy shuffled in her chair with controlled enthusiasm.

"Too early to say. The woman in One, Contessa LaPerla, said she witnessed a shakedown between two unidentified males and her boss."

"A shakedown? I would have never pegged Miss Miller to be involved with the underworld types."

For a beat, my eyes stayed on their faces, before I said, "I don't believe she was, captain. Miss Miller was an accountant or something of that nature. Hired to find missing company funds. The witness gave a statement that The Groove Factory was going bust. Her boss, an individual by the name Charles Isles, might have stolen the money," I explained.

"My my. You think Dana Miller discovered where Charles Isles hid the money? And he killed her to keep her quiet?"

Before I could utter a word, André swooped in, greasing the wheels. "I think Frank Ricca and his bone crusher, Marcello Santoro, killed her. The witness plucked them from a photo lineup with no problem. Her story's on tape. She heard one say he'd slid the bitch's throat."

"That definitely sounds like a threat we can't disregard. And given Miss Miller's role in the company, I can see how you can suspect Frank Ricca of killing her."

I moved closer to Mercy's desk and locked my arms in front of me. "We're jumping to conclusions here." I gave André a wrathful glare. "There's a lot to the story we don't know."

"I called SID; they have a file on Ricca so long it sits on its own shelf."

"Frank Ricca could be the killer, but he might not be. The Halloween mask, the white dress — all oddly specific details. Doesn't scream your usual mafia hit job. If they tossed her off a bridge or burned her body in her car, I'd be down to play."

"And yet, Frank Ricca and Marcello Santoro are your strongest suspects. Motive — Dana Miller found money they wanted to hide. Opportunity — a witness places them in the same building where Miller worked. Means — slit the bitch's throat. I will leave it at that." She pointed a stern finger right at me. "Bring them in, run down their alibis. And I want you to talk to Charles Isles. Get his side of the story. He had just as much motive to kill Dana Miller as these two other fools." She cast her wandering eyes on the clock above her door. "That's all the time I have for tonight. Write it all up, Temple. I want to read your notes at home. Then you are free to go. Good job today."

"Captain," I started to object, "I'd like to send a car to pick up all three suspects, start interviewing them."

Mercy stood up, shoving files into her briefcase.

"Isn't your wife pregnant, Temple?"

"What's that got to do with anything?" I asked, confused, looking between their perturbed expressions. "She is, I meant to say. And Shelly's doing well. Thank you for asking, ma'am."

"Go home, Temple. Before your wife kicks your scrawny butt out and you end up like all the other washed-up, overworked, talented cops who never learned how to balance their work and home life."

"But..."

"Ah ah ah, if you make me repeat myself one more time, I will become very irritated. Do you want me to be irritated, Stone?"

"No, ma'am."

"Look at that nasty weather. And I didn't bring an umbrella. The tunnel will be a mess with rushing, distracted assholes who don't know how to drive," she said as we left her office. Mercy cut the lights.

"I can stay as long as you need me," Lem offered.

"Stay on the van leaving Franklin Park. Get the license plates. I want the name of the owner. And figure out if the driver has any infractions we can pick him up for."

"You got it."

"Mercy said to go home," André reminded us.

Lem hung back, confused over who his boss was. Technically André outranked Lem and me, but I would eagerly choose to ignore his rank, especially if he dicked me on my first homicide investigation as the lead.

"If you order your detectives to work late, at least explain to them who approves the overtime pay." He casually glanced back at Mercy's dark office. "People don't like to work for free in my experience."

"Two hours. Give me two more hours on the clock, André," I said. I quickly nodded at Lem and added, "One more thing — Charles Isles. I'd like to start with him first. I want you to get me everything we have on him. Where he lives, shits, and fucks. Everything!"

"You got it, boss!"

"Don't ever call me that again."

André laughed, his gaze focused on Lem as he slipped out the door. "Aww, look who's got himself an apprentice."

"Who me? Lem and I are hunkering down in the same boat. Helping each other out."

"Maybe for you, but for young and energetic Lem Needham, it's more than that. He admires you."

"You're wrong. And officially wasting my time. It seems to me you can use some busy work. Find Georgie Stavros, the hot-blooded Greek God, and line up an interview. I'd like to hear what he thinks about Charles Isles's entanglement with the mafia."

"You got it, boss!" André chugged his coffee, balled up the paper cup, and tossed it in the wastebasket next to my desk. It hit the side, landing on the hardwood floor.

"Do that again, and I'll ban you from my office forever."

"Power's getting to your head," André snickered.

I worked for a few more hours, typing my field notes and status report. When I sent it off to Mercy, I decided I had enough for one day. I tossed Dana Miller's file in my bag and headed out.

But before I stepped out the door, I made a call to another unit.

"Patrol division, Officer Karen speaking." She sounded sleepy or bored, or both.

"Karen — Detective Temple Stone. I need you to run the plates on a dark-blue BMW. Owner's name — Brad Connolly. Missing five days tomorrow morning."

"Plate number?"

I gave her the information.

"What do you need to know, detective? The CliffsNotes or the works? Pick your poison."

"Find out if anyone spotted the car in the last week, would you? Not just Boston, okay. Go wide."

"How wide?" She let out a chill yawn at the end.

Brad Connolly resided in Connecticut while his fiancée Dana Miller lived in Charleston. To make the relationship work, I suspected they each commuted to see each other. And if I wanted to map out Brad Connolly's movements, Connecticut PD should be looped in.

"Go as wide as Connecticut," I instructed.

Karen sighed, irritated, but didn't object.

"Don't give Connecticut PD any specifics."

"What should I tell them then?" she asked.

"Ugh, tell them Brad Connolly is a person of interest in Boston. We're just running leads. I will give them a call when we have something solid to share."

Outside the rain had slowed down to a dreary mist that soaked the air. The desolate streets made Boston feel empty and spacious, two things Boston could never be.

My body ached from lack of sleep and the long hours behind my desk. It felt good to stretch my legs. Two late-night joggers hustled by me. We exchanged courteous nods.

Envy rose in me watching their laid-back dash. In a grim mood, I unlocked my car, fighting off a dry cough, pretending I could go for a run too if I wanted; I chose not to. As I buckled myself in, out of nowhere, a sharp, slashing pain in my chest sent a warning — the bullet fragment could be shifting closer and closer to my heart, ready to kill me.

Chapter 16

The next morning I left before dawn. I didn't want to face Shelly and confess about the sudden chest pain I had experienced after work. She would insist I call Doctor Hoffman and Doctor Giovanni to report it to them. But how could I solve a murder stuck in a hospital bed?

Besides, the pain had resolved on its own. I woke up feeling fine, tired, and maybe a little sapped, but nothing a strong black coffee couldn't help me get over.

Before heading to the station, I popped into the crime lab to check on things. The lab consisted of walls painted in neutral colors. No sunlight got in. It resembled a dull holding box. Techs in long white lab coats hunched over microscopes, paying me no attention.

It was dead quiet aside from the occasional fingers typing on a keyboard.

At the end of a curved hallway, I spotted the thick, smoky gray mane of Callum Baker, head of the CSI department. He spotted me too and broke into a friendly smile. He beckoned me closer.

Unlike the rest of the techs in the lab, he wore a two-piece suit — indigo over a silky, eggshell-white shirt. He'd paired the outfit with an olive-green tie.

His office smelled of warm, gooey apple pie, but I didn't see where he'd stashed the baked pastry.

"Wondered when I'd see you," he said.

"Ah you know — if the mountain doesn't come to you — you go to the mountain," I replied.

"The lab's slammed. Meant to call. Take a seat." He pointed at a chair next to his desk. "The media's eating this one up, huh? But they don't know half of it. Bloodless corpse, weird mask, and unfortunately not much physical evidence at the crime scene."

"Not the most straightforward case I've worked on, I'll give you that much." I crossed my legs.

"Congratulations on the job, by the way. Between us, Bradley Walker has not been your biggest fan and cheer-leader," Baker said. "You always had my vote!"

"Walker's feelings are the least of my worries. If you ask me, he needs to worry less about me and solve a case, any case."

Baker placed a perfectly golden, flaky apple pie on his desk and pointed at it, asking if I'd like a slice. It looked too scrumptious to resist.

"Some cops like Detective Walker lose themselves in their tunnel vision. Don't let it happen to you." Baker cut two slices.

"Appreciate it. Though, I don't know how long they'd keep me on if I bungle the Bloodless killer investigation. So far, the progress I've made has been less than impressive by my standards. Took us days just to learn her name — Dana Miller."

"Oh? Miss Miller suffered tremendously. I read Doctor Wu's autopsy report. Cruel and unusual killing."

"And we are all over the suspect list. She had a fiancé, currently presumed missing. Both were to spend a weekend in Paris before she was killed."

"You think the fiancé did it?"

"Could be him or the guy she worked for."

"What kind of work did she do?" he asked.

"Of what I can piece together — she was an accountant. Hired by someone to go through The Groove Factory's ledgers. Her boss, Charles Isles, has been accused of hiding millions, practically bankrupting his own company."

"She found the money and he killed her to silence her." Baker made coffee.

"That'd make sense, right? But — Charles Isles might be laundering money for the mafia. A charming guy by the name of Frank Ricca was spotted with Isles the night Dana Miller was killed. One of them threatened to 'slit the bitch's throat.'"

"Awe, sounds like a strong motive," Baker said.

I exhaled, drained. "Not you too, Callum. Mercy and André think Ricca and Isles are good for it."

"And you don't, I take it, based on your reaction."

"The mask and the white dress. The public display of her body. None of it smells like a mafia hit. Even if she found the stolen money and threatened to expose them, it still makes no sense that the mafia would end her. The heat her murder would bring on them — it doesn't fit in my mind." I scooped up some apple pie. "Do you have something for me?"

"Checking." Baker donned a pair of heavy black-rimmed glasses and studied his monitor. "Take a look. The lab ran an analysis of the embalming fluid found in her. It contains formaldehyde, sodium nitrate, glycerin, methanol, and sodium borate. High grade, professional. And it's not cheap."

"Doctor Wu believes only funeral homes could get their hands on this type of embalming fluid."

"I concur with her opinion. Also, the solution he used contained a pink coloring agent. He used a diluted solution of water and alcohol with an added fruity scent to bathe her in."

"Why do you think he did it?"

"My best guess? To kill bacteria on the body. A funeral home might be better qualified to give you an answer," Baker said. "No fingerprints or fibers on the stage. He probably wore protective gear. Careful and meticulous would be my classification of his work."

"I agree. And Wu thinks Dana Miller's not his first," I said as I took another scoop of apple pie.

"Considering how well her body was preserved, the lack of amateur mistakes first-time killers make, I see how she arrived at that conclusion."

"More reasons why a mafia hit doesn't fit." I put my plate down.

"Might be though. The mafia's ruthless. Take a look at how they killed in the eighties and nineties. A lot of innovative imagination. It could be that Frank Ricca killed Dana Miller to send a clear message — sing and you die."

One of the lines on his desk blinked. "Hang on."

Baker answered. He listened, then said, "Bring it in."

He took his glasses off. "We bagged some evidence from a trash can near the staircase. All the rest were emptied; trash bags replaced."

A knock followed; a woman entered, dressed in black pants, a dark blouse, and a white coat. Her blonde hair was pulled into a bun atop her head.

"Thank you, Willow. I'll take it."

She turned around and nodded to us. "Don't expect shockers."

Callum spent a few minutes reviewing the folder. "Hmm. The can contained a half-pack of nicotine gum and a plastic spray bottle. Both items came back positive for partial prints," Baker murmured. "Unfortunately, the evidence was compromised by someone puking in the trash — we can run additional tests to develop the prints more. It will take some time. Patience." He gave me the folder.

"I don't believe this." I glared at the notes. "For the love of Jesus!"

"The lab identified the DNA in the throw-up."

"Who? Who does it belong to?"

"Officer Danny Stevens. Assigned to Patrol. I can give you his badge number if you wish to speak to him."

I was fuming — Westcott and Stevens were the two cops first on scene. Judging by her stellar report, I had given them an A plus. But because Stevens had purged in the trash, he compromised evidence most likely connected to the Bloodless killer.

Furious about the mega screw-up, I dashed to my car. I thought of the many ways I'd like to make Officer Stevens's life a living hell, and then I reminded myself — cops could screw up like everyone else. I loosened my tie, already deciding Stevens won't learn through punishment. But a call to his supervisor might be the more appropriate approach. Let his division work it out.

From my car, I sent off a text to André to add funeral homes to our list of leads. I sent another text to Lem, telling him to call the national suppliers producing embalming fluid and request that samples be sent to the crime lab. Callum Baker could compare them to the fluids used on Dana Miller.

At the station, before I even reached my desk, a much bigger screw-up by one of my own had spread like metastatic cancer.

"It's as bad as it gets, Stone," Mercy declared.

Chapter 17

I stepped into Mercy's office. Lem Nedham was quietly sitting on her sofa, hands tensely folded in his lap.

"Remember when I told you a woman from the media wanted to do an exclusive with you?" Mercy shut the door behind us.

"Yeah. Okay." I shook my head. "You have to stonewall her some more, captain. We can't go public with the rest of what we have. A killer draining his victims of blood and embalming them will freak everyone out."

"I'm right there with you, but staying quiet is no longer an option." She shifted her attention to Detective Lem Needham.

"I'm sorry Stone. I screwed up. Fucked it all up." He sounded beat-up. "Someone kept calling your line this morning; eventually the operator kicked the call to me. She said she was from the lab. Wanted to know if you want to run additional DNA tests on the Jane Doe. I wasn't thinking straight when I told her there's no DNA to compare. The killer squeezed all the blood from our vic."

I flexed my fists and clenched my jaw as I threw out-raged eyes at Mercy.

"Sorry again, sir. I don't know why I even said it. I wanted to show you I can do it. That I'm a good detective. Solid cop. You gave me a shot to be part of the biggest murder investigation of my career, and I bombed it."

"Go wait for me outside, detective." I opened the door. "Don't go anywhere and don't speak with anyone."

"It was your job to watch him." Mercy didn't waste a second after Lem walked out.

"I thought I did," I objected.

"There is a reason why we don't let green, inexperienced detectives in the field, handle evidence, interview witnesses, or run down leads for us."

"He screwed up, captain. Admitted to it and came clean. What else could he have done?"

"It's your job to mentor him, show him how the job's done, how to handle an investigation A to Z. This media leak is as much your failure to lead your detectives as it is his." Mercy straightened the jacket of her uniform.

"I'll talk to him. He won't do it again," I said.

"No, he won't, and you know why? Because I'm sending you to handle the reporter."

"You can't be serious?! What am I supposed to say to her?"

"Don't come to me for advice, Stone. You're a big shot. Lead Homicide. This is me teaching you a lesson. A lesson that you should listen better, train harder, lead these men in the bullpen smarter."

"Ma'am," I tried to wedge a word in.

"Now I don't want to hear another word. Meredith Sawyer from Channel Six is in your office."

A woman in her early fifties, with short gray hair, dressed in a black suit and heels to match, was perusing a day-old copy of the *Boston Herald* in my office.

"Anything good?" I asked. I dropped off my bag at my desk and hit ON on the coffee maker.

"Gossip and lies," she said with a smirk. "So I hear you're the man I'm looking for."

"Is that so? Well, here I am at your service. What can I do for you?" I bit back.

She regarded me with a spark of disdain. "I love funny cops. Good B-roll."

"This funny guy has a murder to solve, and I don't remember calling a press conference." I took a sip of my coffee.

"Detective Stone, according to my sources, Boston Homicide hasn't been completely forthcoming with the media. The Jane Doe murder in the park wasn't just a random stabbing. It's so much more. So much bigger than what you made it out to be. Isn't it?"

"Every murder is much more and bigger to my detectives. We are not the ones chasing headlines. We chase murders. If that's all you needed..." Amused, I glanced at the door.

"Why did you lie to us? You told us she was stabbed."

"She was stabbed," I said.

"You omitted to say the killer drained her blood. Jane Doe was a mummy more than a corpse. And don't try a bullshit department line with me."

"Testing clickbait headlines on me, hm? I'd stick with reporting the facts. Leave the mummy bit out. It makes you sound insensitive, Miss Sawyer. How's that for a bull-shit department line?"

"Is that how it's going to be from now on? Us against you? Detective Stone, you're newly promoted, and you don't know the ropes entirely well, but the chief and the mayor are on my speed dial. Do you think they will stand by you as soon as I break the story? Expose the evidence you hid on purpose? Huh? It looks like I have your attention."

"If you are after my attention, I'm afraid I will have to disappoint you. Jane Doe," I pointed at a photo of Dana Miller, "is the one I'm dedicated to. She suffered unlike another human I have seen. And the man who did this to her is still out there. It's not uncommon for us to hold back information we don't want the public to know. It's not lying. It's preserving the integrity of our investigation. Giving us a fighting chance against men who stabbed a woman and watched her die as her blood slowly seeped out of her."

She grimaced with disgust. I could tell by the way she cranked her neck that I aggravated her.

"I'm happy to forget you used a false name to entrap one of my officers to gain inside information. You illegally obtained evidence we didn't permit you to use. I doubt your viewers will like you very much after my press office issues a statement of how you circumvented the law. I might clear the rest of my afternoon to speak to every camera and every reporter who shows up asking me about you.

"Oh, and because you're new to how I run the homicide department, last year I was shot three times by a man who'd shot his wife in the head in front of their baby. I shot back, cuffed him myself, all before my backup showed up. So knowing you have the mayor or the chief of police on speed dial doesn't scare me at all." My voice cut like ice. "Go public with what you know and you'll make an enemy of me."

"Or?" She sounded curious.

"Smart woman — or as soon as I have the perp arrested, you'll be my first call. B-roll of the Bloodless killer walking into the station. Splashy like your headlines."

"I don't know, I will have to think about it. It sounds tempting, but it's too much risk. I got Detective Needham to sing; who's to say my competition won't get to him too?"

"They won't. You'll just have to trust me." I put my hand out for her to shake.

Lem zoomed right in after Meredith Sawyer packed up and left. Worry was plain on his broad forehead, his eyes tense and nervous, showing honest remorse.

"Sir, how bad is it? Will she run with it?" he asked, keyed up.

I gulped my coffee. "It happens. Sawyer pulling one over you — part of the game. There isn't a cop on the force who hasn't been burned by their big mouths for talking to the media. You got to learn. Part of the game." I put a reassuring hand on his shoulder.

"Yeah? For real?" He put both hands on the back of a chair and let his head hang low. "Captain Mercy wants me off the case, doesn't she? I could tell — in her office — she thinks I suck at my job."

"Lem, becoming a good homicide detective takes time; years. Some devote their entire career to Homicide, and they never grasp the job. Catching a killer requires a cop to make personal sacrifices." I picked up a framed photo off my desk and stared at it.

"Is it worth it?" Lem asked.

"It's the only thing I've ever wanted to be. It's worth it to me," I replied. "Where are we at on the van? Did you run the plates?"

He shook off the fear. "Meant to do it this morning when I got in. But that reporter lady called, and then shit rolled down the hill."

"Go. Do it. And send me whatever you have on companies selling embalming fluid," I said, stepping outside my office. Mercy stood at the other end observing the bullpen. Our eyes connected for a quick glance, long enough to exchange mutual respect.

Chapter 18

"I was down at the hospital, and you'd never believe what a nurse told me." André brought lunch. Two subs, fries, and cokes.

"It must be good if you're that giddy," I said.

"In the hospital, Danzel Fierra showed doctors his kill list. His ex-employer, Jenny, the wife, a couple of randoms, and you. Fierra had bumped you up to the top for slamming him to the ground." He laughed.

"That's what I get for trying to help him out."

"His wife, Jenny, said the psych ward won't release him quite yet. Not until he's stable and back on his meds. They think he could have seriously hurt someone in the mental state we arrested him."

"He brought a knife and a Halloween mask. He probably would have attacked, injured a person, killed — it's a big maybe for me." I chewed on my fries. "Imagine how bad it'll get if we tell the public that Bloodless is out there and we haven't caught him yet?"

André shook the ice in his cup. "I heard about Meredith Sawyer playing spy. Tried to tell you, Lem's not ready."

"Give the kid a break, will you? It's not like you and I don't have our sins," I said and set aside my lunch.

Detective Chester Panzoli interrupted the silence with a knock and poked his balding head in.

"Am I interrupting?" he asked.

"Not at all. What is it?"

"Dana Miller's phone records. Her cell phone provider expedited our request after I emailed them her death certificate."

I took the folder from him. Skimmed it over.

"But I'm hitting a wall with Brad Connolly. He's not dead, and the cell provider's refusing to give me anything without a warrant." He pointed at the file. "Brad's phone number's all over her data. They spoke frequently. Calls and messages."

"Anything useful in their messages?" I asked, pausing to read a line of text here and there.

"No arguments or fights. She was head over heels for Brad. The last month they mostly talked about Paris. Hotel and plane info. It's in their texts. Oh yeah, and the ring. She talks about her ring. She seemed to love the diamond he chose."

"A diamond ring should be forever. Not in Dana Miller's case. The killer stole it from her. He took everything he could from her," I said. "Thanks Panzoli. I'll read the rest."

"Don't thank me, just catch the weirdo. My daughter's wedding is next month. Her diamond ring looks a lot like your vic's. Can't think what I'd do if I were Dana Miller's father. Would break the little fuck's neck with my bare hands." He left.

"This case is freaking us all out if Chester Panzoli is giving a crap." André shrugged.

"Time to get back to work. Talk to me about Georgie Stavros."

"He recognized Dana. She was in the office Friday night before she left. Around nine." André consulted his notes. "Saw Dana packing her bag. Didn't watch her long enough to tell me if she was upset or not."

"What about Charles Isles and Frank Ricca? Did Stavros see them with Dana?"

"Nope. But I showed him the van," Andrew said.

"And?"

"He thinks he saw a van on the street, could have been white. From talking to him, I gathered Stavros is not the sharpest. More there for his looks. A male model helping out The Groove Factory between gigs. Officer Westcott scared him straight."

"Did she?"

"Our boy Stavros is not our guy."

"Check his alibi. Worth digging deeper to be on the safe side. Any connection between Stavros and Frank Ricca?"

"None. In fact, when I brought up Ricca, Stavros looked like he wanted to drill a hole in the ground and hide."

"Okay. Seems like we can soon clear him off. Did he see anyone else in the office that night?"

"Besides the janitors and the security in the lobby — only Dana Miller packing."

"Add Stavros's statement to the murder book. Take two detectives and send them to The Groove Factory. Have them interview the janitor staff and security. Collect video from the building."

"Who can you spare?"

I spotted Bradley Walker strolling in. "Walker's currently without a case. And anyone else you choose." I shuffled through the files on my desk. "I'll work on Dana Miller. Put together a brief. If everything goes to plan, you and I can ride to her house tonight."

"Nothing ever goes to plan," André mumbled as I drew a straight line on the murder board with a black marker. Above it, I wrote 'Timeline'.

It took hours to piece together a partial picture of Dana Miller's life. She had stayed off social media. I couldn't track any friends of hers who would help me understand her. Miller had chosen to live a life of total solitude, and soon I realized why. The reason saddened me. The lonely existence she had worn like a robe could be pinpointed to a single event. And just as she had started to break out of her shell, met Brad, and started to socialize, she ended up murdered in the most heinous manner Homicide had ever investigated.

I stepped away from the board, examined the details, and told myself it was as good as it was going to get. I called Lem first.

"Be ready to brief," I instructed him, hanging up before he could protest.

Then I called the rest of the team to the conference room.

Captain Mercy led the charge. The room suddenly started to feel snug.

"You get this hyped up if you're about to score some points for our team," Mercy observed.

"Yes, ma'am."

"Excellent. We're expecting a guest. The Mayor's Office insisted on sending a rep. Meredith Sawyer's name was dropped in my conversation with City Hall." Mercy unbuttoned her jacket with attitude. "The rep is to watch and listen without interfering, or so I'm told."

I glanced at Mercy. "Ditto." Then I asked, "I'm ready to go now, or do you prefer to wait?"

"The floor's all yours, detective."

Wasting no more time, I walked them through the basics. "From the DMV, we learned Dana Miller was a lifelong Massachusetts resident. Her address is listed as 112 Hancock Street, Charleston. The only child of Martin and Elena Miller."

I briefly consulted my notes. "No criminal record on any of them. Martin, also from Massachusetts, was the president of Charleston Central Bank from 1976 to 2001. He met Dana's mom, Elena, on a trip to Eastern Europe in the early eighties. Brought her with him, and a year later, they had Dana. Elena was a homemaker and, by all accounts, a doting mother. She volunteered as a math instructor at the Charleston Library, tutoring students in math."

"Why haven't the parents filed a missing person report on Dana?" Dissatisfied, Mercy shook her head.

"They couldn't have. Martin Miller died in a car accident in 2001. A semi ran a red light and plowed into Mr. Miller's vehicle."

Lem took over. "The police report from the accident states that the front of Martin's car absorbed the blow from the semi. He died instantly. The first responders mentioned a second passenger, a small female child. Dana, most likely. They found her clutching Martin's hand through a broken window. She refused medical attention. Eventually, at the hospital, the ER docs treated Dana for a dislocated shoulder and minor concussion."

I continued, not allowing the rest to dwell too much on Dana's early childhood trauma. "Her mother never re-married, and from property records, it seems she raised Dana in the family residence on Hancock Street. The deed was transferred to Dana's name one year ago by Elena Miller."

"Did Elena go back to Eastern Europe?" André inquired.

"Elena moved — but not to her birth country. She was diagnosed with early-onset Alzheimer's and checked herself into a memory-care facility in Boston. I left the facility a message that I need to speak with them. I as-sume Elena doesn't know Dana's dead. After work, I plan to stop and visit with her, if her caretakers allow it," I said.

"I'll go with you," André volunteered.

"Dana followed in her father's footsteps and went into finance. But she opted out to form a small, private com-pany that did forensic accounting. Once I knew her name, looking her up was a breeze. She's done work on behalf of the IRS, banks, the private sector. It seems she built a rock-solid reputation for being discreet and thorough."

"If she exposed powerful men, she potentially made some enemies. People with means," Mercy said.

"She could have. We know her last job was at The Groove Factory. A big question mark over her role there. According to a witness inside the company, someone hired Dana Miller to expose Charles Isles's financial crimes. Allegedly he was draining the business accounts, driving the business into the ground. But that's unsubstantiated. More evidence is needed to back it up."

I told the group about Brad Connolly, the fiancé. From their texts, I had learned that Brad was the protector. He told Dana he loved her often. They had spent a substantial amount of time discussing Paris, their travel plans, and what to do in Europe. I came across no arguments spelled in words. If they fought, they didn't express their anger in the messages. From what I could tell, Dana had been happy and content with how her life was shaping up.

Her fiancé could still have killed her and ditched the country, insisted someone in the gathered crowd in the conference room. I admitted to not knowing Brad Connolly's location. We hadn't found the dark-blue BMW he drove. Technically, anyone could be the killer, including Brad, but I countered as I referred back to their texts.

"Miss Miller mentioned a weird guy hanging around the office. Brad wanted his name. Dana replied saying he's harmless, I *think*." I stopped to give the group time to catch up. "She never mentioned him again to Brad. It sounds like her killer stalked her, but Dana might have disregarded the red flags until it was too late to do something about it. There's also the mysterious white van leaving Franklin Park. And now a possible witness might have spotted the same van parked in front of The Groove Factory around the time Dana Miller left work."

A peppy knock on the door quieted us down. A fine-looking woman in a black fur coat wearing shiny black high heels stepped in. A black leather legal brief dangled from her dainty wrist. Don't-fuck-with-me attitude oozed off her.

I caught Mercy rolling her eyes at the late arrival. Her head looked ready to explode.

"River James, chief of staff for Mayor Avon Tower. I see the party has commenced. Start from the top."

"How nice of you to finally join us, Mrs. James. Nearly a half hour late. Anyone else in your shoes would sit down and try to keep up. Most certainly not waste any more of this department's time by demanding we rewind the tape." Mercy went after River James in a tone of voice reserved for cops about to have their ass handed to them on a platter. "If the mayor expects the police to catch this killer while you breathe down our neck, then at least have the courtesy to arrive on time."

"Captain — "

"I'm not done yet. Your office assured me you are here simply as a guest and an observer. So sit down, and I ask politely — stay out of the detectives' way."

"Are you done?" River stepped up to the table.

"Not in the least. I'm warming up." Mercy bulldozed River James. "Going forward, if you ever decide to come back, I expect you in class five minutes before go time. Show up a minute late and I'll toss your bony ass on the front steps — and since you're such close friends with Meredith Sawyer, please tell her I have the power to ban people from this building. I am sure she'll know what I mean."

With a quivering chin, River James seemed to swallow a string of piping-hot words lodged in her throat.

"Any questions?" Mercy asked.

"Nope. Got it. Five minutes early. I apologize to you all. Please go ahead with your brief."

But I didn't get the chance. Gina flung the door open, panic written all over her face.

"Temple — go home!"

"What's the matter?" André jumped up.

"911 intercepted a call from one of his neighbors. Four units are headed there..."

I shoved bodies aside to clear my path. River James said something, but I didn't hear a word. I rushed out, dialing Shelly — no answer. I called the house phone, and on the fourth ring, her sweet voice picked up on the answering machine.

Behind the wheel, a tingling pain stabbed my chest, shooting an electric bolt through my tapped-out body. A warning of sorts. Life's funny that way — it landed in my shot-to-hell heart. An instant explosion on impact. I felt the boom — boom — boom. But as long as I was still breathing, I would ignore it.

Chapter 19

Once I arrived at my house and found the threat of danger to be low, my pulse leveled out, which eased the pains in my heart. Yet my thoughts moved in a hazy rhythm.

As it turned out, Shelly wasn't in imminent danger.

Thankful for the good news, I reached for her and leaned down to kiss her. The last thing I remember was saying 'Shelly' before my world shut down. In the dark corners of my mind, I saw her. Quietly seated in a chair, white dress sprawled, her lifeless eyes begging me for help. I couldn't escape her. Out of nowhere, it started to rain. Blood. Tiny droplets, then torrents. Drenched, I reached out to her. I wished to protect her. Hide from the flood together. I grabbed her hand, but she was stiff like a piece of wood. She had died a long time ago. Long before I found her. I stood in front of her, soaked in blood, staring helplessly at her. Suddenly, she jerked upright, and it freaked me out.

A tearful scream pierced my ears as I woke up and found myself spread out on my front lawn. Shelly sat up in the stretcher, clutching the metal railing like she had expected to hear I had died.

"Temple, baby! Oh no, God, please. Help him. Help him," she pleaded with the medics. "Are you okay?"

"I'm fine. What happened?" I pulled myself up, rubbing the back of my head, where I felt a radiating headache.

"You blacked out," said André, who had followed me in a separate car. "What are you waiting for?" he told some firefighters. "Do your job." Of me, he asked, "Can you stand up?"

"I'm good. Look." I wobbled some, but I managed. "Okay, everyone," I pushed away their hands, "I'm feeling fine. Leave me alone."

André studied my unsteady gait, irritating me.

"My wife's the patient. Let's all worry about the heavily pregnant lady on the stretcher." I guided their attention back to Shelly.

"Me? I'm not hurt. Thatcher insisted on notifying the fire department over my protests," she told me. "Have the fire department check you out before they pack up."

"No. Forget about it," I replied. "Thatcher, huh? Smart of him to call — and clever to use my name to get attention. It worked." I studied the departing firemen.

"We see it all the time in spring — unpredictable season. Finicky." A burly fireman finished up placing Shelly's wrist in a splint. "It's because people forgot how to move their bodies locked up at home all winter. The good news is, Mrs. Stone, the wrist will make a full recovery. Give it twenty-four hours before moving it. And it should be alright."

I scanned her for missed injuries. "Won't hurt to drive you to the ER. Have the baby checked on the monitor."

"Excuse my husband, sir, he gets overly protective. Especially now, since I'm an incubator. I hate all the fuss, Temple. It's more of a pain in the butt than the bruised wrist."

"She's good. A couple of minor scratches on the left shoulder and behind the right ear. None required medical intervention. The wrist will feel sore. Tylenol and a cold compress should take care of it. All fine and good." He clicked off the safety belts on the gurney. "Call your OB on Monday," he threw me a sympathetic glare, "for his sake."

As soon as the last firetruck packed up and left, Thatcher, calm yet concerned, crossed the street. His wife Merrill padded along a few steps behind him. He rested a shoulder on the Chevy by the hood. And that's when I saw it. The hood opened, the box of tools by the tires. My eyes shifted back to Thatcher and his stained fingers. Car oil, I assumed.

"Don't be mad, okay?" Shelly put one hand on my chest, holding my arm with the other. "He meant well."

Thatcher grinned. "Don't thank me. I was able to fix the engine — for now. She'll need extensive work if you want to keep her on the road."

"I don't remember asking for your help with the truck or my wife."

"Oh, come on, Temple," Merrill quipped. "You don't expect us to leave Shelly stranded. What kind of people would that make us?"

"The mind-your-own-damn-business kind," I hissed.

"Temple, cut it out," Shelly said, mortified.

Merrill shriveled at my reply. Her husband's bright smile lost some of its shine, and he started to pack his stuff. "We meant no disrespect, but I can tell we've overstepped your boundaries."

"Thatch...Merrill — please don't go. Stay for dinner."

"I don't think so, Shells. And besides, the shape you're in — you shouldn't be on your feet for long. Rest. You know where to find us if you need somethin'. Given that you're alone all the time."

The unhappy neighbors bypassed me like a bad case of the flu. "See ya, girl," Merrill said as she walked back to her house, arm in arm with Thatcher, who called me a dick under his breath but loud enough so I could hear him.

Feeling especially irritable, I lifted my eyebrows. Shelly lifted hers. "Would it kill you to be nice to people?"

"I'm nice."

"Nice to the dead, yes. But anyone with a pulse you can be a — "

"Dick."

"Well, yeah. You said it, not me. They're nice. And if you hadn't gone off on Thatcher, he might have told you what he found under the hood of the Chevy," Shelly said as I inspected the situation under the hood.

She winced. I dropped the hood quickly and helped her to the house. She stretched out on the couch. On autopilot, I approached the sliding door to the deck. In a lousy mood, I spent a rotten moment surveying the damage in the backyard. The headache was still there, but less stabbing.

"It's not that bad. We can call a company on Monday to clean up the broken branches."

I placed my hands on my hips. "Not the point. You could have been killed. Gone. What were you doing in the backyard? In your condition — "

"Stop right there — nothing's wrong with me or my *condition*. The water looked beautiful, and I wanted to go for a stroll. So, I stepped outside. Accept it and move on. We should be discussing your condition."

I pretended not to hear the last part. "I'll move on after I cut down the damn tree myself. The branches look thick. Haven't noticed them before, have I? What do you think — twenty pounds, give or take a few? Maybe even more.

"You caught a lucky break when the lighter end smacked you in the back. That's the only reason why you walked away with minor dings. If the heavy end landed on top of you...I'd be having a life-or-death convo with a hyped-up ER doctor right now."

"Jesus, do you even hear yourself? You must have smacked your head harder than it looked. My accident is not on you and not on me. It happens. I mean it — the fireman wasn't worried. Said it's fine and good. And it is. And for the record, it'll have to be something bigger than a tree branch to knock me off." Shelly stretched her arms out to me. "You've been home for almost an hour, and you still haven't kissed me. A direct violation of the marriage contract. I'm giving you a ticket and a hefty fine."

I wrapped her in my arms and twirled her, pulled her head away to expose her neck, and planted a kiss there

— then another. I decided to ignore my blackout episode for the rest of the night.

The next morning, Sunday, I woke up to the smell of something burning in the kitchen.

Outside the window the weather was radiant. I could see the edge of the azure water glistening under the brilliant sunlight. Bathed in warmth, I sent a quick work text, threw the phone on the bed sheets, and forgot about it.

After a five-minute cold shower to wash the last reminder of sleep off me, I followed the charred aroma of ham. Shelly had tried to hide her tracks by sprinkling some eggs on top; or at least I hoped it was eggs. My stomach flipped several times and eventually tied itself into a knot, saying don't even think about it.

I glanced towards Shelly, dressed in a cotton candy pink robe and fuzzy pink slippers. Her shoulder-length hair, usually slicked to one side, was in a tight bun.

The turntable was playing Little Richard's 'Long Tall Sally.' Shelly's head bobbed and dipped with the high notes. She swung her hips, the frying pan in one hand, using the spatula for a microphone with the other.

"You're making Little Richard proud babe!" I said to her, clapping and hollering at the impromptu performance.

"Go back to bed! You'll ruin my surprise."

I ambled to her and kissed her good morning. When she wasn't looking, I snagged a piece of toast and scarfed it down.

"The food looks too good to wait for it in the sack. And I want to be close to you." I poured a cup of coffee, amused by yesterday. Merrill, the neighbor, had said something to me that struck a chord. Shelly had been all alone as I chased Bloodless. And who knows how long we had together as a family? I had been feeling the bullet fragment shifting in my chest more after Doctor Hoffman said it could kill me if I didn't remove it. But the surgery could kill me too because my heart had not healed well after the shooting. Overwhelmed by guilt, I loaded my plate with food, not daring to look at it.

"Should I even ask how the case is going? Every five minutes, Meredith Sawyer teases a breaking news development in your investigation. She's thrown your name around a few times like you two are close pals. Is she my competition?"

I snorted.

"Would it make you hot for me?" I said with a wink.

Mock shock opened her lips.

"You're sick. Pervert."

"If desiring my wife makes me a pervert, then that's who I am."

Shelly shut off the music. "It makes you the most amazing husband in the world." She picked up her cup of tea. "Don't be mad. Promise?"

"What?"

"Say I promise."

I put down the fork. "Okay, I promise. What's up?"

"I called Doctor Giovanni. He called Doctor Hoffman for a second consult."

"Shelly," I balled up the used napkin in my hands, "I fainted. It lasted fifteen seconds tops."

"Don't put that on me, Temple. There's a bullet in your chest. I'm worried, scared. Damn it — I am afraid that I will have to raise our baby alone. You're overworked. Too stressed. Hand off the homicide to someone else."

"I see — that's what this is about. My job."

Her lips trembled with disappointment, her accusing stare fixed on me.

"What can't you understand, Shells? Last year another woman died because I sided with my partner against my better judgment. She's dead today because I let her down."

"Why am I so jealous of a dead woman? I don't know. But I am. You should be home with me more, with the baby, and yet you're still trying to repair what you never broke to begin with."

"You weren't there Shelly. You never saw the look on her face. Fear. Lots of fear. It haunts me. She comes back, you know, in my dreams, asking me why I didn't do more to save her. I have no answers for her. And now this victim shows up too. I see them both. Cold and gone. But very much alive to me."

Shelly reached over for my hand. I pulled away as I told her, "Homicide victims are bodies to everyone else, but to me, Shelly, to *me*, they are more than that. I failed once. I won't let it happen again. And I might not be able to prevent murder, but I can at least catch their killers." More tenderly, I added, "I love you. I have only loved you."

Shelly studied me behind the steam of her tea.

"I know that. But loving you means a part of me walks in the shadow of death. And I'm frightened."

Now, I reached for her. She allowed me to bring her closer. Head to head.

"I'll keep the monsters away. Do you believe me? Hey, look at me. Do you believe me when I say I won't let the monsters near you and our baby?"

Shelly nodded her head, sucking her lips, fighting tears. I insisted, "Say it — Shells!"

"I believe you. Always. I believe in you."

I spread butter on the burned toast as I explained, "Dana Miller lived a lonely life until she met someone who loved her, only to be murdered soon after. Not just killed, but violated. He took her blood, put her on public display, placed a Halloween mask over her head. I shouldn't have but I made a promise to her — to bring the nutsack who killed her to justice."

Shelly returned to preparing breakfast. "Dana Miller — tell me more about her? Who was she?"

I munched on a second piece of toast, picturing Dana Miller and Brad Connolly together. A good-looking couple. It could make someone jealous; I saw it in my mind.

"She was a forensic accountant. Independent contractor, and apparently a well-respected one. Her specialty was tracking missing funds. Millions gone at her last gig. An entertainment company — The Groove Factory."

"Did you ever figure out how she ended up at Franklin Park?"

"The Groove Factory was hired by the running convention to throw a concert. We found Dana on the stage they built. It's a connection. Not an obvious one, but it ties together. The guy who started the company, Charles

Isles, is about to be bankrupt, but he won't be poor. He stashed away a fortune. Or so we've been told."

"Where did he hide the money?"

"Offshore, maybe. There are tons of other possibilities. Dana Miller was hired to find exactly that. Where did the money go?"

"And did she?"

"So far nothing on that front. And I have no physical evidence implicating Charles Isles in her murder. He might be fronting for the mafia. A rough character — Frank Ricca. We are working leads. But the special investigation unit, according to André, knows Ricca well. They are more than familiar with his organized crime operation. When I go in tomorrow, I'll meet the detectives investigating Ricca for his mafia crimes. There might be something to overlap. A thread between our investigations I'm not seeing yet."

"Oh, that's dark and twisted. Better than any *Dateline* episode they show on TV," Shelly said.

"I always knew you were a little dark and twisted, Miss Stone."

She bumped my shoulder. "Have you told Dana's family yet?"

I put the dirty plates in the sink and turned the water on.

"Yeah, about that — she only has a mother, and she lives in a nursing home. Alzheimer's. Need to drop by and tell the staff, interview them, and speak to the mother too if the nursing home lets me. Maybe she'll have a good day, lucid — remembers Dana."

"Ah, that's so cruel. The mother must be completely alone. She has no one left in the world. How utterly sad. Don't wait — go now. I have nothing special planned. I'll sit around and watch the science channel. They have a *Supernova Galactic* marathon."

I brushed my hand against her chin. The corner of her lips trembled with devotion. "I called out. It's officially my day off, and I'll spend it with the most beautiful girl in the world."

"Do you hear your daddy, baby girl? His charm's be-witching." She snuggled against my chest.

Chapter 20

I poured myself a strong cup of coffee after Shelly went to bed. Then I sat down in front of the computer in the den and logged into my police email. There was a message from André saying he'd cleared most employees at The Groove Factory. He asked if we should tail Charles Isles. I replied not yet. The second email was from Lem Needham. The white van, he wrote, belonged to some company — Pelican Bay. He couldn't find anything on Pelican Bay, but he said he's staying on it. I sat back in my chair, mulling over the latest development. The white van kept popping up in the investigation, and it bothered me. So far, I had nothing on the vehicle but the company that owned it. Pelican Bay. Did the driver of the van stalk Dana Miller? Did he kidnap her from The Groove Factory, kill her, and then ditch her at Franklin Park? Why? Was there some obscure connection between The Groove Factory and Pelican Bay that Dana Miller came across in her own work? Did she die for what she knew about the stolen millions? It certainly looked fitting. Exacerbated and not convinced, I turned in.

It felt like I had been asleep for a short while before I killed off the morning snooze of my alarm. Barely alert, I checked the time — seven forty.

For another blissful minute, I lay pretending to be at the beach — Shelly and I, her head on my shoulder — sinful bliss. Not a bad way to kick off the day. But the house phone rang. Shelly answered it, and from the way she called my name, I could tell it was work-related.

"Coming," I muttered, hustling out from under the flowery bedspread.

Shelly, clipping baby formula coupons, nodded to the phone from the kitchen table. "A woman. Didn't give me a name. Asked for you and said you've left messages for her to call you."

"Okay."

I cleared my throat. "Hello. Detective Stone."

The person on the other end started with a brief introduction. A woman, in her early to mid-fifties, I imagined, well-educated by the sound of it — measured, tight voice, punctual, and what I classified as restrained.

After no more than five minutes of back and forth, we said our goodbyes.

"Who was that? She sounded pleasant enough but reserved."

"You picked up on that too? Her name's Melisa Flynn. The director of Pleasant Valley, a high-end care home in Boston. It's about Dana Miller's mom. The nursing home will let me see her today before work."

Shelly stopped clipping. "They didn't tell her, did they?"

"The honor will be all mine and mine alone."

"So sad. And that makes it tough on you."

"But I get to come home to you, so it's a battle worth fighting."

Pleasant Valley resembled an overpriced apartment complex with private balconies painted in calming colors like ivory and wool gray. The front lawn — mossy, green meadow, budding dogwood trees. I felt an instant sense of peace ahead.

An upbeat receptionist with a blonde pixie cut and a streak of purple peek-a-boo, welcomed me on arrival. "And how is our lovely visitor doing on this fine Monday morning?"

"Like I'm on cloud nine. Temple Stone for Melisa Flynn."

"Absolutely. I can arrange that. Can I get you to fill out the visitor form? And here is a brochure about Pleasant Valley — your forever home."

"That's not necessary."

Pixie-cut looked confused but hid it with a restrained shrug. "We offer private tours — "

I opened my badge holder and let her take a look. "Melisa Flynn, please, and thank you. I got off the phone with her about an hour ago. She's expecting me."

Pixie-cut escorted me from the bright reception area to the back of the admin building where the sunlight was less prominent. Carpeted floors, water bubblers, and a communal lunch area begging for an upgrade.

She stopped at a pair of double glass doors. "Your final destination. And don't forget to have a *pleasant* day."

I saw a heavy-set woman with white GI Joe hair, a sharp chin, and pointy cheeks swipe a key pass across an ID reader.

"Melisa Flynn. Thank you for coming. You want to chat in my office before I take you to see Elena? It will give her time to eat the rest of her breakfast, clean up, and get ready for visitors. The sweet woman was hell on wheels last night. She could use some time to gather herself. I checked with her therapist, and he suggested we don't tell her you're coming. Best to play it by ear."

"What happened? Something ticked her off?"

"With her condition, it could be anything or anyone. The night nurse — one of my regular girls — irritated Elena by setting up dinner on the balcony. Lovely weather last night. She thought the patient would like a breath of cool spring air. Unfortunately, Elena took offense to that. She threw a plate of food at Janice." Melisa unlocked her office. It was a large space, filled with potted plants like bamboo trees and philodendron. Posters of inspiring quotes. A large beige sofa paired with a light, natural wood coffee table.

"Mrs. Miller has been off and on ever since her daughter stopped the visits. Keeps asking us questions; we started to run out of things to say to her." Her stern brown eyes offered me a seat.

She lowered herself into her desk chair. "To be honest, telling our patients they don't have any family left is one of the tougher aspects of my job. So, I'm asking you — are you sure it's her, Dana? Because if you're not — you're about to put a fragile woman with an even more fragile mind through hell. I wish there's some other avenues you could explore. I'm worried telling Elena her child, only living relative, is dead will virtually kill her."

"Regretfully, it's the only option at my disposal. You have my word — I'll treat her with kid gloves."

"I'm afraid even if you try to use anything but kid gloves, you might discover quickly that Elena's mind is like a child's. A very young adolescent. There is no room for a mistake."

"We confirmed it using her fingerprints. The woman in the city's morgue is Dana Miller. Elena's daughter."

"Oh, shoot. I know you're probably telling me the truth. I wanted you to be wrong. But everyone on our staff at Pleasant Valley felt that there was more to Dana's absence."

"Why didn't you report her missing?"

Melisa Flynn let out a frustrated breath. "Why would we? There was no direct reason to suspect something bad had happened to Dana. Nothing jeopardized Elena's care with us. The monthly checks cleared. The only bell to go off in my head was the call from you. If you hadn't sounded so compelling on the phone, I'd have said forget about it and written off the request."

"But you felt there was credibility to my words?"

"Dana visited Elena evenings, Monday through Saturday. From seven to eight for over a year and seven months. She never struck me as the type to walk out on her obligations. Ask anyone who works for me, they'll tell you the same.

"She likes to set things up herself. Very good head on her shoulders. Maybe because I've met her, I don't believe she'd willingly break up with her mother, in the dependent state Elena's in."

"Were the two of them close?"

"I'd say so."

"It'll help the investigation to interview some of your staff who knew her. Things they picked on that they didn't report because they didn't think it was important."

Melisa Flynn shuffled in her seat. "Dana was a shy woman, friendly when she had to be, but you quickly realized she valued her one-on-ones with her mother. They ate early supper on the balcony in Elena's room, rarely exchanging a single word. I figured they spent a lot of time in silence."

"How come?"

"Whatever communicating they did, it happened through movement. Dana always anticipated what her mother wanted and needed, and she was always spot on. Silence is our society's most overlooked virtue."

On that note, Melisa Flynn walked me to Elena Miller's private suite.

Outside her door, we heard *Wheel of Fortune* blasting.

"She likes the bright lights and the sound effects on the show. Watches the reruns for several hours a day. It relaxes her, so we put up with it."

Melisa Flynn marched in. "Yoo-hoo, it's Melisa. How's my favorite girl doing? You okay, baby? Breakfast good?"

The room had all the comforts of a nursing home — cozy green recliner, a nice flat screen, a decorative fireplace framed by a white mantel. And everywhere my eyes moved, I noticed photos — mostly black and white; old, definitely. All from Dana's childhood, several from a modest wedding in front of a courthouse. I assumed the woman with thick black hair, heavy eyeliner, and a bewitching smile was Dana's mom, Elena.

"Melisa — did Dana call? I must discuss important private family matters with her. She and her dad should be on their way back. Make sure you leave the door open — " Her glassy eyes transferred to me. She studied me, debating if she knew me. After a tense beat, Elena let her guard down.

"Well, don't stand there, Martin, help her? Dana already upstairs? Tell that child to come down after she's done her homework."

Melisa tried to step in, but I sat down beside Elena, up to the task. "I told her, so you don't have to."

Elena nodded, grateful. Someone understood her. Martin was home. So was Dana. Loneliness had left her room.

As Melisa sneaked out, Elena pointed to the screen. "The last three words are missing. And he doesn't look like he has the smarts to guess the rest. I'm usually spot on, Martin. But my mind..." She chuckled. "Forgot the butcher's boy's name again. He had to tell me. How embarrassing?"

"It happens. I'm sure he didn't have a problem with it."

"If you say so. It's annoying. I don't know what's going on with me. Do you?" She tapped my shoulder playfully. "Dana and you had fun? I would've loved to be there with you. But I understand she can be more like you — chatty, smart. I'm too old school for her. Too foreign."

"Dana loves you. Loves you very much."

Elena's tortured eyes flared with happiness. "My girl — I felt a hole in my heart like I haven't felt before when she left with you. The fight was stupid. Silly. Mother-daughter nonsense."

"What was the fight about?"

"A boy. She likes a boy. No, wait till you hear it — she insists it's love. They'll get married. Kids. What do they know about marriage? What it takes to make it work." She lost her train of thought. Switched the timelines with no hitch. "It's been hard on her, Martin — she refuses to take me to Eastern Europe. Refuses to take me home. And I don't know how long I can hold on…"

The TV host yelled 'E.' "Oh, shut up, you little shit. Don't you see I'm talking to Martin? Entirely your fault my husband hasn't been around to visit me."

"Elena — Dana told you about a man she's seeing? What's his name? Where did they meet?"

"At school, of course. His father's in finance. Asian markets. She picked a man after her father. That should make you happy."

"Right, she mentioned that. I forget his name."

"Brad. His name is Brad. We said no to them going to the dance together. He's too old for her. Dana should be more careful about those boys. Stay on top of her studies. Don't rely on a man to give her a life."

Another sad breath. "I want to go home, Martin. And don't say 'Boston's home.' Dana promised."

I stayed with her for fifteen more minutes. The conversation lingered on Martin and Dana. Sometimes it made sense, otherwise it was snippets of her life from a long time ago. At some point, she began to drift off.

As I got ready to leave, Elena let out a tired snore. I noticed more photos of Dana and Martin on the wall. Elena in thick black eyeliner, a contagious smile. There would be justice for Dana. I'd see to it.

A squeaky plank on the floor aroused Elena, not so sweet and innocent anymore. She shot up — her eyes wide, confused.

A tight yelp followed, filled with fear and dread. It caught me off guard. Elena picked up a porcelain dove figurine from a side table. She aimed for me.

I improvised. Shouted, "Elena — it's Martin! It's me. Look, we were watching *Wheel of Fortune.* I got up to use the bathroom."

Elena lowered the dove, held it in her hands. "What's the damn missing word? I used to be so good at guessing them."

Words flashed on the screen. A busty girl flipped around another letter, and another one. The audience shouted at the excited contestant.

I read it to Elena. "Loneliness remembers what happiness forgets."

"Right, Martin. Loneliness." She returned the dove to the side table. "Tell Dana to come down for dinner, would you? We're...I am...*waiting* for her."

Chapter 21

After seeing Elena Miller, I headed to Hancock Street in Charleston. André Jones met me in front of a three-story brownstone with black shutters. It looked stately. Comfortable living.

"Nice place," André said, exiting his car. "You look okay. How're things? I mean with you."

"Rested. I got the key. C'mon"

"Three shots in the chest. A year later you're on the street. Are you sure you're good to be back — in the field, on the force? With what happened to you, no one will fight you if you choose the desk. You can write your own ticket is what I'm trying to say."

"Are you my mother now? Cut it out. I get an earful at my house. I don't need to hear it from my partner." I turned the key in the lock and entered.

"What happened at Pleasant Valley? Did you tell Mrs. Miller about Dana?"

"The woman lives in a nice place. She has people looking after her. The lady who runs the show there struck me as honest. She won't nickel-and-dime Elena. Her living expenses will be covered thanks to a very generous trust Martin left her.

"There's not much of a physical resemblance between Elena and her daughter. Lots of photos of the family. They were happy. A happy family. You can tell Elena did her best to raise Dana as if Martin was still alive. I caught a whiff of a small rift between them — too much alike it seems. Martin was the balance. After he died, the communication between them had to be forced. But Elena did her best. You can tell she loves Dana."

"Elena took it hard, then? Couldn't have been easy to look her in the eye — tell her she got no one else left in the world to hold her hand?"

"I couldn't even if I tried. She was barely lucid enough to carry on a casual conversation. Random sparks of reality, but overall, her mind's gone. Lives in the past. Safer there. Happy memories. Happy family."

Inside, the brownstone was mostly white walls, white kitchen, and marble countertops to match. Friendly. Neat as a pin, I decided. Dana had kept up with rules, chores. Elena had seen to it that Dana learned responsibility because life could spin on its head and change on a dime. It happened to them. Martin. The crash. A fractured family.

Maybe not the warmest of moms, but Elena, I mused, cooked a warm meal for Dana every night. They had dinner together. A tradition they upheld even when Elena moved to Pleasant Valley.

"Tidy, clean — seems Dana ran a tight ship, like her mother. More alike than she'd ever tell Elena. Maybe for Dana, tidy and clean meant more than a housekeeping rule. Easier to keep track of things, ain't it?

"She was very young when Martin died. Saw it with her own eyes. Lived through it. The report from back then said a 'small female' was found on the scene with him. Clutching his hand. Goes along with what Elena Miller told me about their relationship."

André opened the cupboards. "No song and dance for Elena raising Dana all alone. She didn't take the child to Eastern Europe. No. They stayed here. Martin's roots. Tradition. Family mattered."

"Apparently, Dana showed an obvious preference for her dad. Two peas in a pod. Martin and Dana out, having fun. Elena — strict, rules, alone in the house. She mentioned Dana thinking of her as old school and foreign. Maybe the two had a falling-out when Dana was a child."

More photos of Martin's sweet-natured smile. Standing next to him — Dana in Mini Mouse ears, smiling as wide as the sky. Elena out of the shot. Taking the photo.

"It doesn't take long to figure out Elena assumed the bad-cop role. Disciplining Dana — it dinged their bond. Some friction between them, nothing major or serious to stop Dana from caring for her mother.

"Melisa Flynn, the Pleasant Valley director, said Dana took care of every detail when it came to her mother. Painted her as a doting daughter. Punctual. The staff didn't know Brad Connolly. Dana never mentioned him to the staff at the nursing home. And no ring. The engagement must have been recent."

"Or Dana took it off before every visit in case it would upset her mother," André said. "Yesterday, Lem dug more into Dana's personal stuff. Wide search — as far back as college. He found a single incident, sophomore year at UMass. She was almost nabbed for protesting in front of the state capital, calling for tougher prison sentences for drunk drivers. The cops gave her a citation and cut her loose. Nothing in our system with her name after that." André walked and talked.

"Losing Martin — probably her only friend in the world, the one parent she felt connected to, drives her to act out. Understandable. Kids with similar experiences take up drugs or struggle with addiction. Survival guilt. Not Dana. She has some Eastern European in her. Some of Elena Miller in her. Her mother doted on her, maybe even smothering her, steering Dana with an iron hand."

"Check this out." André pointed to a built-in safe in the master bedroom. "Older model. The dial is analog. So, Martin put it in to keep what?"

I scanned the space. Matching heavy antique furniture, gold velvet drapes, and paintings of small mountain villages — I assumed places in Eastern Europe.

"Looks like this was Martin and Elena's bedroom. Very eighties; high-end, but older. Well-maintained but again, older. Massive bed posts — you can't find this type of craftsmanship on the market today." I hovered over André tinkering with the dial on the vault. "Call the techs. Have them search every room in the home.

"From what I've seen, I don't think her killer has been here. No signs of a struggle, and nothing's tossed. He abducted her elsewhere. And what? Took her to his place? Hancock Street's quiet, but there are lots of houses on the block. If he grabbed her on the street, neighbors would have called it in. She never made it home after work Friday."

"We have the phone logs from her cell. She talked to Brad while she was in the office. Dana Miller must have left shortly after. No one has heard from them since that last call between them. We might never know what they discussed," André said. "I'll have some officers canvas the area. See what shakes."

I headed for the second floor. "Dana owns the home. Her name's on the deed. But she didn't take the master. Left it as if her parents lived here. She must have occupied another room."

I found Dana's bedroom. She had removed a wall between three rooms to create a super master bedroom for herself. Decorated it in lots of wheat, barley, and cream. On the feminine side, but not girlish or over-the-top. And again, neat as a pin.

André hoofed up the stairs. "The techs are on their way. Got anything here?"

"Dana made sure she filled the place with things she liked. Totally her own identity. Yet respectful of her parents' space, even though she was within her rights to move into the bedroom downstairs. She rightfully owns the home."

André started to go through the drawers. "The house has an alarm. Again, an older model, but a good choice. Remote activated. Dana could arm it using a fob or an app. If we contact the company, they should be able to give us the logs. Nail down the last time the vic engaged it."

I ran a hand over the nightstand by her bed. Light dust. "She's been gone for a while. Even before she was killed. Gone, but where? A business trip? Seems unlikely. She was stuck in the office the last two weeks, investigating Charles Isles and his company — The Groove Factory. Yet her home doesn't feel lived-in. Barely any food in the fridge."

"Maybe she ran out and didn't bother shopping before her Paris trip," André said, looking into double-wide dressing drawers. "A jewelry box." André placed a wooden box on top of the dressers. A flock of birds painted in gold adorned the top. When he lifted it, a tiny ballerina twirled to the sound of a sweet melody.

"What you got?" Under the light streaming in through the window, I inspected the few chunky rings, some pearl earrings, and a gold necklace. "Nothing that looks remotely close to an engagement ring."

"Maybe Brad took it back because they broke up." André closed the box and put it back.

"Before their romantic European trip? They were in love — it's in their texts. Brad's not missing. We're missing a body. The killer wanted Dana. She was his fantasy. Brad was an inconvenience. Eventually, we will find him, and her engagement ring won't be on him," I explained.

André circled the three-monitor computer. "And what do we have here? Expensive. Fast and..." He paused, annoyed. "Damn it. She encrypted it. Might take us some time to unlock the system. Doable, but it'll need time."

"Anything in the desk drawers?"

"Office supplies. She probably mostly worked digitally or worked in an office at whatever company hired her. No paper copies of any kind."

"If her death was a mafia hit, wouldn't Frank Ricca send people to her house to look for the report? Break the case downstairs? Take her computers with them?"

"Maybe she told Frank Ricca where she kept it after he told her what he would do to her. So, no reason to break into her house."

I found the home gym and instantly grew envious of all the toys in there. "She liked to exercise — weightlifting and yoga. Hiking when the weather was nice. No signs of marathon training or running. Our vic preferred the comforts of her home gym but liked to push herself to her limits. Some serious weights. Explains the stellar shape she was in."

"But she never fought her killer. Wu found no self-defense wounds on Dana," André said from the office.

"Not because she didn't want to, I bet. He collapsed her lung and fed her copious amounts of drugs," I pointed out.

I moved back to the office. André remained at the computer monitors studying the password portal. "Hmm. Sophisticated. The vic spent a lot of money on security. Quality IT. Off-site corp maintains the servers. Add them to the list of places to subpoena. Gaining their records could be a game changer for the investigation."

"She worked for the IRS, banks, and some on the Fortune 500 list. Makes sense Dana wanted to safeguard their secrets. Protect them. She protected her mom, always in charge of the details. Had the final word. Maybe she felt she failed Martin. That his death was somehow her fault," I said as I gathered my thoughts.

"She was only a kid when he died."

"But then she became a woman. And a good-looking one at that. With mom living full time at the nursing home, Dana would have craved something to protect. Nothing in the home screams a relationship, even a casual one. Brad's nowhere in this house. Did you see a bathroom?" I left André to deal with the computers.

"Third door to your left."

In there, more things women liked and purchased — plush towels, various skin potions, migraine medication. All neat as a pin.

I donned some gloves and picked up a bamboo toothbrush. "Hers is the electric one. His, the all-natural — no frills. And cologne, travel size — sandalwood and sage. Masculine. But no clothes of his in the closets. Not even a pair of socks or boxers. I don't think they spent much time in her home. Too much of Elena and Martin here. Too many memories Dana wished to leave behind."

"Brad's father should be able to shed light on their relationship. Did Dana tell Elena about Brad?" André said.

"Hard to tell. Dana might have confessed during one of their balcony dinners. But Elena's slipping away fast. Her recollections are broken fragments. Almost impossible to believe them. And Melisa Flynn said Elena has become aggressive lately. Threw a plate at a nurse. Probably because Dana stopped coming around.

"Although, when I spoke to Elena, she thought of me as Martin. Her husband returning home with Dana after a day of fun. Said she and Dana fought over a boy. Dana said she loved him; wanted to marry him. Naturally, Elena rejected the idea. Said his name — Brad. Has to be the same one." I removed the gloves.

"And you think it's credible?"

"Elena's not reliable, but yeah. I do. Elena was mad at Dana for not taking her to Eastern Europe. And I think Dana was starting to let go of her parents and accepting she owed herself a life. Maybe not as neat as a pin like her mom would've preferred, but a life of her own.

"The boy — man — might be the reason for the final rift between them," I said, feeling as thought I had seen enough of the house.

The techs unpacked in Dana's office. Work was under-way to collect her electronic equipment. To give them space, I moved to the window, pulled back a lacy curtain. I saw a tight street, but nice. Well-maintained homes packed together. But quiet, green, with mature trees. I walked downstairs and found Lem by the kitchen counter inspecting Dana's mail.

"The mailman stopped delivering. There's a notice to collect the rest in person at the post office," he said, sorting through the ads and bills. "Clean life she lived. In order. Did her best on her own," he said.

"Maybe Bloodless likes women who obey. Is attracted to their soft side. Something about Dana reminded him of someone else. He went through major trouble to stage her in a white dress, the mask...and he brought the chair with him too," I said. "That indicates a level of familiarity with his victim's habits, the rhythm of her daily life."

"He's been watching her." André picked up a piece of mail.

"If the killer was familiar with Dana, her schedule, he knew she lived alone. From what I have seen, Brad didn't spend every evening with Dana," I said.

"Yeah, so?" André mumbled.

"Why kill Dana when she was with Brad? Why not kill her when she was alone, more vulnerable?"

André shrugged. "Why, why, why. Lots of them."

I spotted a woman, older, mid-seventies, standing on the steps of the house across from Dana's. She had a tiny brown dog on a leash, sniffing a patch of peonies.

"Excuse me, ma'am..." I approached her.

She was a small woman, stout, with pink cotton-candy hair that lay flat over a pair of pointy ears. Her misgivings about me were clear in her pastel-green eyes as she tugged on the leash and the dog to go in.

"I don't have time," she replied curtly.

I showed her my badge. "Detective Stone, Boston Homicide. Do you mind if I ask you some questions about your neighbor?"

Her gaze skimmed past me, towards the wide-open door, flooded with cops, where Dana Miller used to live. "Is something the matter with Dana?"

Her misgivings gave way to anxiety. The teddy-bear-looking pup sniffed between her feet, trotting about, excited to be outside.

"We're investigating her death. Sorry to take up your time. It will only be a minute."

"Lord! Of course. Anything I can do to help. My name is Josephine Whitney. What do you need to know? Though I must warn you, Dana, as sweet and polite as she was, kept mostly to herself. Once she bought a gift for Mr. Darcy. That was nice of her."

"And Mr. Darcy is..." I asked.

Mr. Darcy let out a confident bark, jumped on his back paws, and stood upright, apparently quite fond of his name. I patted his head, and he licked my fingers.

"You two knew each other somewhat, then?"

"Yes. Wonderful young lady. She grew up on this block, you know. I knew her parents — Martin and Elena — very well. Things changed, and not for the better, after Martin's death. Elena kind of shut off Dana from the world. I barely saw her play outside. Always in the house, doing chores, homework. If you ask me, Elena took it too far with Dana. But there was no talking to her." Mr. Darcy jumped into her arms. She nuzzled him with her nose. "I kind of understand why Elena laid the law thick on Dana, but I wished she'd allow some room for fun. But, hey, I never had children of my own, so maybe I'm wrong."

"When was the last time you saw Dana?"

"Friday, several weeks ago. I don't know the exact date. She'd been leaving to go to work late, like night time. So, finally, I caught her as she was leaving to ask her about it. She said some Boston businessman hired her to examine his business books. I guess he suspected one of his employees was stealing from him. Though, Dana didn't come out and say it."

"Did she tell you anything else about her client?"

Josephine Whitney fed a treat to Mr. Darcy. "Like what? Dana was an extremely private person. Those walls her mom helped build. It was hard for her to trust, connect. Even basic human interaction could give Dana a panic attack."

Mr. Darcy was still licking the flavor of his treat from her fingers. She shifted. "Hang on. There was something she said — Dana asked me if I had seen a car parked in front of my house?"

"She asked you that?"

"Yes."

"And had you? Seen a car?"

"Uh-huh. Thursday night. A white one. A work van, older vehicle. Not from the neighborhood. It idled for an hour. Its bright headlights woke me up."

"Did you happen to take down the license plate? Make? Model?"

Josephine Whitney dropped Mr. Darcy, who scampered to the peonies and lifted a leg. "I was so tired. It was the middle of the night. I opened the bedroom window and yelled for the jerk to kill the engine or I'd call the cops. He left practically that second."

"If we show you some photos, do you think you'd recognize it?"

"That'd be a waste. I'm looking at the car right now." She pointed at a white van parked at the bottom of the street.

"Is that it?"

"It's the same model, but newer. They kind of all look the same to me." She buried herself in her coat.

"What about this man? Have you seen him with Dana?"

"Oh yeah, dark-blue BMW. Very polite. Took my trash to the street a few times in the winter. It looked like they were a couple, but good luck making Dana tell you anything private. She just wasn't wired like that." Josephine Whitney shook her head. Dana, she repeated, stayed private, always, because Elena trained her to be.

I thanked her again for her help. She asked some questions of her own. Mr. Darcy barked as she let him in.

André had stayed on the street by his car waiting for me.

"Dana's neighbor might have seen the white van Alice Hatchet and her neighbors saw leave Franklin Park. Georgie Stavros spotted it on the street in front of The Groove Factory. Seems to me Dana had a dedicated stalker," I said.

"Did she give you a license plate?"

"Negative. But she confirmed Brad Connolly drove a blue BMW and occasionally stayed with Dana. Called him polite. They looked like they were together." I pointed at the van on Dana Miller's street. "Find out who owns that vehicle and have him checked out. The neighbor could only give me the color and the make."

"SID are waiting at the station for you."

"What do they want?" I paused. "Frank Ricca? I don't see him capable of draining anyone's blood." I opened the car door.

"Hear them out. I've talked to a few old timers who knew Ricca's uncle back in the day."

"So what?" I shook my head.

"They said the Riccas were messed up in the head. Capable of helluva more than draining your blood," he replied.

Chapter 22

Warm weather had melted the afternoon, and people were strolling along the streets. I peeled off my jacket as soon as I stepped foot in the parking lot at the station. André bought a sandwich from one of the food trucks that parked there full time feeding hungry cops.

"The detective from the special investigation unit's a strong cop from what I've heard. Clean record. Has been on the force for twelve years."

"How did he know we're looking into Frank Ricca?" I asked.

André sank his teeth into his sandwich. "He found out on his own when I called asking around about Ricca."

"I'll hear him out, but..."

André chewed his food as he answered, "If SID says they can help us, it doesn't hurt us to at least hear them out."

Before we split up after stepping out of the elevator, André said, "I'll be in with Lem. See if I can give him a hand with finding the owner of the white van. We'll wait for you in the break room."

Shouting could be heard from the captain's office. Bradley Walker and Mercy were working out some issues. It didn't involve me until it did.

I pressed down on the handle. No knock, full of attitude — and not the good kind.

"You have something to say to me, Walker? Say it to my face," I hissed.

"Fine. I will. Someone should." He threw an accusatory glance at Mercy. "Someone said you had one of your episodes, blackouts, yesterday. A bunch of people saw it. One must wonder if you're alright in there." He pointed to my chest, and I was about to clock him.

"Is that it then? You're concerned about my health. How sweet of you. No, see, I don't think that's it. Why don't you come out and say it — be a man about it."

The last part got him riled up. He pushed the chair between us like he might throw a punch. And if he did, I would let him have it. I had grown tired of him.

"Detective Walker — out, out, out," Mercy ordered.

"Ma'am, what did I do?"

"I'm not interested in explaining my orders to you. Go back to your assignment."

He pushed by me, refusing to look me in the eye.

"And you? What right do you think you have to interrupt my meeting?"

"He has an attitude problem he should fix," I replied with an unhealthy dose of attitude of my own.

"Okay. Last I checked your job was to manage the Homicide detectives, not fix them. Correct me if I'm wrong, but you wanted this job. You lobbied for it, you fought for it, and you ended up on top. I still have the nice email you sent me when I recommended you to the chief," Mercy said.

"I'm fine. I need everyone to leave me the hell alone to do my job. You know? The job, captain, I was hired to do. And I can't do it if everyone always questions me." My voice cracked at the end.

"We are just worried about you. First, you blacked out at the promotion ceremony, and now you passed out at your house. Put yourself in our shoes. Some of us feel responsible for your sorry ass getting shot."

"So it's my fault."

"No you damn fool — we want to make sure nothing happens to you. This is me asking not as your boss but as your friend: are you okay? No one will hold it against you if you sit this one out until you're ready to jump back in the game."

I thought about coming clean. It would be wise to do so. Bradley Walker was marching up and down the bullpen. If I stepped aside, he'd take my spot as lead. No chance I'd allow it.

"They changed my meds. It's sorted out. The blackouts are gone."

I slammed the door to my office and went to stand in front of the murder board, fuming.

"Come on Dana, help me out. Who did this to you?" I mumbled under my breath. If I kept my mind on her, I wouldn't have to think about my problems. The bullet fragment shifting closer to my heart, the experimental surgery I had to undertake if I wanted to stay alive — but it could also kill me.

The phone on my desk rang. I answered it holding my eyes on the Halloween mask, wondering why the killer chose it. He could have had his pick at the party store — any mask, but he selected the Grim Reaper. What did the Grim Reaper represent?

"Detective Stone," I said.

"Captain Berry, Winslow, Connecticut. I just received your notice. Are you still searching for a blue BMW?"

"Yes. Brad Connolly's the owner according to our records. Did you find it?"

"Sorry, no. But we have a gentleman in our lobby who says he's Brad Connolly's father. He's refusing to leave until we tell him what's going on. Figured I'd give you a call, get details. What's the skinny? Is his son a suspect in something?" Captain Berry explained.

"Tell him to go home."

"I've tried that," Berry replied.

"Then tell him I'll have a car pick him up tonight and bring him to Boston."

"Okay. Anything I should know?"

"The blue BMW hasn't turned up yet. It's not stolen, no report of it, and Patrol hasn't spotted it in the city. It could be Brad Connolly might very well be dead, killed along with his fiancée. But it's still iffy."

"Understood. The father tells me the son lives with them. Forty years old and still lives at home. But I can't put my finger on it — his parents, the dad, looked wrecked over his disappearance." Berry coughed away from the handle, cleared his throat, and resumed his thought. "I'll put a car on their block and call you if we see suspicious activities, how does that sound?"

"Thank you, captain. I'd appreciate it if you kept our conversation private. I'd prefer to tell Mr. Connolly Senior in person."

In the break room, I shook hands with SID Detective Vargas. He was short, wide, and completely bald. His upper lip was guarded by a fluffed and buffed graying mustache Vargas liked to pet often, I noticed. The dark-indigo suit he wore complemented his tanned features.

"Right...Frank Ricca. What can I tell you about him? Boston's man-made monster if monsters existed," said Detective Vargas as we settled around the card table by the vending machine.

"He could be our perp," André said.

"That remains to be seen," I said on autopilot.

"Ricca's brutal, bloody, and oh yeah — a complete psychopath. I like him for a dozen murders. Including his uncle's, the last Cosa Nostra Don — Antony 'Tony the Iceman' Ricca. He liked to freeze his victims to death. Threw them in an ice box; twenty-four hours later, the family gets a delivery from a refrigerator company. The ruse was to tell them they won a new appliance.

"They open it and discover so-and-so's croaked, encapsulated in a block of ice. Iceman Tony — a remarkably cruel creature. I, for one, didn't shed a single tear when we collected his body parts, scattered across the country like garbage."

I perused the brief on Ricca, stopping long enough to connect with his isolating stony face. The slicked-back ponytail, skin smooth as highly polished marble, the vacant stare. A natural-born killer, I summarized. I would give that much to Vargas.

The SID detective pointed to Frank's mugshot. "I remember the nephew, Frank Rica making a name for himself on the streets — his uncle's brutal enforcer. I chased after Frank Ricca for years. It cost me two marriages. I'd have given one of my nuts to put him behind bars. I'll never forget Frank Ricca's appetite for blood."

"Why do you think the uncle never tried to stop him? He had the power. He had people who could do it."

"Frank was effective. Everyone paid on time. Even those who didn't owe money, paid. In the end, Tony the Iceman lost his life because he was blinded by trust. His nephew, Frank Ricca was always after one thing — the Cosa Nostra's crown. And boy! He got his wish. Come hell or high water."

"The Italian Mafia stood by idly? Sicily can't be pumped about special investigation detectives breathing down their neck. Keeping Frank Ricca alive and in power's more trouble for them."

Vargas considered my question.

"One would think so. The Cosa Nostra struggled to fill their ranks with new Italian blood, and business revenue started to dry up. Not as many Italians immigrating over here, and Europe has a strong hold on the Italian Mafia over there. For a very long time, mobsters were in decline, dinosaurs by gangster standards. Money came in mainly from running bookies and illegal gambling. Until — ”

“Frank Ricca,” I said.

“Yeah, Ricca. He burst on the scene; changed the rules of the game. Got in bed with Eastern European pimps, sex trafficking. Women and gambling go hand in hand.”

I glanced at André. “The ties between Charles Isles and Frank Ricca are starting to make sense. Not much to do with our homicide, but I can see their partnership playing out in my head.”

“Ricca’s crazy paranoid. Doesn’t trust anyone. His inner circle is limited to his top two. Unconfirmed reports suggest Ricca sleeps in a four-by-four cement cell, underground, with bolted doors. A rack of high-power rifles locked and loaded, ready to go. Bringing him in has been a logistical nightmare for us. No good way to prevent casualties of our men.”

“I agree Ricca likes to kill. Paranoid control freak’s written all over your file, Vargas. Most of what I see — Ricca kills the competition. He goes to the extreme in his murder rituals, and he’s brutal. Somehow messy. His murders don’t feel tight, clean like the killing in Franklin Park,” I said, examining the thick file on Frank Ricca.

“For seven years, Ricca’s been running circles around us. His crew’s petrified of him. Last year, we bagged one of Frank’s. Small-time delinquent, nineteen years old, errand boy. In court, he’d have beat the charges. Only we didn’t want it to go that far. The idea was to flip him. Get him to CI on Frank. In return, SID would look the other way on his rap sheet. Cut him loose after the twenty-four-hour hold to make it look like he kept his mouth shut. The DA signed off." Vargas slowed down.

"We screwed the pooch. The daft runt never agreed to see us. Acting out of fear, the chump hung himself in a cell. That's how much power Ricca has over his squad," Vargas finished.

I read further into Frank Ricca's background. The nephew of Tony the Iceman Ricca, immigrated with his family to the States from Sicily. His father, Andrea Ricca, petitioned for asylum protection, alleging the mafia had a hit on his head. Reasons unspecified. But I got the feeling it had something to do with his troubled son — Frank. Dad settled the family in Southie. Fresh start. No criminal record on the father.

So, Andrea Ricca ran away from the guns, the violence, and the mafia life in Sicily. He wanted his children, Frank, and his little sister, Carmena, to have a shot at a normal life. It seems things worked out for Carmena, a nurse at Boston Children's. One marriage, no divorces, three kids of her own.

Andrea Ricca died less than ten years ago. I skimmed over the cause of death; my eyes met Vargas's.

"Yep. It's true. Andrea's wife and Carmena woke up to a freezer delivery. We pursued Tony Ricca relentlessly for the murder of Andrea Ricca, his older brother, but we couldn't get the charges to stick. All circumstantial, and the DA wanted to nail Tony for more than just one murder. We cut him loose. Six weeks later, the first body part, a left ear, showed up nailed to the front doors of

South Station. It belonged to Tony the Iceman Ricca. DNA confirmed it.

"We all figured Frank Ricca got a piece of his uncle as revenge for Andrea's murder. But then we started to get calls from every major city in the country. Frank Ricca got more than just a piece of his uncle. He dismembered him one pound of flesh at a time until there was nothing left to carve."

"Sadistic. He justifies murder if he feels it serves him a purpose. Given his extensive criminal background, Frank Ricca comprehends the law. This gives him an outstanding knowledge of police inner workings. Good enough at least to clean up a crime scene and dispose of evidence," André chimed in.

"There's more...it's mostly unconfirmed chatter, and we were never able to get him for it. One of our own, undercover, good cop, received a tip saying Frank Ricca offed his father and pinned it on the uncle."

"Tony the Iceman suspected the truth," I said. "Most likely knew what Frank had done to Andrea. Went to confront him. Uncle to nephew. Family takes care of its own. Frank showed up prepared with a rock-solid plan to neutralize Tony. The Cosa Nostra ends up under Frank's control. No dinosaurs left after Tony."

"You got to give Frank Ricca credit. Sheer genius," André mused.

"In the course of our investigation we've come across this van." I positioned the photo so Vargas could see it. "Have you seen it before?"

"Organized crime uses them. White and black, popular choice."

"How about Pelican Bay? Ever heard of it?"

Vargas shook his head. "No. Why?"

"I don't know yet. Small things have big parts in homicide investigations," I replied, eyes locked on the white van.

The three of us agreed to keep SID in the loop. Whatever evidence we uncovered implicating Ricca in other murders — we'd hand it over to them. Dana Miller stayed with me. Vargas left after that to attend to other business.

Sitting across from each other, André and I studied our murder book, the investigation mapped out in photos.

"Frank Ricca, the showman. There's a flair of the macabre to his methods," I said, reluctant to admit it. "Andrea Ricca murdered and stuffed in a freezer. Tony the Iceman Ricca dismembered; body parts sprinkled around the country. You heard Vargas, a pound of flesh at a time. The last dinosaur wiped out. There's a message in every kill."

"Dana Miller probably didn't know what she was involved in. Who she would expose with her report. Frank Ricca flipped on her and killed her. Murdered her fiancé too. What's one more body to Ricca?" André said.

"Then why not put her in a freezer, dump her outside of town? Hack her to bits like he did his uncle?" I asked, troubled by Ricca's file.

"Good question to ask Ricca when we arrest him," André countered.

"I see your point; I'm not trying to discredit you. Frank Ricca's officially primary until we find the owner of the white van. Lem, what did you find?"

Lem, who had stayed silent till now, replied, "Pelican Bay — a dummy company, or at least, I can't find any records of it. Offices in Philadelphia and Boston."

"Take another detective and go check out the local office," I said.

Lem curved a brow. "I looked it up on Google Maps. It's in the middle of a field, managed by the city's waste-man-agement department. Smells to me whoever's driving the car doesn't want us to know his name."

"Pelican Bay's trouble for us. Lem, keep at it. Find out who owns it. André — you stay on top of the techs search-ing Dana Miller's computers. I want to know if she ever finished her report or turned it in — and who has it."

Chapter 23

The detective from SID had painted a vivid picture of Frank Ricca and his cruelty. It almost convinced me — Ricca could have killed Dana. Between the pages of his criminal file, I saw a man who killed out of pleasure, out of necessity, for the fun of it. He could justify taking a life, I suspected, with a clear conscience, if he even had one. I doubted it.

But what about Charles Isles, the bankrupt owner of The Groove Factory suspected of stashing millions away as he watched his own company perish? I started with him, waiting for the techs to go through Dana Miller's computers. If her report proved Isles stole the money and Ricca helped, they had a compelling motive for her murder.

Charles Isles came from modest beginnings. He was not the brightest student or especially gifted in any particular subject. According to his school records, Charles Isles appeared to toe the line of mediocrity. And his less-than-dazzling grades carried him over to a community college somewhere out in the Midwest. I uncovered no surprises in his chosen field — general studies. He stuck with it for about two years, his grades benching below average. Four times he was placed on probation; the last one resulted in Charles quitting off his own volition. After a semester, he returned, and it seemed the tide had turned in his favor.

A graduation date was listed two years later — the degree in business management. His grades had jumped enough to get him on the president's honor roll, and young Charles Isles headed off to Fordham University.

I located a six-page rap sheet from his college days. He was arrested eleven times for running illegal underground gambling tournaments. Every time, however, a judge looked the other way, and Isles got off with nothing more than a slap on the wrist.

His streak of good luck continued in the form of a job offer from *Rolling Stone Magazine* to run their ad and sales department. Charles Isles proved to be a skilled manager and a money-whisperer, if the glowing recommendation letters singing his praise were to be believed.

So, he has the smarts, I mused. Good people skills, essential to a killer preying on unsuspecting women. And some money. Selling ads pays well according to his property records. Isles showed a promising aptitude for the real estate market. Bought cheap homes, flipped them for a profit.

Around that time, his fortune sprung, Charles Isles met a vivacious socialite named Tamara Sullivan. Her great-great-grandfather started Sullivan Electric, a public company worth billions today. Charles and Tamara married after a short courtship and settled their little family in Fairfax, Connecticut.

I skimmed over the rest of Charles Isles's history. For the next five years, Charles worked for Sullivan in the capacity of adviser. I'm willing to bet the farm that Tamara's father set up Charles to take over the public relations part of the company. What loving in-law wouldn't?

By now, a decade had rolled over since Charles Isles graduated from Fordham University. And my main suspect had tasted trouble.

In the ten years working for Sullivan Electric, three women had filed sexual harassment reports implicating Charles in sexual misdeeds. The first two settled out of court, but the third one pushed for a hearing. Reading over her deposition, the lady saw no point in receiving hush money. She told a room full of feral lawyers that Charles Isles was a monster for what he had done to her. In open court, she accused him of drugging and raping her. Without her consent, he tied her to a bed and raped her repeatedly over the span of several days. When he finished with her, he shoved her in a cab and sent her packing. To keep her quiet, Charles blackmailed his vic with a sex tape recorded without her consent.

Drugging his victim bothered me. Tying her up — pained me. It was hard not to think about Jane Doe and the drugs discovered in her bloodstream. The dark purple bruises on her slender body from the cuffs he used to lock her up.

I continued to read. Charles's wife, Tamara, picked up the scent of her lying, cheating hubby and kicked him out of the home they shared. Sullivan Electric speedily disposed of his job. And Charles Isles found himself flat broke.

In his financial records after the split from Tamara, I came across one bankruptcy filing and several judgments against him for forged checks.

I skipped through the lengthy list of dead-end jobs Charles held. Somewhere along the way, however, he began promoting gigs. First small, then the occasional visiting act, and eventually he monopolized the Boston concert scene as the number-one promoter. And two years later, The Groove Factory officially opened for business.

About then, I moved away from Charles Isles. You don't have to be a cop to know it takes money to open a first-class entertainment company, which is what The Groove Factory positioned itself as.

But where did the initial capital come from?

In the prison records system where Isles had served time, I found a possible answer. A strong connection between two individuals who lusted after money and women.

I phoned André to come in. The dark half-moon circles under his eyes told me he didn't miss the days of working the beat.

"You summoned," he said, tilting a cup to his lips.

"See for yourself." I slipped a printout toward him. As he read, I told him, "Charles Isles served time with Frank Ricca. Bunk mates. Ricca left first. When it was time for Isles to check out, look at the name he listed as his pickup."

"Frank Ricca," André said. "So we've established a connection between them. Years back. Good pals."

"Business partners too. Charles Isles and Ricca didn't hide their business relationship well. I discovered at least a dozen bank forms showing Ricca footing the bill at The Groove Factory."

André rubbed sleep away from his eyes. "Probably glad to do it. He had dirty money to launder. For a while, their partnership seemed to work, as we know. Until Charles Isles's greed soured things between them."

I shrugged, agreeing with André's assessment up to a point.

"Could be."

"What's bothering you?"

"Contessa LaPerla's statement. I pulled it up. She told us Isles stole money from the company. Wanted out. Bankruptcy filing loomed over their heads."

"Yeah, so? He was stealing. Prepping to jump ship before it went down," André replied.

"She also said someone hired Dana Miller to investigate. How come we haven't been able to find out who hired her? Should have been pretty straightforward."

"What are you getting at?"

I didn't say anything for some time, giving myself another minute for my contradicting thoughts to agree. Eventually, I explained my position.

"Think about it, Jones — Charles Isles owns The Groove Factory together with his wife Tamara Sullivan, a stupidly rich woman. More about her in a minute. Frank Ricca was also in the mix, but he's not part of the business dealings.

From what I have been able to piece together, he likes his whores, drugs, and the occasional murder. So who hired Dana Miller? Who had the most interest in exposing The Groove Factory as a failing business? Why?"

André leaned back in the chair and rested one hand on top of his forehead, turning over the information. When he didn't give me an answer, I continued.

"I think it's fair to say we can eliminate Frank Ricca as the person who hired Dana Miller. He seems like the weapon, but not the hand wielding it. That leaves us with two choices — Charles Isles or his wife Tamara Sullivan."

"Why would Charles Isles hire a top-notch forensic accountant to investigate himself? It's not him. Tamara Sullivan is all we have left," André said.

"Their marriage isn't particularly good or a happy one. Lots of separations and reconciliations. Her father owns Sullivan Electronics."

"No shit? Really? My wife tried to make me purchase one of their smart washing machine combo units. Three grand. Can you believe it? Cops don't have that kind of money." André cracked his neck, locked his fingers together, and stretched like a floppy cat. "It's getting late. I don't think the techs will have time to go through Dana's computers. Will have to push them tomorrow. Lem already checked out. I think I'll do the same. You?"

"I want to interview all three — Charles Isles, Frank Ricca, and Tamara Sullivan. One of them hired Dana and has been staying quiet after her murder."

"If they're smart, they'll lawyer up. Forget about Frank Ricca showing up on his own at the station, lawyer or no lawyer. You heard what Vargas said — the paranoid mafia boss sleeps in an underground cell and has loaded guns hidden everywhere."

I drank more coffee until the middle of the night. I had examined over a hundred pages, and my eyes burned. I stood up to use the bathroom and give my legs a stretch when I felt a cramping pain in my chest. It knocked the wind right out of me. Suspecting I might faint, I threw my arms out and gripped my desk, knocking some papers to the ground. After a minute of taking slow breaths, the cramps stopped. I was able to let go and pick up the paper spill. Before I filed it away, I glanced it over — an arrest photo of Frank Ricca. It was several years old.

In the police database, I pinged Frank Ricca. I studied his gallery of mug shots while waiting for the printer to produce a hard copy. A remorseless face, I concluded. Flat-nosed, as if a hot iron had flattened it at birth. Oil-black hair slicked back in a rattail, tan skin, coffee-brown eyes.

Contessa LaPerla had called him Tony Soprano, and as it turned out, she wasn't wrong. Frank Ricca — the Big Guy — ran the show at the Boston branch of the Italian Cosa Nostra.

Some of the crimes he was accused of committing chilled me. It seemed breathing fear into others was Ricca's zest for life. His smile dripped wickedness. A sinking feeling overwhelmed me as I put his picture on the murder board next to Dana Miller.

The Bloodless killer could be him, I told myself. *Could be. Then prove it.*

Chapter 24

Karen huffed up to the break room as I stared with boredom at the microwave nuking my hot pocket.

"How long will they keep you on the graveyard shift?" I asked, making small talk.

She wiped her damp brow with a paper towel. "I like the overnights. None of you are here."

The microwave beeped. I burned my fingers grabbing the hot pocket. I tossed it on a plate of napkins and stuck my finger under cold water.

"I don't think you'll have time to eat," she said. "I tracked down your BMW."

"You did what?" I asked. "Where?"

"Don't get excited. It's a pile of burned metal. But the plates are a partial match." She fetched a cup of water and drained it to its last drop.

"C'mon, Karen. I've been waiting for a break in this homicide."

"Alright, Jeez. Haven't you been told not to bother someone who's drinking?" she asked. "Your BMW's at the state police lot. Here's the address. State's sending an officer to meet you there.'

I read her note. "I could kiss you right now."

"And I can kick you in the nuts. The hot pocket's looking good — ham and cheese."

Officer Highback had the markings of a career cop who came from a long line of other cops. His Irish-tinted hair was a dead giveaway of his heritage. I could see him drinking dark ale at some bar called O'Malley's singing The Rocky Road to Dublin.

"Are you the Boston cop I'm supposed to let in?" he asked, training the alley light of his cruiser on me.

I showed him my credentials. "That depends — are you the state patrol who's supposed to let me in?" I shoved my wallet back in my coat as he killed the blinding light. "Dark-blue BMW? Where did you find it?"

"In a field, burning. The fire department had to let the fire die on its own. They couldn't extinguish it."

He wasn't exaggerating. The BMW's right side had caved in and melted into a new shape. The passenger side remained in a less damaged form, but the heat from the fire had scorched the leather seat to the metal frame.

"How long has the car been in the lot?"

"It says a tow truck transported it at 4:30 a.m. Friday into Saturday. Someone saw the fire off the highway. Called us to report it."

"Do you have a name for the caller?"

"A truck driver out of Denver passing through Boston. We cleared him. The beemer's been sitting in storage ever since. And before you ask about the body, let me make it easy for you — the medical examiner's backed up, and until they release their autopsy report — "

"Body? There was a dead vic in the BMW? Male, female?"

"Didn't they tell you?" He looked annoyed at the lack of communication. "The driver veered off the highway into the field. No tox report yet, but probably a drunk driver overestimated how narrow that turn is. At night time it's hard to predict when you're impaired, and when you try to correct the wheel you end up rolling off. It happens. We've had about three such accidents in the past six years. All resulted in fatalities."

"And how many resulted in an inferno?" I asked, reaching into the glove box using a napkin to protect my fingers from disturbing any physical evidence.

"The BMW's the first," he mumbled back.

"Anything else you have for the driver? ID, phone, wallet?"

"Male. White. Early forties, or at least we think that's how old he is. Connecticut plate." He shared the file with me. "There you go. His car exploded on city land, but no one at City Hall knows much."

I walked to the trunk and kneeled with my flashlight to inspect the license plate. It had fused to the body of the BMW from the extreme heat. I identified two numbers matching Brad Connolly's.

"We've classified the fire as accidental pending tox and autopsy. But it looks to me like drunk driving."

"You're wrong, officer. This is a murder. Double homicide."

"Murder? Could be, but we found no second vic. Where did you get a double homicide?" He folded his toned arms in front of his chest, protected by a bulletproof vest.

"The male will most likely be Brad Connolly. The missing fiancé of my murder vic," I replied, scanning every line in the report he handed me. "If there's no objection from you, I'll be taking over your investigation. Thank you for letting me in."

André grumbled when he picked up. "What's wrong with you? Can't you go home and sleep like everyone else?"

"How long will it take you to get to the repo lot on I495?"

"It's three o'clock in the morning. Give me another four hours and I'll see you there." He yawned as his wife told him to take the call outside their bedroom.

"You have an hour. I found Brad Connolly's BMW. Brad's body is at the morgue. Wake up Sleeping Beauty, it's time to go to work. I want you to oversee the transport of the BMW back to our garage. I'm going to the morgue."

"Screw you."

The next call I made was to Lem. He sounded less aggressive when I woke him up and ordered him in. A woman moaned in the background for him to come back to bed, but he told her to go back to sleep.

At the front desk of the state morgue, a droopy-eyed man with black-rimmed glasses and a tired white medical coat checked me in. He led me to the freezer room.

"Number 45671, male, car accident. Should be right here," he said, pointing to a fridge door. "It's pretty gruesome. He was in bad shape when we got him."

"I want to see him," I said.

The gurney sounded like a tornado ripped apart a tin metal roof as he dragged it out of the freezer. He lifted the white sheet and draped it over the vic's shoulders.

"Told you it's bad. One of the worst burn victims I've seen since I started working here."

I stepped up to the gurney, staring at the disfigured face of a male. The skin had been completely seared off, exposing yellowish bone beneath. Patches of dark hair still remained on the skull. The neck and the chest area had been consumed by the fire, with more yellowing bones protruding.

"The rest of him looks pretty much the same. Ninety percent burn trauma."

"Is that the official cause of death? He died in the fire?" I finally asked as I motioned to the assistant medical examiner to cover up the body. I had seen what I needed to see.

"Doctor Lavrov hasn't performed the autopsy yet. We have more pressing cases ahead of this guy. Why are you interested in a dead drunk driver?" He walked me to the lobby. "He's a relative? Friend?"

I ignored the question. "Boston Medical Examiner Tessa Wu will take over the autopsy for Doctor Lavrov. I'm sure he won't mind if we take a body, given how backed up the state morgue is."

There was hesitation in the guy's expression; his mouth hung open some until he closed it. "I can't let you walk off with one of ours. It's against our rules." He leaned toward me and whispered, "I mean, I personally don't care. I only took the job to pay for grad school, but Lavrov will cut my balls off if I don't get his permission. He's the biggest douche in the world."

A phone rang somewhere in the hallway. "Hey kid, you should answer it."

At the station, around a pot of hot coffee, I initiated my brief.

"Tessa Wu's performing the autopsy as we speak. We should know pretty soon if it was Brad Connolly in the BMW. But I think we found Dana's fiancé. According to the state police's timeline, Brad drove off I495 Friday into Saturday morning. A truck driver from Denver spotted the burning car in the field and called in to report the accident.

"That suggests Dana and Brad never made it out of Boston, not even as far as Logan Airport. They were probably grabbed by the killer shortly after Dana left The Groove Factory. I think the killer murdered Brad first, staged the BMW to look like a car accident, setting it on fire, expecting the body to burn so we can't ID the victim," I explained my theory.

"If the timeline is correct — and nothing suggests it's not — Bloodless had Dana Miller to himself for forty-eight hours, during which time he bled her, embalmed her body, and then left her jazzed up in the white dress and the Halloween mask at Franklin Park on Sunday morning before the running convention. It's still unknown if the convention has anything to do with her murder."

"Officially, we can count out Brad Connolly as a suspect. He didn't kill his fiancée. Like you've said, the killer wanted Dana Miller for himself. And we've seen what he did with her." Lem stirred sweetener into his coffee.

"The state processed his BMW. Stay in touch with them, I want their evidence brought in. Have our garage do a thorough examination of the BMW. Couldn't hurt us to go through it again. Things could get missed. I'd like to be sure we have extracted every piece of evidence from the car. State started a tox screen, but again, they never received the panel. André, I'm putting you in charge of that. I want the BMW dusted for fingerprints. Lem, phone Callum Baker at the crime lab and have him send a team down to the garage," I said.

I produced photos taken by the state police the night of the fire. Lem and André studied them for a long moment. It had been a mess — there was a black ring of singed earth around the BMW. Looking at the car, I could feel the heat of the fire. And from their exasperated sighs, I gathered they had felt it too.

"The killer cremated Brad Connolly," Lem said.

Cremated, I thought to myself. The car had been used as a crematorium.

"That's it!" I exclaimed.

"What?" Lem flinched as if he was lost.

"The killer cremated Brad Connolly. The medical examiner suggested the killer could work for a funeral home. And what do funeral homes do? They cremate people."

"Shouldn't we first confirm it's Brad Connolly in that BMW before we spin theories?" André asked.

"I want to talk to the fire department. Get our hands on their report. Knowing what type of fuel the killer used to start the fire might help us add another piece to the murder investigation. The killer could be a mortician. That would explain the clean cut to the lung on Dana and the postmortem work with the embalming fluid." I switched between murder files. "Lem, talk to me about the funeral homes you interviewed. Anything pan out?"

"They all sang pretty much the same tune — no problems with an employee," he replied.

"Well, in our line of work, we know how everyone lies when they want to throw suspicion off them." From the murder book, I extracted a list and offered it to Lem. "Funeral homes outside Boston. Twenty miles. There are sixteen of them. I want you to beat down their doors and interview as many of them as you can. I'll get you help, don't worry."

"Why don't we wait for the computer geeks to go through Dana's computers? If she finished the report, Charles Isles and Frank Ricca killed her to shut her up. You heard Vargas from SID. Ricca will cut your throat and send you packing in a fridge for less," André insisted.

"You want to sit around and wait, Jones, be my guest. But if those two turned out not to be Dana Miller's killer, we would have wasted time working good leads. And unless you have signed confessions from Ricca and Isles, may I suggest you don't waste time but help me solve this murder? Isn't that why Captain Mercy put you on me? To watch, help, report back? Then report this." I pointed at Bradley Walker strutting in the bullpen, well rested, clean-shaven, fresh out of the shower. "Walker."

He glared in my direction. Approached.

"You're riding with Detective Lem Needham today. Help him interview the funeral homes on the list I gave him."

"You look like the three musketeers. I hate to break up the band." He turned on his heels.

"That's the last and final order for you, detective. Disregard it and I will make it my life's mission to jam you at every turn. The way I see it, Detective Walker, you have another twenty to twenty-five years to pension. I will jam you hard."

André stared after Lem and Walker scrambling out of the bullpen. "You might be the only person on the police force who can make pretty boy Bradley Walker shit his pants."

"Go, André! We don't have time to gossip like we're retired in Florida playing an eighteen-hole."

I picked up the phone and dialed the Connecticut Police. "Captain Berry, can you have an officer drive Brad Connolly's father to the state line? We found his son, and I'd like to speak with him in person."

Chapter 25

I glanced at the clock, agitated. Where were they?

I mentally calculated the time it took to drive to Connecticut, over the Massachusetts border, past the casino, several small insignificant towns, wide highway. Then the city of Winslow, a bigger, more populated college town. Add in traffic delays, maybe roadwork. That could be the reason why it was taking them so long to haul him in.

I stood by the murder board, digesting the details I had come to learn about Dana Miller and Brad Connolly. When talking to a grieving parent about their child, the smallest things could build rapport, connection, trust. And trust was paramount in a homicide investigation. If people didn't trust you could catch their child's killer, they'd resent you for the rest of their lives. So I stood at the murder board — digesting the details.

"Dana Miller. DOB: 01/18/1981, forty-two years old." I logged her address as a Massachusetts resident of Charleston, education — UMass, and last employment — self-employed contractor. On the same board, I had pinned more photos of the white dress. Lace, pretty; a summer frock against the cold April sky. Meaning? I couldn't conjure up one. Not yet. Not at the moment.

I glanced at the damn time.

The Grim Reaper mask was another why the killer planted and I couldn't quite figure out. But it carried weight in understanding him. He could have chosen another mask, another dress — no, the props were as important as the murder itself to the killer, I speculated.

Gina, the civilian assistant, knocked and entered.

"André called from the parking deck. They're here. Where do you want the *guest*?"

I gave the murder board another serious look. Considering the best option. Let him see it? Rattling him this much might be too soon. In the end, I decided against it.

"Mercy's office. And get us some coffee. I imagine we all need a round after I'm done with him."

Another five or so minutes passed before I caught a real glimpse of him. The guest. The Connecticut visitor. André had let him walk first; Lem trailed behind them. All three looked gloomy. The two cops had the solid faces of men who have seen too much, done too much in their lifetime, because murder wore you down to the bone.

"Truman Connolly. Boy, it's nice to finally meet you. I've been waiting quite a while for the police." He stood up; wanted to shake my hand.

His hair — short, combed to one side, white with a sprinkle of last red in there — framed his round, worried face. His eyes sunken with upset and heightened fear, he examined me thoroughly before he sank back down.

I dragged the captain's chair over to sit beside Truman Connolly. Intimate, in close proximity. Build rapport. Trust. Only I was after the truth. And if I had to exploit

Truman to gain stride in this homicide, so be it. He could lie to himself, but don't lie to me. That's how I looked at it.

"You found something, then?" Truman Connolly gazed at me. "The Connecticut officer who drove me said nothing. Only to go with him. It's about my son, I gathered. It has to be, no? Why else would Boston PD spend money and time to invite me in?"

Despite it all, polite, I thought.

His lower lip trembled out of nerves, fear, or maybe agitation. He said, "Homicide — you're looking for bodies, not missing people. I told myself there was still hope. Some. Even the slightest hope. But that was before the call, your call."

He exhaled and held onto the last breath as if holding onto his last shred of hope. "Homicide — bodies."

"Let's take a step back. Forget about homicide. Start from the beginning."

"Yeah. Alright. Roll back." He took a brief sip of coffee. "I'll make some educated assumptions since y'all tracked me to Winslow. You found him? Or her? Or both? Haven't you?"

"Remember to breathe, Mr. Connolly. Focus on the facts, the pertinent ones first. If not, tell us whatever comes to mind."

"Right. Right. My boy's name's Brad Connolly, forty-seven. He went missing," he paused to gather his thoughts and some emotions, "weeks back."

"Before or after the Paris trip?"

"They never made it to their plane. I've checked. Fought with every worthless rep at the airline. They didn't want to give me anything. Said they'd talk to the cops. But I couldn't get the cops to talk to the airlines. What a damn freaking mess."

"When did you last see them — Brad and Dana?" I asked as I handed him a box of tissues from Mercy's desk.

"Friday night, around ten-ish. More like ten thirty. They were taking the red-eye to Paris. My wife and I had drinks with the kids. A spur-of-the-moment celebration. Brad asked Dana to marry him. Went down on one knee. The entire place applauded." He produced a photo of Dana and Brad embracing. She had a wide, warm smile full of kindness. Brad had put a protective arm around her shoulders, grinning like a man proud of his life.

I examined the ring on Dana's finger. A clear diamond cupped in the center by smaller diamonds on a white gold band. It reminded me of the engagement ring I had pined over for Shelly, but it would have cost me eight grand. On a cop's salary, that's like eighty thousand. I had gone for a smaller, less bright diamond and a thinner band.

"They were perfect for each other. You know — with some couples you can tell they will stand the test of time. Brad and Dana would have stayed together for the rest of their lives." Truman Connolly folded his head into his hands and sniffled, defeated.

"This next part is not easy. Okay?" I displayed a sketch of Brad Connolly drafted by an artist on our staff, since the fire had destroyed Brad's face.

Truman swallowed aching tears, took the drawing, and stared at it for a while, though he didn't have to say a word. Agonizing pain spilled into his eyes.

"My boy. That's Brad. What — what happened to him? Where is he? I'd like to see him. Oh, God! You have to give me something, okay? I can't face Brad's mom. No answers. I'm afraid the not knowing might kill her."

"I'm very sorry to inform you Brad Connolly was discovered in a burning car. Dark-blue BMW. Our medical examiner's performing the autopsy. We should know more about what killed Brad shortly. If you need a moment alone — "

"No, no, no. Stay here. Tell me the rest. I have to be strong for Brad, Dana...my wife. Our lives have been completely destroyed. Who would hurt them? Do you know? Can you tell me?"

I glanced at Lem and André before I explained how we had first found Dana — left at Franklin Park wearing a white dress and a Halloween mask. Truman Connolly listened, tuning in and out, blowing his nose in a tissue, fighting his grief in front of us.

"White dress you said?" he asked, interested.

I gave him a crime scene photo. He forced himself not to look away.

"Friday she wore dark pants and a black sequined blouse. Heavy coat; it was chilly outside that night. She had a box of her stuff. She was done with her gig at the company she worked for. We were all so happy for the kids."

I made a mental note of his statement. Asked him, "We were hoping you can tell us more about Dana and Brad. Their lives. Habits. If they had enemies?"

His face drained of color. Dread smudged under his eyes. "Who would want to hurt her? She was sweet, wonderful. She made Brad so truly happy."

"We're still trying to figure it out. What can you tell us about Brad?"

"My son? Chipper, smart as a whip, and he loved Dana. Worked as a financial investor in the private sector; his specialty was the Asian markets. Always working, traveling, he put his career first for years. His mom and I stopped wishing he'd settle down. Then he brought Dana home.

"My wife saw it before the rest of us — she said they'd get married. They got along great. Anyone who saw them could tell they were meant for each other. I can't...who'd do such a thing?"

"Did you know if Brad and Dana fought? Arguments? Couples fight," André suggested.

"Hold on a minute. Give me space. Dana's been murdered. My future daughter-in-law — dead. And you want to know if Brad and her had problems. Don't even think of pinning this on my son."

"Sir, Brad's not a suspect. We pretty much cleared him after we found his body. My partner's asking out of formality. It's for the lawyers when we catch the perp who did this to your son and his fiancée."

"No. Of course. I'm sorry. Terribly sorry. They were happy. In love. Very much so. No arguments. I'd tell you if they fought. Brad lived with us, Dana stayed at our house most nights. I think she liked to have people around her. She was split on what she should do with her house. She felt selling the property would be letting go of her parents. Since you're investigating her murder, I assume you know what happened to Martin, her father."

"Yes."

"Okay. And her mother — the nursing home."

"We've spoken to Pleasant Valley. Elena's condition is logged in our report."

"Dana thought it was too soon to let go. Brad was more pragmatic about things, but he too understood the emotional connection tying her to the property. He didn't push it. Their main residence was Winslow. They decided to sell the house after she took her mom to Eastern Europe, sometime after the wedding. Dana told me she started to track down distant relatives of Elena but had to put it on hold."

"Did she ever mention why?"

Truman Connolly shrugged, sipped more coffee. "A job came up. Some company in Boston hired her to investigate the books. Speculation of stolen money. But she didn't like it there. Tried to walk away, but they put more money on the table to keep her on. She was that good at her job."

He shook his head in disbelief. "God Almighty. Dana. I can't believe it."

"We have a report she left work on Friday night upset? Did she and Brad maybe have a quarrel? Lovers' spat?"

"A quarrel — you got it backward. Yes, Dana was upset. She'd reached a breaking point at work. If you're thinking of asking me why I'll make it simple for you — I don't know. Dana was private, extremely. Something Elena instilled in her. Hardwired. But Brad was working through tearing down some of her walls.

"On Friday, Brad phoned us at home. Asked me to bring the ring with him. Said he was ready to surprise Dana. Didn't want to wait till their Paris trip. His mom pressed him, that's how we found out about Dana's work issues."

"And you have no idea what might have been the issue at work?"

He exhaled, frustrated, polite but breaking. "Look — some guy came onto her hard. Wouldn't leave Dana alone. Pestering her. Asking her out on dates, even after Dana told him she was steady with another man. He wouldn't take 'no' for an answer. She told Brad her boss promised to check on things for her." A sigh of regret. "A lovely girl. Shame. What a shame."

"Has Brad had any issues at work? Someone he didn't get along with?"

"What? No. Absolutely no. Brad was a private contractor. Kind of like Dana. He got a fee. Bonuses. It was a steady gig. And it gave him the opportunity to hike."

I nodded to Truman Connolly to go on.

"Always outside. Climbing something since he was a boy. He got Dana into it. It helped ease her social anxiety. It wasn't easy on Dana growing up with Elena — she wasn't a warm woman. Alone. Raising a child. And Dana had to earn her mother's praise at every turn. It grinds on a young person. And it did on Dana. I'm not judging Mrs. Miller. She tried her best. Martin's who Dana missed and had a hard time getting over. She felt his absence, especially around the wedding.

"Father of the bride. Who'd give her away? And with her mom in a nursing home — Dana worried she had no close family to invite.

"Of course, that didn't bother us. We loved her just the same. More for it. Martin dying on them sure broke Dana. Maybe Elena thought emotions were a waste; better to redirect them into something useful, school and career."

"Marriage?"

"I don't think Elena was especially thrilled with Dana getting married. Hard to say, her mind's not all there."

"Can you remember anything else? Enemies? Ex-lovers making trouble for them?"

"Nothing else. I have to call my wife. What do I tell her? Brad was our only son. That will shatter her. I'm afraid the news will kill her."

Lem took a decisive step forward. "Tell your wife, sir, that Boston's smartest cop is on the case. He won't allow a killer to go free. Tell her that. He will deliver justice for your kid and Dana."

Justice will be served, ran through my mind as I stared at the clear diamond ring Brad had given Dana Miller. Oh yeah, Lem nailed it. I'd never stop looking for the killer — not until I found him and not until I sent him to rot behind bars for the rest of his pathetic life.

Chapter 26

"Make copies of Dana's ring," I told André. "Give them to Patrol and ask officers to check pawn shops. Talk to the owners. See if anyone recognizes it. Maybe the killer tried to wash his hands of it.

"And send a car to the restaurant where Dana and Brad had drinks with his parents. Show them the white van. The killer must have taken them after the parents left," I said.

"What should we do with him?" André threw his chin towards Mercy's office, where Truman Connolly had been speaking on the phone with his wife. His head hung low as he cradled the receiver with tenderness and care.

"Offer to drive him to a hotel. He's not in shape to drive himself," I replied. "We couldn't even show him a photo of his son. The body had been almost cremated. Let's get back to work."

And while André circulated the diamond ring to cops, I shifted my focus. As I waited for the garage to tear apart the BMW, I examined the murder book, particularly the props left by the killer. A ghoulish mask and a white dress. What was the connection between them?

I worked the phones like a phone operator. Talked to every party store in Boston, quit after they closed for the night. I got nowhere.

The Grim Reaper, one helpful manager informed me, was a bestseller. Popular and in high demand. His store sold out the masks as fast as they stocked them. He practically laughed when I asked if he could think of suspicious customers buying the mask in bulk. "Sorry man, they're all weird," he said. I pretty much got the same response from everyone else. By eleven o'clock it seemed the Grim Reaper would be another dead end; another unanswered question.

When I shut down my computer, I had no more energy to give Dana Miller. I had no more energy to give anyone else.

I was shutting the door behind me imagining the rest of my night at home, when the phone line blared. I hit the light switch. *This better be good*, crossed my mind.

"Homicide," I said.

"May I speak with Detective Stone, please?" a male voice asked. He sounded like he had a hand over his mouth, talking low, hiding the call from someone.

"Speaking. How can I help?"

After a moment of silence, the voice replied, "I'd like to talk to you. To discuss things."

"About?" I leaned against the edge of my desk, worn out, and crossed my feet.

"About the dead chick. The one from the park. You're still investigating her murder, right?"

Well, his reply caught my attention. It punched me in the gut, waking me up faster than a double shot of espresso.

"What's your name, sir?" I probed him.

"I'd rather not with names. You see, there are people, people who hurt people who have means. Do you get it?"

"I think I do. Which type of person are you? The type who hurts others?"

"Goodness no," he punched up the no, "not at all. I am not the killer type. I wouldn't kill a roach if I didn't have to."

"Then give me your name. Come in to the station and we can talk."

More silence, a longer pause. "He's watching. He'll have me followed. I can't risk it. If he finds out I called you, I'm tomorrow's latest murder headlines. And I like to live. Not my time. I don't want to end up in some park, dressed up like a Halloween freak in July. This was a mistake. Forget it."

I could tell he moved away from the receiver. "I hear that you're scared. You took an enormous risk calling me. It couldn't have been easy. But you mustered some courage because you wanted to help the police. I am not wrong, am I?"

"I knew her, you know? Of course you don't. I didn't give you a name. But yeah, I knew her. She didn't deserve any of it. I feel bad."

"You feel bad because you want to help. So help." I was working every trick in the book I could think of to win his trust, to get him to agree to meet me.

"Okay, do you know the Old Mill Factory?"

"The one by the docks?"

"Fifteen minutes. Can you make it?"

I checked the clock. I could have, but I preferred to convince him to come to me. To the station, where I could extract a confession on a recorded line in one of the interview rooms.

"Fifteen minutes," I pretended to calculate the drive, "It's kind of far. Come to the station. We will talk here."

"The Old Mill Factory. If you're not there, I'm never talking, and you can't make me. Do I make myself clear?"

Lem had been standing by the printer waiting for the machine. He finally noticed me waving my hand in the air for his attention.

"I'll be there. Okay? Don't jerk me around. That's not what we do."

"Who were you talking to?" Lem asked me like cops do when they want in on the action.

"I don't know. He didn't identify himself." I rang up the tech department and ordered a tracer on the last call. I opened the top drawer of my desk to collect an extra magazine.

"Wow! What's going down?" Lem said as he tensed up.

"All I know is this guy calls me, says he won't identify himself but wants to talk. Rambles on about people hurting people who hurt others..."

"Gotcha. I'm familiar with the type. Little off, but not enough to let them fall by the wayside." Lem followed me to the bullpen.

"...Right...he's on the edge. High wired. Pressed him for details. He's evasive. Insists if he talks to the cops he'd end up like Dana Miller. A Halloween freak in July, to quote him."

We jumped in the elevator. I dialed André; it went straight to voicemail.

"He's gone home," Lem said as I put the phone away, checking the time on my watch.

"We're meeting at the Old Mill Factory. The one a couple of pyro-loving juvies set on fire a few years back."

"Uh-huh, we boarded the place up after the homeless turned it into a camp. Neighbors started to complain about the rampant drug use and parties at the factory. But the city didn't have the money to demolish it, so they had the Roxbury precinct kick everyone out."

I fetched my car keys. "He chose the Mills for a reason. I tried to persuade him to come in. Talk to me at the station. But he wouldn't budge. If I don't go, he said we'd never get him to talk."

"I'm going with," Lem said.

The nice weather from the afternoon didn't carry into the night. If you lived in Boston, you developed your own sixth sense about the weather. It was that hard to predict. You could be hot one minute, freezing your ass the next. I cranked the heat up as I gunned it.

A detective from the tech division informed me they had captured the caller's location. East Bridgewater and State Street. The North End. Little Italy.

"Just perfect," I mumbled to myself.

"What did they say? No luck with the caller?" Lem asked.

"The asshole used a burner. We have his location. Little Italy. Corner of Bridgewater and State. A unit's headed there to check it out."

"Nonna's. I could go for Nonna's," Lem said.

"You know the spot?"

"Nonna's."

"Yeah, you already said that. Nonna's what?"

"One of the first Italian restaurants in Boston. Because of Nonna's, we have the North End, Little Italy, and some of the best Italian food in the country," Lem said, looking hungry. "Nonna's is owned by a Greek family; I bet you didn't know that."

"I'm about to throw you out of the car for making me hungry."

"Maybe he'll bring some Nonna's pizza we can have after," Lem snickered.

"Get your head in the game detective, and call for Patrol to meet us there. Warn them to kill their lights. I prefer that he thinks I'm alone. And when his guard's down, take him down."

An eight-foot fence guarded the front entrance as if it were a medieval fort. A punched-up sign said 'Private property. Police take notice.'

The factory fire had started after some kids decided to have harmless fun with gasoline and matches. The blaze engulfed the bottom level first and ripped through the rest of the building before a single firefighter showed up. The event sparked a multi-agency operation to put out the searing fire. No amount of effort to extinguish it seemed to stop it or slow it down. It continued to burn for twenty hours and stopped after it had roasted the entire building, leaving no corner unscathed.

Deemed unsafe, Boston officials closed it down, but like all forbidden things, the Old Mill Factory became a main attraction first for the addicts, then the homeless, and then the addicts and the homeless joined forces to turn the Factory into a lawless camp.

Police had been activated and tasked to clean it up. Patrol had evicted everyone, boarded up the windows, and padlocked the fence for extra added security.

On occasion, a cruiser drove around to boost community morale. It deterred trespassers from breaking and entering, and yet, tonight I prepared to trespass.

"It reminds me of my patrol days. The nights I spent at the gas station over there," Lem pointed to a run-down KwikMart, "parked before I'd head out on patrol duty. This neighborhood could be tough, but good people," Lem said with a detectable note of nostalgia.

"Good, so you know your way around the Factory." I scanned the barren area. Dark and open.

"Yeah. I can lead you on."

Inside the yard, I maneuvered around a section of boxes stacked together like tiny homes. Past them, someone had left behind shopping carts packed with garbage.

Nights always seemed sinister at abandoned buildings. The moon glowed in dull yellow as gray fog hugged the crowns of the leafless trees.

"Where is he?" I muttered to myself, checking my watch for the time. Fifteen minutes had passed ten minutes ago.

"I'll take the back. There's another entrance from the side street. No fences to scale. I'll call you."

We split up.

Alone, I kicked into hyper-vigilant gear. Every noise sounded intense, time stood still, seconds dragged on, and minutes felt like an eternity.

Behind the set of trees closest to me, I thought I caught the glimpse of a shadow. An outline of a man. Hoodie and pants, but I could have been mistaken. The sound of feet stomping prompted me to reach for my gun.

I no longer treated this call as routine. Years of police experience told me to watch my back. And then I began to worry about Lem — as green as they come as a detective. I had sent him alone when we should have stuck together.

"Show me your hands. Come into the light." I inched forward, thinking of Lem. Was he okay? Hurt? What had I done?

"I want to see your hands. I know you're there. I only want to talk." Three more steps forward.

"You have nothing to be afraid of. I'm here to talk." I put my gun in the air to entice him to give himself up.

The shadow moved. Quick, rapid, faster than I had expected. It startled me. I locked my weapon in front of me, but by then, the shadow had withdrawn into the black void and I had lost visual.

"Son of..." I mumbled, putting the gun down and grabbing my cell phone to check on Lem.

Before I could dial, a man in an oversized hoodie drawn low over his face high-kicked me in the chest. I lost my balance. He cut me in the back of my knees, and I landed face forward in a bed of soiled clothes.

The intensity of the slam stole my breath away. I coughed, gathering strength. My thoughts raced with no order. Where did he come from?

I pushed off the ground, but Hoodie threw an elbow into my lower back. I winced in pain. Biting, roasting pain spread quickly up my spine, rendering me paralyzed. It hurt worse than I could have suspected.

I rolled over, scrambling to get back up on my feet. A sharp one-two punch landed in my jaw and my nose. Temporarily blinded by the throbbing ache of my nose, I cupped my face, completely defenseless. What I should have done was put my fists up and swing. Swing fast left and right, trying to hit him back if I expected to save myself.

Hoodie allowed me only a second before he delivered a deadweight punch I could tell would have knocked me out cold if I allowed it. But I blocked it with my shoulder. My bones absorbed the brunt of the strike. Powerful enough it could have flatlined me, but I managed to suck it up. Sitting, I threw a foot out, pushing my attacker to the ground. Flat on his back, I snagged his ankle and reeled him in.

He thrashed, struggling to free himself. Once I locked him in my arms, I landed a right fist in his stomach, followed by a bony elbow in the groin.

He folded into the fetal position, hands cupping his junk to protect it from more attacks. I used that moment to reach for my holster. But I discovered it empty.

"You looking for this?" he said, holding my gun pointed at me. Instantly I recognized the voice.

"Put it down. You don't want to hurt a cop," I said, trying to remain calm and in control.

"Aw, look who's scared now." He threw something at me. It landed in my lap. "Put it on."

I picked it up. No way. "Let's be rational here. What's your endgame? More cops will be here any second. Let me talk to them on your behalf. Deescalate the situation."

"Put the goddamn mask on, Detective Fuck Face!" he shouted, smacking the side of his head with the hand holding my loaded weapon. "Do as I say. Do it."

My hands trembled. I stared at the Grim Reaper mask.

"What's the matter? You don't like it? I made sure I bought the right one this time. The exact one. What are you waiting for?"

The wave of wailing police sirens approaching surprised him. Alarmed, he strained to listen for the sounds. I imagined he was calculating how much uninterrupted time he had left with me.

"Hey you!" I shouted at him.

He jumped back, jolted. I seized on his anxiety by throwing the Grim Reaper in his face. He pulled back, staggered.

I pushed the gun-holding hand to the side, away from me. Twisted his body around, locked him under me, one foot pinning his lower spine, crushing it as I used the weight of my entire body.

He struggled, trembled, flinched, choking on his spit.

"Stop. Stop," he pleaded.

"Drop the gun. Do it now," I ordered; measured, decisive.

The gun got loose, and it slipped from his grip, but it looped around a finger. The weapon dangled for a split moment, then it flopped on the ground. I fetched it with my free foot. Reunited with the gun, I slowly lifted it away from him.

"Don't twitch a muscle, you understand?" I trained my gun on him.

On the ground, sprawling, legs and arms in each direction, Hoodie showed he'd cooperate.

Lem scrambled over the fence as I cuffed my attacker.

"Holy shit, Stone! Are you okay?"

"Go get the others. Now!" I shouted.

Lem didn't reply. He sprinted towards the front gate to let the cops in.

I stood him up and pulled the mud-stained hoodie off his face. "Danzel Fierra, you have the right to remain silent. Anything you say will be used against you in the court of law." I continued to Mirandize him as uniforms surrounded us.

Catching my breath, I propped myself on the front of a cruiser and watched as transport drove Danzel Fierra to County. Grill lights illuminated the Old Mill Factory, and under their bright lights, I thought the place continued to look just as sinister.

Chapter 27

"Nice of you to wake up," a female voice said before my eyes fully digested my surroundings.

I turned my head to the voice. "What are you doing here? Where am I?" I asked, staring at a room that wasn't my bedroom.

Meredith Sawyer remained focused on her tablet as I stirred in bed.

"At the French Riviera on our honeymoon," she giggled. "What does it look like to you —– Boston Medical."

I didn't reply, recalling sparse memories of the night before. Danzel Fierra had attacked me at the Old Mill Factory. Bad fight between us. Eventually, I arrested him, but I could hardly call it a victory.

"The ambulance dropped you off." Sawyer stood up, walked to the head of my bed, and fetched my chart. She read from it, "Concussion to the head, bruised ribs, several minor lacerations. You'll live." Sawyer paused and added, "Hmm, interesting."

"Put my chart down and go. Who even let you in?"

"Spoilsport." She returned the chart but stayed. "So what's wrong with you anyways?"

"Do you care this much about every cop who gets injured on the job?" I sighed, fed up with her, scanning the hallway for Shelly.

"Uh, your wife. She was here. She went to the cafeteria to grab a bite. She must be what — about eight to nine months pregnant. She looked worried for you. They all did. The bigger cop and the kid detective — "

"Leave." I readjusted, my ribs feeling extra tight as I moved. "And don't come back."

"Hit a nerve. Okay? I will stay away from your family. Fair is fair."

"I don't think you know the true meaning of fair."

"Be nice to me. I played fair when you asked me to back off and not run the Bloodless tip. Do you know how hard that is for a journalist?"

"Yeah, I bet — you're twisted up in knots inside. And as I recall, we made a deal. You'd be my first call when we make an arrest," I said.

"And you did. Last night!" She sounded rattled. "My sources say lots of lively police activity at the Old Mill Factory. A transportation van took someone up to County." She leaned on the bed rail. "I planned on going Breaking News last night. I panicked you'd screwed me over."

"Why didn't you?" I asked.

"My hospital connection told me you were admitted in rough shape. I had to see it for myself. So that's the second time I've cut you a break, but the last. Talk, or if I walk out the door, I am reporting every wild rumor about this freaking homicide waiting on my desk."

"You can't...you can't tell a word of what you know," I said as politely as I could.

She rolled her eyes and fetched her black python purse. "Good luck with your recovery Detective Stone. By the look of your medical chart, it will be lengthy."

Meredith Sawyer started for the door, high heels hammering the floor with determination.

"Stop," I said as she ignored me. "Stop, please."

"Why should I? Give me a reason to stay."

"You're right, we made an arrest, but it's not our guy. It's not the Bloodless killer. And if you go on air and you talk about Bloodless, you might hamper the investigation."

"It's your job to make sure you catch him, Stone. I'm walking out in three, two..." Her phone jived in her hand. "Would you look at that — my producer waiting with my cameraman at the ER bay."

The tightness in my chest felt like restraints, shackles. I thought of Dana Miller, the terrifying bruises around her feet and arms. Bloodless holding her down as he took her life away.

"Look, the man in custody is a mental psych patient. A sick man with a violent imagination. He was supposed to be under medical care. I don't know how he got released so fast, but he's not our killer. There's a second victim."

"Oh!" she replied and backed off the door.

"His name's Brad Connolly. Forty-ish. From Connecticut."

"A male? Same MO as Dana Miller?"

I shook my head no. "Cause of death's pending. Brad was Dana Miller's fiancé. They both went missing. They never boarded their flight to Paris, a preplanned trip to celebrate their recent engagement."

Meredith Sawyer frowned. "Crap. How did he die then?"

I glanced at her, revolted by the image of Brad Connolly's seared body. "Cremated in his BMW. Or almost cremated."

"Oh Heavenly Father, you must be joking right? Tell me you just made it up to get me to back off running the story at prime time."

"Wish I did. But no, it's true. Bloodless is unlike other killers I've sent to supermax since I earned my homicide shield. Do you see now why it's important to err on the side of caution in this investigation? We can't tell the public too much. Tip him off and he's gone. We might never find him."

"Or you, detective, want to control the investigation for personal reasons," she said.

"What personal reasons could I have? I want the sonofabitch off our streets more than anyone else."

"Why is there a cardiovascular surgical consult attached to an MRI in your chart? What's going on with you?"

"In case you didn't pay attention last year, I was shot three times. Sustained severe injuries but made a full recovery. The consult is simply a consult," I said, staring down Meredith Sawyer.

"Okay. If you say so." Her phone lit up again. She glanced at it, then glanced back at me. "I have to give my producer something. Otherwise, I won't be able to stop him. He was in my office when my sources said you'd arrested a man at the Factory. He thinks it's the killer."

A shadow loomed in the door of my hospital room. Doctor Hoffman, tailed by my wife Shelly.

I thought of the white van registered to a sham company called Pelican Bay. Lem Needham couldn't track the owners. All we knew was that it operated out of Philadelphia and Boston, but the local address came back as a plot of barren land managed by Boston's waste-management department.

"There's a way you can help, but it means keeping your producer in the dark. Can you do that?"

"Kent?" she huffed. "That's easy. I do it all the time. He's harmless."

I told her to use her sources in City Hall to track Pelican Bay. The driver of the van, I explained, stalked Dana Miller at her home in Charleston, according to an eyewitness and her workplace. And we believed the same car had dumped Dana's body at Franklin Park.

"Let me see if I have this right — find who drives the work van, find your girl's bloodthirsty killer?"

"There's more to it, but essentially, if we have his identity, then he's at the top of my suspect list."

"Visitation hours are over, ma'am," Doctor Hoffman said as she approached my bed. She checked the heart monitor.

Shelly placed a brown plastic tray on the table beside me. "For you. I thought you might be hungry after your well-deserved nap."

Meredith Sawyer watched our interaction like an anthropologist studying a new species.

"I'm going. I'll be in touch. And when this case is over — Stone — you owe me a special."

"One-on-one with you — never gonna happen." I laughed.

"Oh, don't be like that. I'm growing on you, kid. Admit it."

"Like a diaper rash on a baby's butt," I replied as I rubbed the top of Shelly's hand.

"Friend of yours?" Doctor Hoffman asked, making small talk.

"More like a necessary evil," I joked.

Hoffman examined my chart and the monitor, her expression strained. "We need to chat. A serious conversation without beating around the bush."

Shelly and I exchanged an anxious glance. We had still avoided the topic of my heart condition and our future. We both acted as if it didn't exist, only it was creating a huge stone wall between us — I blamed myself for it.

"The bullet has shifted its position," she said matter-of-factly. "It's alarmingly close to your heart. There's absolutely no way of predicting where it will end up if we don't extract it immediately."

Hoffman trained her penlight on my pupils. She jotted a note in my chart.

"Your urine sample shows your kidneys are in distress. And your blood work is less than promising. Naturally, your body's fighting the foreign object, but in the process, it has a negative effect on your organs."

The doctor was frowning and not betraying a single emotion. "Even the best hospitals in the country equipped with cutting-edge technology could be powerless to stop it. Your case might soon become inoperable."

"I thought you already said it's inoperable," I declared.

"No, sir. I said the surgery is experimental and carries a lot of risks. Dying on the operating table is a strong possibility, but it's better than not fighting to save your life," she snapped.

"Temple — please. It's not the time to give up," Shelly said.

"Sage advice. You should listen to your wife, Detective Stone."

"She got the brains and the looks. I'd be a fool not to. Even a dolt like me doesn't need his wife to tell him it's not looking promising. In all honesty — it feels like I'm fighting a lost cause," I told Dr. Hoffman.

"Have you been taking care of yourself? Sleeping a full eight hours? Drinking plenty of water? By the look of your pee, I know the answer, so don't lie to me." Hoffman checked the IV bag above my head. "I won't even mention the reasons why you are in a hospital bed right now."

"Everyone at work is under constant stress. I have a full load on my plate with the latest homicide. All hands on deck. Catch my drift, doc?"

Shelly shifted nervously and gave me an irritated stare.

"At our first meeting, we talked about desk duty. Actually," Hoffman pointed out, "I told you I needed to admit you for more testing and observation. Correct me if I'm wrong, but you explained to me that you had to speak with your wife. Well?"

I straightened up. "All I'm asking for is a few extra days. The investigation's at a crossroads. We discovered a second victim. And it's bad. This killer is the real deal. If I walk out, it means I'm letting the police force down, the vics, and their families. The man responsible for all the hurt is still at large. I can't take the guilt of that to the grave with me."

Hoffman pursed her lips and stuck her hands in her white coat. "Overly sentimental matters aren't my area of expertise. Your life is yours to throw away."

"There are others who can take over," Shelly said, on the verge of tears. "Think of the baby and me. What will happen to us if, God forbid, something irreversible happens to you? We don't even have a reliable car anymore, Temple, because you're too stubborn to let go of things."

In her emotional state, she was stirring the conversation into private matters I didn't think we should involve Hoffman in. "Dana Miller belonged to someone. Her fiancé belonged to someone. They were people, still are to me until I close the investigation. And I can't do that yet. So much work's left. Give me three days, Doctor Hoffman. If on day four, I've made no progress — I'll step down as lead investigator and check in at the hospital."

Hoffman interjected. "As much as I don't like to do this, I'm afraid the surgery has to wait. Give your body extra time to heal. We have to closely monitor you."

"Tell us what you want him to do, and he'll do it!" Shelly cut in.

I breathed a long, stressed-out sigh. Not the news I expected or hoped for. I glanced over at Shelly — over-anxious. Told myself to think of her. Reticent but with tenderness and care, I reached for her hand and pressed my fingers into hers.

"Tell me the plan. I'm all ears," I said.

"The outpatient clinic. Four days a week. Blood work and kidney ultrasound. And meds. Lots of them. Can you manage that?"

Before I could reply, André Jones and Lem Needham interrupted.

"Detective Stone, sorry for the intrusion. We have something you'll want to see." Lem handed me a file labeled 'BMW Evidence Report.'

Chapter 28

"Good to see you back on your feet so fast, Stone," Captain Mercy said as we exited the elevator and headed into the bullpen. "Another wet evening. Gloomy Boston night. I'm ready for this to be over. The whole year. Hey, on the ride over I spoke with the DA's office. They filed attempted murder charges on Fierra. Judge denied him bail." She tossed her newspaper on her desk and started the coffee machine.

"So," she nodded to me, "where are we on the Bloodless case? I heard Brad Connolly's father was a mess. Took the news of his son's murder hard."

"True," I said as I stirred cream into my coffee. "After the Connollys celebrated Dana and Brad's engagement, the killer took the happy young couple. Killed Brad. Slit his throat. Fast, effective. It's in Wu's report." I offered Mercy the ME's file. "We checked the restaurant too. No one saw anything out of the ordinary. It's a small Indian joint. No cameras. Back-lot parking. The tech unit didn't spot a white van near or around it on traffic cams. So I'm thinking the killer waited for Dana and Brad by the BMW parked in the lot."

She picked up the file, opened it, and started to read. "Tsk tsk tsk. Wu thinks the killer used excessive force with the blade across Mr. Connolly's throat."

"Yeah, I read that paragraph too. Two-inch blade. Most likely a scalpel."

"Scalpel fits. We've speculated the killer has some medical experience; rudimentary, but it's there," Mercy said.

"He's skilled, no argument. And the murders are different. Complete 180 from Dana Miller," I said, thinking of Brad and Dana.

"What does that tell you?" She turned to the next page.

"I feel the killer's rage in Brad's murder. He cut his throat. Forceful. Bloody. Then buckled in the body, drove it to the middle of nowhere, and set the car on fire. According to the fire department, the car would have melted in front of their eyes. And there's something else," I said.

"The floor's yours," Mercy said, eyes on the report. "What's on your mind?"

"Wu found no drugs in Brad's system. Not even an aspirin," I said.

"Should that mean something to me?"

I drank more coffee, thinking about the tox screen panel on Dana Miller. She had been drugged out of her mind.

"Dana Miller could have ODed if the killer gave her a little something of something else."

"He has access to drugs. Lots of 'em...and your point?"

"Doctors give drugs to their end-of-life patients to help with suffering," I said.

"Stop right there...if you say the Bloodless killer's merciful, I'd like to remind you of the fact that he drained that poor woman's blood," she said, upset.

I put both hands in the air to stop her. "Far from what I'm suggesting, captain. I think he murdered Brad first, dumped him, set him on fire, then took Dana away. Her lung had been collapsing by then. She couldn't have screamed or fought him off," I explained, troubled by the visuals of Dana gasping for air. "But say she wasn't dying as fast as he calculated. He might have grown worried someone could hear her moans for help — I could see him then rush to silence her. It would explain why he used the drugs. Overloaded her system because he doesn't have a medical degree. Like you said, rudimentary knowledge of medicine."

Mercy held my gaze without saying a word for some time. Fingers crossed together, index fingers pressed to her lips.

"Okay, so he obviously hates males. And I hate to say it, but he likes to take care of the female. The woman seems to be the object of his affection. I am only saying that because the killer bathed her, brushed her hair, and put a coat of makeup on her face before he hid his evil work behind that hideous Grim Reaper mask." Mercy shoved aside the ME report. "Last we spoke you suspected two males — "

"Charles Isles and Frank Ricca," I said.

"Correct. Have we examined their connections to this case?"

"As a matter of course, ma'am, but I haven't had the time to check it out myself. The garage found a pack of nicotine gum in the blue BMW. Brad Connolly's car."

"Significance?" she asked, perplexed.

"Same brand as the gum the crime lab fetched from a trash can by the stage in Franklin Park. Brad Connolly didn't smoke."

"So the Bloodless killer's battling a nicotine addiction. Interesting. Prints?"

"Not from the pack in Connolly's car. Partials from the can, but Baker hasn't been able to lift a good match to run through the system. He says it will take time."

Three sharp knocks on the door put the discussion on hold.

"Come in Gina," Mercy said.

"Sorry to bother you, Detective Stone. Two detectives from the tech unit said they'd like a word with you."

"Go. Talk to them. I'm heading home. If you need me, I'll have my cell on me."

At my desk, I talked to the detectives about a batch of emails recently uncovered on Dana's personal computer. I agreed to read them as soon as they emailed me. As I waited, I listened to a message from Lem Needham — he sounded urgent, asked for a callback. Never said why, and I quickly put it out of my mind when I logged in to my email account.

I read each email thoroughly, stopping often to un-derline some parts. They provided a narrow window into

Dana Miller's work at The Groove Factory. She had communicated with one person in particular several times. Charles Isles. Their conversations had been professional. A single email stuck out to me. Dana had been worried about a man at work. A man she referred to as the stalker type. She never gave his name.

"The geek squad tracked you down?" André said, bringing with him more coffee and two plates of crispy bacon, toasty hash browns, and scrambled eggs, smelling heavenly. Or as I thought, the answer to my silent prayers.

He hovered over my shoulder. "Someone at The Groove Factory freaked her out."

"It would have been helpful if she said who," I said, wishing Dana had said more in her emails. "Matches her cautious personality though. Avoid conflict at all costs. If her stalker realized Friday night was her last night at The Groove Factory, that probably pressed him to act out. If he didn't take her, she'd be gone. The murder of Brad Connolly makes a little more sense now. The killer ran out of time. Kills Brad to remove him from Dana's life. Keeps Dana for forty-eight hours or for as long it takes for his sick fantasy to dispel, then he bleeds dry Dana because he's done with her."

"Did you receive the street-camera notification? It went out almost an hour ago," André said.

"No. What?"

He pointed at my computer. "I sent you something to print," André replied as he dipped his toast in his runny yolk. "Street cam alerted us to the van. Lem said he got it covered."

The printer churned out four pages as I inhaled the aroma of fat and butter. "Nothing but hospital food for two days. Who did you muscle into getting us food?"

"I ran into Chan leaving Country Dog. He wobbled some, no doubt from the beers he consumed. Didn't have to say much to him to get him to walk to State Street Dinner. Even gave me back my change."

I picked up a slice of perfectly cooked, still sizzling bacon. "To Chan, and to getting busted by a lieutenant."

André reached over and collected the document. Glanced it over — something on page three intrigued him; skimmed the rest. He handed it over and returned to his plate.

I rolled a napkin between my fingers, dabbing the grease from the bacon while reading. "The City of Boston contracted Pelican Bay to clear out trees fallen in recent wind storms from several city-owned fields. One is north of I495," I said, face red with shock. "How did you get your hands on this?"

"I have an old friend who works in Records at City Hall." André didn't elaborate further. "The van in the video is registered to Pelican Bay as a company car. But we don't have a name for the owner. Lem couldn't break through the maze of paper to unmask the sham company."

"I have someone else helping me dig up intel on Pelican Bay," I replied.

"Who?"

"An old friend who works in Records at City Hall." I smirked.

André waved a hand. "Pelican Bay keeps popping on the radar. The van, the field — two for two. My money's on Charles Isles. He owns Pelican Bay and The Groove Factory. Uses the concert promotion business to bring in capital, steals the profits for himself, then dumps it in Pelican Bay, safeguarded in an offshore account where we can't touch it. If Dana Miller exposed Isles, he would serve good time behind bars. No DA in town would cut him slack. Motive for murder, how I see it," André said as he polished his plate and turned his attention to mine.

I put my coffee down and studied the now-empty squad room, my mind churning over this latest discovery. The evidence made no sense to me. Why would Charles Isles hire Dana Miller to find the missing funds? He owned The Groove Factory; his wife had some shares too. Someone else had to have hired my vic. Someone who wanted to catch Charles Isles double-dipping.

"Are you done with your eggs? It will be shameful to let perfectly fine food go to waste." André was practically drooling.

I scooched the half-eaten meal towards him. Returned my attention to Dana's emails.

"Keep your chin up. We'll get him, eventually." André wasted no time loading a forkful.

Judging by the emails, Charles Isles depended on Dana's report. He wouldn't let her quit. Why? What did he hope Dana would uncover by tracking the stolen money?

"Have cops sit on Isles. Call me directly when they get a visual of him," I said to André. "And I want the tech unit to keep working on Dana's computers. Charles Isles ignored her stalker fears, pressed her to finish her assignment. We need her report if we want to solve her murder."

Until we located Charles Isles, there was nothing else to do for the night. I closed the door to my office, hearing the faint ringing of the phone on my desk. But I ignored it.

In the parking lot, just as I was shedding my jacket, André burst through the exit door and whistled to catch my attention.

"Come on. Hurry."

On instinct, I followed him, utterly confused, but the panicked expression in his eyes told me something had gone sideways.

The tires on the cruiser squealed when he peeled out of the parking lot and lit the grill lights. Driving like a man with a death wish, he took a sharp turn on Margin Street, almost licking a parked fire truck.

"Will you slow down? Holy Cow!" I finally muttered.

André dodged the night traffic, slowed at a red light long enough to clear the intersection, and gunned it. Eventually, he drove us to Dorchester, slowed to the allowed speed limit, and confirmed the address with Dispatch. He parked the cruiser on the curb.

I stepped outside into a breezy night, perfect for a heavy sweater. The wind stroked the tree branches lining the dank street. I recognized this section of the neighborhood. Lots of bars, house parties, and hookers.

"Not in our jurisdiction." I trailed André to a single-story bar decorated with neon pink lights in the shape of a woman with big boobs and a cowboy hat. "Nips," the sign above read.

I pushed through the door. '*Come for the cold drinks, stay for the naked ladies*,' a label sparkled at the front entrance.

'All Night Long' blared from the speakers in the empty main hall. It was hard to see with the dimmed lights and the smoke. But soon enough, my eyesight improved. They spotted a man, young, fit, and strong, cuffing another male in a dark-red suit.

"Let him go, detective," André ordered with a cold voice.

Lem Needham pushed off the red suit, but not because he wanted to.

"May I have a word with you?" I nudged Lem away.

He exhaled, agitated, one leg resting on the front of the cruiser. "What the hell?" I laid into him.

Somewhat shocked by my reaction, Lem straightened up. "I thought you'd be proud of me. Of the bust. I've been sitting on him for hours."

"Found who, Lem? What are you talking about?"

"The white van. Charles Isles drove it all around town tonight," he said. "Didn't André tell you? Shitcan, I told him to loop you in, detective."

"He did. Watch your mouth. He outranks you and me. That still doesn't explain why I saw you attacking a suspect? On what grounds did you execute the arrest? Did you stop and think about it? Or do you go with the flow?"

"His rear light's out. I lit him. He didn't stop. Rolled two blocks with me behind him. Parked, entered the bar. I approached, asked him to step outside so I could talk to him. He told me to wait till the stripper finished grinding against his crotch. We exchanged a few cross words. He refused to identify himself. You showed up for the rest," Lem said in his defense.

A certain four-letter word slipped from my lips. But otherwise, I kept my hot temper at bay. I couldn't reprimand Lem Needham for something I would have done the same.

My jaw clenched when I spotted André exiting Nips. I was sure he wanted to read the riot act to Lem Needham, so I decided I should be the one to dish it out with one of my detectives.

"How's Isles?" I asked André.

"He won't press charges and gave us permission to search the car. Denies harming Dana. Said they parted cordially on Friday. Amicable. She never completed the report, decided to back out. Didn't give Isles a reason."

"Well, that's a pile of hot shit. But I'll address it with him at the station. Start going through the van." I pointed a finger at Lem Needham. "I want you fifteen feet away, detective. Fifteen feet away from the vehicle. By the book," I told André. "Record it in case a lawyer dings us on the search."

Charles Isles stood on the curb and watched as cops went through the van. I sent a cop to wait with him. Isles seemed sloshed, his feet apart, steeling himself, but not well.

"Over here," someone called out.

I approached. In the back of the trunk, I spotted a woman's black sequined blouse. I picked it up — size small. Dana Miller had worn something like it at dinner with her future in-laws. The real surprise was tucked inside the blouse. It tumbled down as I handed the delicate garment to be cataloged as evidence. A two-inch scalpel slipped and landed on the ground between my boots.

I gloved up and picked it up with care.

"Light," I grumbled.

Someone placed a flashlight in my hand. The edge of the scalpel seemed dipped in blood. A strand of long hair, brownish in color, stuck to it. My stomach churned. Uneasiness stirred in me.

"Rush the weapon to the lab. Priority one. Be careful with the hair. It could be our victim's," I told the cops holding the evidence bag.

I clicked the light off and shifted my attention to Charles Isles. He puffed on a smoke, carefree, bullshitting with the cop by his side.

"Sir, I need you to come with me to the station," I told Isles.

"What for? You wanted the car. Take it. I can fetch a lift home. You boys know how to ruin another man's mood," he said, exhaling a lungful of cigarette fumes in my face.

"Mr. Isles, it's in your best interest to come with me. We can talk about the items found in your car — "

"It's not my car. I borrowed the wheels for the night. Mine's gone," he said and winked to a female officer.

"You were driving it, and by law, you are responsible for what's in the car. Station, please. I'd like you to tell me what happened to Dana Miller."

"Dana," he said, the cigarette between his fingers, trembling with anxiety. "She didn't deserve to die."

Chapter 29

A gaggle of pushy reporters blocked the entrance in front of Central. They had staked the steps leading to the building, stretching as far as the parking lot. Cameras rolling, lights trained on me. I felt like prey, vulnerable and naked.

"No comment," I repeated several times, dodging them like killer wasps.

But that didn't sway them from shouting more questions until Meredith Sawyer practically whacked me in the face with her mic.

"Is the man in lock-up — the park killer? What can you tell us? When will you release his mugshot?"

"Nothing to say," I replied.

"Is it true a junior detective tried to make an illegal arrest? Will he be fired?"

I froze, pivoted on my heels, and glared back at her, infuriated by the supposition. I wondered how I had forged a pact with the devil. Aware of the ticking seconds, I cleared my throat and said, "Always twisting and turning the narrative, right Meredith?"

She flinched, I noticed — unsuspecting I'd bite back. "If by twisting and turning you mean telling the truth, then I suppose I am."

"No one's being fired. And we didn't make an arrest yet. The man in custody is detained." I regarded the rest of them. Stony faces starved for a tip on the homicide investigation. Be nice, Temple. Problem was — I was already in a mood.

"No further comment, Meredith. You'll have to wait for an official announcement like everyone else. Now, excuse me," I rudely dismissed her with a wave of the hand.

Captain Mercy waited for me at the bullpen by the elevator doors. I could tell she was agitated by the way she paced. Wasting no time, Mercy went after me for my unprofessional attitude toward the media. Especially so with her majesty the ice queen, Meredith Sawyer.

"We want them on our side. This job hits us hard some days."

Her words rolled off my shoulders, high-strung by Meredith Sawyer sticking her nose in police business. "I wouldn't worry too much about Meredith Sawyer. She's showing off."

"She might be, but she's making Homicide look like we don't know our ass from our head. What happened out there, Stone?" Her serious glare pinned me down. "The shitshow ran up the flagpole so fast I had my ass chewed up by the chief before I could drag myself out of bed."

"It got out of hand," I mumbled.

"It or him. From what I've been told, Detective Lem Needham played a central role in the whole fiasco. Why on God's green earth did you allow Needham to tail a suspect in a major homicide alone, with no backup?"

I let us into my office and threw the overhead lights on — Meredith Sawyer was reporting from the station steps, I saw on my flat screen. I cut her off before she could irritate me further.

"That was all him. On his own. Street cams spotted the van and sent an alert. Lem intercepted it. He had a justifiable reason to pull him over. Isles ignored him. Drove to the bar. If I tell you the rest, you will be obliged to write an official report," I said. "Can't fault Detective Lem, though. I would have done the same."

"Therein lies the problem, Stone. Two of you dodging orders is not what my legacy will be."

"He's a good cop who trusted his instincts. Without him, we wouldn't have found a bloody surgical scalpel and a female jacket in the trunk of the van. I can't write him up for it. Can't do it."

Her shoulders softened. She joined me, leaning against the edge of my desk. "You should and you will. It's how he'll learn. Rules bring order to an otherwise chaotic world. Have you wondered if things would have played out differently if you waited for your backup? Last year, maybe your attacker wouldn't have fired off three rounds in your chest? Rules. Order," Mercy reminded me.

"If you allow Lem Needham to believe he could do the job all alone, he'll never trust anyone else on the force." She walked to the door, pulled the handle down. "That goes for both of you, Temple."

I surveyed the hectic scene of fellow cops on the other side of my office window. Rules bring order to the chaos. I pressed my hand against my stiff neck. "Mind telling Detective Lem I'd like a word with him?"

When Lem Needham showed up bearing a long, frowning face, I had already finished writing him up. I only needed his signature before I filed the paperwork in his personal file.

"Did you talk to Charles Isles yet? The captain won't even let me in the control room to watch. What was I supposed to do? Let the van go? It might have been our only chance."

"We've got to have the talk." I pointed to the other chair in my tiny office. "I've recommended you for a day suspension, docking your pay. And the incident's going on your record. Here's the incident report. Read it and then sign it." I sounded dry.

"You serious? Why? It was the right call. We finally intercepted the vehicle after weeks of searching." He pushed the notice, and it fell on the ground. "Maybe Bradley Walker's right — about the wrong man sitting in this office."

I snapped. "Watch it detective — you're on thin ice." As I said it, I nearly shriveled at how much alike Captain Mercy and I sounded.

Wide-eyed, stare full of rage, Lem Needham snagged the paper, smacked it down on my desk, and inked his name. A hint of regret probed me under my ribs. He had a natural instinct for the job, and I wished to mentor him.

I told myself to give Lem space to cool off, wait for the right moment to talk things over with him.

Lem turned towards me. "What I did was wrong. I now realize my actions were careless. Are you kicking me off the case?"

"Absolutely not. And, hey, for the unofficial record, I would have done the same thing had I been in your shoes. I suppose it's my fault as much as yours."

The phone rang. Gina was on line one, asking if I could accept a call from Callum Baker, the head of the criminal lab. Meredith Sawyer waited on line two. I told Gina to hang up on Sawyer and keep dodging her calls until I said so.

"Hey, Callum," I said.

His thick Irish accent sounded fresh as he said hello. "The jacket's Dana Miller and the hair on the scalpel came from her." Callum Baker inhaled loudly. "The blood's human. Male and female. Brad and Dana's. You scored big tonight kiddo."

"We have the murder weapon and clothing from the victims. Fingerprints? Any physical evidence in the van tying Charles Isles to their murders?"

"Sorry, Temple. Your killer wore gloves. No prints anywhere in the trunk. Lots of Isles's prints in the front of the car."

"Then we can't tie Charles Isles to the murders of Brad Connolly and Dana Miller. The murder weapon and the jacket's not enough. Hell, the van he drove's not even in his name. He's walking."

"We just started processing it. If anything else comes up I'll find you. Keep him talking. I'll expedite things on my end."

Discovering the murder weapon was a big break in the case, I reasoned with myself. The killer had used the scalpel to cut Brad's throat and used the same weapon to puncture Dana's lung. Callum Baker had been concrete. Finding her blouse was another small victory I welcomed. But it didn't explain why Charles Isles would leave incriminating evidence in such an obvious place. If he pulled off a double homicide at two separate locations and left no traceable evidence, logic dictated that he'd be more careful. Yet, he happily agreed to the car search as if he had no idea we'd find the scalpel and the blouse.

Chapter 30

I discovered Isles pacing in the interrogation room. Someone had taken the cuffs off. Hands behind his back, fingers linked together, head hung low. No lawyer to defend him.

Charles Isles had a plump, meaty face that had never been handsome.

He wore several thick, silver rings on his fingers and two diamond studs in each ear.

Dressed in a terracotta suit with an apricot shirt, he reminded me of a reformed hippie trying to play the role of an established businessman but not quite nailing it.

"Finally. I asked to speak with you several hours ago. Another cop told me I can't leave until you allow it," Isles fired off.

"You're detained at the moment. Why don't we discuss a few things first, then I'll see about cutting you loose," I replied.

"Detained? What for? I haven't done anything wrong."

"I will explain. Take a seat."

"I prefer to stand if it's alright with you. Your explanation should be rather quick."

"The blood found on the scalpel came back positive as human. Two people. Male and a female. Brad Connolly and Dana Miller. The hair's also hers," I told him, my eyes lowering him in the chair. "You've dodged our calls, refused to meet with us in person for weeks. And I have been a patient man, Mr. Isles. But my patience's wearing thin. Dana Miller consulted for The Groove Factory. Friday evening she left your office, and no one ever heard from her again. Until Sunday morning that is — her body turned up in Franklin Park wearing a white dress and a hideous mask. We've cleared everyone who works for you but you. What you have done or not done wrong is to be determined, hence why I've detained you. So sit down. Recorder on. State your name for the record," I said.

Charles Isles spelled his name, confirmed his DOB, and provided his home address. I wrote his information in the murder book.

"I didn't know about those things...the scalpel and her blouse. My God. Her blouse. It's not my car. Mine's — oh well — repossessed by the bank." He sighed with embarrassment.

"Who owns the van?"

"I can't say," he said, reserved.

"Let's try Pelican Bay?" I asked. "Who owns Pelican Bay? I want a name if you ever want to see the outside of this room."

"Come on — no. I can't."

"Since you want to play this game — Pelican Bay manages a number of fields, highway land. In one of them, we discovered Brad Connolly, killed and burned to the bone behind the wheel of his BMW. Two crimes, one company — Pelican Bay." As I explained, Charles Isles started to grow smaller in his seat.

"No. I — I didn't know. Wait a minute. It's a mistake. Wait one second. I have to think."

"Think? We have you behind the wheel of the van. Same van in which we discovered the murder weapon, human blood, and clothes that belonged to one of the victims. The only thing you should be thinking about is how to get me to believe you're innocent. Otherwise you're looking at life at best. The needle is a strong possibility," I pressed him.

"Wait. Stop. Please. I don't know anything. That's the truth. Look, I didn't want to get involved with Dana's murder because I wasn't sure what to do."

"What to do about what?"

"What to tell you about Dana consulting for me." He slicked back a piece of his hair. "She seemed like a nice enough girl, but I didn't know her well. She worked in the office for three weeks. Nights mostly, her choice. I spoke to her a few times. Phone mostly, again her choice. She seemed," he paused to gather his thoughts, scratched behind his ear like men do when they are about to say something not nice, "jaded."

"Jaded?"

"Yes, well, maybe jaded is not the exact word, but it was like she was afraid of people. To talk to them, make friends. No people skills. Don't get me wrong, I'm not judging, it's just I didn't know her that much. Still, gray area for me why cops would need a statement from me. The van — it could be anyone's. Lots of people drive it."

"So, you don't deny you're tangled up with Pelican Bay, but you won't talk. Take a look at this email. Is that your personal email address?" I asked.

"It is. Yes."

"And who did you send it to?"

"Dana Miller," he uttered.

"Right. Why did you hire Dana to investigate you? The job offer's right here in your original email to her. Citing personal reasons, Dana turned you down the first time. But you paid her a premium. Double her regular fee."

I opened my murder book. "What did you hire Dana Miller for?"

Isles scanned the walls, stalling.

"You seem lost. Maybe I can help — Miss Miller was a forensic accountant. A very thorough one at that.

"Let me make it clear to you sir, that I know the answers to my questions. Taping your answers is a formality. And if you lie to me, I will know. And since I know the truth, then I have to charge you with a crime. Should I charge you, sir? Then we can have lawyers and judges involved. Do you want a lawyer present with you?"

"No, no, I can't go back to that hellhole. Three years in was plenty for me. I want to help. I do."

"Who is behind Pelican Bay?" I demanded.

As pale as the snow caps of the White Mountains, Isles pressed his lips together.

I stood up and collected my folders. "I told you not to lie to me. Now, see Mr. Isles — I can't help you. I can't.

A detective will read your rights, take you to Booking, where you can make your call. Why am I wasting your time explaining things you know? You remember how the system works. When you're in, it's always harder to get out."

"Wait. Give me a chance, okay? I want to tell the truth. But I can't talk about Pelican Bay. If I do, I am done." I felt the fear in his voice.

"Why did you hire Dana Miller? Tell me about her assignment. The truth, Mr. Isles. Tell me the truth, or I don't see a reason why I shouldn't file charges against you."

He agreed. "Money missing from the company business accounts. For the past two years. Twenty-eight million dollars in total. I couldn't make last week's payroll because the company is broke."

"Twenty-eight million. No chump change."

"No, it's not," he said, looking at his hands, disgusted.

"Who stole the millions?"

"I don't know," he replied with conviction.

"Why didn't you contact the police?"

"I planned to, soon."

"Why not as soon as you found out?"

Isles raised his shoulders, dropped them low.

"Is it because you are the main suspect? Word in the office is that you took the money and stashed the millions in offshore accounts to avoid paying your taxes? Are you hiding behind Pelican Bay?"

"Filthy lies. I never took a dime from The Groove Factory. It means everything to me. Built it from the ground up. Dana's report would have cleared my name. Would have. Pelican Bay — might as well kill me because if I talk, I won't last five minutes in jail. They'll kill me."

"Who will? Frank Ricca? Did he murder Dana Miller because of her report? His name would have been all over it. I told you I know the truth. Ricca's been laundering mafia money using The Groove Factory." I handed Isles a printout of the money wire Ricca had paid Charles Isles to open The Groove Factory.

Isles glanced at it, quickly looked away. Next, I showed him the prison record proving Ricca and Isles shared a cell.

"Who did you want exposed so badly with Dana's forensic report? Frank Ricca? You knew she'd find his name mixed in with your company and he wouldn't have liked it. Did Frank Ricca kill Dana? She was an inconvenience to him. After her murder, it was business as usual for Ricca. What's one more body added to his long list of victims?"

Isles couldn't bring himself to look me in the eyes. "Did he kill Miss Miller? Murder her fiancé too — Brad Connolly?"

"What?" he asked, his guard down.

"Play dumb one more time and I will charge you as an accessory to a double homicide."

"Wait a minute, here. I've never met anyone called Brad Connolly. His death, murder, whatever it is, I have nothing to do with it."

"But you have Dana's blood on your hands, don't you?"

"I don't know..." He wetted his lips, nerves getting to him, I suspected. "Possibly," he said.

"Let's see if this document refreshes your memory. A week before Dana's murder, she emailed you," I said.

He read the email I handed him.

"She shared with you her fears over a man at the office. She called him a stalker. Informed you of her intention to quit, suggested you find someone else to finish the project."

Isles dropped his head between his trembling shoulders.

"I read your response to her," I said.

He didn't reply.

"I will if you don't. You told Dana that you would take care of it. No one will disturb her again. That you will protect her. And she believed you, as jaded as she was." I pulled back, calmer. "Who was stalking Dana?"

"I don't know," he mumbled.

"You didn't take her seriously. Did you even try to look into her concerns?"

"No. I had other things going on. Pretty much forgot about the email immediately, didn't remember until she was killed."

"All you wanted was the report? To clear your name."

"Yes. It's terrible when you say it like that. But I couldn't let Dana quit. She was getting close. And I needed answers."

"Help me understand something — if you didn't steal the money, that leaves Frank Ricca as the other obvious suspect. But it makes no sense. Why would he rob himself? If The Groove Factory closed down, he couldn't launder his mafia profits. But Frank Ricca killing Dana

Miller to shut her up, to show you how far he's willing to go to keep your partnership going — that makes sense." I watched Charles Isles nod his head. "Someone else then left you in the red? Someone else needed Dana out of the picture? Was it her stalker? The man you promised to protect her from? Who are you protecting now Charles? Who?"

The interrogation room door swung open. An over-powering cologne scent clouded the air. An aver-age-sized man in a tailored navy suit and white shirt, swinging a leather briefcase, marched right in. "You must be Detective Stone, Boston's latest choice for top homi-cide cop, if one believes everything reported in the news. Oliver Buzzworth — attorney for Charles Isles — how do you do?"

The intrusion threw me off balance. Judging from the startled expression on Charles Isles's face, he felt like me.

"Usually when a person's imprisoned, charges are filed, lots of paperwork. Not the case with Mr. Isles, I see. Is it because you have nothing on my client? Illegally detaining people now, Detective Stone? That's a new low for this police department."

"We detained your client after we found a bloodied scalpel in the back of his car. And a woman's blouse that belonged to my dead victim. And I could have arrested him for failing to pull over when a cop signaled."

"Was the car his? No. He used the car after his personal vehicle was taken. My client had no idea you would find anything incriminating in there. That's why he gave you permission to search it in the first place.

"Your vic's blouse doesn't prove murder. It could have been left there by a number of people for a number of reasons. Did you find my client's fingerprints on the scalpel?"

"No."

"No, you didn't because my client's innocent. He had no reason to kill Miss Miller." Buzzworth put a reassuring hand on Isles's shoulder. "This is too easy. Don't say another word, Charles."

"Mr. Isles hired Dana Miller to investigate millions gone missing from The Groove Factory. A fact he didn't deny. Her report would have exposed your client's ties to the mafia, particularly Frank Ricca," I said.

"Which proves absolutely nothing. Where's the so-called report? Do you have it?"

"We will get it."

"So you can't prove another claim. More speculations. The mafia angle is a stretch. Haven't heard you boys bring up organized crime in a while."

"Why were you arguing with Frank Ricca on Friday night?" I asked Charles Isles.

"Don't answer that, Charles. You don't have to answer any of their questions," Buzzworth insisted.

"What about the statement — someone will slit the bitch's throat? Dana's, someone else's?"

"Unfortunate choice of words, we will admit to that. And let's be real, you can't possibly prove my client said it. Miss Miller died of a collapsed lung, read the autopsy report. Slashed throat is not the same as a collapsed lung. Hope we can agree on that. Admit it detective, you are on a fishing expedition trying to trick my client into saying something you can use against him. Well, I have news for you. I won't let it happen."

"Last chance, Charles. Did Frank Ricca kill Dana Miller? The police can put you in protective custody if you co-operate. Give me Frank Ricca. Give me Pelican Bay. You promised Dana you'd look after her."

Charles Isles cranked his neck, visibly uncomfortable.

"Talk to me, detective. Leave my client out of it."

"Don't be a coward. We can take Ricca away for life with your help," I said.

"What is this? Make a wish at the Boston Police Department? You know the game. Ask your questions, or if we're done here, which I'd imagine we are — my client and I walk."

"You might not have stabbed her, Isles, but you are just as responsible for her murder as your mafia business partner."

"Where are you getting all of that? Some storybook?" Buzzworth rolled his eyes at me.

"Dana Miller's computer. Lots more bedtime stories to follow."

Buzzworth walked Isles to the door.

"Hey, Charles, did you ever tell Frank Ricca you were putting him out of business with Dana's report? He might have gone to jail over it. Is that what you two argued about? He told you what he'd do to Dana. He carried out the threat. How else will he keep you in line? One thing I can't put my finger on. Why did he hide her face under the Grim Reaper mask? A gag? Frank Ricca's latest sick trick?"

But Buzzworth wouldn't allow Isles to say a word.

"Enough of this, Charles. We're leaving."

Before he left, I said to Buzzworth, "Dana Miller and Brad Connolly are dead, and your client could help us."

"Spare me how the truth could set you free. Most of my clients who trusted cops ended up in a cell wishing they'd kept their mouths shut." He switched his briefcase between his hands. "Stay away from my client, Detective Stone, for your own good."

"Is that a threat?" I said through a clenched jaw.

"No. No. Just a friendly suggestion."

Chapter 31

"Do you believe him?" André asked me in the break room.

"I won't believe anyone involved in Dana and Brad's murders until the tech unit shows me her report. Isles hired her to clear his name. But did Isles hire her to expose Frank Ricca? Without Dana's report in hand, we won't know." I raised my shoulders, wondering about Charles Isles's emails to Dana. "I think Isles wanted to talk more before his lawyer Buzzworth put a tight leash on him," I replied.

"Go figure." André took a mayo, lettuce, and salami sandwich from the fridge. "A lawyer of his caliber would. On the law firm's website, Oliver Buzzworth's listed as a founding partner. He'd get you off for three hundred an hour. Probably more if, like Charles Isles, you're facing murder one," André informed me.

"Wow, how much? Where did Isles find the money to pay Buzzworth? He said he couldn't cover payroll last week." I took a sip from a cold bottle of water.

"I think I know the answer. I did some more digging into Buzzworth. The fancy attorney's been keeping Frank Ricca out of jail for years." André shared his notes with me.

"I saw it in Isles. The total shock. He hadn't expected Buzzworth to show up. Someone on the streets snitched to Ricca that the cops scooped up his business partner. Ricca's smart. Stepped in by sending his personal lawyer to shut up Charles Isles," I said as we moved the conversation to my office.

As I dropped into my chair like a dead weight, I continued, "Let's keep a unit on Charles Isles. I'm worried Isles was ready to tell me a lot more but was afraid."

"Of what?"

"Of Ricca, will be my guess. If Buzzworth tells Ricca that cops suspect him in the murders of Dana Miller and Brad Connolly, I think Charles won't be alive for long. Same goes if the lawyer shares with Ricca how Charles Isles hired Dana to take Ricca out of business with her accounting report."

"Say the word and SID will bring in Frank Ricca. They want him as bad as we do," André said.

"As much as I want to arrest Frank Ricca, there are outstanding issues with the murders of Dana and Brad. No fingerprints to tie Ricca to the weapon. No word yet on Dana's report. And Pelican Bay remains a ghost company. Unless we have answers to these questions, I am afraid we don't have probable cause to detain Ricca," I explained.

André washed down his sandwich with some black coffee. "Something will shake. We have the van. The murder weapon and Dana's blouse are in custody. The tech unit's working around the clock to break the encryption on Dana's computer drives. I'm willing to bet a month's worth of pay — Frank Ricca isn't smarter than the entire police force. We will get him."

Listening to André, I studied the murder board. The picture of Dana and Brad hugging each other a moment after he proposed to her. The ring was a nice-sized diamond, a carat and a half surrounded by a cluster of smaller diamonds.

"How much do you think a piece of jewelry like that would cost?" I pointed to the ring.

"Thirty grand for a real diamond and about seven for a lab-grown," André replied as if he was an expert.

"You work at the jewelry store on the weekend?" I teased.

"I should be. My wife's been asking for a new diamond ring for our fifteen-year wedding anniversary. The carat size keeps going up every night I come home late," he joked back.

"Lem said no movement on Dana's ring. The pawn shop owners he interviewed haven't seen anyone pawning it. So the killer's not holding on to her ring because of its monetary value — it's out of sentiment. He likes to remember, relive her murder." I stayed on Dana's ring for a few more minutes. "Why would Frank Ricca take Dana's ring? Money's no issue for him. Plenty of women around him to satisfy whatever deprived needs he has..."

"Maybe Ricca's waiting for the heat to die down before he sells the ring," André said. "Or maybe he tossed it in the Atlantic Ocean off the Zakim Bridge and we will never find it."

"Yeah, maybe," I mumbled, glancing out the window into the dark night. "Or maybe something's not adding up. Investigation wires crossed over, and we've lost sight of the killer. Buried somewhere," I said as I motioned to the stack of files on my desk waiting for my signature.

"Who else but Frank Ricca? He's a master expert in killing. He has the underground network to move bodies and dispose of his enemies, not to mention unfiltered access to drugs. Considering all the evidence we have — his name rises to the top." André used Face ID to unlock his phone. "The employees at The Groove Factory are clean. A few misdemeanors, car accidents, and one arrest for a bar fight, otherwise no hard time."

"One of them stalked Dana. Freaked her out so much that she complained and asked to step down," I pushed back.

"Then we go to Charles Isles. Talk to him away from the station. Get him to flip on Frank Ricca. You said it yourself — you had him talking until Buzzworth made Isles shit his pants," André said.

"Check the names of everyone at The Groove Factory against stalker complaints, peeping toms, revenge porno. In case, again, anyone was lost in the shuffle." I fetched my interview notes from a folder and placed them by my computer.

"Are we beating a dead horse, Temple?" André propped a shoulder against the ajar door. "Dana Miller sounds like the type who jumped at her own shadow. Someone could have said hi to her and she — "

"What? She what — overreacted?"

"I mean, yes. Overreacted. Gosh, Temple, her neighbors barely knew her. It's like she was a ghost. What's next, order every stalker in Boston arrested?" André said.

I shot up from my chair. "If I have to," I paused, "I don't think Dana overreacted, I think someone inside The Groove Factory really put the fear in her heart. Killed her. And I know I don't have all the evidence yet, but I don't think Frank Ricca's our guy."

The screen on my phone lit up. A message from Shelly wondering what time she should expect me and reminding me of my mandatory doctor's appointment early the next day. It was pushing one o'clock in the morning. Suddenly, I felt tired, ready to turn in and call it a night.

"Have Lem Needham type up the notes from our interview with Charles Isles. We'll go over it again tomorrow, make sure we didn't miss something. In the morning when I come in, we will start reinterviewing the employees. We ask everyone if someone at the office is a stalker. This type of behavior didn't start with Dana. It has been there all along. Others would have picked up on it." I yawned.

"You can be compelling when you wish to be." André put his coat on. "Till the morning then." He walked out.

Chapter 32

"André, hold up?"

"Yeah?"

"I have to take the morning off. Shelly and I have a thing..."

"Baby checkup. Can you reschedule?"

I stuck my hands in my pockets to hide the nervous jitters. So far, Shelly and the doctors were the only ones who knew about my grim future. I didn't want to wait until it was too late to tell André in case the doctors chained me up to a hospital bed. Feeble and sick in a windowless room, forsaken by all, but kept alive by stubborn white coats playing God...it petrified me. In a hurry, I dispelled the image from my head.

"Something else. I might need to be in and out of Central for several weeks. The heart doctor found out what's been wrong with me. The reason for the sudden weight loss, the weakness in my joints...the mood swings."

Weariness and contrition washed over André's face as I talked. I noticed the tightness of the muscles around his eye sockets. With each word, his face sank further, until he reached the same glass-half-empty conclusion I had when I heard Doctor Giovanni explaining about the ever-shifting bullet fragment in my heart for the first time.

"Shit," he said.

One word that perfectly summed it up.

I sighed and gave him all the time in the world he needed to process and figure it out for himself. It took a while. More than it had taken me at the doctor's office. Back then, I was full of questions, arguments, and bargaining.

"The union will back you up a hundred and ten percent on your sick time if anyone upstairs tries to jerk you around. Sheldon Curly's the head of the union. I know where he drinks his coffee." He paused to pat down his pockets. "If I wait another hour, I might meet him there. Go over the situation with him. He's one of us. Don't you worry, Temple, you're not alone in this dogfight."

I appreciated the consoling words.

André called the elevator. "After coffee with Sheldon, I'll pay a visit to Captain Mercy at her home. Get it done before someone from the Mayor's Office puts her in a rotten mood."

The elevator doors parted. He stepped in. "Alright, good luck with the morning stuff, and when you clock in, Lem and I'll have some more interviews prepped for you."

Before the doors closed, I stuck my arm in to push them off. André glared at me.

"Should I take it we're not done?" he sighed.

"You can't tell the captain. Not yet. Give me time to bring in the rest of the evidence. Another few days. Dana's killer bled her to death, filled her veins with embalming fluid, then staged her in the park as a showpiece. I want to nail him to the wall for what was done to her and Brad Connolly. But if you tell Mercy, the brass will sideline me. I'm too much of a liability for them."

André shook his head, comprehending the weight of my words.

"Anyway, anyhow, Mercy..." he said.

"I want a piece of the killer. Justice has to be served. For her. She was nobody to Bloodless. But she's someone to me.

"And — "

"There's more?"

"And you owe me."

The last part stung him like a provoked wasp.

"Damn it. I owe you. A day hasn't gone by that I haven't thought of the night of your shooting. Understand — I got there as soon as I heard. Everyone did."

"But it wasn't fast enough."

Heavy, suffocating silence drifted between us.

"After this," I said eventually, "after this — you're off the hook. You've paid off your debt. I'm letting go."

"Can I — let go? That call was mine. You went."

"We move on. We don't bring it up. We live with it, but we move on."

André left to drink coffee with Sheldon Curly, the union director.

I returned to my desk and my murder board. Dana Miller's photos pinned there. I studied her delicate features, petite in stature, slender physique. It hadn't taken the perp long to overpower her.

"You're not alone in this dogfight, Dana. I'll get him or them. And then I'll close your book, and you can rest peacefully."

The phone on the night desk hooped as I walked out. From the corner of my eye, I spotted the night clerk saying goodbye to his young wife bouncing a fussy baby. To give them a few extra minutes of family time, I reached over and answered.

"Homicide. Detective Temple Stone speaking," I said.

The pause on the other end after I stated my name felt deliberate. The heaving breathing of the caller filled the silent void between us. Odd.

"Hello? Is someone there?" I asked, electric sparks traveling down my back and body.

I checked the bullpen — the night clerk jingled his set of car keys in front of the irritated tot refusing a pacifier. Another several seconds of no answer before I decided the caller must have butt-dialed the station by mistake.

"Detective Stone."

"Mr. Isles?" I said, surprised to hear his voice.

"I want to talk. To explain." He slurred some of his words; I suspected he had relied on alcohol to give him courage.

I checked my watch. "I was actually on my way out. If you'd like, I can meet you somewhere and we can talk. Just the two of us. No recorder, no police."

"And no Buzzworth. Freaking A-hole."

"If you don't want his services, you can fire him," I said.

"Shit, yeah, alright. He won't allow it."

"Frank Ricca? Is he threatening you? I told you the truth this afternoon. Boston PD will protect you. We do it all the time."

"Protect me, no. No. I didn't believe — Dana. Or didn't want to believe her because I'm a selfish screw-up. Have been my entire life. How else would you explain someone taking twenty-eight million away from me? I let it happen.

"Uh-huh. Tried to believe it wasn't true. Not real. But yeah, pretty much let it happen. Woke up too late to do a damn thing about it. So I hired Dana Miller. A well respected, smart-as-a-whip forensic accountant who had a reputation to be discreet. She could track anything with a money sign in front of it. Brilliant."

I turned my head towards the photo of Dana and Brad hanging in my office. "Do you know who killed her? You can tell me."

Charles Isles sniffled.

"Charles, talk to me. Dana came to you for help. I can help you. But I can't do it if you don't work with me. Did Frank Ricca murder Dana and Brad?"

"Ricca kills everything and everyone. Never should have trusted him. We served time together, you know that? Of course you do, you have the records. He had a big mouth on him in jail, but because his uncle was Tony the Iceman, everyone steered clear."

Gulp. Gulp. Gulp.

"Frank threatened Dana," Charles Isles muttered.

"To slit her throat?" The muscles in my neck tensed. My mind spun in all directions. I had to keep him talking long enough for the tracker to lock on to his location.

"Oh God. The bitch. Slit her throat. I wish things were different."

"I'm sending a car to pick you up, sir. Where are you? Give me an address."

"*Pfff*...good luck getting past Buzzworth."

"Is he with you? Is Frank Ricca there? Think about helping Dana. Tell me what you know about her murder. I will protect you," I insisted, growing alarmed for his safety.

"Dare to swear on your life? Cross your heart and hope to die?"

Sweat dampened the collar of my shirt. I had to keep him on the phone a little while longer. The tracker would find him.

"I do. I do care for you, Charles. And I care about catching the killer who murdered Dana and Brad. But I can't do it alone. I need your help."

Silence returned. Long and uncomfortable. I wondered if he'd dozed off on the line or if he couldn't talk because the lawyer might be listening to the conversation.

"Big promise you've made, Stone. I'm undeserving of the gesture. But I'm flattered by how much you believe you can help me. Stop Dana's killer."

Our conversation neared the one-minute mark. Several seconds to spare, and the tracker could give me his precise location. *Keep him tied up, Temple. For God's sake, don't let him off the phone.*

"The Grim Reaper mask — how didn't I see it sooner? How?"

Click. He disconnected the call.

"Crap." I dropped the handle on the desk and slumped my head between my shoulders, reeling with anxiety. He had sounded delusional, emotional, totally paranoid.

My knees wobbled. But I managed to cool my nerves. I knew I had to find Charles Isles and keep him away from Frank Ricca.

And if I wanted to keep my promise to Dana — I crossed my heart — I had to hurry, because I was running out of time.

Chapter 33

The next morning's doctor's appointment sucked, I quickly concluded. Listening to Doctor Hoffman discuss the heart surgery to extract the bullet fragment and the small odds of me living through it was as depressing as expecting a broken watch to give you the right time.

The brain fog after made me irritable to the slightest infractions. Shelly was glad to rid herself of me when she ditched me at Central. I watched her weave through traffic in the Silverado, which was coughing a cloud of threatening smoke.

By now, the unit assigned to Charles Isles somehow had lost him, and no one had seen him after he'd left his home last night, Gina the civilian assistant informed me as I entered the bullpen.

The sun intruded into every corner of my office, and I officially hated daylight. The head fog decided to stay. And a large bloodstain materialized on my sleeve in the fold of my arm where the nurse had stuck me with a needle. Wanting to hide it, I rolled my sleeves up, letting out a breath.

I tried to focus on typing the notes from my phone conversation with Charles Isles, but I couldn't. My thoughts centered around Isles's last words to me before he cut off the call. He had recognized the Grim Reaper mask, or so he had admitted. *Why didn't I see it sooner?* he had told me. And now I found myself wondering if Isles had seen the mask before, and if so, where? I felt like I should know, see it, but for reasons I couldn't explain, I was failing.

It was possible Isles had spotted the mask on the news. The details of Dana Miller's murder stayed with him because he felt responsible for her murder, I speculated. On the phone he sounded hammered — he mumbled a lot, spoke in broken half sentences, and most of it made little sense. Except for the Grim Reaper mask. The other possibility I considered — Charles Isles participated unwillingly in Dana's murder. Ricca, I summarized, could have extorted Isles into taking part. And the guilt of watching Dana die might be eating Charles Isles up. It explains why, despite the risk, he reached out to me. Some significance there too? But what? He admitted to hiring her, paying double for her services. Didn't try to wiggle out of his responsibility. With a somber, straight face he fessed up to have let her down. He disregarded her reports of a stalker, promised to take care of it, and lied about it afterward. But he didn't lie to me. From the interview, I gathered Charles Isles carried a heavy load of guilt in him over Dana Miller.

As I examined the interview transcript, something else popped up in my mind. Dana Miller's neighbor reported a white van on their block watching my vic's home. Could it be the same white van owned by Pelican Bay, driven by Charles Isles? Yes, I felt convinced. But Isles refused to give up Pelican Bay, shut down when I pushed him over it. I saw fear in his eyes at the mention of Pelican Bay. Who did he fear so much that he would go back to prison for? I could only think of one name — Frank Ricca. Unfortunately, if Frank Ricca owned Pelican Bay, I had no evidence to prove it.

I took a coffee break from my thoughts after an hour of back and forth between reports and reading field notes. My nerves were stretched to their limit. Between the doctor's appointments, the stress of waiting for the birth of my child, and working the biggest murder case of my career — I didn't think I could carry on like that for long.

Gina knocked, holding a jumbo iced honey bun and a soda. "For you."

I closed my eyes and eagerly sipped from the can. "Needed that."

She was examining the bloodied stain in the crease of my shirt. "You alright?"

"Routine stuff at the doctor's. The nurse was new. Missed the vein."

It didn't look like she believed my explanation. "The woman you asked me about — Tamara Sullivan — "

"Yeah? What about her?"

"She can meet with you this evening after her spa appointment ends at six. Took me forever to get some bitchy assistant to finally return my calls after leaving a gazillion messages on her dumb voicemail."

"Persistent as always. Thanks, Gina."

"Anything for you, sweets." She flipped her raven-black hair. "Hey, you sure you're alright? I can go across the street and get you something else to eat. Something with protein and veggies. Nothing loaded with so much sugar to give you a heart attack." Her dimples smiled.

I had taken a bite of the bun, feeling the spirit-boosting effects of sugar pushing through my bloodstream. "Don't you dare."

But not even the delicious bun could flip my ire into anything else positive — the lab ran into a snag. The em-balming-fluid samples produced no conclusive results. Another setback.

Plan B, then.

Tamara Sullivan, the wife of Charles Isles, owned a small share in The Groove Factory. She could help me understand why her husband hired a forensic accountant after someone stole millions from him. I also wanted to hear Tamara Sullivan's take on Dana Miller. Did they meet? In my police experience, women were natural ob-servers. They caught subdued social changes, shifts in mood, which men rarely paid attention to. Maybe Tamara Sullivan knew the office stalker.

What else did Tamara know? Her husband's connec-tion to the mafia, Frank Ricca laundering money through the company, the other women in her husband's life? Most women would slam the door right in my face and tell me to go to hell. Shelly, my wife, would.

But what other choice did I have? Tamara and Charles were family. Husband and wife, married for twenty-two years. The marriage had been turbulent; it was all spelled out in the paper trail. *In a long union like theirs*, I mused, *there are not many secrets left untold.* And yet, despite their documented unhappiness with each other, those two had stayed together. *Interesting dynamic*, I admitted.

I impatiently waited around another hour or so for Lem and André to show up, but neither clocked in before Callum Baker walked in.

"Thought you should see something." He opened his tablet, flipped through photos of the Grim Reaper mask worn by Dana Miller. "It's of common low-grade cotton, polyester particles, and cheap paint. Not handmade. It has a UPC on the back along the edges. We lifted no DNA or fingerprints left behind by the killer. He wore gloves. Careful, assiduous in his handling of things. I'm fairly certain the mask was in a plastic package the killer removed and placed directly on the victim."

"So, he buys it in bulk, at least several at a time. I could check the universal product code database. Get a company name. André could work on obtaining customer records and shipping. This is huge! Anything else — what does it mean? Bloodless is a fan of horror movies?"

Baker punched a few keys. The screen changed to a picture of a gathering; people dressed in funny costumes, large floppy hats, lots of colorful masks. In the center was a tall, mysterious figure dressed in a dark robe and holding a curved scythe.

"The Grim Reaper's a European figure created in the mid-fourteenth century. Its exact origin's unknown, but some scholars believe the symbolism is rooted in the plague. From what I could find, the scythe he's holding has to do with him reaping human souls. The robe connects him to a priest presiding over a funeral service."

I did a double take. Cleared my throat. "Funerals? Are you absolutely sure?"

"As sure as God made little green apples. The Grim Reaper has been around for centuries. Symbol of death, harvesting the souls of others, plucking them from this world, sending them to the netherworld. The underworld."

"Evil," I remarked.

"Ah — some might believe what he does is evil, but that would be false. Think of him as the undertaker. Takes your soul under. In myths, the Grim Reaper's neutral. Nature's enforcer of law and order." Baker pointed to the black mask on Dana Miller's face.

"If what you're saying is true, then Bloodless views himself as the Grim Reaper. It fits him, it fits how he staged Dana Miller — a body left in the park, in a central location — it's a message telling us he's come to reap human souls. He removed all her personal items, including her ring. We don't get to learn her name or where she's from. You don't need material possessions in the underworld. Back to the chilling mask — he could pick another. Why this one? A happy one, no. A colorful one, again no. Black, dark — what's he trying to tell us? Sending us a threat — I'll take your soul like I have taken hers," I said. After some further reflection, I continued, "The Grim Reaper mask, the white dress, and funerals are all parts of the killer's identity."

"I hear Frank Ricca likes to reap human souls," Baker said.

"Yes, he does, doesn't he? And yet, I keep thinking we're chasing after the wrong killer."

Chapter 34

It had rained. Muddy water was pooling in the flower beds in front of Central when I stepped out. Thunder clapped in the distance, predicting more stormy weather.

I flipped the collar of my coat to stop drizzle from wetting my neck and dashed to my car parked on the curb. I unlocked the door and jumped behind the wheel. *Nature's enforcer* — Callum Baker had told me. My mind tried to imagine Frank Ricca as nature's enforcer, keeper of law and order. My logic rejected the assumption. His lengthy criminal record showed equal anger toward men and women. Prone to violent outbursts, Ricca would put anyone in the hole as he pleased. There was no room for forgiveness as long as Ricca deemed you unworthy. A few of his psychological attributes fit Bloodless, but not quite — at least not in my head.

Whoever killed Dana Miller loved and hated her for something. Her murder felt deeply personal. But why did Bloodless choose her? A quiet accountant with no friends who had found her happily ever after with Brad Connolly, her finance, a guy well-liked by his peers. Why drain her blood? Why sever Brad's throat and set his body on fire? Rage and hate, I envisioned.

I jammed the key in the ignition. The car rolled away as my mind flipped through old murder cases I had worked searching for a possible connection. Several stood out. The night I was shot, I had finally caught a break in another case, a string of strangulations — all women, all Caucasian, living in Back Bay. Each body was found clutching a red tulip. And it was a dot of blood on a flower stem that led us to their killer. We smashed his door in and took him down as he tried to choke his latest victim. The tulips — he later confessed — grew in his domineering mother's garden. The woman owned a cottage on the Cape, and whenever her nut-job son dropped by, he'd snip a few tulips to bring with him.

I'd never forget the stoic smirk on that bastard who told me every one of his victims reminded him of his mother. He hated her but couldn't kill the person who gave him life.

My thoughts continued to circle to the Back Bay strangler. He choked women he viewed as surrogates for his emotionally economical mother. His own moral code of ethics wouldn't allow him to go after the real woman he wanted to see dead. His mother. Any other woman was fair play, though. I wondered if Bloodless had his own moral code stopping him from killing the one he wished to see murdered the most.

The rain sped up. Drops began to beat against the windshield, and I considered the ethics binding me to Dana Miller and keeping me chained to the case. I could easily hand it off to Bradley Walker. Freed from her, I could throw myself at the mercy of Doctor Hoffman's surgical scalpel slicing through my heart to extract a bullet left by another killer. The traffic was congested up ahead. An impatient driver laid on his horn, giving the rest of us a piece of his mind. He was over it.

But I wasn't — Dana Miller wouldn't let me off the hook as easily as I wished. I had given her my word. Swore to deliver justice. I would see to it she received a dignified end. Images of her bruised wrists caused by the chains he held her in flashed behind my eyes. She'd been through a raw deal. She had no one left in her life to fight for her. But me.

I could catch Bloodless. My gut instinct told me not to give up. The evidence was in front of me, but for whatever reason, I couldn't see it yet. The cruiser chugged right along the Zakim Bridge as I devised a plan. For one, push the lab to hurry the hell up with the embalming fluid. Call Meredith Sawyer — press her on Pelican Bay, find the owner. Go through old arrest records. Maybe I had arrested Bloodless in the past — look at the MO, couples gone missing together. And if that didn't work, then I'd go back to Charles Isles, have a word with him again — where had he seen the Grim Reaper mask? If Isles cooperated, I was willing to offer him a deal, put in a good word with the federal witness protection program. Relocation, new identity, new start — all on the government's tab.

Hooked to the dashboard, my phone chirped. "Stone."

"Looks like Vargas and his team are moving in on Frank Ricca," André fired off. "They responded to a tip from one of their CIs who gave Vargas an address. Told cops it was Ricca's latest hideout."

"What? Where?"

André said the street name and house number. South Bay, old neighborhood, mostly blue-collar families, occasional drunken brawl, but for the most part, we rarely responded to calls there.

I threw on the grill lights and zapped between cars as fast I as could in this damn traffic. "Meet you there," I told André.

SWAT had breached the main door of a navy-blue, single-story home facing a tight street lined with homes looking less than pristine. A tan-colored Pitbull in the yard over was tearing a lung out watching the action unfold. Residents stood on their porches, buried in heavy jackets. Boston was experiencing another late start to summer.

"SID just missed him." André pushed through a slanted, rusty white gate. "Eyewitnesses confirmed Ricca has been staying here. The residence belongs to Marty Conti, ninety-two-year-old male, who's serving two consecutive life sentences for his involvement in the gunning down of Viktor Kostov and his entire family in eighty-three."

"What's the connection between Conti and Ricca?"

"Conti's a card-carrying member in the Cosa Nostra. Served with Ricca's uncle. Apparently, even behind bars, once you're in the mafia, you stay in the mafia." André clucked his tongue.

I climbed a set of weathered wood stairs squeaking beneath my feet. The door had taken the brunt of SWAT's ire, judging by the pile of smithereens. At the end of a short entryway, I spotted SID Detective Vargas waving his hands, gesturing to others. Something wasn't executed to his liking.

"Sonofabitch," Vargas greeted me, though I was certain he meant Ricca and not me. "He's in an unmarked red minivan. Last seen traveling eastbound on I495. And he's not alone."

My throat burned. "Who did Ricca take?"

"A woman. The neighbor heard her crying. Asking Ricca not to hurt her. Pleaded with him to leave her alone and she won't call the police." Vargas glanced at a second-story window next door. "The lady who lives there is visually impaired. Legally blind in one eye. But she told another officer that Ricca slapped his hostage across the face and threw her in the back of the minivan. She thinks the girl wore a dress, no shoes. Black hair, petite."

The description matched Dana Miller. But too general to be sure.

"Detectives, come see." An officer led us down a dinky staircase connected to a basement equipped with chains bolted to the walls. I saw a metal-framed twin bed, partially hidden behind an oil tank. The sheets were crumpled in a pile. It looked like she had been sleeping before she was yanked out. I touched the mattress, figuring out the scene for myself.

"Still warm," I told André. "Make sure the crime lab bags the sheets. Swab the mattress for DNA."

Beside the bed was a workbench, cluttered with common tools found in most homes. Above it a hanging rack — more tools with sharp edges hanging from hooks on rusted nails. I glanced at a knife, recognizing it. We found the exact same one in the back of Charles Isles's trunk — a scalpel. Curved blade, sharp enough to slice your skin to the bone.

An industrial sink still filled with filthy, murky water dried my throat as I discovered a severed index finger with a chunky silver ring.

Pointing to it, I asked, "Doesn't it look familiar?"

"Holy cow!" André muttered.

"Charles Isles wore three silver rings like this. One on the index finger. The ring's strikingly similar," I said.

"Wouldn't surprise me. Ricca loves his sharp tools. We think he cut up his uncle while keeping him alive. But we could never prove any of it in court." Vargas snapped several photos of the crime scene on his cell. He spotted a brownish stain on the slab of cement near the pipes under the sink. "Maybe blood. The entire floor's probably covered in it."

"Bag the finger and the ring. I want it in the lab stat. Call Tessa Wu to examine the finger, see if she can extra DNA and a fingerprint match," I told André.

To Vargas I said, "You need to get on the phone with the prison warden. Formally interview Marty Conti — push him to give up Frank Ricca. If he has a woman with him, it could be his next victim. And have the crime lab examine the water pipes for blood."

"Conti's been in solitary confinement since early 2018. The prison deemed him a threat to other inmates. And Conti would never talk. Old school. The last of the dinosaurs," Vargas replied.

I studied the basement — underground and in the home of a loyal mobster. Chains to keep his victims from escaping when he had to step out. I imagined Dana Miller lying in the twin bed, zonked out on pills and God knows what else Ricca pumps them with. Transforming them into zombies.

"Go through the medicine cabinet. Bag everything," I told the cops around me.

I nodded to André. "If Vargas thinks Conti's a dead end, we need to find Charles Isles if he's still alive. He didn't seem like the old-school loyal type. A slimy bastard, more like it, but he loves his freedom, and if Ricca cut his finger off, then Isles has more reasons to trust me."

André threw me the car keys. "You drive."

On the street, I quickly swept the neighborhood. Bristling with fear, nervous people huddled around, smoking and whispering to each other while kids pedaled their bikes to the edge of the cordon tape and dashed back.

Someone had to stand up for her — Dana Miller; others if Bloodless killed more. My own moral code of ethics wouldn't allow me to move on until justice — I sighed — was served.

Chapter 35

This time I drove, fast, my foot heavy on the pedal. Boston traffic had thinned out several hours ago. Getting out of the city was as easy as easy gets.

"Charles Isles's home is another half a mile up the road," I told André, glancing at my phone. "Grove Glenn Hill, Westford. Nice town, old money. Suits him."

"I suspect you'll give him another chance to flip on Frank Ricca for our protection," André replied.

"It's the right call. Ricca's on the lam. According to Vargas's witness, he fled in a dark-red minivan, unmarked. Judging by everything I saw in the basement, Charles Isles might not be with us anymore. On the phone with me the other night, Isles alluded to Ricca keeping tabs on him. Using Buzzworth, the lawyer, to watch Isles and report. Like we suspected. You read Ricca's file — the arrests in his youth, the pure desire to inflict pain. On his own kin too — murdered his father, packed him in a freezer, and sent him over to Carmena, his sister, and their mother." I nodded. "The basement we just left could be where he killed Dana Miller if he's Bloodless."

"If? I'm pretty certain he is," André said.

I glanced at him. "I won't pretend I have every detail figured out. But I think something Callum Baker told me today about the Grim Reaper mask will eventually lead us to Bloodless."

"What?"

"The Grim Reaper is nature's enforcer. The undertaker. The one who takes your soul to the underworld. Somehow, and I don't know why, but I don't see a soulless killer like Frank Ricca pretending to be the keeper of dead souls."

"It fits him like a glove if you ask me. Watch any horror show and you'd see it too. Ricca kills you without remorse for his actions."

"There's more, André. Photos Baker showed me of the Grim Reaper in a black robe. Callum thinks it's an association for someone presiding over a funeral."

My phone dinged. I let it go to voicemail. Whoever wanted me would have to wait. After Charles Isles. It rang a second time, but the caller hung up before my recorded message could tell them to wait for the beep.

André's phone went off. He answered immediately. "Captain?" A short pause. I could hear Mercy tearing into him about something I had no vested interest in until André unglued the phone from his ear and handed it to me.

"She'd like a word with you."

"I tried calling you." Her voice sounded like a melting snow cap. "Spoke with Detective Vargas — he filled me in. Frank Ricca's considered armed and dangerous. The BOLO was issued a couple of minutes ago."

"He might have a new victim with him. A woman. The description is a close match; similar to Dana Miller but too generic. The next-door neighbor believes Ricca got physical, roughed up the vic to get her inside the minivan. The woman was crying, pleading for Ricca to let her go. Logic dictates that he still needs something from his latest target. But with the heat on him, I'm afraid she doesn't have a lot of time left." I paused as I briefly concentrated on the dark, wet road.

"The finger came back as a match for Charles Isles, the lab informed me. What's your next move?" Mercy asked.

"Charles Isles might be the only person who could help us track Frank Ricca. They've been in business together for five to six years. Laundering money for the Mafia for that long, I think Isles knows where a few of Ricca's skeletons are buried. I'd like to have a word with him. I'd go as far as suggesting lesser charges for him if he helps us out. If I find him still alive."

Mercy expressed her reservations with my plan by letting out a short *hmmm*. "Hold off on making any promises before I've had a chance to clear it with the DA's office."

"Okay. But I'll need to give him something. He's not as stupid as he looks."

She sounded exacerbated, burned out; feeling the hefty load of the Bloodless investigation. Mercy finally replied, "Stall by promising Charles Isles a basket of newborn puppies if you must. If you don't hear from me in thirty minutes, consider the deal off the table. Is my message getting through to you?"

And though I said yes to Mercy, part of me was already thinking how I could circumvent her order. The moonless night stretched in front of the car. And while the tires chewed up the miles, I thought back to Frank Ricca smacking his vic, so brazen and out in public. She must be going out of her mind with fear.

"Lem texted to say Ricca and the woman tried to pawn a diamond ring. Could be Dana Miller's. Ricca's finally flushing out evidence. Told Lem to stay with Vargas. Keeps us informed if SID brings Ricca in."

"Selling Dana's ring when every Boston's cop's looking for you — that's gutsy," I replied.

André found the police file on Charles Isles. He opened the front page and read for some time as I pushed on the gas. "His wife, Tamara Sullivan, looks pretty solid on paper."

I asked, "But how solid? She stayed married to someone like Isles. A long way off from an upstanding citizen."

"Maybe it's the money. At age forty-seven, Tamara Sullivan's listed as a paid consultant at her husband's company, The Groove Factory." André coughed in his sleeve, cleared his throat.

I continued to gaze into the blackness of the night, eyes trained on the unknown ahead. "Tamara draws a salary to the tune of two hundred thousand a year, for no work. They've been married for twenty-four years. I read most of what's in the report."

"Long marriage." André flipped through the rest of the fanned-out pages.

"And not a happy one. They've been separated at least three times in the past from what I could find. I bet there have been more breakups than that. No kids listed for either one of them, illegitimate or otherwise," I pointed out. "It wouldn't have surprised me — he cheated on her multiple times. I suspect she stepped out on him if only to level the scoreboard between them. So, far from a happy coexistence? And yet they stayed married."

"Some couples prefer to take the hurt and the pain because they don't understand happiness. That could be their situation," André suggested.

I exited the highway and pointed the wheel in the direction of a gritty, rock-strewn path splitting the thick woods down the middle. Dour night had fallen when I parked the squad car in front of a sprawling chalet of timber and glass. Modern and rustic.

"This place is beautiful," André remarked.

"Showman's digs. Why am I not shell-shocked by the size of it? Somehow, it makes sense, the business arrangement between Isles and Ricca. One has an ego the size of Texas, and the other has a boatload of dirty money in need of a good wash."

"I'm in the wrong line of business. Listen — "

Nothing but stillness and overwhelming sensory darkness, the occasional chirps of night birds.

"Serenity," André mumbled.

"If you're done dream chasing, I'd like to move on. Offer Charles Isles a one-time deal. If he doesn't take it — it walks out the door with us. I still need to file my report before I can go home to a bargain supper paid for with money earned, honestly."

I stepped up to the home and pressed the Ring button. A digital camera eye trained on us.

"Cheap security for a chateau this luxurious," I observed.

"I imagine you can't find the house unless you're invited by the owners. It's a good six miles off the highway, amidst impenetrable green trees and overgrown nature. Why drive out here unless you know where you're going?"

The front door snapped open, and a man in his late sixties dressed in a white suit and a black bow tie said, "Good evening."

"We're looking for Charles Isles. Is this his residence?" I asked.

"It is. And who might you be?"

The formal stiffness of his voice grinded on my nerves some. I fetched my badge and flashed it in his face.

"Boston Homicide Detective Temple Stone. My partner André Jones. We'd like a word with Mr. Isles."

"Please wait," he said before he gracefully, but not uncongenially, I noted, closed the door in our faces.

"A butler? Are you serious? Who still employs butlers nowadays? Decked out in a uniform to match the job," André said.

"Formal. Charles Isles didn't strike me as the straight-laced type. More hippie, free love, let's get down and boogie type. But formal, that must be his wife — Tamara Sullivan. Old money. Old tradition. Brought up to respect her rank in society and uphold it in her own home, even if it's miles away from civilization."

The white-coat butler returned. "This way, please."

I stepped into a palatial foyer — black and white tile, cascading grand staircase, crystal chandelier with icicles dangling above us.

We took an elevator two floors down to an underground floor, which was more industrial — masculine, cold gray walls matching the cement floor, low iridescent lights. The butler left us to wait by an Olympic-sized pool.

"The gap between the rich and the poor. I'm dying to see what's on the ground floor if this is their pool house. Didn't think Charles Isles was that filthy loaded," André said.

"Rich man, poor man, beggar man, thief. Dirty mobster money paid for the swanky accommodation."

I studied the water in the pool — the prettiest blue I had ever seen. My thoughts wandered off to the Mexican deep-sea fishing trip I had taken André on. We spent the days on a small fishing boat, bare feet up, a cold beer never too far off. Suddenly, I longed for those carefree days when André and I were the lowest grunts on the cop ladder.

Around then, the pool waters splashed, and a statuesque woman wearing a tiny silver one-piece suit swayed her hips towards us. She casually tossed a white satin robe over delicate shoulders, leaving it open in the middle, I noticed, offering a glimpse of her large, firm breasts.

"Leo said you were with the police. I'm Tamara." She extended her hand to shake mine. "I wasn't expecting company; excuse the outfit."

"Mrs. Sullivan — Detective Temple Stone, this is Lieutenant André Jones, we're with Boston Police. Is your husband around?"

"Charles?" She sighed, irritated, her eyelashes fluttering. "Why? Is he in some kind of trouble?"

"We need to speak with him personally regarding our investigation — "

"Why am I not fazed by this? Trouble follows him wherever he goes. I feel like it's never going to end," she said, flipping her dripping wet hair downwards before wrapping a silky towel around it.

"Come sit. It's a long drive from the city. Leo will get us drinks — "

"On the clock. None for us," I said.

"Of course. How about a bottle of water?"

"Fine. Thanks."

She crossed her smooth bare legs; I got the impression Tamara Sullivan was comfortable and then some showing off her body to anyone with two eyes.

"So, tell me, what mess has Charlie gotten himself into now? And don't try to hide it from me. It's not the first time cops turned up at my front door wanting to interview him. In a long marriage like ours — far from perfect — you learn a thing or two about your spouse."

"It's a private matter. We'd like to bring him to Central with us. Clear up some things we discovered after our initial interview. But we're up against the clock, so if you don't mind telling us where he is, we'll get out of your hair and let you go back to your night swim."

"Ah — detective, has anyone told you — you suck at lying?! No, but you do. I hope you forgive my frankness." Her seductive, aqua-blue eyes casually slid to my ring finger, searching for my relationship status. "Married, huh? Mrs. Stone should be thanking the Lord her husband's so bad at it.

"My husband isn't terribly good at it either. He was better when we first got together, but as the years trickled away, he either stopped trying hard or I learned every play in his playbook. Charlie and I separated some time back. Couldn't take it any longer. I found no more comfort in him. Whatever was left of our relationship, I had to let it go."

"Separated?" I glanced at André, then back at Tamara Sullivan. "On the paperwork he filled out at the station, he listed this address as his most current one."

"Don't take his BS personally, detective. My poor husband is pathological. I used to get mad at him, now — I've accepted it. He stops by sometimes, but I don't bother myself with asking where he sleeps or with which skank. It's none of my business frankly."

André tried to call Isles on his phone. It was dead.

"What's new? Lately, he's been secretive, which is unusual for Charles. He's one of those men who wears their heart on their sleeve. Blabs like he has diarrhea of the mouth."

"When did you notice the change in his behavior?"

She bit her lower lip, thinking. "Two to three months ago. Work-related stress. It changed him so much that I hardly recognize him anymore. But love's blind, or whatever people say. My father used to say about Charlie and me — a fool in love with a fool. How does something so good get so bad?"

"We're investigating the murder of a woman. The killer left her body at Franklin Park at one of your husband's gigs. Did he mention anything to you?" I said and waited for her reaction.

Not a wrinkle or fold appeared on her forehead. "The running thing — I heard about it," she replied like we were gossiping. "Charlie fumed that the negative publicity would ruin the company. I could tell he was in deep. Broke again like before. But if any man could dig himself out of a hole, it would be Charlie. That man can claw his way to the top. I admire that in him; maybe the only thing left to admire."

Listening to Tamara Sullivan left me unconvinced by her lack of interest in Charles Isles. I suspected she was lying to our faces. But why? Was she protecting him? Or had the love between them truly fizzled out, and I was witnessing the dying flames of their union?

"Do you know where he's staying during your separation? If he has a room in this house to sleep or change his clothes, we'd like to take a look. It could give us an idea of where to look next?"

Tamara gulped water. "I don't think so. That's prying, and well, my husband and I are on the brink of divorce, but still, somehow it doesn't feel right."

I reached into my inner pocket. "Have you seen this man? Do you recognize him?"

Tamara Sullivan shuffled in her seat. She tightly closed her robe and tied it around her waist. I witnessed a storm gathering behind her ocean-blue eyes. What was she so mad about?

I waited for her to answer, and when she didn't, I said, "His name's Frank Ricca, an Italian mobster with a reputation as a cold-blooded killer. Someone saw Ricca take a woman against her will tonight. Things turned violent. I'm worried if we don't catch Ricca soon, it might be too late to save her."

She handed the photo back to me. Picked up her bottle of water, swung her feet over the armrest, and dangled them, untroubled. "I've never seen this man. What's his connection to Charlie?"

"Police matter." I bounced on my feet. How could Tamara Sullivan be so casual about the whole thing? "Now, will you help us track down your husband? I have solid evidence he's hurt, badly. Or was this trip a waste of our time?"

Pouty, Tamara shifted her attention away from me to André. "Try any of the low-rent slumps in Chinatown. He has drained all of his accounts; my soon-to-be ex-husband can't even afford a night at a decent hotel. And if you need an exact address — oh well then, you'd have to interview every rat pimp along the way, they all know my husband's name. It shouldn't be a problem."

Light rain rapped on the windshield as I pulled out of the parking spot.

"Hell hath no fury like a woman scorned," André said. "And Mrs. Sullivan's scorned. Charles Isles has done her wrong for the last time. And she's incredibly attractive — who in their right mind would cheat on a woman like that?"

"She's totally pissed at him. I agree. Did you feel anything off with her?"

"Her pain from the dissolution of her marriage seemed genuine. No children to fight over. But there's always a fight when someone's divorcing the other. That leaves the house. It's all she has left, especially if she was telling the truth about Charles Isles being broke. Her husband must have seriously wounded her during their decades-long courtship, and she never got over the hurt. So, where to now?"

I bumped onto the highway. By now the rain was pelting us. "You heard the lady — every rat pimp in Chinatown knows her husband, and they're about to know us."

Chapter 36

Even on a rainy night, Chinatown buzzed with people from different backgrounds, transforming the neighborhood into a seasoned blend. It was a world far removed from Tamara Sullivan's wonder-to-behold exclusive woodland chalet. Around these parts of Boston, Chinatown residents lived on little and expected even less in return. Uneven, cramped streets, low-lit window displays advertising 'spicy chow mein,' 'bowl of ramen noodles,' 'pork dumplings,' dishes of that variety. Random men as thin as a match smoked on grungy stoops and pitch-dark street corners, seemingly disengaged from the passage of time. They measured life one tobacco smoke ring after the next.

Since Tamara said Charles never gave her an address, we had no choice but to track him down by going door-to-door. The first three watering holes said they'd never seen Charles Isles after they barely examined his photo.

"Might have to call for reinforcement," André said, letting out a long, drawn-out yawn. "He could be anywhere. And it's not like Chinatown advertises their prostitution services. Nabbing him would take all day and night."

I nodded in agreement. "Chinatown is not what I imagined for Charles Isles."

"What did you expect? It fits him rather perfectly. Not the first time he's been broke. Ten years after Sullivan Electric fired him for sexual misconduct, Isles lost everything. His lucrative real estate business, the cars, the social status; it all went up in smoke. He was working dead-end jobs just to make ends meet."

"True. But he came back from it. Built an impressive entertainment company. Managed to run some of Boston's most beloved events. By any account, Charles Isles was a redeemed man worthy of society's forgiveness."

"And how did he repay us — laundered money for the Cosa Nostra. Forged a partnership with Frank Ricca, a homicidal maniac." André dodged passing cars to cross the street. "These two had a long partnership before they went into business together. Jail mates. Watching each other's backs. Who did Isles call after prison? Frank Ricca. They've been together as friends and partners ever since. Maybe cutting off the finger was a mafia initiation ceremony. Isles repledging his loyalty to Frank Ricca. It happens. It's not unheard of. We have no evidence Ricca removed Isles's finger, and you know Oliver Buzzworth will bring it up if we ever catch Ricca. If I was him, I'd be halfway to Sicily by now."

"I don't see it. You should have heard Isles on the phone. He sounded scared, frightened of his lawyer and Frank Ricca, his so-called best friend in the world. No, I think their partnership soured over the missing twenty-eight million. Dana Miller coming on board, sticking her nose where Frank Ricca didn't want anyone sniffing. But I don't know yet why Ricca would steal his own money? That's a small but integral element to solving Dana Miller's murder."

Walking beside André, I chuckled. Fear was what I saw in Isles's eyes when I brought up the Grim Reaper mask. He had clammed up, refused to speak. Why? Maybe to protect Frank Ricca? It could be? But again, Charles Isles struck me as someone who looks after his own interests first and always. I didn't feel a great deal of loyalty in him, especially not for Frank Ricca.

"We ain't never gonna find him on our own." André pointed at a twenty-four-seven noodle shop. "What do you say? It's on me. You look like you could use a bowl."

I turned down his offer of wet, overcooked noodles and told him to find me at the fish market on the corner. The place looked unusually active for the hour.

I walked inside to the chime of a bell placed above the door. Some joyless faces looked up from their phone screens and watched me carefully as I approached the market counter. A petite, ropy, gray-haired male scolded at me before I spoke. His expression changed to less enthusiastic after I flashed my badge.

He quickly rebuffed any attempt at conversation. But he stopped short of asking me to get the hell out. And so, I hung around, mostly for warmth, but also natural curiosity.

"You missed out on the noodles — pillow soft and a hint of zest," André said.

"I'll take your word for it. If you don't mind, can we get back to searching for our suspect now? What do you think of this place? There seems to be some action near the back room. Lots of visitors going in and not that many coming out. The female-to-male ratio's three to one. Could be an illegal brothel."

"And if it is — how do you want it to go down?" André asked, hand placed over his handheld radio.

"We're checking things out. I most definitely don't want to make any enemies. Bust them on prostitution charges and none of them will ever give up Charles Isles."

I hustled down the dimly lit hallway and discovered a large, heavyset man ogling a titty mag. He was minding a battered door with a sign indicating 'limited access.'

"Do you mind?" I said to the bouncer and motioned for him to step aside.

"And what if I do?"

He flung the dirty mag to the ground, leisurely swinging his jacket enough to reveal the butt of a Glock.

I took a bold step towards him, held my badge up. His face drained of color.

"Look, it's not real," he said, handing the Glock over to André. "It's a good deterrent for rowdy customers. They see the piece and tend to leave quickly and quietly."

"What's going on in there?" I asked.

Dead silence, then he gave me a line. "It's a massage parlor. Busy night for the girls. Lots of men with tight knots in their necks. How about you? Your neck tight? I can grab a girl for you. Twenty bucks. Police special. Interested?"

A clash of voices erupted and escalated to an explicit tirade. Someone smashed a bottle on the ground. I could hear the sounds of a physical struggle, fists, and kicks. The battered door flung open fast. A voluptuous woman in a coal tracksuit shouted for help.

"Get in here! The dirtbag in room four is refusing to pay again." Her startled gaze fell on me. "Who's that?"

"Cops," the bouncer replied and gladly vanished from sight inside the back room to break up the fight.

Arms crossed, examining me head to toe, the woman asked, "Is there a problem?"

"Several. But the most pressing one's this man." I handed her Charles Isles's picture. "Have you seen him before?"

"Charlie? What's he done?"

"So, you know him, Miss..."

"Kai-Ming — everyone calls me Lola."

"Lola, then — when was the last time you saw Mr. Isles?"

"Don't take this the wrong way, but how do I know you are who you say you are? All day, every day I meet people who come in, pretending to be someone else. And Charlie is a good friend. Maybe you lie and you hurt him."

André dialed Dispatch. "Ask for Captain Mercy. She'll confirm our names for you."

Lola looked down at the cell phone, hit disconnect, and shifted, visibly uncomfortable speaking to us.

"He's a regular. Sweet man. Comes in at night. Spends several hours with a few girls he sees regularly. Not the best tipper. But he's harmless, and that's something women in the massage business don't take for granted. Why's the police looking for him?"

"We're not at liberty to discuss that with you. Have you seen him tonight? Has he been in?"

She folded her arms in front of her body, looking like she wouldn't talk anymore.

"I'm not looking to cause any trouble for you," I glanced around the fish market, "or your family."

"My father runs an honest fish market, detective. The massage parlor is out of necessity. We have family back home who survive off the money we send them. And Charlie's honestly a harmless older gentleman — lonely and alone. He's flat broke. My dad's gearing up to kick him out too if Charlie doesn't pay rent this month..."

I stopped her. "Charles Isles rents from you?"

"A single room in the motel out back. He's supposed to pay weekly. Like the rest of our tenants."

"If he's that much behind, how come you haven't evicted him yet?" I asked.

Lola blurted out, "He promised to give us a cut when he found his money — two million. My father, of course, believed him initially, but weeks went by, and Charlie never delivered the money. Tonight, Dad finally confronted him about it. Threw him out. They argued some. I stepped in and tried to tell my father to show some compassion. But he wouldn't hear it. Told Charles to pack his crap and clear the room."

"How did Isles take it?"

Lola cracked her fingers, one finger at a time. I thought she looked genuinely concerned for Charles Isles.

"Fine, I assume."

"Fine?"

"Alright, maybe not fine. He's Charlie, you know. A big, bright smile on his face. Never heard him say a bad word about anyone. Well, almost. He didn't like his wife very much. From what I've picked up, Mrs. Isles was a lot of work, and she always belittled him. When her name was mentioned, that sunny smile on Charlie's face faded in a blink of an eye. Last I saw him, he called someone asking for a ride. I think his car was repoed, and he had no other means of transportation. I offered to give him money for a cab, but he said after tonight, all his money problems will be gone. Hang on," she put one arm on her hip, chin propped on the other, "gave him three Tylenol. His left hand was wrapped in a dirty rag. Wouldn't let me take a look."

"Can you show us the room he rented?"

"Sure. Right outside this door and across the pool. Second floor. Room 614."

"When did you say he moved in?"

"Two months — no, more like three months. He said his wife and him split up. I was left with the impression they did that a lot, but it never lasted because he explicitly asked for a month-to-month deal. My father was happy with the arrangement until — "

"Isles stopped paying his bills."

The back of the fish market was walled off with over-grown shrubs wrapped around a crumbling iron fence. On the dark side of the side street, Lola pattered ahead of us, jingling a large key ring.

"What do you want with him? Is he in any trouble? He's a goofy wise ass. Whatever you think he did, you're making a mistake."

I wanted to warn her about trusting Charles Isles — his close ties to Frank Ricca made him a danger to others. Dana Miller had trusted him. Reached out to Isles for help with a stalker. But Isles never lifted a finger to help her. Fed her lies so she stayed on board. To find the money. The stolen millions. I speculated if human life had a price, it would be twenty-eight million. At least, that's how much Dana was worth to Charles Isles. I suspected he knew more than he told me during our interrogation, more than what he gave me on the phone. And now, another woman was kidnapped, and my only hope to save her before Ricca could kill her was tracking down Charles Isles, the so-called goofy wise ass.

Lola pulled on the worn-out gate to the pool and took one step in. Then froze.

"Oh, Jesus! No! Sweet Jesus."

I pushed her out of my way to jump in the pool's soiled water. The body weighed easily two hundred pounds. I hugged his neck tight and paddled to the narrow stairs.

"Call 911. Do it now. Request an ambulance."

"It's a freaking mistake!" Lola cried out.

André muscled me out of the gunky swamp so I could gather my breath at the ledge.

"It's Charles Isles," I wiped my mouth, "no pulse."

Chapter 37

André dragged him out and laid him flat. He positioned Charles Isles's head in a neutral position and partially opened his mouth. Air gradually wafted from Isles's blue lips.

I yanked the tie from his neck, tore his soaked shirt, and pressed my ear to his unmoving chest.

"I can hear shallow breathing," André said.

I didn't need a second prompt. I started chest compressions.

"Ambulance's three minutes out," Lola sniveled. "Will he be alright?"

"Wait for them at the fish market. Tell them we're back here. And don't let a civilian past the side door. This is an active crime scene."

André told me to stop; he leaned into Isles and forced air into his mouth. "The shallow breathing stopped."

"Is he okay? Oh, Charlie!"

"Damn it, Lola. Go. Go now. And get the medics."

"I'm going. Yes. Please, just help him."

I refused to give up; born stubborn and thick-headed, I forced every ounce of strength into restarting Isles's heart.

"Effing breathe. Don't die on me, man." Heavy sweat dripped off the edge of my chin as I grumbled to André, "Someone held his head under that mossy bog. If we pressed the bouncer more, we might have found Isles sooner." I kept at it, forcing my weight onto his rock-hard sternum.

André slapped his mouth on Isles's lips and blew, blew, blew, until he had no more air to give.

"Whoever killed Isles, he's long gone, and that's all that matters at this moment. No cameras on the way in, no cameras on the way out." André drew in a breath. "We might get lucky and lift a fingerprint from the gate and the fence. Make sure the sweepers don't rush it. Big man like Isles would have fought the attacker. No visible self-defense marks, pending medical. Then, he knew his assailant — "

I stripped his shirt off and tore apart the undershirt. "No stab wound to the ribs, no bullet hole. Where's the damn ambulance? If we don't take him to a hospital now, we'll lose him."

As I said it, the sirens grew closer and closer. I exhaled, relieved to hand over resuscitating Isles to someone more capable while I examined the crime scene. I'd try to figure out first what happened, second, who did it and why? Though I already had a pretty good idea who could have killed him. In my mind, I saw Frank Ricca, recalled his remorseless face, cold features — those of a killer. A blast of frigid air brushed over my freezing shoulders. I shivered.

The high-pitched horns of the sirens arrived. Tires squealed; howled. Lola was crying but talking to Fire and Rescue; I could hear her giving them directions.

"Run to the car and get the field bag. I want everyone in disposable booties. And get officers to cover each entrance. Start a crime scene log, stat. No one in and out without signing their name and rank," I told André.

He left me with Isles as the medics burst in. One placed a stethoscope on the lifeless chest while his partner peeled off the shock paddles of a defibrillator. Things weren't looking up for Charles Isles, I began to suspect.

"How long has the patient been without a pulse?" the medic asked.

"We found him in the pool about six minutes ago, CPR for about four. No visible change in breathing."

They zapped Isles several times while the medics kept adding voltage, but with no positive result. They discussed intubating him, but eventually ruled it out as a viable option.

"Sorry detective — he's gone. I can't pronounce him dead. The ER will do that. I can only provide transport if that's what you'd like."

On my feet, I punched the misty air in frustration. "Dammit!" Then to the impassive medic, "Leave him. Will get someone to phone the ME."

"Again, sorry I couldn't bring him back for you."

"Yeah. Alright. Not your fault. He was dead and gone when we got here. Someone made damn good sure of it."

Captain Mercy and André showed up.

"Detective — give me all you've got. How bad is it?"

"Charles Isles — dead. He was gone before we got to him."

"Drowned? Murdered?" she asked, brows hiked up.

"Seems likely. No other visible life-threatening injuries to the body, pending the ME's ruling." I glanced down at the half-naked body of Charles Isles. "Homicide seems the most obvious."

"Any links to Frank Ricca?" Mercy swept a piece of her hair behind an ear.

"As of right now — no. Frank Ricca's in the wind. At large. With a hostage. When Doctor Tessa Wu examines the body, I'll know more about the manner of death. In the meantime, I want the entire place shut down. Start going door-to-door." I pointed to the deteriorated motel attached to the pool. "It's late enough. A lot of people are home from work. Best-case scenario — one's willing to talk, give us a statement."

Mercy said, "If it helps, I can offer a willing witness a night at a decent hotel and twenty-four-seven around-the-clock police protection. But nothing else. I'm afraid I'm all out of favors in this city, boys. The best I can do."

"It's something. Let's start there."

With gloved hands, I returned to the body and went through his pockets. All I found in his coat was ten dollars in ones and a key pass that looked like the motel's. I patted down the pants, fetched his wallet. Credit cards, driver's license, small-dollar bills, and several day's old receipts. Nothing seemed stolen.

"What's that?" André was looking over my shoulder.

I examined the wet paper. Ink smudging off. Parts tearing off. "It looks like a slip from the post office and a receipt. He ate dinner at a sandwich shop."

We placed his personal belongings in separate evidence bags, sealed and tagged them. Then moved on to examining the crime scene. As I checked the ground for other evidence, I wondered about Charles Isles and the night of his arrest. In the van, we discovered Dana Miller's black sequined blouse and a bloodied scalpel, the murder weapon. Solid incriminating evidence against him, but the charges wouldn't have held up in front of a judge. He would have walked free in a day or two if not sooner if Oliver Buzzworth did his job. I told myself I couldn't have saved his life, couldn't have stopped Frank Ricca from attacking Isles, cutting his finger off, drowning him. None of it was on me, yet, I felt responsible, guilty for not pressing him harder to come in and accept police protection if he gave up Frank Ricca.

The nagging feeling of overlooking something needled me between my shoulders. But what? I couldn't put it together, not yet. And with Charles Isles dead, I feared I had missed my shot of catching Bloodless before I had to give up the case and try to repair my broken heart.

"While we wait on Wu, why don't we go up to his room?" I suggested to André.

Room 614 occupied the second floor of a dead-end corridor, overlooking the worse-for-wear pool. Inside, there was no room to swing a cat. I found it hard to imagine a big guy like Isles sleeping in a bedroom the size of a matchbox.

André hit the light switch, but the yellow glow didn't help beautify the place. On the contrary. Charles Isles lived like a dog, surrounded by piles of garbage. A pack rat.

"I want to say the killer tossed the room, but I'd be lying," André said.

"Gone to seed. I'm starting to understand Tamara Sullivan's predicament. Snowball's chance in hell she'd reconcile with him."

"By his own account, he was worth at least twenty-eight million. For a piece of the pie, she might've."

"If Tamara Sullivan had any sense in her, she'd have declared him incompetent." I covered my face with the back of my arm.

André turned a box of crumpled, frail files over onto the bed. "It seems Isles was investigating a case of his own. Twenty-year-old tax records, real estate deeds to homes, business filings. Whatever it was, he put a lot of work into gathering it all."

"He said to me he didn't realize someone was stealing from him. He carried heavy regret with him. I felt it. Maybe Dana Miller died before she shared her report with him, and Isles attempted to solve some of it on his own. He was trying to track the millions using whatever's in all these boxes. Why do I get the strange feeling Charles Isles might not be the person we thought he was? Odd behavior. And more questions for us to answer." Exasperated, I side-stepped a tower of papers leaning against one foot of his bed.

I opened the door to a shanty bathroom. "More boxes in the tub. They look different, though."

Organized and labeled. Like office boxes one uses to store files. He kept them stored away from the rest. I wondered why.

I studied the walls and the floor with my flashlight. The glaring beam hit the smirched blue-gray tiles, and I spotted it. I knelt, hovering the flashlight directly over the single piece of evidence.

"André, send up a sweeper. Find Lola for me. I'd want to speak with her again. See if you can track down the building super if they've got one. Highly unlikely, but check. And I need a phone. Mine died, it seems like a lifetime ago."

André passed me his device; I took several photos and enlarged them.

"It's a partial. Callum Baker should be able to clean it up to run a comparison against Charles Isles's footprints. See if they'll match."

"Or," I stood up, "could be the killer's. This means the perp drowned Charles Isles first, then rushed to the room. Looking for something? But what? Something in the paperwork, the files. Nothing else here but old records. Finally, the killer walks to the bathroom, one last place to check. Like us, he discovers where Isles kept the important files. He takes a step, doesn't realize his feet are wet, and leaves a print behind on the tile floor."

André looked at the dimly lit courtyard as I continued, "Get some boots to transport all four of these boxes to Central. Seal 614."

I started for the door, turning the events of the night over in my mind.

"Where're you going?" André asked behind me.

"To chat with Lola. She said the massage parlor was especially busy tonight. I wondered if she saw the killer but never realized it."

Chapter 38

The sweeper, a youthful-looking guy in a white disposable one-piece suit, marched through the door lugging a digital camera and a field kit. I decided to stick around for a while to hear him out.

"Wow. Small, crowded spaces — bad for you, detectives. People like your vic stuff and hide gross things in lots of questionable places. Seen it before. What's that smell? Mildew — judging by the water-damage stains on the walls. Black mold on the top right corner of the bedroom ceiling. Perfection." He dismissed it with a frustrated wave. "Take a look at the carpet, littered with rodent particulates and random bits of trash. Typical low-rent slum. The honest truth, it's going to take a miracle. So much room to miss things."

"Then think twice and act once. This crime scene should be one of the most important ones of your career," I snapped.

He picked up his equipment and nodded nervously. "Understood sir. Callum said you discovered a print to be documented. Can I see it?"

"It's in the bathroom. My partner took photos on his cell, but we want it preserved. And guard it if you have to until Baker shows up and takes over," André said.

The tech shuffled to the stinky bathroom, bent one knee, and snapped the floor with a super-size flash.

"It circles back to Lola. Get her official statement on tape. She seemed to have a soft spot for the vic. Wonder if Charles Isles opened up to her? How much did he tell her? I'll show her the Grim Reaper mask. Isles said he recognized it; maybe he mentioned it to Lola. After I wrap it up with her, we should stop by Tamara Sullivan to notify her. She's still his next of kin. We should move."

Doctor Tessa Wu arrived as I rounded the corner and ducked into the fish market.

"Stay with Wu. See what she says. Have her sign off on COD. I can handle Lola on my own."

Lola jerked upright when I showed up at the now-emptied fish market. Her father and bouncer brother stayed seated, choosing to ignore me. To their outrage, Lola rushed to my side with anguish painted on her face. Her brother got to his feet, but their father lowered him into the chair with a frown.

"Did he make it? The ambulance left without Charlie. And I didn't know if that's good news or not. Cops didn't let us leave before we spoke to you. When can I see him?"

"I'm sorry to inform you, but Mr. Isles didn't make it. He was gone when we pulled him out of the water."

She flinched, then started to pace in a small circle. Her father lit a thin smoke, saying nothing to comfort his visibly distraught daughter.

"How could that happen? He was just here. He spent several hours at the bar. Talked my ear off about the future. How it would fall in place. Mentioned you."

"Me?"

"Yeah, the murder cop with the grayest eyes he'd ever seen. Said you'd catch him. Make him pay. Some bullshit about justice and more empty blabber about taking back his millions."

"Did he give you a name?"

"No. No names. He never gave details. Talked in circles. To protect me, he'd say when I called him out on his shit. Now he's dead. And you're certain he was murdered, not some freak accident?"

"Based on initial evidence — homicide seems most likely. I'm not sure how much you know about his past, but I assure you he was mixed up with troubled people. To him, keeping their names out of his mouth meant protecting you. I can see it."

"You're talking about the women and sexual harassment lawsuits against him — that was ages ago. Ancient history. There's more to any story, you know?"

"It was far from ancient history for his victims. But it sounds to me like you and Charles shared quite a bond. He obviously trusted you. Did he ever talk to you about other stuff? Things and people in his life? His business?"

"Sure, yeah. Charlie was a talker. Never shut up for longer than five minutes. Always a story and a line. But underneath the funny-guy act, he struck me as lonely; emotionally starved for any positive human interaction. Half the time I thought he was lying about some of the things he said." Her stare bounced around the room. I could tell she was holding back. "I'll miss his company."

I waited to hear what else she'd tell me on her own. Her father blew a black cloud of smoke over our heads. When the ring of smoke drifted off, Lola spoke again. "We never," she cringed, glancing somberly at her relatives, "dated. None of the romantic crap. Friends, mostly he talked — I listened. It gets lonely cleaning up the whole place by myself. Charlie kept me company, then walked me to my parents' apartment upstairs. Always the perfect gentleman."

"Did he have two key passes issued to his name? The killer might have used a second one to enter without Mr. Isles's consent."

Lola gathered her hair and twisted it in a knot on top of her head. "Sure. Yes. We give you two keys at check-in. Twenty-five-dollar fee if you lose one and we have to replace it. But he never brought anyone with him. His wife wouldn't be caught alive in a place like ours. I'm not sure if she even knew or cared where Isles stayed. Once she learned about the woman he hired to find his money, his wife flipped, threw him out on the street for good, and told him to get lost. He wasn't allowed back at their house. She sounded like a lot of work." Through clenched teeth, she said, "I can't get him out of my mind. Who would do such a terrible thing to this nice man?"

I handed her a picture of Frank Ricca. "Have you seen this individual before — maybe with Charles Isles, or alone?"

Lola's father snatched the photo from my fingers and stubbed his cigarette against a half-empty beer can.

"Enough chit-chatting," he said to me, stood up, and took one step in front of Lola. "Go upstairs — your mother needs help."

"We have reason to believe this man might be responsible for Charles Isles's murder. He evaded the police earlier today, fled in a dark-red minivan, and took an innocent woman with him as his hostage. Can you take another look at his photo? You might be able to help us save her life."

His dominant demeanor overpowered any objection Lola might conjure. She obeyed him with speed.

"If Frank Ricca threatened you or your family, we can protect you. He killed a man in your backyard in cold blood. It won't be the last time he murders," I pleaded.

"No one saw anything. And we don't want to answer any of your questions. My son and I decided to close the market for the night. I expect that's sufficient to conduct your investigation before we open in the morning?"

"Okay. But here's my business card. My personal number is on the back — your daughter should call me if she remembers anything else."

Out on the cold, damp street, I spotted Lola watching me from the second-floor window of her parents' apartment. She slipped behind their tattered curtains as soon as our gazes met. Straight away, the window went dark, and Lola vanished into the black night.

Chapter 39

"I wonder if Tamara Sullivan will fight us on searching her house and Isles's office. She didn't seem very keen on us snooping around when I first asked. Get a warrant ready in the eventuality she raises a stink. Didn't see too much personal belongings in the motel room Charles Isles was renting, which means he hadn't completely moved out of the marital home." I rolled down the window and let the fresh breeze of the late night cool off the heat in the car.

Shadows of trees outlined the stretch of road when André murmured, "How much should we tell her? Tamara. Do you think she knows about her husband snooping around someone else?"

"Best if we don't bring up Lola when we give Tamara the news. Lola mentioned a possible reason for why Isles stayed in Chinatown — Dana Miller. The wife found out Isles hired a forensic accountant to investigate the missing funds, and according to Lola, Tamara blew a fuse. Ended the marriage on the spot. What do you make of that? We don't know what the story is and how deep and dark it goes between the spouses. Something's fishy with Tamara Sullivan. Call it a gut feeling or whatever. But I don't think she was completely forthcoming with us. It seems Charles Isles kept secrets from his wife — didn't trust Tamara Sullivan. She's more a suspect in my book than a grieving spouse."

"I agree. Money is a great motive for murder. And it could be just me, but she recognized Frank Ricca from the photo you showed her. Kind of hard to believe Tamara Sullivan never met him. According to several employees at The Groove Factory, Frank Ricca dropped by. And Tamara's listed on the company roster as a consultant. They crossed paths. But she didn't admit to it."

I ran my hand over my sweat-dampened hair. My breathing was slow and labored, but I couldn't pull over and allow my body to rest. "She lied to us, André. Looked us in the eye and lied. Simple as two and two equals four. Why, though? What is she hiding?"

André's phone beeped with a text. "Vargas from the SID unit says his men struck out with their CIs. No one wants to snitch on Frank Ricca. If anyone has seen him or knows where the police could catch Ricca — they aren't talking."

I imagined Frank Ricca's latest victim shackled to a wall, sleeping off the high of the drugs he force-fed her. *He won't keep her alive for much longer*, I thought. She was dead weight to him while he was on the lam from the law.

I rounded the U-shaped driveway of Tamara Sullivan's eye-popping mega mansion, illuminated by a ribbon of moonlight.

"Then let's not spend more time than we need with Tamara Sullivan. The death notification is only a formality. She wasn't that torn up about him when we spoke to her before. Why would she care if he's dead or alive? Love had long left their mega mansion."

"She might be asleep." André eyed the stone path leading to the wood-paneled front doors.

"I hate death notifications. Not once do they go without a hitch."

"Without a hitch? Really, Temple?" He curved a questioning brow.

"Oh, don't give me that judgy look. Some people don't want to be bothered with it. And it makes me uncomfortable when adults cry. I'm wasting time holding their hand when I should be on the street looking for the person who killed their loved ones." The motion lights turned on automatically, spiriting the darkness away.

I knocked several times. Tamara Sullivan appeared in a silky strappy dress that hit the floor and spread out from there. Her hair was glazed back in a small bun at the nape of her neck. A yellow-diamond tennis bracelet dangled from her wrist. She directed a malignant stare at me.

"Detectives?" She placed arms around her shoulders. "Is something the matter?"

"Can we come in? My partner and I need to speak with you." I peered behind her; the home seemed set up for a romantic evening, party of two.

"At this hour? I don't expect the news to be good. Is it Charlie? Because if he needs money to post bail — tell him I said he's barking up the wrong tree." She followed my eyes, tightening her grip on the door handle, pulling it near her hip to block my view of the lit candles. "I've planned a relaxing evening for myself. Soft music, a hot bubble bath, and an excellent bottle of vintage Bordeaux. For once, I'd like it if Charlie's dumb decisions don't spoil my plans."

The automatic lights in the yard shut off, transforming Tamara Sullivan into an ambiguous silhouette.

"I'm afraid it can't wait," I replied.

She threw open the door, swiveled around on her bare heels, and showed us to the living room. Tamara Sullivan pointed to her expansive beige couch.

"Anywhere you like, I suppose. Make yourself at home. I presume you're still on the clock, so I won't ask if you'd like a drink. If memory serves me right."

"We won't be staying long, ma'am." I unbuttoned my suit jacket.

Tamara Sullivan left us and returned a few minutes later wearing a heavy bathrobe. Her self-care evening had been ruined.

"I'm a first-rate fool for allowing you in my home again. Say what you're here to say and leave. Let me make it clear to you — Charlie stops coming to me for help. I'm exhausted from cleaning after him. Whatever crap he's involved in, I'm not entirely sure I want to hear about it." The air in the room grew cold.

"Mrs. Sullivan — it's my duty as a sworn police detective to inform you Charles Isles was discovered dead this evening," I told her and waited.

Unable to speak, Tamara Sullivan placed one hand over her chest. The other one covered her open mouth.

"Excuse me — what? You said Charlie's dead? My Charlie? What kind of bullshit is that? I don't believe you.

Another one of Charlie's impractical tricks to milk me for money."

I wouldn't swear on it, but something told me she wasn't really devastated over her husband's death. She was trying too hard to sell me grief and sadness . And she wasn't incredibly gifted in the faking department. But it's not a crime in this country to stop loving your spouse. And Charlie Isles had given Tamara Sullivan plenty of reasons to want out of their union.

"I'm sorry to be the bearer of bad news; unfortunately, yes, it's true, Charles Isles died at approximately eleven forty this evening."

"I'm speechless. Utterly speechless. It's unimaginable what this man has put me through, and I still have a soft spot for him in my heart."

"My partner and I found him in a motel pool in Chinatown. Did you know he was renting there month to month? Maybe it slipped your mind?"

"A motel in Chinatown — he's lost his mind. As I've told you, we opted to avoid each other. Our home is big enough, so that wasn't especially hard. What happened to him? I don't know why I really want to know."

"We performed CPR until paramedics arrived to revive him. Their efforts were unsuccessful. And nothing we did could bring him back."

A single lonely tear rolled down her cheek, her skin glistening under the candlelight. She was fussing with her diamond bracelet.

"Oh. Wow. WOW! Okay." Her voice trembled, but I felt note of ice in there.

"Legally — you're next of kin, Tamara. And we must inform you of his passing. Does he have other family members we can call?"

"I'm it." She fussed again with the bracelet, then finally left it alone. Straightened herself up, wiped any remnants of tears lodged in her eyes, and sniffled. "His folks cut ties with him ages ago. Things from before. No reason to bring back the past. I was the last one standing beside him. But even I had to face the music. Charlie was never going to change. Once the accusation of money gone missing from the company made the rounds, I told him it was over between us. We fought over it. Eventually, he left." A defeated smile colored her lips. "Lying was part of him, it was who he was. Years ago, I'm sure you know, other women. Gosh. He was a fool. The damage the Sullivan brand sustained because he dipped his pen in the company ink." Tamara leaned backward against the snug cushions and put a hand on her forehead. She shut her eyes but allowed one more tear to escape.

"What a coward that husband of mine. To swindle that much cash, bankrupt The Groove Factory, and leave me to pay off his debts. Are you sure he didn't stage it — the murder? Maybe he's jetting off to the Caribbean to spend the rest of his life living in luxury? God damn you bastard. I hope your soul never finds rest."

"He's dead, ma'am. We're sure of it. Why do you think he stole the money for himself? He told us he loved The Groove Factory. That he was good at running it." I spotted the slightest quiver in her shoulders under the weight of her bathrobe.

"Once a thief, always a thief. Who else would do it? He had access, means, and opportunity, as the police say," Tamara replied.

I glanced at André, who had a probing glare directed at the now-widowed Tamara Sullivan. "He wasn't the only one with means, motive, and opportunity, was he, Mrs. Sullivan? Why would he hire Dana Miller?"

"Who is she? Never heard of her. What is her involvement with my husband?"

"Sorry, of course, I forgot you two split up. So insensitive of me. Charles hired Dana to dig up the money. Did he ever mention her report to you? Maybe he showed you a copy?"

"You've lost your freaking mind, detectives. If I knew where the money was, I'd go get it myself. I'd secure the finances better than my husband. Charlie was incredibly depressed, and shall I say confused about the next chapter in his life. Midlife crisis, I can only assume. If Charles hired this woman — Dana Miller or whatever her name is — he did it to make himself look like the good guy. Something to tell a bankruptcy judge. Make it look like he searched for the money but he only found a wall of shell companies leading to absolutely nowhere."

"You sound informed. Did he find a wall of shell companies?" I reached into my pocket and took out my notepad and pen.

"I'm only aware of what time it is. It's late. Two homicide detectives just informed me my troubled but beloved husband is dead. I must make some phone calls, inform people. I'd hate for the family to find out from the morning newspapers."

"Again, we're sorry for your loss. Don't mean to keep you. Last question — when was the last time you stopped by the office? You were listed as a consultant. Paid for your services."

"Honestly, I stopped going to the downtown office a long time ago. Couldn't show my face, not after Charlie was accused again of stealing. And you're wrong detective, Charles wasn't the only one who loved The Groove Factory. The business means as much to me as it did my husband if not more, because I'd never take a red cent from it. Please, I don't want to take any more of your time, you have a killer to catch. My husband's."

She showed us to the door. The butler had left for the night. But there were two tall glasses on the kitchen island, a single red rose by an open bottle of red wine.

"Expecting someone?" I nodded towards the wine.

One brow arched, she said softly, "Not really. Drive safe. The road becomes wet and slick at night time." She gestured to the door. Her eyes were locked on the edge of the night as if she was waiting for someone to stroll in and rescue her from us.

"One more thing before I forget — did your husband have a will that you knew of? Might come in handy to know who will inherit his share of the company."

"Best if we leave those questions for my lawyers. Charlie's dead, and as long as I have a say — The Groove Factory's a family business. I assure you I'm perfectly capable of managing it on my own. It's a financially healthy organization with plenty of clout in the entertainment industry. A solid name and build-to-last reputation. Despite the recent bad publicity, I believe the company will weather the storm."

"Your husband told us he couldn't make payroll. With twenty-eight million in the red. What will you do? Take a business loan?"

Tamara Sullivan unclipped her hair and flipped it sideways. "Typical Charlie. Always a complainer, a man with no vision or creativity to dream bigger and bolder."

"In that case — we discovered some boxes with papers your husband stored in his motel room. Groove Factory documents, I presume. It might help us understand what happened to your stolen millions. If you don't mind, we'd like to search his personal home office if he's got one here?"

"What good would that do? I'm not the queen of stupid, detective Stone. Whatever you're fishing for will have to wait until I consult with my lawyers." She pattered to the edge of the steps, her eyes long dried; Charles's already laid to rest in her mind, I imagined. "But if you don't mind, I'd like the boxes you found in my husband's room back. I can wake up someone from my staff to follow you to the police station, collect them from you?"

I buttoned up my suit jacket. "I'm afraid, Mrs. Sullivan, the boxes are official evidence in the homicide investigation of Charles Isles, which makes them the property of Boston PD until the case is solved, closed, or the DA decides otherwise." I gazed back at the tall glasses, bottle of wine, and lit candles. "You have a good rest of the night, now, ma'am. And again, I'm sorry for your loss."

Chapter 40

André and I didn't speak as we entered the deserted highway. My thoughts drifted to Charles Isles. His supposedly loving wife displayed no love lost for him. I decided she'd reached a place in their tumultuous relationship where loving him meant hating herself, and a clever woman like her couldn't bear it. Tamara Sullivan, I concluded, was nobody's fool, even if she tried to play one.

"What did I tell you? Death notifications — never without a hitch." The wipers glided against the wet windshield as I thought of Shelly sticking by me even if my time on Earth remained short.

"Hate admitting it, but you're right. Tamara Sullivan exhibited some initial shock. I suspect a part of her had expected one day we, or others like us, would visit her. Deliver the news. Charles Isles is dead. She certainly looked prepared for it. Didn't see a lot of wasted emotion. Practical. Economical. Some pain. Mostly over how he treated her. To her credit, he wasn't husband of the year. Cheating, lawsuits, bankruptcies. He put the big hurt on her."

"Didn't ask a lot of questions about her husband's death? She couldn't care less. Others in her shoes would want to know details, make arrangements, ask to see the body, begin to think of the funeral service. Not Tamara. No, sir. She did a lot of talking about The Groove Factory, getting the company straightened out. That's my take on it."

I continued, "She suggested Charles Isles faked the drowning to get away from the heat on him. Strange thing to imagine. Means, motive, and opportunity, she said of Charles taking the money from his company."

André stuck his thumb under his chin. "Yeah, true. She denied ever hearing about Dana Miller, but Charles Isles told Lola his wife kicked him out after she learned about Dana. Way I see it, Tamara Sullivan likes the smell of money and power. Strong motives for murder, what do you say? We've seen it done before by other calculating spouses. Could be the play here. And Frank Ricca? What do we do about him?" André asked as he typed a text.

"Not much we can do until we locate the hole he's lying low in. But I can't shake the feeling we're chasing two killers. Is Frank Ricca the Grim Reaper? The undertaker? I don't know. Look at Charles Isles's murder tonight. Body in a pool — mafia style. Sloppy comes to mind. And Dana Miller's killer wasn't sloppy. Cleaned her, prepared her for the underworld. The white dress makes more sense, don't you think? Pure, clean, free of the human world. The mask's also a connection, but I don't understand its meaning quite yet."

"Maybe you look too deep into things — symbols and signs. Maybe Ricca's fucking with us. The dress, the mask — props to show he's still got it. Still Frank Ricca, the scariest mafia Don on this side of the ocean. A warning to anyone who tries to remove him from power. Think about it. He runs the largest underground organized crime unit. Underworld's same as underground." André peered out the window, eyes locked on the consuming darkness.

"Same but different," I countered. "I want to speak with Vargas from SID again. Have him go through old cases associated with Frank Ricca and his top guys. See if he can find any similar cases to Dana Miller."

"Why can't you accept it's Frank Ricca? He killed Dana Miller because she would expose him in her report. And he drowned Charles Isles because he talked to you, told you the truth."

"But he didn't, André. When I brought up Frank Ricca, Isles clamped up. Shut down like a dead lightbulb. He only spoke to me when I hit him with Dana's messages. His failed promise to protect her," I pointed out. "Killing Dana Miller because of her report is not good enough. Isles was facing murder charges and he wouldn't flip on Ricca. No, Dana Miller died not because of her work, but because of where she worked. She came in contact with someone at The Groove Factory, and he grew obsessed with her. But why did he kill her and Brad Connolly? He could have killed her any other night. Stalked her house, stalked her at work. But he murders Dana when she's with Brad. Together. Happy. Celebrating. That's when Dana's stalker couldn't take it. The happily ever after," I said.

André and I didn't speak for some time.

"Why do you think Tamara Sullivan wanted the boxes from Isles's room so bad? Told you she'd send someone from her staff to collect them from the station," André mumbled. "Not collect her husband's body, like you said, but the boxes."

"I've been thinking about that too. Can't be sure until we go through them. But something tells me we'd be fools to underestimate how conniving Tamara Sullivan can be."

"But is she capable of murder?"

"The marriage was irrevocably destroyed. Tamara Sullivan kicked Isles out to the boulevard of broken dreams — Chinatown. And I think she's seeing someone new."

"You picked up on that too?"

"Yeah. I did. The wine, the candles — I'd say Mrs. Sullivan was expecting someone else to show up at her doorstep tonight."

The outskirts of Boston blossomed in the distance. A city adorned in a million and one tiny lights, shimmering under the midnight sky.

"Back at Central, I'll give Tamara Sullivan to Bradley Walker to run a full background on her. Let's get her story nailed down. I want him to go as far back as the first time she met Charles Isles. And see if we can find names for her lovers, some of them at least. She had them," I said.

"Bradley won't like that," André replied, fighting hard against exhaustion.

"He'll come around. I need her vetted fast. See what we are up against. Look for a connection between Tamara and Frank Ricca. She denies ever meeting him, but that's obviously a lie. A big one too. And she's smart, she felt our suspicion. Lawyered up pretty quickly."

"Who knows, maybe Oliver Buzzworth will defend her and you'll have a second go at him," André said with a laugh.

I shrugged. "Something else bothers me. In the interview, Charles Isles struck me as a slow-to-catch-on character, but even a broken clock's right twice a day. On the phone with me, Isles sounded as if he might have expected someone to take out a hit on his life. I couldn't put my finger on it until I saw him dead in the pool. Had he tried to tell me, but I didn't listen? Did I write him off like he wrote off Dana?"

"One day you will die from stressing too much. Why should it be on you if Frank Ricca took out Charles Isles? The bad blood between them started long before you and I entered the scene. Probably way before Dana Miller agreed to work for The Groove Factory. We aren't responsible for them. We're only cops, only humans," André said.

I pulled up to the curb next to André's darkened townhouse. As he stepped out, his next-door neighbor hurried to his idling Tesla, wearing purple scrubs.

"The rest will be up soon. I might get a few hours of sleep if the house stays quiet," André uttered, hopeful.

André had a family, people. I had Shelly, a new baby soon. My family would grow. Before Brad, Dana had no one and nothing but rules and loneliness. The surrender in her eyes haunted me when I was awake and when I was asleep. I envied André's disconnect from the victims. I couldn't do my job, chase after killers, if I shrugged off their pain. *And that's why I can't let go of Dana Miller's case. I feel sorry for her.*

He closed the door and leaned into the open window. "Hey, I almost forgot — Sheldon Curly, the head of the police union — said you have their full backing. They won't let the brass screw you on sick time, especially since it's the result of an injury on the job. He said to tell you to keep your chin up. In his eyes, you're a rock-solid cop. In all our eyes. You might be owed some compensation from the department and the city. He's looking into things for you."

He pushed off the car.

"One last thing," I said.

"Oh? Shall I go in and start a pot of coffee for us?"

I drew in a breath and let it out gradually. "No. Go ahead. I need to clear my head anyways. We'll renew the knockdown, drag-out fight for justice after some well-deserved rest."

Chapter 41

I made my way to Tessa Wu's morgue. Her assistant buzzed me in. I found the medical examiner in the autopsy room, wearing a heavy blue protective gown over olive scrubs.

With one hand, she worked a staple gun to close a shoulder blade to shoulder blade cut on a male splayed on the cold examination table.

Pleasant tones of birds chirping and wind humming in the woods pushed through her sound machine.

"Your timing's impeccable, detective." She lifted her head, eyes hidden behind thick goggles. "I'm just finishing up with your pool vic."

I approached, examining Charles Isles — the vic, as she had referred to him. I gave him a quick scan; his matted, long white hair, his face bloated, the shade of a purple tomato. The rest of the body resembled granite, chalky white, with deep bruises in spots around the legs, thighs, and some parts of his belly.

He had a tattoo of a leaping tiger on one arm, and right under it, three small gray-black Chinese symbols — no clue what they meant. A pin-up girl in a revealing outfit, winking as she straddled a grenade named 'Big Boy,' adorned his other arm.

I spotted the nicks on his knuckles and scratches inside the forearm. He wasn't in good physical shape before he died, I concluded. He carried about eighty pounds on him. Maybe the drinking, maybe the fast food we lifted from his rundown motel room.

"Dragging him from the pool was a living hell."

Wu nodded thoughtfully.

"He suffered from high blood pressure, which he most likely ignored. I checked with his PCP, who said Charles came in ten years ago for a physical." Wu removed the goggles and the cap. Her silky hair stayed up in a knotted bun.

I noticed the minimal makeup — black mascara, a puff of brownish stuff on her cheeks, and a dab of red lipstick.

"Date night? Tell him I owe him one for letting you work late."

She rolled her eyes to say 'as if.' "My parents' wedding anniversary. Fifty years. My brother and I took them to Strega."

"Strega? Prime rib and buttery mashed potatoes. Fancy people."

"It was really wonderful to get the whole family together. With work and life stuff, we don't do many Sunday suppers anymore."

"You were one of those kids — Mom helped with homework, Dad fixed your bike. Sunday afternoon — throw a ball in the backyard, let the dog chase his tail."

"Can't pretend they weren't great. Pretty impressive parents actually. And loving. And attentive. It wasn't idyllic. Everyone has something going on, but yeah, my childhood was close to picture perfect.

"Maybe that's why it's taking me so long to take the plunge and get married. Because they made a relationship look effortless. Unhurried. Always there for each other. Which hasn't been my experience. Dating in Boston is not effortless and most definitely hurried. You seem solid with your wife. Think you'll be ringing in the fifty?"

I quieted. Fifty? According to Doctor Hoffman, I might not make it to the birth of my child.

Wu caught on. She lifted a tray of surgical tools and submerged them in a chemical disinfectant.

"Hey! What can I tell you doc, I'm a lucky man. Don't know why Shelly ever said yes to go out with me; it must've been in a moment of weakness. But as long as she wants me, I'm jumping for joy."

"Well, your vic wasn't doing much jumping of any kind before his death. His X-rays show bone fractures caused by the excessive weight. The bone density indicates he gained all that weight rapidly. Fast — within months. You're looking at four to six, around then. His body took a toll in the last inning."

"Matches the time frame. His bundle of trouble began with the discovery of misappropriated funds; domino effect after that. He could have hit the drive-throughs — stress eater, or because the food was easy, cheap. He gorged on cheeseburgers and coke every meal. What about the injuries to the knuckles? Too small to be defensive."

"You are correct. He never attempted to fight his attacker. Those are from the pool. He scraped his hand when he fell into the water. Based on their position, it's my conclusion he slammed his hand against the interior wall of the pool. I found embedded particulates in the wounds. Waiting for the lab results to confirm my findings.

"Something else I uncovered that's interesting — bruises from cuffs. His killer had them on him for several hours, not as long as Dana's. Can't say for sure if it's the same cuffs, but the pattern's a match."

She showed me an enlarged image on the video monitor.

"He was a big guy. Makes sense why he didn't fight back. The cuffs stopped him from defending himself. Like Dana Miller. Tox screen?" I pointed to Wu's computer.

"None. Alcohol. He had a few glasses of something. Not drugs. And his severed finger was removed while he was alive."

"What's your official ruling?"

She gave me the ME report. "See for yourself."

My eyes searched for the COD box. Zoomed in.

"This was a homicide, detective. Your guy died of asphyxiation. The killer held Isles's head under water until he stopped breathing." Wu rolled the sheet over the Y-shaped cut on his chest and stopped right below the neck.

"I found the presence of pool water in his lungs, enough to make me believe the vic struggled for some time. And it took a lot of force to keep him under. See the pooling of blood on his back here and here." Another photo on the screen. "It indicates his attacker used an excessive amount of force to keep him down. I imagine Mr. Isles thrashed in the pool like a fish in a net."

"Canvassing the neighborhood produced no reports of ruckus. No one saw or heard Charles arguing with anyone. After he left the fish market gambling hall, he vanished, until he turned up dead in the motel pool. Something else has been bothering me the whole time about Charles Isles — it goes back to the night I tried to rescue him.

"André and I initiated chest compressions immediately after we called it in. I was up first, pumping his chest to restart his heart. There was something off about it, unlike other vics I've worked on. I figured it was me, tired and weak from working overtime. He was hard as a rock."

"For the record, by the time you got to Charles Isles, nothing could've been done to bring him back — unless you know how to turn back the hands of time. He had expired anywhere between thirty to forty minutes prior. And the swampy pool you found him in wasn't where he died."

I looked at her, running through other possible locations in my mind. Where else? I missed something. But what?

Wu rested her hand on a rolling cart with test tubes, flasks, and weird-looking glass bottles.

"Maybe this will help you." Wu nodded at a small tube with azure liquid. "Drained it from his lungs — water."

"Water? That color?"

"Yeah. Water mixed with sapphire-blue dye. You add it to a pool to give the water a specific color. And this is a custom job. Produced by a company in New York. A personalized color is not cheap. It takes an extra someone to shell out that kind of dough for their pool water." Wu shed her white coat.

"I've seen a pool like that," I said. "Ground floor of a mega mansion."

I saw her clearly in my mind — a femme fatale emerging from the water, dripping wet, sipping a glass of whisky, the expensive kind. Minutes before her butler had let me in to collar her husband for murder.

Chapter 42

"Alright, alright, here's what we have so far," I said. One by one, Lem and André filed into my office. "Tessa Wu found pool water in Charles Isles's lungs."

"Yeah, so? He drowned," André cut in.

"Based on her findings, Charles Isles drowned in a different pool."

"Where?" André shuffled his feet, intrigued.

"The pool you recently admired," I said as I pointed at him with the dry-erase marker. I wrote a name on the murder board. "Okay. It's official. Isles was killed in Tamara's gigantic pool. The company she used to customize the color of the water fed us her name. It's a positive match for the water Wu drained from Charles Isles," I said.

"She convinced no one with her act. No acting chops. I've seen gang bangers put on a better show than Tamara Sullivan," André told us.

"There's about twenty miles of highway between her home and Chinatown. She couldn't have killed her husband, transported the body to Chinatown, and returned home to answer the door for us," I said. "To pull it off, someone must have helped her. Transported the body." I examined the crime report from that night.

"They tossed the room and tried to lift something from the boxes in the bathroom," André added.

"Wu also discovered cuff marks on his wrists. Like Dana Miller. But the medical examiner couldn't tell me if they matched. She thinks Isles was held captive for less time than Dana Miller."

"Without your hands, you can't defend yourself," André pointed out.

"What do you want to do? Take Tamara Sullivan into custody?" Lem chimed in.

"Soon. But I'd like some more clarity on a few outstanding issues. And I think Isles's texts will help us," I said and lifted a folder off my desk. "The last person Isles texted before he died was Frank Ricca." I handed a copy to Lem and André.

André read, "Fine. You win. Wish you both happiness."

Lem read the reply, "Keep your mouth shut or I'll cut off something else."

Then it was my turn. "How many more must die? The Grim Reaper? You knew." We studied each other. Frank Ricca had sent no other replies. And from what I knew, a few short hours later Charles Isles had been murdered in his wife's pool.

"Isles recognized the mask in the interview but said nothing. His lawyer's on Ricca's payroll. But Isle brought up the mask on the phone with me."

"And he never gave you a name...why would he? He hated Ricca, was supposedly wrecked over Dana Miller's murder, and yet he said nothing." Lem threw his arms in the air.

Facing the murder board, I stared at the photo of Charles Isles, remembering our conversation. "He said someone's coming. Ricca's men were watching him. Maybe he wanted to confront Ricca first. But why? Why would he do it? It seems to me he wanted to stand up to Ricca. The mafia boss is a notorious bully." I clicked the cap back onto the marker and put it down. "There could be countless reasons why Isles didn't snitch, but we can't let that distract us." I took down Dana Miller's photo. Held it. Mid-length brown hair, some honey-blonde highlights. Quiet. Reserved and responsible. Had to act like an adult after her father died in the car accident. No breaks for her in life.

I said to them, "Isles might have realized who killed Dana Miller, and I will too. It's obvious Isles didn't suspect Ricca in her murder, judging by their final messages. It was someone else. Someone close to Ricca. Another person. As perverted as Ricca, but who stays out of sight."

"There you go again. Different day, same tune. Based on what? Isles sent a single text to Ricca questioning the mask. No name mentioned. Ricca could still be Dana's killer. He could have murdered Isles to shut him up," André countered, elbows resting on his bouncing legs.

Lem stood up and circled to my desk. "The lab hit a match on the embalming fluid. It's a factory out in the Midwest, serving the New England region. Mostly smaller funeral homes. The company person I spoke to at their regional office faxed me a list of funeral homes. A total of one hundred and sixty-two."

"Crap. Too many to go door-to-door. We will need to narrow down the parameters," I said, checking out the list.

"I mentioned to the manager that the killer used a fruity bath to wash the victim. Asked him if he was familiar with the solution. Turns out his company sells that too. But it's expensive. Not all companies buy it. So he faxed me a second list."

"That's good police work Lem. Forty-nine," I mumbled. "The killer works for one of these forty-nine. Let's divide them. André, how is Vargas doing? Any luck linking one of Ricca's cases to Dana Miller? Couple gone missing together?"

"He agreed to check, but he won't. And who could fault him? Grunt work. Waste of time. His team has the itch bad for Ricca. And we should too."

At that moment, Bradley Walker knocked. "Tamara Sullivan background as you requested." He tossed the file on my desk and rushed for the door.

"Run it by me," I said in a stern voice.

"Fine." He cracked his knuckles, giving me a death stare. "The lady is flat broke, but you would never know it by how much she spends. Her trust fund dried up a long time ago. Years ago. Her husband's supporting her lousy ass, but I think she spent more than he gave her."

"What makes you say that?" I searched for the evidence in his report.

"I found three boats in her name, one house in Umbria, that's in Italy, and a villa in Madrid, Spain. Her husband's name is not on any of the deeds. Weird, right?" He cleared his throat.

"So she has a spending habit. We can't arrest her for that," André said.

"Four months ago she took out three large life policies on her husband. One's for six million, one for eight, and one for ten."

I didn't reply for a beat as I mulled over the evidence in front of me. Tamara Sullivan had kicked out Charles Isles after learning about Dana Miller investigating the company's finances. Probably to put pressure on him to fire Dana Miller. But he didn't. Dana probably told Isles about the insurance policies, the European homes, the boats. She told him about his wife's lavish lifestyle behind his back. It started to make more sense why Isles had wanted the final report so badly. To show the court. To sue his wife. And if Tamara stole the twenty-eight million, Dana's report could send her to jail.

But what about Frank Ricca? What was his role in this whole mess?

Maybe Tamara had told us. The night we notified her of Charles's murder. She showed no grief for him. But she spoke of The Groove Factory. How she'd turn it around. Keep it going. I had asked her about taking out a loan. Who would give it to her? She couldn't have been less concerned. I suspected Frank Ricca would feed her cash, just like he did with her husband. And with Isles dead and out of the way, Dana Miller murdered, her report seemingly missing — who would stop Tamara and Frank Ricca?

"You said four months ago she insured Charles Isles?"

"Yeah. Three policies making her the beneficiary," Bradley Walker said.

"But Charles Isles waited another three months to hire Dana Miller. Why did he wait? We are missing something. The catalyst that started it all. What pushed Charles Isles to bring on Dana Miller? Something else must have happened that's not here?"

"I don't know if this will help you, but Tamara owns the house. Paid for the land in cash; contractors, architects — all cash transactions," Bradley said, sticking his hands in his pockets.

"How much?" I asked.

"Nine mil for the land alone and seven more she put in the house."

André's phone chirped. He answered it. Talked fast. Hung up. Gave me a nod like cops do when they receive a tip.

"The tech unit downloaded a trove of documents from Isles's computer. It seems he was less paranoid about security than Dana Miller."

They left shortly after. I sat back in my chair, seeing all the moving parts coming together. Not lining up exactly. But I understood the landscape — Charles Isles suspected his wife stole the twenty-eight million, but he needed the proof. He hired Dana Miller, one of the best forensic accountants around. Paid her double. She dug up Frank Ricca, the mafia laundering money using

The Groove Factory. Tamara Sullivan and Frank Ricca had a side hustle going. But Dana's report could spoil their plan. So what could they do? I believe if Charles Isles had left things alone, backed off, quietly divorced Tamara, he might still be alive today. But I paused considering Dana's faith. Finally, I decided she would have been killed not because of what she knew but where she worked. Someone saw her. She probably reminded him of another woman. Stalked her. Fantasized about her. It had freaked Dana out. Even if she distanced herself from The Groove Factory, I speculated, her killer would have found her and killed her anyway.

The white dress, the Grim Reaper mask, the drained blood, the embalming fluid — it would all point to the killer, I reminded myself.

Charles Isles had already figured it out. He knew Ricca killed and killed to terrify you, but Dana's murder is not Ricca's. Who? I looked at a photo of Charles Isles pinned on the murder board. "Where did you see the Grim Reaper mask? One of Ricca's men? Has to be." I walked to the door. "Lem."

"Yeah?"

"Get me the names of everyone we know who has a link to Ricca."

"You want pimps and low-level drug dealers too?"

"No, start with his inner circle. The ones he trusts. Someone connected to Ricca killed Dana Miller, but he's letting us think it's Frank Ricca. We need to find him, and we need to do it soon. We're running out of time," I said as I lifted my phone and saw an alert reminding me of my appointment with the heart doctor.

Chapter 43

I sucked sugary juice from a straw, shaking off my sluggish thoughts as I waited for Doctor Hoffman to see me.

"Get me another one of these if you see the nurse," I told Shelly.

Feet propped on the back of two chairs, she replied, "Still a 'no' on Charlotte? I think Emma's okay, and Harper's not quite what I had in mind for a girl's name."

"So, it's decided — we're having a girl. Isn't that something the doctor should confirm and not your crazy cousin down in Alabama?"

"Laugh all you want, but Morgan's so good at that stuff. She predicted the gender of every baby in our family and her husband's. The ring trick works," she declared. "I did it three times. Girl. Every time. So, Charlotte or Harper?"

I spotted a nurse in pink scrubs and waved my empty juice box in the air.

"Neither. Charlotte sounds spoiled, and Harper's what you call it — trendy. I want my baby girl to have a strong name because she'll be pretty like her mama," I blew a kiss to Shelly, "and stubborn like her dada."

"Okay. Let's see what Google gives us when I put in a wise-ass husband — well, well, well — a picture of you. What do you know?

"I don't hear any suggestions from you, and the baby's due soon. You are, aren't you baby girl? Mamma feels like a giant tent." Shelly glanced at me, pleading. "I miss seeing my toes. I don't think I'll ever see the bottom half of my body."

"'Course you will, darling."

Doctor Hoffman appeared by my bedside holding my medical chart in one hand, the other partially tucked in the pocket of her white coat.

"Good morning, Mr. And Mrs. Stone — how is the patient feeling? Any persistent coughing or prolonged blurred vision?"

"If I get more hydration, I'll be significantly less grumpy. Other than that, I feel alright."

Hoffman walked to a nursing cart and handed me an apple juice.

"Pregnancy seems to be progressing nicely. Due date is nearing."

"You really think so, Doctor Hoffman? Oh, I hope you're right. I can't take it anymore. No one tells you the third semester's the longest. Time's standing still. Anxiety and excitement take turns wrecking my psyche. Both of which fill me with dread of the unknown."

"It's normal to feel this way."

"See Shells, you're not a bad mother for having those emotions. I tell her that all the time, doctor."

"If those emotions start holding you back from completing your daily activities and you can't find joy — speak to your doctor. They'll be able to tell you what to do, run tests. But I think the anxiety, the excitement, and whatever else you said — the dread of the unknown — the rest of us simply refer to as — motherhood."

Hoffman angled her head towards me. "And how about you? Any feelings of dread I should be aware of?"

"None connected to the state of my health."

"That's good to hear. I looked over your last round of labs. The urine production has improved. It tells me your kidneys are able to move the volume of waste. Your body's been filtered from the toxins. The treatment plan's working."

Shelly clapped enthusiastically. "Doctor Hoffman — this is not a joke? Does that mean you won't have to cut him open?"

"No joke. The honest truth. I will keep you on the meds you're on. They seem to help you in general." Hoffman pressed her cold stethoscope against the horizontal scar on my chest. She listened to my heart. "Persistent murmur on the right side of your heart. Not what I like to hear, especially in your case."

Shelly kissed me and reached for my hand. I gave her fingers a slight tug and a hold-it-together squeeze. Far from joyous, Hoffman crossed her arms and waited for Shelly to settle beside me on the edge of the examination bed.

"As we discussed before, the bullet fragment is not going anywhere. It has to come out. Yes, your labs look good-ish. But you're not healed. And now might be our last chance to get in there," she pointed to my heart, "and remove the sucker. Repair the damage to your heart. You're a young man. You can have a full life, see your kid grow up. But we must act."

"How come I feel better? The headaches are gone. I swear I think I put on some weight. Energy's back," I said.

"The meds have carried the brunt of the load. Think of them as heavy-lifting helpers."

"Can't be all meds and machines, doc? Maybe the bullet's not moving. Lodged somewhere and wants to stay there. It doesn't hurt. My dad used to say why fix something if it's not broken."

"Your heart's broken, sir. Oh yes, it is. It's the miracle effect of the modern-day meds, I'm afraid, Mr. Stone. Your condition hasn't been cured. The pills are only a," she placed X-rays under a lamp, used her pen to show me the fragment, "patch. It's like slapping a Band-Aid on a leaking dam. When the dam bursts, oh and it will, expect a flood of Biblical proportions. I won't be able to repair you."

"Ugh-mmm, I feel dizzy. So, what then? Now what are we supposed to do? How bad are we talking?" Shelly impatiently tugged on her ear.

"The original thought was to admit your husband to the hospital. Perform a complicated heart surgery. Experimental. The position of the fragment makes the procedure especially risky. And your husband's heart is already compromised from his previous surgeries. My other two patients survived, but they were in better shape than your husband.

"And, we lost time we can't get back waiting for you to heal. I've looked at your case from every angle — your age, under forty, is a bonus; the fact that you don't smoke or drink is also a plus. What worries me is your present occupation. Stress kills far healthier people than you every day, Mr. Stone, and you have a noncompliant streak."

"I won't argue there. Being a cop's what I do, all I know how to do. Every day a dead woman on my murder board stares at me, asking why I haven't caught and punished the monster responsible for her death. Her fiancé's too.

"The victims' families want, deserve, justice, and I'm all they have. It's not a question of whether I want to live — 'course I do," I stared at Shelly holding back tears, "but once a murder cop, always a murder cop. You can't change fate."

After taking a second to contemplate, Hoffman replied, "I suppose I can see your point. I've known I was going to be a doctor since I was a kid performing heart transplants on my dolls. And quitting medicine would surely put me in an early grave. Let's not change fate — just slightly alter it."

She handed me a script. "I'm putting you on some trial drugs. Fair warning — there are nasty side effects — bad night sweats, exhaustion, double vision, and low blood pressure. But if they work and we get your heart rate up, fix the murmur, then you improve your odds. Remember, no amount of drugs will fix you. I'm afraid you have maybe another few days before some ambulance drops you at the ER. If that ever happens, your only other option's a heart transplant. And where will you get one from? People wait months, years for a heart, so don't wait that long for someone else's; fix yours while you still can."

"I'm scared, Temple. I'm freaking out. What will I do? The baby?" Shelly frowned.

Hoffman chuckled. "Things are piling on. I get it. Keep your blood type in mind. That's another major complication for you, detective."

"What's wrong with your blood?" Shelly whipped back her head, demanding an explanation.

I couldn't face my wife.

Hoffman stepped in to explain. "His blood's the real kick in the pants. I've put feelers out to colleagues around the country asking for blood donors — but it's a long shot. We all have patients we don't want to lose, and the blood shortage is real."

"Gloom and doom, then." Shelly sniffled. "Temple — I can't raise our baby alone."

Hoffman nodded at us. "I'll give you two some space. My office will be in touch."

After Hoffman left, I put my arm around Shelly, stroking her face and hair. "Day by day Shells. We take it day by day."

Before I stopped at my desk, I hit the break room and made myself a fresh pot of coffee. Gina popped in.

"The queen of mean dropped by asking for you. Told her to hit the road, but I gathered she might make an appearance again soon. Wait. Where did she go?"

I poured myself a cup and took a big sip. "Who?"

"The woman from the fish market. She was just here. I told her to wait for you. Gave her a water."

"Lola's her name. She was looking for me? Did she say why?"

Gina shrugged. "She barely said two words to me. Asked to speak with you. When I told her you're not in yet, she tried to bolt. I thought she might be someone you've been trying to track, so I offered her a seat here. The homicide unit can be stressful for some civilians."

"You did the right thing."

I rushed to my desk. Not a trace of Lola. "Damn it," I uttered as I dashed down the stairs.

"Garry, Josh — you heading out?"

"Yes, sir," Garry, a street cop, said.

"Do me a favor — keep your eyes open for this woman. Kai-Ming. She goes by Lola. Left Central about five to ten minutes ago. Possibly on foot. Or a bike. Alone. Try to make contact, but don't detain. She's a witness in one of my murder cases."

They left in a squad car. I crossed Trenton Street to a park. Saw some benches, patches of grass, and swings. Not a whole lot of people. I canvassed the park, hitting a dead end. Showed Lola's photo to some food-truck cooks on a smoke break. They told me no woman matching the photo had been around.

About to give up, I spotted a kneeling woman wearing black linen pants and a gray hoodie, petting a small white dog tied to a streetlight.

She waved goodbye to the yapping furball when I was close enough to make a positive visual.

"Lola?"

Startled, she flinched. "Detective. I meant to come back."

"Even if you didn't — I'm glad I found you."

"I tried waiting for you, but I started to feel paranoid. My father would flip out if someone told him I'm speaking to the police."

"Why?"

"He doesn't trust strangers. Thinks everyone's out to get us. Wants my brother and me in front of his eyes at all times, like we're helpless children."

"It can't be easy to have a life of your own. See people. Do normal things people your age do."

Lola studied the line of passing cars. "It isn't. And you sound very much like someone I cared for deeply." She sighed. "I feel awful for what happened to Charles. And I lied to you."

"It's okay. We'll take down Charles Isles's killer. It's not a matter of if, but of how soon."

"Then I hope this helps your investigation." She passed over a legal-size yellow envelope addressed to her. Charles Isles was listed as the sender.

"It came in the mail yesterday. I haven't opened it. I couldn't really — I saw Charles's name on there, and you understand. I thought it might be important, might help you catch the killer. He never mentioned sending me anything before he died."

She waved a meek goodbye.

In Central, I dialed Callum Baker's internal line. "Come down now — Charles Isles sent us a package from beyond the grave."

A reflection of a shadow spilled on the wall as I readied to hang up. Meredith Sawyer slowly shut the door behind her and swayed herself to a chair.

"Got him," Sawyer said, flashing me a smirk like a black-mailer who has the upper hand.

Chapter 44

"But first," Meredith Sawyer crossed her legs, "I need something from you."

"Imagine my surprise," I replied as I covered Lola's package with paperwork from my desk.

"Is it true the dead male from Chinatown is Charles Isles? And don't lie to me."

"It is," I admitted.

She leaned back, watching me carefully with her dark eyes, thinking of something to say. "Okay. Murdered?"

"Yes. And before you ask — I have a suspect, but I can't give you his name."

She waved her hand in the air. "Connection to the dead woman in Franklin Park?"

"Maybe. Some think there might be," I said, scanning the bullpen.

"But you don't. What do you want with Pelican Bay? How does a dummy company tie in to two murders?" She unclasped her purse.

I stood up and walked to the window. It was a sunny day, spring in full bloom. "That I can't tell you. It's confidential. If I give it to you, I'm compromising the progress I've made." I stepped forward towards her. "I keep my word, Miss Sawyer. Once I have the killer in custody, you'll be the first to know. Now you were saying you have intel you'd like to share."

She let out a frustrated sigh. "You're testing my patience, Stone. For whatever reason, I have a soft spot in my callous heart for your gray eyes, but I can't keep giving you preferential treatment. I have a reputation to uphold, and that reputation is on the line right now. Because of you."

"I'm close, okay? I can feel I'm getting closer to the killer. You won't have to wait long. Just between us, there is an internal battle of minds in BPD. A power struggle. Some think the same killer committed both murders. Others don't, if I make myself clear. Pelican Bay? What can you tell me?"

She didn't reply, taking her sweet time, messing with me.

"Lookit, lady," I directed her attention to the picture of Dana Miller and Brad Connolly on the night of their engagement, "there's something we decided not to release to the media. To prevent widespread panic in the city."

"I knew it!" She clapped her hands like she won candy night playing bingo.

"Dana Miller was bled dry by her killer," I said.

"Say what?" Shock registered in her flickering eyes.

"After he took her blood, he loaded her with embalming fluid to give her that dead-but-not-dead appearance."

"Fuck off. Nice try, you asshole. I'm not buying it." Meredith Sawyer laughed and closed her purse.

I handed her a copy of the medical examiner's report from Dana Miller's autopsy. Let her read it.

"I'm not lying. We don't know how many more he's killed. But he's killed others. Murdered Dana's fiancé. Brad Connolly. Slashed his throat, burned his body in his BMW. The body was so badly damaged, we couldn't let his family ID him. We used dental records to confirm." I sat down beside her, leaned closer. "Brad was found by state police in a field managed by Pelican Bay. You're a smart woman. You can see how Pelican Bay's not lining up. Still don't believe me?"

I stared at her. "I have photos of Brad's autopsy. Real ugly to see. Seared flesh, exposed bones. Want to see?"

"I think that's quite alright actually, Detective Stone. For once, I believe what you're saying is true." She took a copy of a business license from her purse and let me have it. It was filled out personally by someone I had considered but hoped to be wrong about.

"I was going to give you the runaround. Tell you I have nothing on Pelican Bay. Release the inside information when I went live with the story." She regained her composure. "But after what you told me about — him — their killer... Go get him so we can fry him for his crimes."

As Meredith Sawyer left, André Jones entered before my butt hit the chair.

"You both look like you were on the losing end of a shitty fight."

"Sawyer's alright. Not as crazy as some of the others. What do you have?"

He placed a file on his lap. "Remember the tech unit downloaded a trove of files from Charles Isles's computer?"

"Yeah?"

Before he discussed Charles further, my partner handed me a poster for blood donors wanted with my name and picture on it. I nearly flatlined from embarrassment. "Shelly dropped off a bunch. Gina is spamming the entire station. Making calls to every precinct in the city. She'll go statewide next if she has to. Should I even ask why you didn't tell me you're this bad?"

"There might not be a cure. If I'm dying, and it's most likely going to happen, I thought, if only I put away one more killer, then I could leave the world a little safer for my wife — " I broke off to study three house sparrows nestled on the windowsill. After a minute, I continued, "and unborn baby. My sacrifice is for them and the victims."

"Noble. And stupid. But I won't lecture. It's my fault. I should've been there for you. Have your back."

"Doing this job, I've learned that risk is part of it. Running into a dicey situation blindfolded because the evidence told you to go there. Suddenly something switches. Fast. On a dime. You couldn't have predicted he'd shoot me because hell, you couldn't have. I'm alright, okay? Back to Dana Miller's case. Coffee?"

André cupped the mug with two hands. "Uh-huh. Fair warning. It's a lot of numbers, charts, and what have you. Written in a technical language I don't speak. We had to phone the finance guys to walk us through most of it."

In silence, I examined the document.

"She reached out to him and only him. Reliable to the bitter end," I mumbled. "Dana Miller was there to prove someone embezzled money. And right up to her dreamy trip to Paris with her boyfriend, fiancé actually, Dana Miller did exactly that. She emailed Charles Isles her report the Friday before she left. Last night at the office. Then, as we suspected — she was killed. Bloodless ran out of time with her. Acted on impulse, but he had planned her murder. Saw it in his mind's eye every day she came into the office."

The report contained mostly Excel sheets, graphs, numbers of accounts. An elaborate maze of money gone missing; Dana eventually tracked down every stolen dollar.

"Dana Miller traced the funds to offshore accounts controlled by Pelican Bay — with holdings in the Caribbean, some in Switzerland, and a few in Asia. Diverse portfolio. Practically untraceable. But Dana stayed on the trail, kept it up until she solved the maze. The money bounced around the world then returned to the States, smaller amounts in multiple accounts. The last deposit was made one week before Dana started to investigate. Tamara Sullivan's listed on the domestic accounts.
"

"His wife was sucking the company dry. Blamed Charles for the whole mess. Makes you feel bad for the guy, doesn't it?" André stirred his coffee. "And I bet it wasn't hard to do. To start the rumor about him, I mean. He had a serious record. Jail time.

"We couldn't find out who owns Pelican Bay in Dana's report. And I'm told Dana was an excellent forensic accountant. Her work speaks for itself. Maybe the FBI can assist us there."

"Meredith Sawyer dropped off a gift for us," I said.

André examined the business license. His lips curved into a winning smile. "Told you Frank Ricca's behind the murders. We can pin all three bodies on him. Let's call Vargas. He could stand to hear some good news."

André reached for my phone, but I placed my hand over it. "Before you go ahead and make a department-wide announcement, I'd like to take some detectives with me and search the fields on the list. The ones Pelican Bay has under contract with the state."

"What do you expect to find?" André scoffed.

"More bodies. The ME suggested the killer had experience. Master-level skills. He collapsed Dana's lung with a single stab. Aren't you at least a little bit curious how many are buried somewhere in there? If Frank Ricca's the killer, he'll get the needle for this."

In the bathroom, I swooshed some water in my mouth before I dampened my face with a paper towel. Frowning to myself, I ran over the newly uncovered evidence in my head. Dana Miller's report exposed Tamara Sullivan stealing from Charles Isles. She fleeced him to the tune of twenty-eight million. The European homes, boats, the mega mansion she lived in — all bought and paid for by her dead husband. I bet she was already pushing to cash in on the three life insurance policies she took out on him.

Greed had played a major role in the murder of Charles Isles after all.

As I had imagined, Dana had discovered Pelican Bay, but her report didn't list an owner for the company. Meredith Sawyer had provided me with the identity — Frank Ricca.

As of now, it seemed Frank Ricca and Tamara Sullivan played Charles Isles, planned to kill him, to remove him from The Groove Factory permanently. But for what reason? After some consideration, I decided they each must have had their own motive. What bonded them together was their lust for money and power.

What I struggled to make sense of was Dana Miller's murder. How did she figure into their plan? If Tamara feared what Dana's report could do to Ricca and her, maybe she told the mafia Don to murder the accountant. There I hit a wall. If Ricca killed Dana to protect himself, to protect Tamara — why would he drain her blood and embalm her? Why leave her on a stage in a public park, wearing a white dress and a Grim Reaper mask? Every element of her murder told me her killer desired to show off his work — Dana.

But I wondered how I would convince the rest to see it as I did. Frank Ricca was their man. And he was guilty of many crimes, murders too; only he didn't kill Dana and her fiancé Brad.

I returned to my office, thinking. Patterns shift, change, emerge, and break, I concluded. Gina had left me two aspirins next to a bottle of water and an apple

Danish. A bright-blue note on my screen asked me to phone Callum Baker.

Before I made any calls, I tossed the aspirins in my mouth with some water. The Danish looked tasty, but I had no appetite.

Callum Baker answered promptly. "Are you at your computer? Check your email."

"What's this about?"

"Smart woman that lady Lola to bring you the envelope."

"That sounds promising."

"Good things come in small packages. Lots of fingerprints — matching your vic — Charles Isles. And the woman — Lola. Nothing else. Clean. The shipping label is legit. Authentic. I spoke with the Postal Service, and they gave me the location of the blue box where Isles deposited the envelope. Hang on."

I heard the noise of pages moving around.

"Washington and Essex."

"That's only a block from the fish market Lola's dad owns. Charles could have walked there."

"Next, we examined the flap — no one tampered with it. Edges sealed. We lifted some DNA off the glue strip."

"And?"

"Positive for the dead male vic. Looking at the physical evidence — Charles Isles made sure he personally handled the envelope. Didn't let anyone else touch it."

"Paranoid about its content. Chose a blue box over the Postal Service. He mailed the envelope to the one person he trusted — Lola. He was drawn to her innocence," I speculated.

"Again. I think you're correct, detective. The vic kept the envelope safe and clean for four months before he mailed it."

"Four months. That brings us to around the time he moved into the motel after his wife and he broke up." I rubbed a thumb over my lips. "Okay. What? What did he mail to Lola?"

"Sending visuals to you right now."

I refreshed my email. Callum Baker's message appeared at the top. No header. Only three attachments.

My ego bruised, I mumbled, "I expected as much."

"Hmm, you okay, Temple? I figured you'd be more — I don't know — enthusiastic. You've been hammering this homicide from each and every angle for weeks."

"It's fine. Good work, Callum. Strong evidence. Can you authenticate them?" I asked, feeling drained as I fired off a text to André and Lem. *Got them both on film.*

Baker cleared his throat. "Already done. High quality. Real. The photographer used a long-range lens. Excellent stability. Most likely a Canon EF100 or something similar. It seems your vic was playing detective on his own. Hired someone for the job. Someone experienced."

"Yeah. A pro. And those don't come cheap. It's quite possible the images confirmed what he already suspected."

The elevator doors parted. André stepped out and gunned it straight for me.

I thanked Baker and hung up.

"Got the text. What?"

"Look at what Baker lifted from the envelope Charles Isles sent Lola."

André glared at the monitor, then shot me a sharp look.

I banged my fist on the desk. "And he sat on them for four months before he used them."

"Life insurance on him." André went around my chair.

"Makes sense now why Isles hired Dana Miller. He would have used her report and these photos — Tamara Sullivan banging Frank Ricca — to bury them," I said. "Send Bradley Walker and some uniforms to bring in Tamara Sullivan. You link up with Vargas. Any movement on Frank Ricca — I want to know. Lem and I will clear the fields on the list. This ends today."

Chapter 45

There wasn't much time to spend at home. I was wearing a pair of jeans and a gray tee. Tossed on my windbreaker and my Sox cap.

"Temple — we should talk?" Shelly leaned against a wall in the walk-in closet as I rummaged for clean socks.

"Not now, hun. I finally nailed them. The wife and her mafia lover. It all came together fast last night." I shoved my feet into my boots.

Shelly handed me the Homicide badge hanging from the dresser mirror. "I understand. You speak for the dead. Stand up for them. And you're one of the best, if not the best."

I kissed her forehead and held her in my arms.

Outside, the weather was sticky and hot. The cool spring weather had melted into a suffocating July. As I slid behind the wheel, I glanced at the Chevy. The hood was still partially open. It made me think of Thatcher, our neighbor, inspecting it without my permission. And Shelly had said he discovered something, hadn't she? But what?

Thatcher answered the door wearing only his pajama bottoms. I saw the restrained anger under the tight smile.

"Top of the morning to you, Temple. How kind of you to stop by."

A little boy no older than three, holding the Hulk, poked his head behind Thatcher and wrapped his hand around his father's leg.

I owed Thatcher an apology. It wasn't his fault my life was turned upside down. In fact, he'd pitched in, stepped up to help my wife, when clearly, he had a full plate of his own.

"About before...I wanted to say..." I muttered.

Thatcher's face lit up as he tousled his son's blonde hair. "Ahhh...don't you dare. It wasn't my place to touch another man's truck. But our wives are close — it felt right. I should be the one saying sorry to you — I couldn't figure out what the problem is. Why it won't start. Everything's brand new under there."

I glanced back at the Chevy. A heaping pile of junk, putting me further in debt with its expensive repairs. "Maybe this weekend I'll call you to move the truck out."

"Your junk removal's my business." His smile remained.

As I started to step back, he said, "Oh, I almost forgot." He vanished behind the door, leaving his son to stare me down with his huge blue eyes. "I found this lodged under the battery."

Why would my father hide a key under the hood? And what is it for? I wondered as I met up with Lem, lugging a heavy-duty link cutter over his shoulder.

"The teams at the other two fields reported nothing but land. One more team's working. This should be the last one," Lem said as he snapped the padlock in half.

Inside, I surveyed the area as I wiped my dusty hands on my pants. Flat land, bedrock, a dense forest in the distance. Three run-down buildings used as sheds to store landscape equipment; mostly small tools, some riding mowers, and landscape stone.

"Let's split up," I suggested. "I will take that one, you see what's going on with the clunkers over there."

Lem headed to a lot of rusted cars and trucks, too beat-up to be anything more than scrap metal.

I circled the smallest of the three structures. Chipped, once-blue paint exposing brick and mortar; nailed-down windows. A brownish metal door with a set of padlocks protecting it. I rattled the locks, checking to see if someone left them unlocked. No luck. I returned with the link cutter.

As I broke the lock, I heard wrestling in the bush behind the building — a rapid movement not made by any animal. Quietly dropping the cutters on the ground by my feet, I reached for my gun and extracted it.

Careful to be quiet, I began to approach. When I reached the back of the building, I hugged the wall, clutched the gun to my chest, and waited. For several minutes I heard nothing but the breeze swishing in the tall grass, bending back the reeds and rustling the tree branches. About to give up and holster my gun, the shape of a man darted across the field towards the woods. His strides were long and powerful; those of a physically fit man. I noticed that he moved with confidence, assured of his escape route, as if he'd walked these parts before.

I sprinted after him. Sweat dripped in my eyes; the salt burned. I rubbed it away so I could see him, but somehow it made it worse.

Squinting, I spotted his camo pants as he jumped over a fallen log then ducked, avoiding an incoming whack from a tree limb. His heavy brown jacket snagged on a branch, which didn't slow him down at all. He wore a baseball cap covering a shaved head, or so it seemed from afar. He never turned back. Not once. Lighter on his feet than he looked, I watched him outmaneuvering thorns, rocks, and exposed roots.

I pushed after him, sucked in air like it was rocket fuel, but I couldn't catch up to him. A tightening shortness in my chest took the wind out of me. If I didn't slow down, I risked fainting on the spot. Couldn't let that happen, and I couldn't let him get away.

In the distance, it looked like he had eased up, no longer sprinting as before. Some kind of issue up there that I couldn't see. For a second, a tiny moment, he glanced back, checking me out. In that moment, I caught a glimpse of his face — sharp jaw, thin lips pressed together, slim nose. Completely forgettable out on the streets, but in the woods, I sensed he was a predator and I, his prey.

Our eyes made contact, and my memories collided. A spark of recognition. I had seen him before. I remembered how cold his eyes had seemed to me in Franklin Park as he observed the empty stage. Dana Miller was already in the morgue.

He had been there. In the crowd. And I had seen him. I had him in my grasp, but I had let him get away.

Not again. I think he remembered me too because a second later he bolted faster than before. Faster than I think he had ever run in his life. Whatever issue he had encountered, he forgot about it.

Between the trees, I saw his shadow darting deeper into the horizon. I couldn't kick it into higher gear. My body ground like rusty brakes. My leg muscles cramped up and soon felt like cement blocks. Some type of heaviness settled on my head, around the shoulders, pressing me harder into the ground with each movement. I heard myself say *stop*, but I didn't, and I don't know why. It's not like I could get to him. In fact, his shadow had gone, totally disappeared where the path ended in a thorny patch.

So focused on what was up ahead of me, I failed to notice the wet ground. One foot slid on a pile of wet leaves, the other getting tangled up. I landed on my right side, hitting the ground with my already bruised ribs.

Agh. I moaned, cleaning mud off my cheeks and forehead. When I finally managed to hoist myself up, I could see no trace of him.

I jogged for a few more minutes and stopped at a bog. The polluted, mosquito-infested marsh emitted a foul odor. I couldn't cross, not without leaving myself vulnerable and exposed for him to take a shot at me.

Fighting to catch my breath, I lowered my head and tried to inhale. Gobbled in air until I felt lightheaded. When my breathing normalized, I surveyed the swamp for any signs of the shadow. Eventually, I had to give up. He was gone. Faster than me, he had either waded through the water to cross to the other side or knew of an alternative route. Frustrated, I kicked the bedrock with my boots, throwing pebbles into the bog. As I prepared to leave, I glanced down at the edge of the wetland. My gaze fell on something that I almost ignored.

My eyes circled back to the black fabric caught on a thorn. I found a pair of gloves in my pocket, put them on, and lifted the wet material. There was no mistake. I held the Grim Reaper mask in my hands.

Back at the field, I gave my officers a general description of the man I had pursued. Ordered them to fetch the forest rangers to assist in the manhunt. I found Lem. He seemed less than impressed with the Grim Reaper discovery when I showed him.

"We have a bigger problem, detective," he said, looking at the clunkers with nervous eyes.

Soon a team of cadaver dogs and their handlers began to discover shallow graves buried across the field. More officers, crime lab techs, and Tessa Wu arrived to take over. I led her to the burned car. She leaned into the driver's seat, examining the remains.

"Male. He was set on fire. And has been here for a while. Months, maybe longer. I'm taking him to the morgue. Should know cause of death soon." She waved to her assistant to give her a hand removing the body from the car.

"Do you think you can ID him?" I asked, thinking about Brad Connolly's murder.

"Shouldn't be a problem. He has a mouth full of teeth. Give me a few hours and I'll get you a name."

Lem joined me at the top of the hill, overlooking the mass operation. "They found another one," he remarked.

"How many's that so far?"

"Twenty-six, someone said, and they're still finding more," Lem replied.

Before dusk, I called Meredith Sawyer. Told her she had ten minutes to show up, set up, and go live before her competition would swoop in.

After hanging up, I stared at the Grim Reaper mask secured in an evidence bag. Same as the mask on Dana Miller. What else were we bound to discover when we cleared the buildings? More bodies? Tools used by the killer? *Probably*, I mused.

My cell then rattled. It was Lem, shouting. He sounded rushed. "SID reports shots fired. Residential home. Possible location for Frank Ricca. Two officers down. Time to roll."

You could hear the choppers buzzing over the neighborhood off the highway. Four, I counted. Later, I learned the number was six. Restricted air space. No one could be in the sky without the risk of digging their early grave.

Lem's initial report had been correct. Two officers down. One dropped by a bullet in the head. The other in critical condition, fighting for his life at Mass Gen.

Frank Ricca had sent us a message — he wasn't playing. If we wanted him that much, he'd draw some blood from us first. Guns blazing.

Lem met me by the cordon tape. Kicked straight into an oral report. Ricca showed up at the ranch-style home — white with black shutters, single detached garage — sometime after two in the morning after a wild police chase. He barricaded himself inside. Reports of others in the house. Women. No kids.

Until about an hour ago, Ricca had rebuffed the hostage negotiator. Then, on his own, he had called back and agreed to let the women out.

"Why?" I asked.

"No one has a clue," Lem replied.

I pictured Ricca, his remorseless face. Shuddered at the thought of his reputation — a brutal, paranoid madman. He'd drop you for looking at him the wrong way.

A sniper pointed a rifle at the house from a rooftop. A SWAT man, running point. About ten others, a unit, surrounded Ricca's hideout in half-crouched sweep.

By the look of it, we were preparing to send him a message of our own — surrender. We won't ask again.

Off to the side, four strung-out women shared a smoke. One called Ricca 'a fucking SOB,' and the others seconded that. They wore lacy bras, black high socks, neon-colored mini leather skirts. Skinny like shoelaces. An officer brought them blankets, water. Ricca's girlfriends chugged the waters but turned down the blankets.

"I'm still trying to nail down the details for myself," Lem said. "But it seems you and I missed some of the action." Lem glanced in the direction of the women. "Bet they won't talk."

"Probably not. Faithful and loyal — that's how they were trained."

"Shame. They could give us the skinny on his movements inside the house. Provide us with crucial info on what to expect. In terms of guns — how many and what kinds? Risky business going in blind. No way to protect ourselves."

I surveyed the line of barricades. A stream of panicked residents removed from their homes. A baby was tearing his lungs out as the family dog let out threatening barks and growls.

"He has a plan." Eyes trained on the street, I said, "Densely populated. Quiet community. Safe streets. Families live here. Houses front and back. Side to side. A play set in every other yard. If you shoot and miss, you're bound to take out the wrong window. Did you say the cops chased him?"

"That's right. Don't know more than that. One of his associates rolled out of the moving minivan — James Bond style. SID detectives cornered him, he shot at them, and they returned fire. He didn't make it." Lem thought for another minute. "Ricca might drag it out. Issue is, he might have that kind of time. To wait. We don't. Look at all these people —who'll take care of them? What a walking nightmare. Men like Ricca always have something to prove. Shot two of ours for the game. For the fun of it."

"He's caged in there for the time being." I rubbed my chest, felt my heart's sluggish thump. "Contaminated."

André Jones approached, resembling a recommissioned World War II tank. Rusty, but operational. It would do.

"Alright — we just got word — Ricca has a hostage."

"Who?" I gazed at the eerily silent ranch lined up in the sniper's scope.

"One of the women." He handed me a tablet. "Maria Shapova. Age nineteen. Recently arrived in the States on a visitor visa. Expired three months ago."

I scrolled through the light file we had on her. Basic background and whatever the feds collected on Maria Shapova when she entered Boston on a red-eye flight from Munich.

"It could be the woman he kidnapped."

"We already attempted to question Mrs. Shapova's girlfriends, but they'd rather eat piping hot nails than cooperate." André nodded to them, chatting carefree. "The captain would like a moment when you're up to speed."

"Sure. Ricca's top priority, though. He won't need the girl for long."

"If she's still alive," Lem added.

"She is. She still has a purpose. But I'm worried he's wrapping things up inside. Whatever the plan is — he won't let her live. To him, Ms. Shapova is only a means to an end, but not the end itself. He might try her as a bargaining chip. Ask us for something ridiculous like a helicopter..."

"Command's not signing off on anything," André replied.

"No. I don't think he wants it, anyway — control is what drives Ricca. He's lusting after calling the shots. That's where we should hit him."

"SWAT's thirteen minutes from releasing smoke bombs. They'll gas the living daylights out of him. Move in and bring him down." André leaned closer to the radio wrapped around his neck. "10-24. Copy?"

"Copy Lou," Dispatch replied.

"Detectives Temple Stone and Lem Needham on scene. Log time of arrival. Notify Captain Mercy."

In the photo, Maria Shapova was slightly heavyset; round, fleshy face, baby-blue eyes, pinched pink lips. Thin straight hair. But I couldn't imagine the white dress on her; the Grim Reaper mask draped over her bloodless remains. In my mind, Ricca didn't stand over her, scalpel in one hand, bleeding Shapova dry. The guy from the woods, now him I could see killing Dana Miller.

In homicide, emotions only cloud judgment. They teach us that early on. So, any decent murder cop steers clear from feelings in case they corrode our brains. It makes us look mechanical. We are not. And given the fact — Frank Ricca — might be the last perp I ever put away, I admitted with relief — I hated him. But I knew he hadn't killed Dana Miller and Brad Connolly. He couldn't have. It had to be one of his men. One of his. Charles Isles had tried to confront Frank Ricca, accuse him of turning a blind eye to the senseless murders.

"Tell SWAT to call it off. It's what Ricca wants. And I won't give him an inch," I ordered. "Only them two in there?"

"Wish it was. But no. We used a body-heat scanner before the shootout. Picked up a third with Ricca and Shapova."

"Do we have any idea who else is with him?"

"Our best guess is the homeowner," André admitted. "Property records show Marcello Santoro. Son of Small Vitto Santoro."

"That makes the most sense. Ricca trusted no one but his top two. What do we have on Santoro?"

"Marcello Santoro — born and raised in Southie. Barely graduated from South High before the Cosa Nostra offered him a membership. Santoro and Ricca are relatively the same age; close family ties, worked the streets together for Tony the Iceman Ricca. When Frank seized control of the mafia, he moved Santoro to the number-two slot."

"Get me a line. I want to talk to Ricca," I said.

The three of us stood in silence for a minute before our radios exploded with nervous chatter. Everyone was talking over each other. The transmission bungled. Captain Mercy stepped in. Ordered a dedicated channel. As the noise started to die down, one of the hostage negotiators said, "Frank Ricca," and handed me a phone. "Let him think he calls the shots and you will do fine, detective."

"My buddy Charles Isles was fond of you, Detective Stone," Frank Ricca said, sounding chatty.

"And see where that got him. In a freezer at the morgue," I shot back.

"That's no way to talk to someone you just met. Haven't you heard of more bees with honey? Why should I talk to you — cop?" he said as I heard him take a sip of something.

"Because I'm the only one who thinks you didn't kill Dana Miller and Brad Connolly. And for you, that's the difference between a life in prison and a needle in your arm. You ready to talk or what?"

Chapter 46

"Put it on." André handed me a 'BPD' bulletproof vest.

I scanned the vest — steel plates, heavy. Instantly rejected the added weight on my already thinned-out frame. "Flying solo on this one."

"Out of the question. Put it on, or I'm ordering SWAT in."

"I know what I'm doing. He doesn't want to shoot me. He's shitting himself in there. The house is surrounded; gun on every roof. It's over, and he knows it."

"If you're so sure — then why go in at all?"

"There are twenty-six bodies and counting in that field, André. Cadaver dogs are still digging up dirt, coming up with human bones. But only one vic burned in a car. Male. Like Brad Connolly. And," I showed him the Grim Reaper mask, "I got jumped by a male, freaking strong. Lost him in the woods. He dropped the mask."

"So? Ricca sent a goon to tidy up after him. You surprised him, and the sonofabitch ran."

"No, you're wrong. I've seen this guy before. In Franklin Park, the morning we moved Dana Miller to the morgue. He was there, standing, blending in but not all the way. Caught my attention. As a matter of fact, I singled him out for questioning, but Danzel Fierra stole the show." I put my hand on André's shoulder. "This is probably my last homicide. I can't let Bloodless get away by allowing Frank Ricca to fry for crimes he didn't commit."

"Don't talk like that. You have more life left in you." André sounded wound up.

"I'm all done — my heart's shot up to hell and back. The doctor," I exhaled, worried, "doesn't paint a rosy picture. Shelly's printing posters soliciting blood donors. Can't let her keep doing this to herself. So this is my first and final homicide case as the lead."

"More cops are signing up daily to test and donate. Hang in there."

"I've hung on for as long as I could. I hung on for Shelly and the baby. For the murdered vics. For everyone else. I'm done hanging in there. Last one." I pointed to the ranch. "If I can't be a cop, I'd rather die."

"Don't talk like that."

"I know it's hard to hear. The alternative's harder — hospital bed, meds, IVs. Can't provide for my family. No dignity in that."

"Dignity's not everything." He rubbed his eyes, moving a few stubborn tears. "Tell Ricca — he tries something funny — I'll be his worst nightmare. He'd wish to have traded places with you."

"Alright guys," a SWAT officer said as he approached, "everyone's in position. Eyes and ears on the house. Your mic's long-range. Good to go. Working and already recording. Give us the signal, and a sniper takes the target out. That's all there is to it. Any questions?"

We stepped onto the lawn, André's stout frame hovering over my rail-thin shoulders. He received a text. Read it. "Tess Wu says she has a name for the guy in the burned car. Do you want to talk to Wu?"

"Not now, but tell Wu good job. We needed to know his name. Start putting together a file. We'll need it," I replied.

By the time I reached the home, a sweaty puddle had pooled on the back of my neck. I knocked lightly, battling an all-over energy shortage.

"Come in. It's open." I heard Ricca's muffled voice.

Inside, it smelled of rotten flesh. Ripped garbage. And melting butter. A bout of nausea ordered me out, but I ventured in, slowly, my gun halfway out.

I scanned the entryway — bare white walls, no furniture. Moved to the next — same. I supposed the mafia saved a bundle by not hiring interior decorators.

Some real serious action had gone down in the living room. I stepped over an empty beer can, surveying the hot mess. More empty beer cans, wine bottles, a stack of pizza boxes. Hot-sauce stains on the carpet.

Ricca had thrown a farewell party for Santoro and himself. At the card table, I spotted a passed-out male; wide shoulders, no neck. He wore a black satin button-down shirt and brown pants, sporting a gold ring on each pinky.

I extracted my gun and pointed it at Marcello Santoro, but it wasn't Marcello who surprised me. On the couch, folded into a ball, Maria Shapova mumbled softly to herself. She had noticed me. Hugging her bruised knees, she gazed at me, pleading — eyes drowning in black mascara, scarlet red lipstick smeared across her pale cheeks. Her puffy upper lip showed signs of a backhand. *He hit her recently*, I thought.

At the sound of pots and pans clattering in the kitchen, her eyes jumped to the ground, her whole body shivering like a goldfish in a shark tank.

I stepped closer to Marcello Santoro. No movement. Not a twitch. Odd. What kind of enforcer was he if he couldn't feel a gun pointed at him?

I stopped wondering once I saw his face lying in a pool of blood. I touched him. Stiff. Cold. And very dead.

"Ciao detective!" I swung the gun toward the voice.

Frank Ricca carried a saucepan; he was stirring something with a wooden spatula, kitchen towel tossed over a shoulder. Casual. Your friendly neighborhood serial killer. His forced expression said the party's not over.

"Ah! I see you've discovered Marcello — lousy card player. I'm afraid he won't be joining us for dinner. Hope that's okay."

Maria Shapova choked on some snot. Frank Ricca glared at her with wild, hateful eyes. There it was — a glimpse of the crazy, murderous perp I'd expected to encounter.

"Behave. Not in front of our guest." Ricca pointed at my cocked and loaded Glock. "Put it away, detective. It's scaring the lady. Dinner in ten. The bathroom is second door to your left — wash up. You look like you had one of those nights — rough and unforgettable."

"Don't think so, Ricca." I checked Marcello Santoro for a pulse. His head lolled back. A through-and-through bullet hole in his temple. "With him — how many is that?

Thirty, forty — does it really matter to you? Yeah, we found your burial ground," I muttered.

He shrugged. "People have an expiration date like everything else. Take Marcello for example — he was a talker! Never knew when to shut his trap. Finally, I shut him up. Well...at least we'll have a peaceful meal — you and I — lots of catching up to do."

"Frank Ricca, you're under arrest for the murder of — "

"Detective, detective — I'm not going anywhere before the cacio e pepe's done. Shoot me if you must." He winked at me. "But I think you won't."

"How can you be so sure?"

"Kill me, and I can't answer your Grim Reaper questions. Isn't that the reason why you came in? I'll be in the kitchen. The meal's nearly ready. Join me for your private one-on-one master class in cooking fine Sicilian cuisine. Care for a glass of wine? You look thirsty. A big glass of red's long overdue."

After he went back to the kitchen, I signaled to Maria Shapova to run. I'd cover her. She shook her head no, dropped her haggard face on her bony knees, and folded into a ball again.

Meanwhile, "Mambo Italiano" played in the background. Frank Ricca belted out the notes off-key, butchering the beat.

"Shut it off, Frank. Where was I — yeah — you're under arrest for the murder of Charles Isles and Marcello Santoro. Turn around and put your hands behind your back. You have the right to remain silent..."

"Cacio e pepe's a simple Italian dish. With just a few simple ingredients, you can transform any pasta dish into an elegant and delicious meal. Hand me the stick of butter. And you missed a vic?"

"Don't think so. Master class is over. Put the spatula away. Hands behind your back. And I didn't miss anyone. You killed Charles Isles. I can prove it. Killed Santoro, again I can prove it. But you didn't murder Dana Miller and her fiancé, but you know who did. And I expect you to tell me."

Ricca jokingly backed off. "She was right about you. Tamara called you a straight shooter, a no bullshitter."

"I'm moving this party to an interrogation room. Less distractions there. More one-on-one alone time." I showed him the handcuffs.

"Pfff. You'll have to shoot me first. Cacio e pepe — you start by melting a stick of butter over low heat. Add the pasta, al dente — " Ricca worked the pot on the stove with expertise. The butter sizzled as he tossed the pasta in. "Sprinkle generously with black pepper. Do you want to know the key ingredient? The secret to making this meal so special?"

"If I say no, would it matter?"

"No." Ricca fetched a jar from a cupboard. "Fresh pecorino romano. I ship it directly from Italy. It smells like," he stuck his nose close to the steam, "hmm — home."

"They have pasta suppers in prison. If you're nice, someone might let you have his cheddar cheese."

"Prison, huh? I have no plans to go back there," he said, and I believe he meant it. Ricca stopped and inspected the streaks of dirt on my face. "What happened to you?"

"Don't worry about me." I approached, cuffs and gun ready. "Worry about the reunion celebration all your frenemies will throw in your honor." The saucepan started to overheat. "It seems your pasta's burning. No more stalling; turn around."

I caught the expression of an angry woman in the window above the sink. She stood behind me. I spun around, gun aimed at Maria Shapova waving a sharp knife in my face.

Distracted by her, I missed Frank Ricca seizing a pot from the countertop. It landed on the back of my head, hard enough to throw me off balance. I dropped the gun and lost it. Pivoting on my feet, I drove a punch into the middle of his face. He laughed, wiping the stream of blood from his nose.

"Stop! Or I'll kill you. Frankie, are you okay, baby? Looks broken." Maria Shapova swayed the Glock like it was a handbag.

"Good girl, Maria. Hold onto his weapon. Detective — I hope you behave better during the meal. Cacio e pepe's ready. Paper plates alright with you? Marcello didn't keep dinnerware. If he couldn't eat it straight from the box, he didn't eat it at all."

Ricca set up the table for the two of us. A plate of pasta each for me and him. Maria Shapova returned to the couch and assumed her curled-up position.

Ricca twirled the fork, twisting the long pasta smothered in butter sauce. "Eat," he ordered.

I pushed the plate away. "There's only one way you can get out of this alive — and it's through the front door, walked by me. Pull another stunt like that," I glanced at Maria Shapova, then to Ricca, "and you're dead."

"I wouldn't waste bullets on you — detective — it seems death's at your doorstep already."

"Might be. Could very well be. But my conscience is clean. Never killed an innocent person. Never murdered another human for the game. You on the other hand — seven acres of bodies. How sick."

"You know what the difference is between your first and second murder? There isn't one. Humans are natural-born killers. You understand, right? Don't expect a man like you to understand."

"Why did you allow it? The murder of Dana Miller. Pelican Bay's listed in her report, but not your name. And from what I've gathered, Charles Isles wanted his wife, Tamara, to burn at the stake. Not you."

"Hold on — Dana Miller wasn't one of mine, but you already know that. Never met the chick. Tamara phoned me, said Isles found out I was sleeping with her. She told me about Dana Miller working the books, snooping on Tamara's spending habits. Pressed me to get rid of the bitch."

"And you did? Are you confessing?"

"She was already dead when I heard about it. The next morning, Charles called, flipping out. Telling me, if the cops come asking questions he will sing. So I took my boys, paid him a visit. Reminded him what a good friend I could be. Sent my personal lawyer to bail him out." He gave me a shallow smirk. "That's what I get for my kindness."

He put down the fork and sipped some red wine from the bottle. "We had a good thing going on. I funded some projects for him — liked the return on them, funded some more. Partnership of sorts. Worked well."

"What happened, then? Why kill Charles? He didn't sell you out to me. Oliver Buzzworth was in the room with us."

"I liked the guy, Isles, alright? Kind of funny-looking, talked all the time. Get him and Santoro in the same room and they'd talk over each other. Mamma Mia!

"Have some pasta. Try it at least. You're missing out. Good food heals." When I refused to eat, Ricca motioned to Maria Shapova. She picked up my cocked, loaded Glock and pointed it at me.

"Eat!" Ricca repeated.

I managed a small bite. Ricca liked that. Friends. Eating a meal together.

"Partnerships sour. That doesn't mean I killed him. I heard through the grapevine that Isles was killed in a motel pool."

"He was killed in a pool, but not the motel's. At his ex-wife's mega mansion. We analyzed the water in his lungs. A tint of blue; a custom-made color. The New Jersey company that makes it confirmed Tamara Sullivan's a client.

"Why did you kill him, Frank? Is it because Charles confronted you about the Grim Reaper? I read his texts to you. He had realized who murdered Dana Miller. Did you know he also called me? Yeah, that's right. He wanted to tell me, but I think he wanted to confront you about it first."

He looked away. *I've hit a nerve,* I thought. *His ego. Keep hitting.*

"Or did you kill him — for Tamara Sullivan?" Maria Shapova hissed from the couch. I continued. "You actually developed feelings for Tamara. She's a master manipulator. You wouldn't be the first one to fall for her game. The two of you together — fire and gasoline. Don't take it personally. From what I hear, she hates every man's guts."

"She's a wild cat. I concede there. We hit the sack several times. So what? I have a soft spot for her. And something else — she loves the smell of money. I can launder twice as much with her as the boss as with Charles. He was always afraid of being caught. Sent back to jail."

"You killed a man because his wife stole millions to pay for a lifestyle she couldn't afford. Tamara threw her husband to the wolves. And she'd known him for over twenty years. She's known you for a hot minute. How do you think her testimony will go in court? Not in your favor, I bet."

The tiny veins around his eyes began to visibly pulsate. I continued, "Is that why you're hiding Dana Miller's killer? Because you fear what he will tell us on the stand?

The city will let you fry. Give him up. Show us you have some excuse for a heart.

"I like your passion. Hot-blooded, crazy Italian passion. I see myself in you. Men like us — don't listen to others. We're so sure of what we want out of life, we're blind to everything else."

He and I are nothing alike, I told myself.

"Confess or don't. It makes no difference to me. I came in to offer you a shot to tell me the truth. But I'm starting to see it's a waste of my time. I will see you on your execution day."

Since I had his ear, I added, "Men like you are too dumb to help themselves even when the rescue boat shows up. Last chance before I walk out." I threw the evidence bag with the Grim Reaper mask on the table. "He was at the field today. Dropped it on the ground running away from me. But I'll get to him. Today, tomorrow — I'll get to him."

"Wow — I contemplated fucking with you. Entertaining myself before the sky fell on my head. Not as fun as I imagined, ain't that right Maria?"

She shrugged.

"Is that why Maria's here? To entertain you? Does she even know what's going to happen to her?"

Maria jumped up, the gun shaking in her hand. I put my hands out as if I could stop the bullets.

Frank Ricca hurled a blade at her. It landed in her shoulder. Blood spurted from her like a well.

"Maria, Maria — what will I do with you?" He rolled his eyes as if we had witnessed a tantrum from her. "She has no manners."

Footsteps gathered outside. The ranch was surrounded. SWAT in position. With or without my signal, they'd shoot. Frank Ricca seemed to agree with my assessment.

"The SOB you're looking for is the undertaker. Okay? He killed your girl — Dana. Those bodies you dug up, he put in there. I pay him to clean up after me. Take care of the mess. He's the silent type but exceptional at his job. Had no idea he killed on the side. See what I mean, people taking advantage of my kindness?

"I don't know why he killed the bitch. Like I said, she wasn't on my radar. I wanted Charles Isles to step down, go away, let Tamara take his place. His old lady and I could go on with the business. If it was up to me, Isles would be still alive, sipping a cold one with his little Asian girlfriend. But he wouldn't shut up. Ran his big mouth. Tamara's not as restrained as me. So she hit him over the head with a bottle. He fell in her pool. I drowned him."

"And the undertaker? Who is he?"

"I got him a job at The Groove Factory. His mom got sick or something like that. Shit, I don't remember, and I don't care. He wanted a steady paycheck. No one complained about his work ethic."

"He killed Dana Miller, bled her to death. Murdered her fiancé. Torched his body in his car. Who is he?"

"A country boy who likes to play with scalpels. His name is..."

Maria Shapova fired a bullet into Frank Ricca's head before he could tell me. The flash blinded me temporarily. My mind spun crazy fast, showing me Dana in the white dress and the Grim Reaper mask. Why?

After the shot, SWAT kicked in the front door. They cuffed Maria Shapova and threw her in a squad car. Lem and André helped walk me out.

"Call a medic," André called to someone. "It's over. It's all over. We have him. You did it."

I snagged the edge of his bulletproof vest. Gripped it. "No. Back to Central."

"Temple — a doctor should check you out. There's blood on you," Lem said.

"Ricca's. It's all his. Took credit for Charles Isles's murder. None of the others. The real killer worked for Ricca. That's as far as I got before Maria blew his brains out. But Ricca called him the — "

"Stop talking. Save your strength. You did your job. Made us all proud." André guided me to a waiting ambulance.

"Ricca said the killer was his undertaker. More work to be done. Call the lab. Have them retest all the evidence from each crime scene. The real killer's not done killing. And well, damn it, I'm not done living."

Chapter 47

"Gather around. Take a seat or stand up. But cut the chatter," I addressed the Homicide bullpen. André on one side, Lem on the other.

Mercy waved at me to keep talking.

"Ricca's dead." The announcement unsettled some detectives. "He confessed to killing Charles Isles for reasons unrelated to the original investigation motive. The murder of Dana Miller and her fiancé belonged to the undertaker, someone Ricca hired to clean up after him. Their murders — still open, active — are still unsolved. Let me say this — every one of you works this case until we catch the perp. Call your wives and girlfriends — tell them not to wait up."

Without pausing, I added, "There's something in our files that we missed. Overlooked or buried. We're starting from square one, as if the case is hot. Look at it with fresh eyes. No killer's perfect. Including this one. He's made a mistake — small on the surface. Reexamine each piece of evidence, call witnesses, and interview them again. Pay close attention to any males between the ages of thirty and forty. Probably attractive, but he doesn't stand out. Women feel comfortable around him until they don't, but by then it's too late. He might seem willing to cooperate at first, but when pressed for details, specifics, he'll be evasive. If you come across anyone who matches the mold — find one of us. That's it for now. Take five before we dive in."

"You sound like your ol' self," André said.

"I chose this case over my own life, my family. I'd better be on my A-game."

"What do you want us to do?" Lem flipped open his pocket-size notebook.

"Call Tessa Wu, ask her to review the remains. The two males and Dana Miller. Let's see if she can tell us anything more about the killer, his methods. Ricca said Isles gave the undertaker a job at The Groove Factory. It's one of the employees," I said.

"We ran backgrounds on all of them. No one had more than a pot bust or a shoplifting mark on their file," André said.

"He's there in The Groove Factory. Isles wouldn't have given him a big role. Nothing like accounts payable. We're looking for something entry-level. I don't think the undertaker's capable of handling a regular nine-to-five job. Women take up a substantial space in his life. He's consumed by ideas of what to do and how to show them his *love*. His paychecks are probably spent on the embalming fluids and the drugs — neither's cheap. So he maybe has several open credit cards at one time to pay for it all. And a sick mom."

"His mom?"

"Yeah, Ricca told me the undertaker asked for a job because his mom was sick."

"We ran the security guards, but we didn't run the janitors because they were all part-timers, I think. It didn't seem pressing at the time," Lem wedged a word in.

"Do it. Go ahead and run their names. Check their home addresses against the list of funeral homes using the same embalming factory. I want names. Let's go."

As I moved around the Homicide room, they followed me. "Call CSI, primarily Callum Baker. The lab should test the physical evidence again, even the extras. A piece of something is what we're missing. He's not smarter than us. Might think he is, but we're better."

"Damn straight." André crossed his arms.

On that note, I fleshed out my profile of the killer. "A country boy, that's what Ricca called his clean-up man. The man I chased in the woods matches that description. Brown jacket, camo pants, at least six feet. So we need to start with anyone who has a home in the country, farmland, even if it's not in their name. The killer probably lives at home, with his parents, especially if he has to look after a sick mother. And something else — where is it?" I flung papers off my desk until I found the autopsy report. "The killer almost ODed Dana Miller." I scanned the list of drugs. "Cancer meds. Maybe he's stealing his mom's meds, or she died and he used the leftovers. It's another thing to add. Shorten the list of potential suspects. But we're close. I can feel it," I declared.

I stood in front of the murder board and briefly examined Dana's picture. The white dress. The Grim Reaper mask. They held significance; a key to finding the killer. I pushed myself to think. What was I missing? My head throbbed. To distract myself, I took down Charles Isles's picture and put it away in his file — stamped it 'Case Solved.'

"Hansen Jackson's the male in the car. Age thirty-eight. Missing for sixteen months. Has a sister who reported him. The case's still unsolved," André said as he added a photo of Hansen Jackson's remains on the board next to Brad Connolly.

"Did he have a girlfriend?" I asked.

"We're checking. Calling Mr. Jackson's sister."

"The upside-down version of the perp — started with the first murder." I pointed at the skeletal remains. "Right now that's him. And if he had a girl or fiancée, the under-taker killed her. But where is she? He didn't leave her in a public place like Dana Miller, or we would have found her by now. So where is she? Where did he leave her?"

"Detective!" Gina shouted. "It's your wife. Your neigh-bor called from the highway. Shelly's in labor."

"Come on, I'll drive," André said. "Priority one. Lights and sirens."

At Mass Gen, a peppy nurse in the maternity ward announced I had become a father. A baby girl. Seven pounds. The sweetest baby on the floor, the nurse said.

I found Shelly asleep — recuperating. Next to her, in a tiny bassinet, I met my newborn daughter. She was sport-ing a white cap hiding an impressive chunk of smooth black hair. She was awake, alert, and twitched with de-light when I picked her up.

Dumbfounded, I said, "Hello. I'm Dad." I didn't like the sound of it. Tried a different approach. "But you can call me Daddy. In fact, I'd like that very much."

She squealed.

"You like that, don't you? Wow! Look at you. The nurse wasn't lying — you're the sweetest, most beautiful baby in the whole wide world. Quick, before your mama wakes up — I need you to know that I love you, and I love your mommy — and...and...and... I'm mad that I'm dying. If I could take it all back, get a chance at changing my mind and flipping the outcome — I would have. Because, baby, you're worth it."

A soft knock. I lifted the baby and brought her closer to my heart.

"May I come in?" It was Doctor Hoffman, hands stuck in her snow-white coat. "Congratulations. I heard your wife was in labor. It seems the delivery went well."

"Thank you."

"Do we have a name for the little princess?"

I gazed into the blue-gray eyes, button nose, cherry-red lips. Tiny feet kicking.

"Shelly should. Whatever she likes, I'll love."

"Her daddy should." Shelly woke up. "Hi, darling. I see you've met the new addition to our family."

"I love her so much. And I love you, Shelly. My two butt-kicking, name-taking girls. Wonder women." I kissed the baby's forehead, then kissed Shelly on her chapped lips. "I can't believe I missed her birth. It's unfair I'll miss out on everything else in your lives."

"Not necessarily." Hoffman stood at the edge of the bed, analyzing our little family. Finally, she said, "There's an open OR. I can admit you and have you under anesthesia in an hour. If you're up to it? I hope you are because we're out of time, detective. I came to tell you that, but I saw you with your daughter. I'm good at what I do. Let me do my job and give you more happy moments with your family, not just this one."

"Temple — darling!"

"I — I don't know..." I said, gazing at my baby daughter.

"If we're doing this, we have to hurry — which means I have to tear you away from your wife and newborn."

"Absolutely. Go. You won't get another opportunity like this. When you wake up, we will be waiting. You can pick a name then."

"What should we call her in the meantime?" Hoffman waved her fingers at the baby.

In the background, Shelly's favorite, the Discovery Channel, showed the formation of stars. I smiled at my wife.

"Nova. We should call her Nova."

"I like it. Fitting. Go fix your heart so you'll never miss another precious moment with us." Shelly reached up for a kiss.

"I love you. Alright — Nova — Daddy has to step out — but I'll be back. Lesson number one — Mommy's always right. If I listened to her all along, I wouldn't be in this sticky mess. If you ladies don't mind, I'd like to stick around for many years. What do you say, Nova? Would you like Daddy to teach you how to ride a bike, throw a ball, play hide-and-seek?"

Nova had already fallen asleep in my arms. Handing her over to Shelly felt excruciatingly painful. *Will I see them again?* swirled in my mind.

A nurse left a light-blue linen hospital gown on the bed for me. She wrote 'Temple Stone' on the patient board and drew a large smiley face in red marker.

"You can change in the bathroom, okay sweetie? Put your clothes and personal items in the bag on the hook. When you're ready, ring the bell, and one of us will come in to set you up with an IV. It's usually several hours before you go into surgery — we have to prep the OR, paperwork, stuff like that. You'll meet with the anesthesiologist soon. He'll go over putting you under, have some consent forms for you to sign. Standard stuff. It's a quiet night on the OR board. Not a whole lot going on. We like it slow and quiet. Questions?"

"Can't think of any."

She laughed. "If only all my patients were that contained. But really, if you think of anything, or you need us to get you something — we're right outside the door. No food or water until after your surgery. See you in a few, hun."

She left, and I sat down next to the gown, my shirt still scented with newborn smell. Two buttons in, my phone jumped. Bradley Walker. I frowned and sent his call straight to voicemail. Did so several more times.

I lay back and shut my eyes when I heard a male shouting. I poked my head out to discover Bradley Walker yelling at a nurse.

"What's happening?"

"Sir, I'll ask you to leave one more time and then I will call — "

"That's not really necessary, ma'am, he's one of my detectives," I told her as I watched Bradley swallowing his pride.

"Why are you here, Detective Walker?"

"You wouldn't pick up your damn phone. Hansen Jackson and his girlfriend, Nelly Klarkson, went missing sixteen months ago after a party hosted by The Groove Factory. She was a wannabe model. Charles Isles and Frank Ricca could have been there — they both liked pretty women. And that got me thinking — the undertaker might have been there too. Maybe he saw Nelly Klarkson, liked her, and abducted her. Killed her boyfriend." He showed me the original report. I looked at the four-by-six picture of Nelly Klarkson. She was a dead ringer for Dana Miller.

"Sir, you need to go back to bed. I need to hook you up to an IV bag," my nurse said.

"Sorry. Not today. I have a killer to catch." I rushed out of the hospital, cursing myself under my breath.

Chapter 48

The pieces started to fall in place. Nelly Klarkson's parents said their daughter had been the light of their lives. She loved the stage since middle school. Cheer captain, class president, homecoming queen. Nelly Klarkson had checked all the necessary social-status boxes to win every popularity contest.

After graduation, she headed off to college, but college wasn't high school, and Nelly Klarkson quit after two semesters. Returned home and hung out with boys she shouldn't have.

"Did she have enemies? Someone she was afraid of?" I asked her father over the phone.

"Nelly? Everyone loved her. She wouldn't hurt a fly. She knew how to work a room. Hold and keep the attention on her with her bright smile." He sighed. "You think she's dead?"

"I don't know, sir. We're investigating. Her abduction has similarities to another murder. A young woman found in a park, wearing a white dress and a Grim Reaper mask. We haven't found Nelly, just her boyfriend, Mr. Jackson. I'll call you back if I find anything related to your daughter." I started to hang up.

"Young man?" His voice trembled. "Did you say a Grim Reaper mask?"

The killer's name was Archer Kniff. He went to school with Nelly Klarkson, or so her father was convinced. Kniff had been an off kid. Always clutching the Grim Reaper mask, even in class. His parents owned the funeral home in town before they both died rather suddenly on the same day, hours apart.

Lem pulled a janitor's file from The Groove Factory records — Archer Ross Kniff, who had listed a PO box as his primary address.

"It's the field of dead bodies." I circled his address on the map. "His parents owned farmland. Operated the funeral home from there. All units, head to this location. Set up a perimeter blocking all access routes."

From the road, I dialed Shelly, but she snubbed my calls. I tried her a final time. I yearned to hear her voice telling me, 'It will be alright, darling.'

But with each unanswered ring, the call started to feel like a goodbye. See you on the other side. I gulped — pick up, pick up, pick up.

As expected, she didn't. But her voicemail offered me a chance to get my feelings off my chest. Somewhat disappointed and seriously afraid, I spoke in a shaky voice.

"If I make it back alive, let's go back to the beach. You were so beautiful that day. The way the wind twirled your hair, your sweet lips stretched in a loving smile. I still feel your head nestled on my chest. If I make it back alive, let's get me a new heart so we can go to the beach more often — take Nova with us. Kiss her for me. I miss you both."

I shut the phone for good. Tucked it away in the glove box. From there, I fetched my gun. Placed it on the seat next to me.

In the next twenty minutes, the sun gave way to a bleak night with a round, dour moon and no stars. I had stopped listening to the cop chatter once I passed the rusty welcome sign, 'Barksville,' home of the world-famous blueberry festival.

"And the world's biggest psychopath," I mumbled under my breath.

I arrived in the dead of the night to a chain fence with a makeshift sign — 'Stay Out.' Everyone else showed up a few minutes later.

"You know what to do," I told my team, and we fanned out.

I squeezed between two barbed wires without getting caught on the spikes. The driveway, packed gravel, curved like a twisting snake. I could no longer see the colorless moon through the broad sycamore trees with their crowded branches intertwined like clasping fingers.

As I approached the end of the path, I heard the screams of a woman. Pleading. Gut-wrenching sobs for help. The darkness felt disorienting, so I used her ear-splitting voice as my guide.

The agonizing sounds came from an old barn. Hiding behind some empty wooden barrels and broken milk crates, I peeked through a web-covered, dusty window. Under the weak light of an electric lamp hanging from a rusted nail, I spotted Nelly Klarkson. Her wrists were chained and suspended from a wall. She thrashed her lean body against the chains to free herself, but it didn't work. Her face showed signs of beating — busted lip, cut forehead, bloodied nose. I concluded she'd done something to irritate Archer Kniff. The guy had a short fuse and explosive temper.

"No. No. No. Please. I won't do it again," she begged a shadowy figure I couldn't quite make out. Judging by his stature, male — six three, about three hundred pounds — Archer Kniff. His size was bad news. He had a full head on me, and two fifty in weight and muscle. Hand-to-hand combat would be child's play for Archer Kniff.

I felt the urge to touch my gun, to assure myself that I still had a chance no matter how slim it was.

Tied up, Nelly Klarkson became even more hysterical when Archer Kniff stepped into the light.

Veiled under an amber glow, I studied him. He had a masculine face, a high brow, and a sharp nose. A baseball cap pulled low. Nothing remarkable or memorable about him, I concluded. Bland like I had suspected.

But he was a monster. And I'd seen my share of monsters before. Frank Ricca, the Italian mobster, was worthy of the title. But he paled in comparison to Archer Kniff. I couldn't find a shred of humanity in him, standing over his latest vic, watching her fight for her life.

She screamed at the top of her lungs. I thought she might rupture a vocal cord. Thrashed harder, back and forth, side to side, tried to throw a kick at him. I could tell he liked this part. It gave him pleasure. Filled him with lust. His eyes sparked with joy when he pulled the cord of the handheld chainsaw. She almost fainted but immediately roused as the blades choked on a gust of black smoke, sparking to life. Its teeth began to rotate towards her, so close, the saw almost took a piece from her right shoulder.

I had to improvise. I pointed the gun at Archer. Aimed. Lowered the weapon, frustrated. A barn post gave him partial cover. There was no good way to take the shot and kill Archer Kniff.

The chainsaw suddenly died. Archer Kniff seemed pre-occupied with fixing the malfunction.

"Sorry, doll. It will take too long to fix. And I'm expecting company later tonight, so if you don't mind, I'll have to hurry us along. Be back in a jiff."

Concealed by the darkness, I watched Archer's looming shadow exit. Nimble, he disappeared deep into the property. She yelled for someone to save her.

Quickly, I sprinted in. The hostage saw me. Thankful tears rolled from her eyes, soaking her torn and sweat-stained blouse.

I managed to release her from the chains. She dropped to the ground but stood up just as fast, shaking like a rabbit.

"My name is Detective Temple Stone. I'm with Boston PD."

"I...I am...I..."

"No time for this now. Here's what I want you to do — race to the entrance. I left my car running by the fence. Do you remember how you got here?"

Her frail shoulders shook. I thought she might be malnourished. Kept in captivity for some time, judging by the serious bruises on her wrists, similar to those on Dana Miller.

"That's alright. If you take the gravel pathway between those old trees and stay the course, you can't miss the *grand* entrance. I need you to hurry. Run. More cops are headed this way. Flag them down when you see them. Okay? Can you do that?"

She bit her lip, tears cascading down her face like race-car drivers. "You're not coming?"

A door swung shut near us. I pushed her out of the barn. "Just you. I will try to buy you as much time as I can. Run. Run. Run. Don't stop. Promise me."

"Okay. I'll try. What if he gets to me before I get to the car?"

She had a point; Archer Kniff might go after her. I held my weapon in my hand. Looked at it.

"Do you know how to use one of these?"

"My daddy's a hunter."

"Take it. Locked and loaded. Point and shoot."

"No...no...I can't. What about you? What will you do?"

Archer whistled a happy, carefree tune. Chills prickled my spine.

"I'll think of something. Go. Now. Before he kills us both."

I didn't stick around to see her outline vanish between the sycamore trees. I nested as deep as I could into the barn, picked up a pipe from a bin of scrap metal, and hid behind a half wall.

His footsteps suddenly stopped. I saw his shadow spill around me until it swallowed me completely. Now what?

I had cornered myself. Four walls and no escape. *Good job, Temple. Very smart.*

"Noooo! Nelly!" Archer Kniff screamed at the top of his lungs.

If I didn't do something to distract him, I was certain he'd chase her.

I stepped out from my hiding spot.

"Boston Police. Put your hands where I can see them," I ordered. "Archer Kniff, you're under arrest for the murders of Dana Miller, Brad Connolly, Hansen Jackson, and many more. You're under arrest for the attempted murder of Nelly Klarkson," I informed him, winded.

Archer threw his head back, laughing demonically. The pipe in my hand trembled a little.

"Laugh all you want, Kniff. But I bet you won't laugh when the state gives you the needle."

He cut the chuckles but remained smiling. Focused those cold, motionless eyes on me. *The lust for blood has been there since birth,* I mused.

"You think you can save her? Nelly and I are soulmates."

I lowered the pipe. "Was Dana your soulmate too?"

"I thought she was. Gave her a chance. But she was unreasonable. Messing around with another man. Couldn't allow it," he said, glaring into the soundless night.

He yelled, "Nelly! Nelly Klarkson, bring your ass back here. We're not done. You hear me? Stupid bitch."

I wanted to rip his head off.

"She doesn't seem too fond of you, huh? None of them did. Dana Miller loved her fiancé. Nelly loved Hansen.

They rejected you. Is that why you bled Dana? Because she didn't want to be with you?"

Archer Kniff stepped forward. I had hit a soft spot. If I talked about the victims, their real identities, I mused, it dispelled his fantasy world.

"I purified her. Made her new. Freed her soul."

"Ahh, of course — how can I forget your creepy obsession with the Grim Reaper?"

He lunged at me, wielding a knife. Missed. Came at me a second time, harder, meaner. Sliced my shoulder but didn't hit the bone. I moved the pipe to my uninjured arm.

Keep poking at him.

"She was a bad girl. Really bad. I gave her a chance to be nice, Nelly Klarkson, but she refused."

"Nelly Klarkson? Huh? She thinks you're a mask-wearing freak. Have you seen yourself in a mirror? A face only a mother can love and a personality only a father can tolerate," I said.

"Good boys don't hurt those they love, but some might," he said on a loop, then stopped. I could tell he was seeing red. He lunged at me again. I barely evaded his butcher's knife.

Shaking his head, he mumbled, disoriented, talking to someone else, but I couldn't risk jumping him. He was stronger than me. I calculated the damage he could do.

"Put the mask on, son. They are just bodies," he said to no one.

Disgusted, I lifted one of the metal chains and threw it at him. It hit him in the stomach. He doubled over, and when he regained his strength, I spotted the wrath flaming in him.

"You shouldn't have done that," Archer Kniff moaned.

He jumped; pounced, more like it. Threw me to the ground. Crouched over me. Knife lifted over his head, about to strike. Wiggling, I managed to create some space between us. Let my fingers sweep the ground around me, looking for something to use as a weapon. Nothing.

His elbow bore down on my side. Tender. I coughed; spat. Wiped the blood from my mouth. Coughed again.

"Daddy let you keep the mask in the funeral home? Archie's scared of dead bodies, huh?" I asked to buy myself some time.

He clenched his fists, wishing he could squish me like a bug, I imagined. "I'm not afraid. Remove their blood so they can't hurt you. Embalm them to purify them."

I broke his fantasy with my raspy coughing. Archer Kniff pulled me towards him by my shirt.

If I didn't do something to defend myself, to end this fight, he would kill me. And I couldn't accept defeat. If I died, I wouldn't see Nova again or make passionate love to Shelly.

I screamed. Roared with pinned-up rage. Fury.

He struck me in the jaw. In the ribs. He was enjoying himself. I wondered how long before the thrill wore off and he strapped me to a table — to bleed me dry, embalm me.

Somehow, I freed a leg and kicked him in the chest. With my free hand, I punched him in the jaw, got his nose too. Blood started to run. Gushing. It stained his mouth, neck, and shirt. The butcher's knife fell from his grip when he tried to protect his broken nose.

I felt my head starting to spin, my mouth dried out. For a split second, all I could hear was the fading thud of my heart.

I had to stop him.

I tried to get up. I couldn't, so I dragged myself to the knife. Almost there. My fingertips brushed against the handle.

"You really are one stubborn SOB." Archer Kniff snagged my ankles, dragged me away.

He threw me on my back. Face to face. His bloodied, mine bruised. Archer Kniff closed his hands on my throat, using his thumbs to crush my windpipe.

As he squeezed the last drop of air out of me, he yelled, "Give me your soul!"

In my hand, I felt the sharp knife. But it was getting harder and harder to focus. Harder to lift my hand. Could I even do it?

I couldn't let him take my soul. I thrust myself against him with the knife. I felt it penetrate him, cut him, kill him. He choked, shivered, then slumped over me.

Then cops, many of them, showed up from somewhere. André reached me first. Shouted, "Medic! I need a medic!"

Two paramedics wheeled in a stretcher. Secured me to the gurney with belts.

"Nelly Klarkson. Did she make it? Is she alright?"

"She's okay. Told us where to find you," André said, waving to the medics to hurry up. He placed an oxygen mask over my face. "Rest now, Detective Stone. This is over."

****

Doctor Hoffman examined me with grave concern in the ER bay.

I imagined she was about to say — I can't do anything for you, Detective Stone. You had your chance, and you blew it. So, I said first, "I'm ready to fight. For my life. Please — I need your help."

My words must have changed her mind. "OR seven's prepped and ready to go," she told the medics.

As they rushed me through a hallway, bright overhead lights blinding me, I felt a soft hand grab mine.

I heard a voice I very much wanted to hear. "I love you darling. Stay strong. Don't leave us. Promise me."

I thought I replied, "I promise," but for the rest of my life, I might never recall what I said to Shelly.

Eventually, I woke up in a sunny room to *Get Well* balloons, flower arrangements, and handmade cards. Shelly walked in with Nova in her arms; Doctor Hoffman came in too.

"Nova — look, Daddy's awake. Hi Daddy! Aren't we so happy to see him?"

I stretched my hand out to them. Touched Nova. Shelly held my hand in hers, and it felt good. Doctor Hoffman picked up my chart. She read some notes, but all-in-all, her face remained neutral.

"Your surgery went well. A success. It seems you're doing well."

"How long do I have with my family?"

The question seemed to puzzle them. "That depends. You will be off work, of course, for several months, gradually back to desk duty while we observe your progress, but in time, I don't see why you can't return to the streets. Most transplant patients continue to lead fulfilling lives."

"Transplant? You fixed my heart?"

Hoffman offered a tight smile. "The night you arrived, I received a patient with a fatal knife wound to the chest. He was an organ donor. A perfect match for you. O negative — same blood type as you. If you don't have any more questions, you should rest."

She started to leave. "Who was he?" I sounded scared.

"I really shouldn't."

"Please, I have to know."

"Okay. The patient's name was Archer Kniff. He died in a fight."

The mention of Kniff's name sent my heart pounding. Machines attached to my chest went off, lights blinking, alarms blaring.

"Temple, calm down." Hoffman sounded concerned. "Calm down. Nurse. I need a nurse."

Shelly said, "Baby, what's wrong, darling?"

My heart went thump, thump, thump as if it wanted to escape my body.

Hoffman stabbed my IV with a needle. The drugs slowed my heart down. The doctor said, "Take a nap, detective." So, I did.

I had been sleeping, stuck in the realm of half awake, half not. Somewhere between dream and reality, a thought struck me. The worry that had been hiding in the back of my mind. Archer Kniff's heart — my body. His blood — my veins. Fused into one. Bloodless and me. How do I make sense of it? Make room for him, because without him— I would've died.

Movement in my darkened room alerted me to danger. Instinct told me to protect myself. I seized a wrist. A woman moaned, more like a startled sigh. I smelled her fruity perfume.

Hot with fever, I mumbled something about '*good boys.*' Let her go immediately after.

"Excuse me?" the nurse said, a little stunned.

"Nothing, ma'am. Sorry. It's my new heart — working through some old baggage."

Chapter 49

Tucked in her carrier, Nova stirred as I put her down to sign the paperwork. The tow truck slowly backed out of the driveway.

"Is that a bullet hole?" Shelly pointed at the hole near the trunk of the red minivan.

"Do you really want to know?" I teased her.

"Only you'd buy an impounded car."

"It runs well, and it's big enough for our growing family."

She chuckled, unconvinced. I said, "I've seen the van in action, it can haul. And you did ask for a new car."

"Yeah, I suppose, but I was hoping we'd get one not confiscated from the Italian mafia." She glanced at me, the late July sun reflecting in her beautiful eyes. "I changed my mind about the van. I love it."

Nova kicked off her blanket, yawning. Shelly lifted her into her arms, and Nova started to doze off. We took her to the nursery. I put down the diaper bag, imagining what the rest of my life would look like, half forgetting that Archer Kniff's heart beat inside my chest.

Shelly leaned into the crib.

"Hang on," I said, reaching for my coat. As I rummaged through my pockets, the secret key from the Chevy dropped onto the carpet. "Oh, come on. Seriously! Not again," I grumbled, probing the beige carpet for the shiny key. I suspected it was lost forever, like all small important things tend to grow legs and disappear.

But I was wrong. Lodged between the foot of the crib and the dresser, I discovered it. As I retrieved the key, I nearly missed the bolt to the crib. The last one that was supposed to keep Nova's bed secured.

After I screwed it into place, she finally had a sturdy bed. Shelly laid her down. I put an arm around my wife and kissed the side of her forehead. She put her hand on top of mine and leaned into me.

"You always know the right thing to do, have I told you that lately?" Shelly whispered. "Dinner?"

"Mmm, sure. What's on the menu?" I asked while my stomach spun in fear.

"How about BBQ beans and tuna bake? I hear it's your favorite." She nudged me in the ribs. "Just kidding. I think we both know — I'm no domestic goddess. What about some ramen?"

Relieved, I relaxed. "Only if I make them. And you get a bowl of your own."

After dinner, André texted, asking if I could drop by Central. Shelly didn't object. And so, sometime after six, I drove Ricca's minivan to the station.

I exited on the Homicide floor and strolled through the double doors. A 'Welcome Back' banner hung on them. It was a gathering. Every cop I knew was probably in attendance. They were loud, boisterous. Swapping jokes, sipping soda from paper cups. Someone cut slices from a big white cake with my name on it.

"Temple." Bradley Walker handed me a slice. "Glad to have you back, sir."

I nodded in appreciation. The grocery store cake tasted like heaven. I took the leftovers to my office as one of the maintenance guys finished fixing my name on the door. "Good as new. Take care."

Lem hurried over, Captain Mercy a few seconds behind him. André strolled in last.

"Thanks to you, Nelly Klarkson will make a full recovery. Her family's glad she's back with them," André informed me.

A stabbing sensation needled my insides. I cleared my throat, pretty sure it was just an adverse reaction of my heart. "Archer Kniff can never hurt anyone else," I remarked, thinking of his DNA altering mine.

André showed me a diamond ring sealed in an evidence bag. "Nelly Klarkson turned it over. Told us Archer Kniff asked her to marry him, but the ring was too small. Made her wear it on a chain around her neck."

"Dana Miller's?" I asked.

"Aha. Stole it from one victim to gift the other. How sick?" he replied.

"From what we've gathered talking to Nelly Klarkson, her story matches her father's. They went to the same high school. He was infatuated with her. She thought he was weird. The Grim Reaper mask didn't help him with the other ladies. Apparently, he suffered from crippling anxiety around people. Wore the mask as protection; at least, that's what he told his class.

"Things went downhill when kids voted Nelly and Archer as senior prom king and queen. The whole school showed up at the auditorium to witness Archer's humiliation when he found out he was the butt of their joke. He ran off the stage wearing the Grim Reaper mask as Nelly kissed Billy Joe Molina, her then-boyfriend. The next night, someone killed the Klarkson's family pet — an old black cat named Cleocatra. After school, Archer walked Nelly to the bus stop as if nothing had happened between them. He convinced her to take a gulp from a flask he brought with him. She did. You want to take a guess what was in the flask?"

"Seriously?" I asked.

"The cat's blood. He bled Cleocatra into a flask and gave it to Nelly," André added.

Lem took up the story. "After high school, Nelly said she forgot about Archer Kniff until he bumped into her at a party. She was there with her boyfriend." Lem showed me a photo of Nelly Klarkson in a white linen dress, similar to the one Dana Miller had worn. "Taken on the night Nelly disappeared. The poor girl couldn't remember how Kniff took her. All she could recall is seeing Kniff kill her boyfriend. Her doctor thinks she's blocked it and might never fully regain her memory from that night. She's been locked up in his parents' basement for sixteen months. Never met or heard of Dana Miller."

"Brad Connolly's father, Truman Connolly, will be here to pick up his son's ashes and Dana's. He's taking Elena Miller, Dana's mom, to Eastern Europe, so they can spread their children's ashes across the hiking trails."

"Dana deserves that. Her obedience and sense of justice led us to two killers — Frank Ricca and Archer Kniff."

Someone popped one of the party balloons in the bullpen. It reminded me that today was a day of celebration. Archer Kniff's homicide case was officially closed. The boxes of evidence related to the investigation had already been taken to storage.

I placed the tall bottle of clear Casamigos tequila on my desk. Poured us each a drink. Raised my cup, and the rest lifted theirs.

"What should we drink to?" Lem asked.

I said, "To the unknown ahead."

Acknowledgments

First I would like to say a big heartfelt thank you to you, the reader. Your support has allowed me to write and share my stories. I appreciate you. And I understand how precious your time is and it means so much to me that of all the books in this industry, you chose OUT FOR BLOOD. It's the greatest gift you could have given me.

Next, I would like to say thank you to my family. My husband in particular for his love, encouragement, and understanding. Often I had to withdraw to my special nook to imagine, write, and edit. My absence meant missing meals together, family activities, and trips. Since day one my husband has been my biggest supporter and my greatest source of strength when I didn't believe myself.

And to our three beautiful children, I also owe a huge thank you. They make me laugh by reminding me daily how important it is to stay silly and to let things roll off my back.

As a mystery writer, I strive for my stories to mirror real detective work. On occasion, I bend the rules to fit the creative narrative. The overall accuracy remains the goal. And when I feel stuck in my research I always seek the advice of the ultimate expert on police procedures — my husband, who has over a decade behind him on the police force.

If you enjoyed, OUT FOR BLOOD, please consider leaving a review on Amazon or any other book platform you chose to shop from. Your words can be transformational.

Happy Reading,

Jolene Grace

Also by Jolene Grace

THE WRONG WIFE
GOING DARK

ABOUT THE AUTHOR

Jolene Grace knew only one thing with absolute certainty when she was a c — she'd become a writer when she grew up. At first, she wrote her stories i journals, scraps of papers, napkins, even her schoolbooks. Writing gave her outlet to create worlds in which bad guys got punished for doing bad thing And the good guys always won.

Fast forward several decades later and Jolene continues to create fictional worlds in which her characters embark on a thrilling journey, navigating a of suspense and intrigue. She loves to wave a web of plot twists and puzzlir clues that leave the readers guessing until the very end.

In her spare time when Jolene is not at her desk working on one of her next b she co-hosts the fastest growing true crime podcast 'The Crime Room.' On th show she shares her unique perspective as a murder mystery novelist on all aspects of criminal behavior, police investigating techniques and psychology.

Connect with Jolene

Free Book

Join Jolene Grace's Readers Club and receive a Free copy of "The Wrong Wife," a pulse-chilling dark romance murder mystery, in which Boston Homicide Detective Long Collins and his rookie partner Rex Hobbs must battle a vindictive killer.

Readers also get free chapters from Jolene's next books, bookish swag, and news about events.

QR Code

The Wrong Wife

Detective Long Collins is Boston's most eligible bachelor. He has the family pedigree, the money, and the looks to make any woman swoon over him. His only flaw is the badge and the gun.

Rex Hobbs is a rookie with a bad past she can't escape. A rotten apple. And Boston PD would love to kick her out.

One wrong move and Hobbs loses the badge she holds dearest to her heart. Without the shield how else would she prove her father never did the awful crimes cops accused him of?

A stroke of faith propels Collins and Hobbs on the same path. One of Boston's richest wives is murdered in her home on the night she planned to reveal a dark secret about her philandering husband.

Now, Collins and Hobbs must tear down their differences and trust each other to catch the vindictive killer or an innocent man could spend the rest of his life in jail.

Only the closer the two get to each other, their attraction grows, until they can't be apart any longer. But their love threatens to uncover some of Boston PD's most shocking secrets long buried.

With the entire police force against them, what would Collins and Hobbs choose — run to save their love or expose the truth?